Outre-Blanc

Outre-Blanc

by
Oksana & Gil Prou

translated by
Sheryl Curtis

preface by
Bernard Werber & Jean-Claude Dunyach

A Black Coat Press Book

Visit our website at www.blackcoatpress.com

ISBN 978-1-61227-743-1. First Printing. March 2018. Published by Black Coat Press, an imprint of Hollywood Comics.com, LLC, P.O. Box 17270, Encino, CA 91416. All rights reserved. Except for review purposes, no part of this book may be reproduced or transmitted in any form or by any means, electronic or mechanical, including photocopying, recording, or by any information storage and retrieval system, without permission in writing from the publisher. The stories and characters depicted in this novel are entirely fictional. Printed in the United States of America.

Table of Contents

Preface 7
OUTRE-BLANC 13
Appendix 329

Preface

Jean-Claude Dunyach: One thing struck me when I read "Outre-blanc", as well as your books too: you love to go beyond the impassable barriers, where no one has gone before you. Beyond death, beyond the depths of sleep and, in this case, beyond the borders of the universe... Science fiction has already sent us into space, far from Earth, sometimes even beyond our galaxy, but there we shift squarely into metaphysical fiction. Where does this desire to cross over the last barriers come from?

Bernard Werber: In the past, science fiction thought we were going to be saved, or at least revolutionized, by machines. Think of Jules Verne, or H. G. Wells. But in the fifties and sixties, a science fiction appeared that began to say: it is not machines that will revolutionize the world, it is our brains, it is our thoughts, our ways of viewing reality. For me, there are three, in order thar started to introduce this kind of ideas: Asimov with psycho-history, where history is conditioned by psychology, which is a way of rethinking it; then Frank Herbert with his reflection on religion and spirituality as forces reshaping the world; and finally Philip K. Dick, with his reflection on the madness and limits of our perception. These are truly three revolutions in thought and not technology. With that, we could cross through all the barriers.

Jean-Claude Dunyach: There were also all literature, comics, the films... dedicated to mutants, superpowers. This also opened up possible paths for free ourselves from our limits.

Bernard Werber: That too. In any case, we have more or less admitted that we will not be saved by machines, because technology is also the atomic bomb and greenhouse gases. Even if rockets carry us to other planets, we start from the principle that things are generally usually worse there than here. Computers, rockets, nuclear power, all these demonstrations of power will not save us.

What will save us –because we want to be saved– is our way of perceiving the world. Our way of dreaming.

And this perception is limited by death... So, there is a new science fiction that appears to be banging its head against this border, which is truly the ultimate border. As much as one can imagine that, in physical space, we will eventually understand everything, or at least have a good vision of things and a far-reaching view, as far as the afterlife is concerned, we must perhaps admit that we will never understand what is going on there and that one will never know anything about it. So, it is an extraordinary and irreplaceable topic for novels.

Jean-Claude Dunyach: I agree with you on the principle. But all these places, the beyond, the sixth sleep you mention in your last book, are uncharted places. We receive nothing, no reliable information reaches us from the beyond (I'm stting aside ghosts and other spiritual manifestations which I don't believe in). Of course, religions have mapped, to some extent, the path that leads to it I'm thinking of the Egyptian Book of the Dead *or the Tibetan* Bardo, *but once there, you literally have to imagine everything... Is it this challenge that appeals you? Or the total freedom that it gives you? The fact that we will never be contradicted, that we can't get it all wrong?*

Bernard Werber: It's true that writers have an advantage over scientists because we never have to prove what we talk about. We just have to propose a credible explanation or scenario, a path the reader will agree to take with us. As you say, this is an uncharted path, which is perfect for the imagination. The work of the novelist consists in saying: since there are no beacons, let's invent them, let's act as if we were able to make the journey. Our status as an author legitimizes our role as a pioneer in this world.

Now, as there are no limits in the interpretation of what may come after death, we must not let ourselves get carried away by this whirlind of possibilities and we must make our way with a great deal of rigor. The Tibetan or Egyptian books of the dead are handbooks with extremely precise descriptions. You will reach this or that territory, you will meet this or that divinity, which is described and drawn, your soul will be weighed on a large scale against a feather... All this is very technical and I believe that the science fiction author must reproduce an approach that is as precise as that of the Egyptian or Tibetan book of the dead. Above all, he must not become delusional.

One of the great dangers of science fiction is that everything is possible at the outset. Above all, this freedom must not be abused. For my part, and I know that you work like this too, I base my work on actual myths, on shamanism, on everything that can be known as explorations of the invisible world. So, even if our message is original, it remains linked to what has been produced by other people who have thought about such matters before us and who have established their own beacon. We don't have a territory created randomly, there is already something similar to maps, even if they are inaccurate.

Jean-Claude Dunyach: If you want to face the inexpressible, where science has not charted anything, where the reader has no landmarks, you have to know how to be an explorer, cartographer and popularizer, all at the same time. As Oksana and Gil have done for that matter. You said it yourself, it takes rigor.

How do you keep from misleading those who read you in these strange territories?

Bernard Werber: We need to talk to them about imaginary worlds as we would a new continent. That's what I did for the *Thanatonautes*. I relied on Christopher Columbus discovering America and I imagined the same mechanism. We land on a beach, we head into a forest, we discover a clearing... I just replaced the beach, the forest, clearings, with levels of consciousness in the world of the afterlife. I also used Dante's Divine Comedy as a landmark. In fact, there is an enormous map of Paradise and Hell. They have been described in many religious or mythological texts, in epics. It is often very precise. Take Greek mythology: we are familiar with the description of Tartarus, there is the Styx, Charon who will take your soul across in his boat, for a fee of course, Cerberus the three-headed dog of the underworld...

Jean-Claude Dunyach: as you present it's almost like a TV report?

Bernard Werber: Maybe not, we have to use our imagination, but at least we have very precise descriptions. Someone who does a little research, even on a subject as bizarre and esoteric as death and the beyond, will find a lot of information, very detailed assumptions. I try not to mislead the reader, I say to him: "See, you already knew all this, you learned it at school or from books, you saw paintings in museums, you look at them like something imaginary, now I suggest you see it as a possibility."

Then, the second approach, apart from myths and religions, is to use science. We have scientific theories, machines that analyze brain function, which helps us to explore our sleep, which materializes our alpha, theta waves and son on. There are also the beginnings of a map, or at least landmarks.

I use both, simultaneously. As a result, my readers who are of a more scientific bent can find landmarks that suit them and those who are more mystical in nature can also find some. The important thing is to leave nothing "in floating". The reader is directed, there is a left and a right, a scientific map and a mythological one. And in the middle there is the reader's personal intuition, depending on whether he has had experiences with the hereafter or with particular states of consciousness, depending on whether he has lost a loved one and has the impression that that person is still there and to him... The very idea of the hereafter resonates differently for each reader and we must give the reader the means to find himself there.

I believe that each book is a mirror that allows the reader to be conforted in his convictions and occasionally to develop them, to enrich his intuitions with what the writer proposes to him. But we need a starting point, a seed of curiosity on the reader's part. I don't believe it is possible to have a reader who completely ignorant of the subject and who says at the end of a book like *Thanatonautse*:

"I'm convinced, I have become a believer, I believe in the existence of heaven and hell..." I don't see it at all like that. If he's already on the path, some books can help him travel faster and farther. If he is resistant to this kind of approach, he will either feel like he is reading a fairy tale or he will be bored. And he will never get lost, which is the first step.

Jean-Claude Dunyach What you say strikes me, with respect to the book by Oksana and Gil. The characters in "Outre-blanc" also start to lose their way; more exactly, they are captured and dragged outside the maps, beyond the reach of surveillance systems and satellites. They are lost in the heart of the Amazon rainforest, one of the places on Earth where it is easiest to disappear. They are scientists, some collapse, others find unsuspected resources in themselves. But each of them experiences it as the beginning of the loss of self.

And that, literally speaking, also involves voluntarily misleading the reader... By warning him: "From now on, we will have to make the maps we need together. And for that, I need you to trust me. "This requires a certain state of mind when writing, doesn't it? There is a jubilant side, at least from my point of view, in telling the reader : "I'm going to take you out of your comfort zone and lead you to a place where sensations, perceptions, the very idea you have of reality, will evolve. And you'll have to do the same". And that also means that the characters we create to explore this type of universe are unique. This is something that has always struck me in your novels: your heroes are endowed with an immense sense of curiosity, they want to know. This is a reflection of what you are, it's the same for me with my own characters. They say to themselves: whatever happens to me, at least I learned something.

Bernard Werber: This also means that the reader must have a certain amount of courage to get into this kind of book and stay with it to the end. I see the writer as someone who is on the edge of the forest and who says to the reader: "Come on, I'll take you by the hand and we'll cross through it together." And the reader says to himself: "Wait, in the forest there are wolves, snakes, all kinds of dangers..." But the writer replies: "As long as I'm there, you risk nothing." This is a reading contract based on trust.

At that moment, the reader says to himself: "I want the forest to surprise me, to frighten me, it's the game, but the author must not let me down. He must explain what is happening and protect me at the same time." There are forests where the reader can go astray, get completely lost, there are forests where he can be bored or understand nothing. And the reader can also say to himself: "I should never have come here, this place is too dangerous..." He will wonder if he has enough strength to turn around and find his way, amid the terrifying noises that come from all sides at once, from above him... He is afraid of everything the author has helped him imagine.

This is the principle of the forest. And the author tells the reader: "Let's keep going, you'll see, it will please you. "*You'll see, it will please you*" is what keeps the reader in suspense, but it is also a contract that can go wrong. The reader may have the impression that the author has lied to him, that the place where he is taking the reader is not going to suit him at all. That's the risk. But, at the same time, it means that a bond has been created between them, the start of a complicity that the author will strive to make stronger.

That is where we authors feel pressure. There is no Writer's Association that makes sure the author has done his job well, there is no writing code of ethics, it's really a one-on-one contract. At any given moment, we must find a way of convincing our reader to turn another, to accompany us a longer. We are all guides in dark forests, but we each have our own.

Jean-Claude Dunyach: It's true that sometimes you take strolls during which, if someone did not hold your hand, you would run away. Yet, when you come out on the other side, you say "Wow! I'm annoyed, but it was worth it."

Bernard Werber: A good novel is a baptism. An initiation. The interest in taking walk, beyond being surprised, is that we come out of it transformed. Someone sleeping learned to dream. Someone who knew nothing, learned to know the forest. And he will be able confidently set out to cross through darker, more dangerous forests.

That's it initiation by book. And it is a real joy for us writers to bring forests into being. And to stroll through them with our readers...

Ce n'est pas du cachot, du puits, de la géhenne,
Ce n'est pas du verrou, ce n'est pas de la chaîne,
C'est de son propre cœur qu'on est le prisonnier.
Victor Hugo – La fin de Satan

OUTRE-BLANC

CHAPTER 1

Tuesday, January 19, 2016 – Mount Roraima
(on the borders of Venezuela, Guyana and Brazil)

Pain. Heat. Stench. Fear.

Above all, fear.

The covered truck had been driving for more than an hour between the ruts of a muddy road that meandered through the Amazon jungle. In the distance, the mighty silhouette of Mount Roraima dominated the plain. A subtle mixture of the smell of sweat, diesel and urine, cyclically invaded the back of the truck where the four prisoners sat, wrists firmly bound.

Phil Caldwell did not understand what had happened. Everything was blurred in his mind. He remembered only one thing: shots and shouts.

Then a violent blow. On his neck. And night prevailed.

The shadows of unconsciousness suddenly dissolved into a hell of jolts, violent jumps and squeaks. All the truck's metal struts squealed like a pig being slaughtered. The perpetual swinging from one side to the other constantly kept the exoplanet specialist off-balance. Each movement pulled at his arms. His muscles and tendons were being subjected to a severe test as they were simultaneously stretched, compressed and twisted. Painful, bruised, his body swung around the anchor point like a crazy pendulum shaken by frantic kids.

Having recently left the prestigious Stanford university to join the Orpheus expedition, he had not imagined for a moment that the study of the fauna and flora at the top of the Venezuelan tepui could have ended like this.

Attacked by gunmen, beaten, tied up and now rudely taken to an unknown place, Phil Caldwell wondered for a moment whether he was dreaming. But the groans of pain of his three companions in misfortune quickly destroyed this illusion.

The entire Orpheus expedition had just been kidnapped by men whose intentions were still unknown. However, the attack on Karin Stockhausen's camp had been extremely violent. Against this backdrop of fear, their current silence did not bode well for the future.

His neck still sore from the blow to his spine, Phil tried to turn his head to find out who was being confined along with him. Tied up as he was, he could see only one of their guides: Luis Urube. The head of the little man with skin browned by a thousand equatorial suns nodded. Leaning forward, he was still unconscious. The cries of pain came from behind. But Phil Caldwell's hands were tied together to a horizontal bar at the top of the truck, his movements hindered. His feet, too, were firmly tied to a rail running from the front to the back of the truck, and the redhead spun on himself like a weathervane. Since he had been confined in front of the tarpaulin that protected the contents of the truck from any indiscreet glances, it was impossible for him to pivot 180° to see the other two prisoners.

He settled for asking, "Who's here?"

"Me!" replied a man with a rather deep voice.

Phil Caldwell immediately recognized Gregory Greensberg. Blond, athletic and good at dealing with the most difficult situations, the experienced logistician had organized the route and the various stages of this expedition, initially dreamt up by Karin Stockhausen, the general manager of the Orpheus Foundation. Specializing in research on biodiversity and ethology in the case of accelerating global warming and the loss of biodiversity, the Orpheus Foundation had been financed for the past two years by the wealthy Stockhausen family of which Karin was the sole heir.

"Who's next to you?"

"Paula. She's not doing well at all."

"What's wrong with her?"

"She vomited and is complaining about pain in her . One of these wretches kicked her in the ribs after pushing her down. That didn't exactly improve her condition!"

It is true that, since the beginning of the expedition, on January 9, 2016 to be precise, the group's biologist and ethologist had been sick. Paula Cavendish had been suffering for almost a week. As soon as she had arrived, the spicy and unchanging food common to that part of the Amazon, which was located at the junction of three states – Venezuela, Guyana and Brazil – had apparently wreaked havoc with her stomach.

The aggressive intrusion of armed and hyper-violent guards into the expedition's base camp had worsened her condition considerably.

"Will we be arriving soon?" asked Phil, taking care to keep from screaming in pain.

His tendons and joints were being tested severely. But it was especially his wrists that caused him horrific pain. Burning like acid splashed on gaping wounds, the pain radiated into his arms, shoulders and chest.

Grimacing more and more, the exoplanet specialist nibbled at his lower lip before continuing.

"Where are they taking us?"

"I don't know," sighed Gregory Greensberg.

"Who are these madmen?"

"I don't know that either," admitted the logistician, whose light gray eyes were dulled by shooting pain.

He groaned for a moment and spat out some drool and blood. The blow he had taken in the face an hour earlier had shattered his right brow and upper lip. The blood had dried a little. But every time the truck, partially mired in deep ruts, jostled, it opened the wounds again.

After a brief moment, Gregory continued, saying "This area is very isolated. We are far from the central power of Caracas. The proximity of Guyana and northern Brazil facilitates flight. This is paradise for all kinds of trafficking.

"Drug? Weapons?"

"Yes. And everything else."

"What do you mean by *everything else*?"

"There are guerrillas fighting for lost causes, traffickers who feed weapons circuits to terrorists on all sides. There are also bandits who plunder everything they can get their hands on.

"Charming! And we ... we're now stuck in this wasps' nest with all our scientific equipment."

"And our dollars!"

"But... but if they just wanted to rob us, why didn't they leave after taking what they wanted?"

"I don't know any more than you do, Phil. They will probably tell us what they really want soon enough."

"When?"

"Before nightfall."

Phil grimaced again because the gashes on his wrists were more and painful. The blood had no time to coagulate because the wounds were constantly reopening. Vermilion rivulets flowed along his arms before disappearing under his armpits and down his torso.

He swallowed painfully and finally asked the logistician, who seemed to be very familiar with the region and its dangers, "Why before nightfall?"

"The jungle is too dense to drive through at night, in the rain and with trucks of this type. We'll stop at the latest within four or five hours."

"Four or five hours," murmured the astrophysicist, telling himself that his wrists and arms wouldn't withstand such treatment for so long.

The minutes that followed were really distressing because the two men knew that this dreadful episode was only the first of a long series.

Next to them, Paula Cavendish continued to moan.

She finally vomited up the few remnants of the previous evening's meal that she had not regurgitated yet.

For his part, Luis Urube was still unconscious. Apparently, the hammering his head had taken from gun butts had been extremely violent. "Hammers" was also the word that best defined the armed men who had assaulted the eleven members of the Orpheus expedition while they were preparing to resume their journey in order to arrive at the foot of Mount Roraima that same evening. The brutes spoke little, screamed sometimes, and hammered their victims all the time.

Desperate, Phil glanced furtively at the man who was watching them, constantly clasping his assault rifle, which seemed to be grafted to his hand. Sitting on a solid bench installed the length of the truck cab, he barely noticed the dreadful jolts that shook the vehicle every which way. Dressed in green, the brute caressed his weapon from time to time. In any case, the Stanford University researcher had no intention of testing their guard's speed and accuracy when it came to dealing with a prisoner trying to escape.

The man had bushy eyebrows and his hair was jet black. A long scar ran across his right cheek, continuing over to his ear. Apart from his fierce and stubborn air, one detail in particular worried Phil Caldwell: the guard had taken no pains at all to conceal his face.

"For hostage takers, that's very foolhardy," he thought. "Except, of course, if their final intention is to kill all their prisoners."

The astrophysicist darted his green eyes towards the grumpy guard.

"Where are you taking us?" he asked in halting Spanish.

The only response he received was the squeaking of the metallic, covered structure at the back of the truck.

He thought it wise not to insist.

"Help me!"

In a frail voice, broken by anguish, the unfortunate biologist beseeched her companions. Her wrists were hurting her. Her belly too. Mud had been running down her cheeks in long silvery furrows since the attack on the Orpheus expedition camp.

Making the most of a brief moment of relative calm in the banging that indicated the shock absorbers were about to give up the ghost, Gregory Greensberg tried to reassure he, saying that the truck was about to stop. The blond logistician with muscular shoulders and an impressive build was trying to put a brave face on and put the scope of the drama that was being played out in this lost place in the Amazon jungle where trafficking of all kinds prospered into perspective. But Paula Cavendish was not fooled. She looked at the man who was trying to dispel her anguish with reassuring words.

Words that were reassuring and meaningless, especially since no one knew when the vehicle along the ruined trail would stop. Above all, none of the hostages could even imagine or foresee the real intentions of their assailants. One thing was certain, they weren't being taken to a vacation camp.

The dark-haired biologist, with desperate dark eyes, sighed. She moaned several times. Then, haggard, her mouth half open, she seemed to sink into a stupor where physical pain teamed up with despair.

In order to avoid counting the minutes that passed too slowly for his taste, Phil Caldwell tried to recall what had just happened.

Unfortunately, everything was blurred in his head. A few images appeared, like lanterns in a stormy night. But they were fleeting, darkness alternating with blinding flashes. And the taste of blood in his mouth. Blood. Always blood.

Waves of blood!

Dominating all these scattered sensations, screams continued to rumble in his mind. Cries, groans. Swearing. Then the dull sound of rifle butts hammering his companions' skulls.

Since the sweet, sickly taste of the partially coagulated blood that had flowed in his mouth obstinately refused to dispel, Phil Caldwell decided to go back over the entire thread of this exciting expedition that was brutally transforming into a nightmare, from the very beginning.

He had arrived last at Manaus. Coming directly from Stanford University, he had suffered a bit from the suffocating equatorial heat that characterizes that large Brazilian city located in the heart of the Amazon and along the Rio Negro, one of the major tributaries of the Amazon River. Knowing that the rainy season ran from October to May he naturally expected to be welcomed by a warm shower. It was completely different from the climate of San Francisco where he had lived for five years.

The other members of the Orpheus expedition had been welcomed warmly at the Tropical Manaus Ecoresort. Karin Stockhausen had chosen this hotel because it was very comfortable and ideally located 10 minutes from the city and 10 minutes from Eduardo Gomes International Airport.

Exhausted by his long journey, the researcher, who specialized in specialist exoplanets and their possible capacities for sheltering strange forms of life collapsed on his bed. Without eating. But, the next morning, he caught up with an enormous breakfast: tropical fruits and the tastiest cakes piled up in pyramids, circles, and mountains of delicious food.

Karin and the other members of the expedition joined him quickly. Amused, they watched the brilliant astrophysicist dig in as if he had not eaten for a week. The discussion began immediately.

Gregory Greensberg gave him an outline of the schedule in logistical terms while Alexander Haffington and Paula Cavendish told him about the current state of their research. Alexandra and Paula were high-level biologists and biochemists who would work closely with Phil on their research into the unique biotope that characterizes tepuis. These *islands in the sky*, as some scientists called them with an innate sense of metaphor and lyricism, formed, as it were, separate

17

worlds in which unexpected forms of life developed without regard for the abundance of vegetation and animals that swarmed 1,000 or 2,000 meters below. Namely, in the thick jungle where heat and humidity multiplied the forces of an exuberant nature tenfold.

This was precisely the aim of this expedition which had been organized and was financed by Karin Stockhausen. Since its creation in 2014, the Orpheus Foundation had specialized in a particular field that highlighted the convergences between ethology and the study of the most surprising forms of life that swarm over our planet, as well as at the bottom of the oceans or in hydrothermal sources. This confluence was by no means incongruous if ethology is applied in keeping with its broadest definition: the biological study of the interactions between species.

However, since the Orpheus Foundation received virtually unlimited funding as a result of the colossal fortune of the Stockhausen family, this ambition now intersected with specific research carried out by NASA as part of the study of exoplanets. That is why Phil Caldwell found himself at the foot of Mount Roraima with a team of biologists, edaphologists[1], biochemists and climatologists.

The link between the study of the most extravagant forms of life that exist on Earth and the hope of one day discovering living beings on a distant planet nestled in the heart of our galaxy may seem tenuous. Nevertheless, reality reinforced the relevance of this experiment. As evidence, some extremophilic bacteria thrive under conditions that far exceed the worst environments within stellar systems. They survive even in a vacuum and under conditions of temperature, pressure or radioactivity, making them almost immortal beings. In Mono Lake, California, a bacterium bearing the sweet name of GFAJ-1, was discovered. This bacterium reproduces and thrives in a bath of phosphorus and arsenic.

This discovery, which was made in 2010 and whose results were modified two years later, led Karin Stockhausen to establish the Foundation. And then to organize this first great expedition, which had just fallen into a trap, even before reaching the first foothills of Mount Roraima.

Still hanging by his arms in a stinking truck that jolted on ruts that ran on endlessly, Phil recalled his surprise when the head of the Department of Astrophysics at Stanford University called him late one evening in December 2015. In a few words, he told Phil that Karin Stockhausen wanted to organize an expedition at the top of the tepuis that run along the border between Venezuela, Guyana and Brazil.

His mouth slightly open and his eyes as round as marbles revealed his astonishment. His lack of comprehension, even. But, when Paul Henderson clarified the joint objectives of the Stockhausen Foundation and NASA, Phil did not

---

[1] Edaphology is the study of soils as a natural habitat for plants.

hesitate. Some stammering – and a "yes!" – rang out at the end of the discussion.

Phil left San Francisco on Monday, January 11 to fly to Brazil. Following a brief stop in Miami, he arrived at Manaus.

After two pleasant days at the Tropical Manaus, the serious work began. As there are more than 600 kilometers of difficult roads between Manaus and Boa Vista – the usual starting point for the tepuis – Karin Stockhausen and Gregory Greensberg opted for a domestic flight with one of the three companies connecting the two Amazonian cities.

Their arrival at the Aipana Plaza Hotel was smooth. The comfort was completely different from the luxury displayed at the Tropical Manaus. But the members of the expedition were not on holiday. And they knew that full well. Moreover, in January the climate is much drier at Boa Vista. It is easier to breathe and the humidity is much more acceptable for Westerners unaccustomed to humidity levels of 98%.

The departure from Boa Vista on Saturday, January 16 was more complicated because it had been necessary to arrange for a bus for the members of the expedition and a large truck to carry all the equipment they needed. Moreover, precautions had to be taken for handling the very fragile and sophisticated scientific instruments they carried with them.

In addition to all these constraints, it was necessary to take the utmost care with respect to the indispensable medical equipment of Linda Griffith, the doctor assigned to the expedition.

The biologists, biochemists and ecophysiologists of the group were maniacs; they kept a constant watch over the comfort of their instruments. At every delicate crossing, they insisted that the driver stop the bus. Then they accompanied Fernando Pinzon, the driver of the truck who also acted as a guide, to make sure that the shocks and jolts of the road would not risk damaging their precious scientific equipment.

Normally, it takes about four hours to reach Santa Elena de Uairén from Boa Vista. But, given the careful monitoring, the trip dragged on for half a day.

Gregory was fuming, but Karin calmed things down by explaining that the goal was to make many observations for a whole month and that it was absurd to take the risk of breaking essential research tools on the false pretext of cutting t ravel time by four or six hours.

The blond logistician repeatedly glared with his light gray eyes to express his displeasure. But Karin was an efficient and wealthy expedition leader. These two qualities prevailed under all circumstances.

Phil groaned a bit just then because the truck carrying all four of them had just bounced heavily over a succession of holes that tortured shock absorbers already in poor shape.

The pain in his wrists was so violent that he fainted for a moment. But he quickly recovered his wits. The juxtaposition of metallic grinding from the structure of the vehicle and the howls of his three suffering companions eliminated any possibility of drowsiness.

The astrophysicist glanced hastily at Luis Urube, who had finally emerged from his lengthy faint. A bloody wound decorated their guide's left temple. His cheek was marbled with a mixture of mud and blood that formed a macabre tree shape that mimed the skein of streams that characterizes the deltas of the great rivers.

But, in this case, it was simply the result of blood from a large wound that continually flowed down his cheek mingling brown and red. The redhead tried to speak to him, but the surrounding noise was too loud. The unfortunate Venezuelan guide opened his eyes like a tortured man being taken to the stake. At that moment, the Stanford researcher that Luis Urube perhaps knew the men who had attacked them and tied them up in this truck stinking of sweat and urine. He shuddered at the thought.

Phil Caldwell stealthily observed the armed guard whose body lolled this way and that to the rhythm of the jolts. His beard was shaggy, his eyes black.

Apart from the scar that stretched over his right cheek and continued to his ear, another large scar ran through his upper lip and chin. All these war trophies indicated a shady temperament. Since the man was still armed, Phil cautiously decided not to insist by asking him a question to which the brute would respond, either with an insult or a blow of his gun.

The unfortunate man then tried to recall the last moments before this brutal drop into a black abyss, his awakening sanctioned by only two words: fear and suffering.

After a night spent in precarious conditions in Santa Elena de Uairén, they continued in the direction of the village of Paraitepuy, where many Pemon lived. This little town is home to the Canaima National Park office and is the transit point for those wishing to climb the steep slopes of Mount Roraima, which is 3,000 meters at its highest point. The Venezuelan government wants to control the flow of visitors while verifying their identity and the amount of equipment they carry.

Unfortunately, the convoy, consisting of a bus and the truck that carried the equipment, never arrived at Paraitepuy. Bogged down in mud, the heavy vehicle came to a halt in the middle of the trail.

Fernando Pinzon cursed in Spanish.

Then he turned to Karin Stockhausen, who had rushed to determine the reason for the unexpected stop.

"The front right wheel broke on a piece of metal that some assholes left in the middle of the road! Worse yet, it really seems like that debris was placed there on purpose!"

"It's not the end of the world. We'll all help you fix it..."

The words of consolation uttered by the head of the expedition stuck in her throat.

Many armed men arrived from all sides and encircled both vehicles. There were more than twenty. Orders were given. Blows rained down on the expedition members.

A large, black cloud invaded Phil Caldwell's mind.

At this painful recollection, tears began to flow down his cheeks. And the pain returned. Atrocious. Consuming.

Almost unbearable.

CHAPTER 2

The vehicle braked brutally. Squealing like a wreck tossed this way and that at the whim of the wind in the shallows, the old truck came to a stop.

The four prisoners tied up in the kidnappers' second vehicle had been positioned face to face, unlike Phil Caldwell and his friends who had a tarpaulin stained with gasoline and grease for their only horizon. But, apart from this meager comfort, their situation was just as uncomfortable. Pain dominated, obliterating any other sensation.

"Where are you taking us?" Karin Stockhausen muttered, staring at the gruff guard watching them.

The young heiress of the family that had made a fortune in nanotechnologies and their medical, military, environmental and industrial applications shook her long red hair, as if this simple gesture had the power to free her from the bonds that dug into her wrists.

"¡Cállate!"[2] replied the man.

The woman in charge of the Orpheus expedition did not insist.

Observing their jailer, she noticed that the large, tousled mustache that made him look a little like a cartoon pirate was only a facade. The guard's face was cold. His dark eyes shone in the semi-obscurity instilled by the brown and green canvas sheets that covered the metal frame of the rocking trailer. The man did not speak. But his gestures spoke volumes.

When Matt Lochner insulted him by calling him *cobarde* which means, cowardly, chicken, wimp in Spanish, the man simply made a gesture with the fighting knife held in his left hand.

As the guard slowly slid the blade along his neck while making a horrible grimace, the cameraman understood that these determined men were not joking and had no qualms about slitting throats.

The pain that devoured their arms and wrists confirmed this simple statement: they had been attacked and kidnapped by bandits who would not hesitate to use the most extreme violence.

"*What will happen later?*" wondered the journalist who was in charge of recording everything that was going to happen for a month in order to make a complete report highlighting the success of the expedition.

Unfortunately,, Karin Stockhausen was not the one to provide a credible answer in such a situation when brute force reigned supreme.

Discouraged, the leader of the Orpheus expedition quickly examined the condition of her two other colleagues.

---

[2] Shut up!

Alexandra Haffington, the team's biochemist, had not been shaken up too roughly by the attackers. But it was difficult to say whether it was simply out of respect for a woman, for both Paula Cavendish and Linda Griffith had been struck with the same force and violence that had been used against the men.

Moreover, Alexandra was young – 28 years – and pretty. Blonde, with superb green eyes and a queenly bearing, the biochemist possessed all the assets that attract men. The glance s of the boors who had attacked them were sufficiently explicit in this respect. Even if the orders barked by their leader were very clear and imbued with a pragmatism with no place for emotions, it was obvious that these hardened bandits could be extremely dangerous to a luscious young woman whose figure alone would damn a hermit.

Sergei Kucharski was not moving. Eyes glassy, his head nodded in pace with the constant shaking of the truck in which they were held prisoner. A climatologist with the Orpheus Foundation, this blond colossus had had a penchant for starting fights, whether in bars, or when one of his many female conquests was bothered.

When the bus carrying the expedition members was attacked by a score of men armed with assault rifles, handguns and machetes, Sergei wanted to resist. His punishment was not long in coming: he was struck in on his head by a rifle butt and then in the chest. The climatologist collapsed. Then he was ruthlessly pulled along by the attackers who did not seem to appreciate resistance.

For two hours the poor man had been swinging, hanging by the wrists likes his three colleagues. Since the bar to which they were tied was high enough, their bodies were tortured by the laws of gravity. Their joints hurt, their tendons were twisted harshly and their skin was carved by knots tied too tightly.

The heiress of the rich and powerful Stockhausen family turned her head to Matt Lochner.

"How is he?" she asked, pointing at Serguei Kucharski.

"Hard to say. He doesn't really seem to be unconscious because his eyes move and his mouth twitches, indicating that he realizes what is going on around him. But..."

"But what?"

"Serguei is giving the impression that he's totally apathetic. And that's not like him at all."

"That's the least you can say," said Karin Stockhausen, recalling his last outburst of anger, just yesterday evening."

"All the same, I'm not a doctor. Linda should take a look at him. But she's in another truck and was also beaten."

For a moment, the groaning and squealing of shock absorbers under strain covered this embryonic discussion which could hardly go on because no one was in a position to examine the climatologist and, above all, no one could say where the damned trucks were heading. To Guyana? To the north of Brazil?

The uncertainty was total.

Despite the overwhelming sense of helplessness, Alexandra Haffington tried to find out more. Naturally, she looked at Karin, who was in charge of the expedition, first.

"Karin?"

"Yes?"

"What are they going to do with us?"

This simple question summarized the situation perfectly and its apparent absurdity.

Friedrich Stockhausen's daughter replied, "The first question that comes to my mind is, why?"

"I don't want to be a harbinger of doom," said Matt Lochner, "But based on my experience as a journalist, one conclusion comes to mind: either this hostage-taking is motivated by a ransom demand or..."

Since the blonde cameraman employed for two years by the Orpheus Foundation did not pursue his sentence, Karin insisted.

"And the other hypothesis?"

"A hostage taking by a terrorist organization wanting to obtain the release of some of its members or to make a mark on people's minds by means of a dramatic attack."

"The criminal theory would no doubt be the least risky for us," said Alexandra in a weak voice, covered partially by the driving sounds.

The young woman shook like a leaf. Her deep purple t-shirt was stained with mud and her large green eyes were round under the combined effects of terror and pain.

Karin and Matt looked at her while wondering if the biochemist could withstand such a trial for long.

"You're probably right," agreed Stockhausen, who, despite her colossal fortune and high rank in a society where money is the only master, was still very close to her direct collaborators and scientists who accompanied them in their ethological research. "I hope it's only for money."

"If that's the case," the journalist said, "They will watch over us and our health because their success will depend on our survival."

"And if not?" cried Alexandra.

"Things will be much more random and difficult for us," murmured Matt who did not really know how to tell a 28-year-old woman that the worst atrocities are possible once madmen are in charge of your destiny.

Silence fell inside this confined space between four filthy tarps. Relative silence, of course, for the old truck moaned like a wounded man abandoned on a battlefield. The soft sounds of the mud squishing underneath the wheels combined with the metallic squeaking of the frame of the rear end of the heavy vehicle which painfully made its way through the thick jungle bordering Mount Roraima.

The guard with the mustache looked at them often. The almost gruff impassiveness of his bovine face cracked when a smirk lit up his brown eyes, digging a dimple in the center of his right cheek. Then he spat on the ground and once again brandished his gun and the long dagger that never left his hands, to halt any attempt of rebellion.

But how can one rebel or try to escape when one is tied up, dangling from a pole, arms in the air and feet constantly swinging around an imaginary axis?

Karin and Alexandra clearly understood the futility of such efforts. But the journalist continued. From time to time.

"When I think that, in less than two days, we would have reached the summit of Mount Roraima and that we would be able to walk between exuberant enclosed spaces bearing the sweet names of *Cristal Valley, Enchanted Lagoon Valley* or *Labyrinth* Valley, I say that it was a piece of really bad luck that brought us into contact with these armed brutes!" Matt said, trying to free.

Unsuccessfully, of course, since the bonds were perfectly tight.

Karin nodded. The tall young woman turned her porcelain blue eyes toward Sergei Kucharski, who seemed to be gradually regaining hisspirits. The unfortunate man stammered a few inaudible words. This comforted his companions who had feared severe head trauma after such a beating. Apparently, that was not the case. That was the only glimmer of hope at that moment.

The Stockhausen family heiress stretched her neck to the left in an attempt to catch a glimpse of a portion of the landscape that scrolled past between the gaps in the dust-stained tarps that closed around the back of the truck. But the crack was irregular and the tilting movements of the vehicle made any clear view of the outside impossible.

In any case, they were prisoners in the middle of the dense jungle that separates Venezuela, Guyana and Brazil. This geographical location had two major disadvantages. First: a tropical climate that is difficult to withstand when all the logistical means that have been carefully prepared for many months have fallen into the hands of a malicious armed group.

Karin was thinking about the field hospital that Linda Griffith and Gregory Greensberg had prepared with utmost care and would be sorely missed if one of the expedition members were to be sick or injured.

The second disadvantage was a corollary of the first: who could free them in a zone located on the extreme outskirts of three states unable to control gangs of traffickers that have been scouring the tributaries of the Amazon River for decades?

However, one important factor had to be taken into account: all the members of the expedition, apart from the two guides, were Westerners working for a wealthy American Foundation. It didn't require an unbridled imagination to understand that this factor was going to play a crucial role in the very near future. Deep down, Karin hoped that the expression *very near future* would bear meaning and hope. She suddenly recalled the atrocious destiny of some FARC prisoners in Colombia who had remained in the jungle for many years.

The head of the Orpheus Expedition shuddered as she considered this gloomy possibility.

"Where are we?" All eyes looked towards Serguei Kucharski.

The climatologist was hard to see. His blonde hair still bore the signs of the beating he had received during the kidnapping. Generally steel-gray and sparkling with mischievousness, his eyes were dull, as if washed by the waves of an impetuous ocean that had wreaked its havoc on him.

Despite the 56 years he proudly acknowledged, this friend of the Stockhausen family was athletic, very muscular and in perfect shape. Normally, people though he was 40-something, because of his marvelous and intellectual energy. Today he looked seventy! With pale skin, drawn features, and blood trails still decorating his forehead, cheeks and chin, like in war paintings of a defeated Indian chief, Serguei was a defeated colossus. A wounded colossus. A humiliated colossus.

Haggard, he scrutinized his three friends without really understanding what was going on.

"We're prisoners," summarized Matt Lochner.

"But who?"

"No idea," Karin said, trying to smile at her old friend despite the pain in her wrists and arms. "But these people are aggressive, brutal. Very determined, too."

"And very well organized," the journalist added. "They seem to know perfectly well who we are and why we're here."

"I see," murmured the climatologist, grimacing.

He remained silent for a moment before continuing, "Where are they taking us?"

"To a place they feel safe and hidden from any outside gaze, I guess," Karin replied.

The young redhead woman had just finished her sentence when a jolt more violent than the others made the truck creak with a disturbing force.

"They're going to break an axle!" Matt remarked, shaking his head.

The guard watched him for a moment, but remained silent.

The shearing effect of this shock, which was intense than the others, revived the pain in the wrists of the four prisoners.

Sergei Kucharski moaned a little. He looked at the guard whose furrowed eyebrows made it clear that he did not intend to comfort his prisoners.

"¿Dónde nos llevas a hijo de puta?"[3]

---

[3] Where are you taking us, you son of a bitch?

The man spat blackish juice on the ground and brandished his long dagger. Then he mimicked a horizontal gesture again across his throat. The meaning was clear.

Wounded by the guard's silence far more than by an insult echoing his own, the climatologist opened his eyes wide. He grimaced, clenching his jaws and grinding his teeth. Then he eased his body downward, which immediately intensified the burning sensation and endless stretching of the nerves in his arms, shoulders and chest.

Karin advised him not to insult their guard because this kind of reaction, totally pointless given their situation, could well cost them a lot later on.

The head of Orpheus did not really have the opportunity to continue her sentence because a sinister cracking sound followed by the violent application of the brakes threw them all toward the front of the truck.

A spate of Spanish curses prolonged this episode which resembled an incongruous mixture of a rodeo and bumper car race. The vehicle stood still and the strong odor of overheated oil washed over the rear end. The conclusions were obvious.

"What was I saying just a few minutes ago?" Matt Lochner grumbled. "These idiots have totally destroyed an axle!"

The journalist was right. Driven too fast and without any care, the truck carrying them had just run over the end of a tree trunk that was lying on the road, partially hidden by mud. The frame had most certainly been affected and partly bent. The driver was immediately swept up in a tumult as he continued to curse to hide the fact that he had not paid enough attention to the road. His ploy did not work and the truck driver at the head of the convoy mocked him.

The two men grabbed one another and a shot rang out, putting an end to the altercation. The man who had just shot was probably the leader of the group because his arguments were effective and precise.

They could be summarized as follows: The first one who opens his mouth again... will get a bullet to his head!"

Precisely and apparently credible, this argument put an end to the quarrel.

While the hostage takers were fighting, the four prisoners in the truck were in very bad shape. The large bonds that held their wrists to the metal bars supporting the tarpaulin were still in place. But the ropes that tied their feet less tightly had given way under the violence of the impact. Immediate consequence: the bodies of the unfortunate captives now tilted towards the cabin. The unbearable pain that had been spreading throughout their wrists from the time of their capture gradually metamorphosed into acid, winding its way along each nerve. Of each muscle.

Sergei shrieked in pain. The veins of his neck and temples swelled and twisted beneath his skin like the aerial roots of a tree in the middle of a swamp. Karin and Matt tried to calm him down. But their own fears were so visible that this attempt failed.

Before climbing out of the back of the truck to determine the scope of the damage, the guard with the big shaggy mustache walked over to the climber who was braced against a large chest that obviously contained weapons. The tips of two M16 and M4 assault rifles poking out made this clear. The man looked at his intended victim for a moment. Then he slapped the other man forcefully without saying a word.

After this mediocre attack on a prisoner who was both bound and wounded, he shoved the filthy fabric aside and climbed out the rear of the vehicle.

The conversation among the hostage takers probably lasted less than five minutes. Yet, it seemed like an eternity to the unfortunate hostages who were stilled tied up, arms raised and wrists damaged.

Suddenly, another guard burst into the vehicle, which was still covered by a tarpaulin that must have been green once. Rain, dust, oil, and mud had, of course, faded it . Now, brown and yellowish streaks dominated.

"Cambiamos of camión. ¡No trate de escaper usted o le deguello!⁴

"Let's stay calm," Karin Stockhausen advised. "there's no point in playing heroes for now."

The advice was wise because, when they were finally untied and able to limp out of the vehicle, the hostages discovered about twenty armed men holding them a gunpoint. The opportunity to finally see their environment was of no particular use.

They immediately realized why their captors had not taken the precaution of blindfolding them before extracting them from their prison on wheels. T there was nothing to see because the narrow path on which they had stopped was surrounded by gigantic trees. It was not even possible to see Mount Roraima, whose high and imperial peak stood up in the middle of the jungle. With no landmarks, it was impossible to know whether they were in Venezuela, Guyana or Brazil.

The four prisoners waited for a moment, parked along a bank of stagnant water. Very quickly the man who appeared to be the commander of the commando group that had attacked the scientists ordered the first truck to pull the second truck out of the way with a long metal wire. The operation was rather difficult because the front axle was broken, the beams had been folded into a V, and one of the wheels of the rugged vehicle was now almost perpendicular to the road and scraped the ground in a thunderous sound. But the truck driver who was at the head of the convoy operated the vehicle skillfully. After a lot of creaking and twisting of the broken truck cabin that looked like an insect drowned in vinegar, the heavy vehicle finally shook.

It left long and deep traces in the water-soaked ground. But it could finally be moved a hundred meters from the entrance of a winding path that disappeared into the jungle.

---

⁴ We're changing trucks. Don't try to escape or I'll kill you!

The road was finally cleared.

"¡Vamos!" shouted the leader of the hostage takers, lifting his M14 over his head like a warrior drunk on power.

The man was as dark-skinned as his acolytes.

His eyes were truly unusual. Large, bright and cold at the same time, his eyes were of an intense blue that stood in sharp contrast to his typically South American skin. This discordance between face and eyes illustrated better than a long speech the implacability of a character prone to anger.

Moreover, a long scar ran across his nose and forehead. Probably a sign of virility that had run wild from the time of childhood, this symbol reinforced the determined and inflexible character of the man who had just kidnapped one of the richest women in the world.

Two guards seized Karin, Sergei, Alexandra and Matt. They waited for a moment as the third truck passed by splashing the ditches with thick, slimy mud.

Another vehicle – there were five in all, not counting the one, of course, that had been damaged – stopped in front of them.

Forcibly, the armed men made their prisoners climb aboard and tied them up in the same way as before. Screaming in pain because the wounds on his wrists were bleeding again, Serguei Kucharski tried to escape from this humiliating and challenging ritual.

A blow to the ribs punished this brief attempt at rebellion.

The climatologist's eyes filled with tears.

CHAPTER 3

When the convoy finally stopped, five of the captive members of the Orpheus expedition were unconscious. Distributed equally throughout the first three trucks, they had all slipped into a sort of coma filled with hallucinations caused by suffering, fear and the incessant swinging of vehicles that hiccupped along the tracks carved in the dense Amazonian jungle, jostling from side to side.

The stop meant deliverance. Or a prelude to Hell.

A few squeals of satisfaction. Sounds of boots splashing about in mud or water-logged soil. And, as always, the heady odor of the equatorial humidity mixed with diesel fumes from old and poorly maintained vehicles.

Then orders were given in a tone that left no room for discussion.

Soon, the tarpaulins covering the backs of the trucks were opened. The bandits seized the hostages, loosened their bonds at last and pushed them unceremoniously towards the exit. Those who had fainted during the journey were quickly revived when buckets of water were poured on them.

Haggard, the eleven members of the expedition directed and financed by Karin Stockhausen finally found themselves all together.

Naturally, they naturally wanted news about one another —especially those who had been wounded in the attack on their camp – while massaging their wrists, injured by ropes that were too tight. But the sinister expressions of the guards, accompanied by a few insults barked in Spanish, and their strong propensity to brandish their assault rifles and adopt warlike postures, aborted any attempts at discussions and comforting.

Since chatter and amiability were not really part of the kidnappers' mindset, the scientists of the Orpheus mission knew that the days ahead would be painful. Formidable. Dangerous.

The guards' behavior immediately confirmed this pessimism. Apparently, their only means of expression were blows and swearing.

Once they had all been taken out of the three trucks and freed from their bonds, Karin watched her colleagues at length, offering words of support to those who were wounded or panicked.

This was the case of Alexandra Haffington. Obviously, the biochemist was more at ease in her research laboratory than in the field. Her friends had had the opportunity to realize this by observing, with an air of mockery, it is true, her uncontrolled reactions when dealing with the animals of the jungle. Snakes especially. But today, the young woman with long blond hair and sparkling green eyes was not afraid of reptiles or spiders. No, she feared the worst predator ever: man!

Karin Stockhausen gently pushed one of the guards with her, moving to stand in front of the biochemist. She examined the other woman for a moment. A simple glance at the distraught face of the biochemist confirmed the intensity of the anguish that gripped her colleague whose luscious figure excited the darkest urges in their captors.

She took her hand.

"What are they going to do to us?" asked Alexandra, clasping Karin's hands in her own.

Karin Stockhausen clenched her teeth as the strength of young woman's grasp clearly illustrated the anguish that was creeping into her heart.

"Don't worry. Everything will be fine."

The biochemist opened her eyes wide. Obviously, she did not share this optimism at all.

"You saw what they did! These monsters beat our friends. They tied us up for hours. I'm scared!"

"I'm convinced that those who have kidnapped us want something from us." If it were only to hurt America or exact some sort of vengeance, they would have slaughtered us. Did you see their weapons?"

"Yes," said Alexandra, shuddering.

"If their only goal was to kill us, they would have done so by now. No, they have something else in mind. A villainous project no doubt."

"So?"

"If that's the case, it's in their interests to keep us alive so as to negotiate."

"With whom?" interrupted Sergei Kucharski.

Karin hesitated.

"No idea. For the time being, we've only heard orders concerning the convoy's movements and some insults in Spanish. It's a little early to form a definite opinion as to the true intentions of these armed brutes."

"True," admitted the fair-haired colossus. "But the kidnappers have chosen this place well. No one will find us here."

"So, we can remain prisoners for months in the forest?" asked Alexandra, who instinctively took Karin's hands in hers.

"I don't know," admitted the expedition leader.

The climatologist about to respond to this admission of helplessness when a few cries sprang out from the jungle surrounding the modest camp.

Phil Caldwell watched his surrounding carefully. His analysis was rapid. A small clearing where the boggy and chaotic road they had travelled for several hours ended. Around them: trees. More trees. And still more trees!

But, not really, in fact. Just north of the forest was a small building apparently made up of hastily cut tree trunks, palms and banana leaves. Quite rudimentary. Fragile.

However, it was from this direction that the man, who appeared to be the chief of the mercenaries who had attacked the expedition, made his way. His martial bearing, his instructions communicated in a dry and brittle tone, and the apparent respect the other guards gave him, left little doubt as to his real role and importance in the midst of this group.

He barked some orders.

A dozen men, still heavily armed, seized the prisoners in order to lead them toward this shed made of vegetation and carefully concealed under the high branches of the giant trees that covered this lush area located between the basins of the Orinoco, Essequibo and Amazon rivers.

Countless tributaries shaped a landscape that was both exuberant and dreary at the same time. Humidity reigned supreme. Moreover, the incessant rustle of insects quickly grew haunting.

Jostled unceremoniously, the captives, including Paula Cavendish, Serguei Kucharski, Linda Griffith, Luis Urube and Gregory Greensberg, who had been injured or beaten during the attack, walked slowly toward the building. They tried to ask a few questions, in English and Spanish, for those who were somewhat familiar with Cervantes' language. But the guards remained silent.

Obviously, the orders were clear: nothing was to be said to the prisoners for the time being!

A flock of macaws scattered overhead. They were chloroptera macaws, giant parrots with beautiful red heads and majestic silhouettes. With their marvelous plumage, all the colors of the rainbow dominated by cobalt blue and moss green, these wonderful birds brought a touch of gaiety to an environment filled with mud, putrefying organic matter and suffering.

But the cries of the large birds soon became unbearable for the unfortunate prisoners who were being pushed into the wooden shed.

Phil Caldwell walked over to one of the expedition guides: Fernando Pinzon. Arms firmly held behind their backs by ropes, the two men were not free to gesture. But as they walked side by side towards the shed, they were still able to exchange a few words in English.

"Do you know where we are?" asked the exoplanet specialist.

"No idea. As these trees block our view. We can't even see Mount Roraima."

"But…"

Looking at the Stanford scientist with his gold-flecked brown eyes, the Venezuelan guide simply said, "In any case, I don't think we're in Guyana."

"How do you know?"

"Although I can't see it, I feel that Mount Roraima is to the east. So, that means we must be in the extreme south of Venezuela. Or north of Brazil."

"You feel? Without seeing?"

"Life in the jungle develops certain senses. But I can't…"

Fernando Pinzon was abruptly interrupted as the guard who followed him twisted his hands violently to force him to keep quiet. As his wrists were sore after the long trip in the truck, he whimpered and looked at Phil.

At the moment, the guide and the astrophysicist both understood that the days to come were going to be very difficult.

Shouts and cries rang out to their right. They turned their heads in unison and saw that Gregory Greensberg had once again been struck on the side of his head. The logistician fell to the ground. Without hesitating, the brute who had beaten him pulled the man back to his feet, insulting him so that he would go faster.

Less than a minute later, the prisoners found themselves facing the entrance to the shed, its walls made of staggered rows of branches lined with giant palm leaves. The structure was not very solid. But the presence of armed, nervous and violent men eradicated all will to flee.

The hostages were shoved unceremoniously into the enclosed space, where a strong smell of old sweat dominated. It combined with the smell of urine and the heady fragrances of fermenting vegetation, making the atmosphere almost unbreathable.

A humidity level of close to 100%, no window and flooring made of freshly cut grasses were now the daily life of members of the Orpheus expedition.

As she entered, Karin rebelled and tried to escape from her guard. But the latter increased the pressure on her forearms and elbows without striking her. The Stockhausen family heiress had a good idea of the underlying reason for her slightly privileged status compared to that of her companions in misfortune. But she locked this thought up deep in her heart. The situation was serious enough already. There was no point worrying her colleagues and friends any more.

Once they were all inside, the leader of the gang spoke in a clear voice. And in English.

"Sit down on the ground!"

"But ..." Serguei Kucharski tried.

Yet another blow with a rifle butt, this time to his right knee, made him realize that these energetic men spoke better with their weapons arms than with their words.

As the "guests" were slow to react, the man who had just spoken made a precise sign. Immediately, the guards seized the captives. Then they forced them to sit in pairs along the walls of the elongated, rectangular building.

Alexandra Haffington and Phil Caldwell were seated very close to one another and they immediately realized that a giant cockroach was quietly walking about among the grass lying on the ground. Just in front of them. The unfortunate biochemist stifled a cry. Phil whispered a few words in her ear to calm her.

The result was disappointing.

Once each expedition member was sitting in place, the gang leader looked carefully at the twelve prisoners seated face to face. He grimaced and left the shed.

CHAPTER 4

Two minutes later, another silhouette emerged in the doorway which brought a bit of light into the sinister place.

The newcomer planted himself in front of his hostages like a bully taunting his enemies.

He stepped forward and said in a thundering voice, "My name is Felipe Maldorano!"

He let out a brief silence. Then he added, "Your salvation or your death depend on me. And you!"

As he spoke, Felipe held a pistol in his right hand and a long machete in his left.

The man who considered himself the gang leader was of Mexican or South American origin. The hostages who had travelled in the damaged vehicle had already caught a fleeting glimpse of him as they were transferred to another truck. But now they could all examine his unsettling silhouette. His dark skin, black hair and large mustache gave him the look of an imitation Emiliano Zapata. But it was obvious that Felipe Maldorano had no intention of fighting any oppressor in order to free people subjected to an unjust law.

His law could probably be summed up in two words that govern the world: money and power. The logic of terror used for power was also visible in his face with the long, blistered scar that adorned his nose and forehead.

One singular feature stood out in the man's body, marked by unshackled violence and raw fury: his eyes. Completely incongruous in the chiseled face, his eyes were a marvelous blue, both intense and pale at the same time. Aquamarine flecked with indigo. But his presence and his weapons immediately contradicted the apparent serenity of his gaze.

The kidnappers' chief stood there, with an arrogant bearing accentuated by the backlight.

The prisoners remained silent. The armed guards did too.

This clearly demonstrated that Felipe Maldorano's natural authority was unquestionable. Absolute. This hold was certainly a result of his strength of character and charisma. But it was also easy to imagine that this almost servile obedience was nourished by a single source: the ferocity that drove the man. Authoritarian. Implacable.

And the fact that Felipe carelessly kept his machete in his extended left arm further accentuated this latent threat.

The man was a wild beast. He proved it immediately.

"If everything goes well, you will be released in less than a week."

"What do you want?" asked Karin Stockhausen, drilling her amethyst gaze at the leader.

Driven by anger, the veins on the man's neck stretched his skin like ropes on a sailboat.

"Money!" replied Felipe, with disconcerting ease. "Lots of money!"

He let it a moment.

Then he continued, disdaining the other ten captives, "If your family is reasonable, and obeys all my orders, you and your colleagues will soon see the light of day. If not…"

"If they don't?" interrupted Gregory Greensberg.

Felipe Maldorano frowned. Obviously, the gang leader gang did not like being interrupted in an almost private discussion that he seemed to want to have between the heiress to the Stockhausen fortune and himself.

Immediately, the guard next to the logistician approached Gregory and kicked him in the ribs. The prisoner's light gray eyes lit up immediately with a flame in which hatred and a desire for murder danced.

But the logistics manager remained motionless. He knew full well that Felipe wanted only one thing: to make an example. It was even very probable that he would enjoy that immensely.

Gregory had no desire to play the martyr and decided to reserve his ingenuity and his hatred for other occasions.

"If they don't," replied Felipe, "You will be executed one by one, until no one questions my determination."

While hammering out his sentence, the man began to spin his machete like a samurai would do with his war sword: the formidable katana.

"This man is crazy," thought Phil Caldwell, pursing his lips to keep his thoughts from turning into words.

The prisoners looked at one another. Despite of differences in behavior, stooped shoulders, terrified grimaces, the eyes did not lie. The scientists all knew that the man standing in front of them, holding a long machete with a shiny blade, could cut their throats with a single move.

His apparent calm hid a tension and a visceral cruelty which the lure of a colossal prize multiplied.

Karin Stockhausen was both responsible for the expedition and the only real bargaining chip because of her family's fortune, which was well-known and which *Forbes Magazine*[5] highlighted every year. The young woman with the flamboyant mane started speaking again, without blinking, to show that the brute pontificating in front of her did not scare her.

---

[5] Established in 1917, *Forbes* is an American economic magazine that annually lists all the billionaires in the world (dollars) by classifying them according to the estimated amount of their fortune. By 2015, the Stockhausen family appeared in 50th position with a fortune estimated at $16 billion.

Since she was the only prisoner who held any real value in the eyes of Felipe Maldorano, she had to act with cautiously so as to avoid endangering her colleagues' lives. Since the gang leader was determined and his associates were armed brutes, it was absolutely necessary to avoid any conflict that could had disastrous consequences.

Karin looked at her kidnapper and simply said, "What do you want?"

"To free you. And as quickly as possible!"

"Perfect. And in exchange for what?"

"I won't discuss that here. Especially not in front of your colleagues."

Felipe sniffed for a moment.

Then he blew his nose in a particularly inelegant manner. The gang leader took on the airs of a lord. But he was essentially a scoundrel prepared to kill his father and mother for money. Apart from the antipathy his character provoked, this showed above all that the lives of others were of little importance to him. If things went wrong, he would not hesitate to put his threats into action.

A skillful negotiator when it was came time to bring forces together and obtain funds from her wealthy friends for the development of the Orpheus Foundation, Karin wondered if this talent would be of use when dealing with a barbarian prepared to do anything for a ransom. She was not sure. Not at all!

However, she had no choice. She continued, "Very good. Let's talk alone, if that's what you want."

"What I wish is for you to you shut up!" he snapped, raising his machete above the red-haired woman who closed her eyes in terror.

"Is he on drugs?" Linda Griffith, the expedition doctor, wondered silently.

The prisoners looked at one another again. They were growing more and more worried. If the kidnapper was unable to control himself after a simple question, that means anything else would go badly. The guards remained impassive, but their flickering eyelid and forced grins showed that they too were suspicious of Felipe Maldorano's violent and uncontrolled reactions.

Madorano began to pace nervously, passing very close to the feet of the captives who were all seated, their legs stretched out and back leaning uncomfortably against along the wall of wood, palms and latticework made from a plant with soft and solid stems similar rattan.

When he finally grew calm, Felipe took up a position in the center of the only opening in the shack concealed under the high foliage of jungle titans. As he stood there, light flowed in behind him, which conferred on his somber silhouette a fleeting and illusive aura.

"We'll discuss all this later. Meanwhile, I'll tell you what you will be allowed to do in the coming days. Everything else is forbidden!"

As he uttered this last sentence, his almost angelic blue eyes lit up with flames that left no room for compassion. If, of course, that word even held meaning for Felipe Maldorano.

Felipe came over and stood right in front of Karin Stockhausen's feet; she was seated closest to the door on the right side of the dusty, stinky shed.

One by one, he observed the prisoners sitting on the ground and continued, "First, all of you, in turn, will give me your name, your age, and the role you play at Orpheus. If you make a comment, ask a question or utter an insult, I'll cut your foot off at the ankle!"

In order to confirm this threat and prove that it was not a simple boast, he slowly slid the tip of the blade of his machete along Karin's legs. She did not flinch. She settled for boldly staring at their captor while clenching her jaws.

Felipe seemed to appreciate the heiress' courage. He relaxed and began provide a brief version of her biography, once again revealing that she was the only captive who would remain alive in case of trouble.

"For Karin, there's no point. I know that you're 34, you're still not married, you're blessed with prestigious degrees from the largest English and American universities, and your family's fortune is estimated at over $15 billion. This information is enough for me. Let's move on to your neighbor."

As he spoke, he pointed his weapon at Fernando Pinzon.

"My name is Fernando Pinzon. I'm 42 years old and one of the two expedition guides."

The unfortunate Venezuelan Orpheus associate was dripping with sweat. He closed his eyes for a moment.

"That's perfect!" Felipe replied. "That's exactly what I want from all of you. Next!"

"Matt Lochner. 49 years old. I'm a journalist and cameraman for the expedition."

"Cameraman!" laughed the kidnappers' leader. "Perfect! I'll need you quite soon."

"But..." said the blond reporter, whose blue eyes widened with countless questions.

Felipe pretended to point the blade of his machete at the unfortunate man's left ankle.

He fell silent.

"Let's continue!"

"My name is Linda Griffith. I'm 36 years old and I'm the expedition doctor."

"You know how to deal with wounds and nasty injuries?" Felipe asked, with a sarcastic tone.

"Yes," Linda replied saying another word.

This laconic reply seemed to suit the maniac parading about with his long machete and pistol. He rubbed his chin energetically. For a moment, the rustling of the thick beard being scratched became the only sound giving rhythm to the infernal flow of seconds in the rudimentary building.

"Continue!"

"Martin Physter. 34 years old. I'm an edaphologist."

"Edapho what?" "Edaphologist."

"What's an... edaphologist?"

"It's a branch of geology. I study soils as a natural habitat for plants. This is very important in the case of Mount Roraima's peak, where the fauna and flora are so unique."

The scientist seemed terrified and the words oozed out of his mouth, rather than being uttered clearly. Having been forced to a little more explanation to make is work understandable, he feared the anger of the man on whom their lives depended 100%.

However, Felipe did not get angry. He merely raised his eyebrows, nodding his head doubtfully and thoughtfully at the same time.

Having questioned the five expedition members who were on the side where Karin was seated, he turned to the other wall. Just for fun, he kicked the second guide in the ankle.

"And you? What's your name?"

"Luis Urube sir," stammered the second guide, who was completely terrorized.

"And?"

"I'm 35 years old and I'm a guide for Ms. Stockhausen."

"Sir. Ms. You're very polite! I don't like people who are too polite. They're often snakes with angels' faces. And I don't like either snakes or angels!"

The unfortunate Luis hunched his head into his neck, as certain turtles do so well. He was waiting for the blow.

But Felipe continued his quiet examination of his new victims.

"Your turn!" he said, examining Sergei.

"Serguei Kucharski. 56 years old. Climatologist."

"A Russian who will tell us why the wicked Americans and the Chinese villains are destroying our planet!" Felipe burst out laughing.

"I'm American," Serguei said. "My father was of Russian origin. But I was born in North Dakota."

"Shut up! I make the comments here!" roared the kidnappers' leader spitting his hatred out in a mist of saliva. "My guards noticed you. You like playing the rebel! If you want to rebel... it's simple. You make a move and I put a bullet in your head. That clear?"

The colossus with steel-gray eyes blinked once in agreement. His friends sitting in front of him could easily see that he was holding back a reply. The muscles of his cheeks and his neck rolled under his skin.

But he remained silent.

Felipe seemed somewhat irritated by this silence, which was eroding his own fury. But, as he had just asked the hostages to remain silent, he could hardly blame Serguei when the man obeyed.

The brute sighed deeply and continued his slow stroll after, once again, looking daggers at the climatologist.

"My name is Alexandra Haffington. I'm 28 years old and I'm a biochemist."

The young blonde with the green eyes had astutely anticipated any question. As she was, strictly speaking, respecting the instructions given by the man who had just kidnapped them, this precaution was intended to protect her.

And it did. Felipe's face split in an enigmatic smile and he settled for saying, "Welcome among us."

Then he headed toward Phil Caldwell.

"And you there, redhead! Who are you?"

"My name is Phil Caldwell. I'm 41 years old and I'm an astrophysicist."

"Astrophysicist! And what are you doing with these people specializing in small animals and stunted ferns?"

"I study exoplanets. As such, I'm interested in all forms of life in extreme environments."

"Why?"

"With water, carbon and oxygen, our planet has developed some very strange life forms that could be found, possibly, on certain exoplanets both near and far."

Phil Caldwell grimaced. The justification for his work with Karin and her colleagues at Orpheus had been summed up in a single sentence, which was a feat on its own. But it was long. Most likely too long for the seemingly limited patience of their new tyrant.

Surprisingly, this was not the case. Felipe stretched his lower lip forward, giving his face a rather grotesque look.

He nodded and said, "Very good. Very good."

Phil breathed a little. No one would cut off his foot – or his hand – today.

The head of the hostage takers stopped in front of the last woman of the expedition next.

He looked at her.

"You?"

"I'm Paula Cavendish. I'm 44 years old. I'm a biologist and I'm sick."

"Tropical diseases?"

"No. Vomiting after the beating I took."

"I'll see to it that your doctor treats you. We have some medicine here. But if any of you intend to have an appendicitis attack, you'll die here because we have no hospital."

After a brief pause,

"Is that clear?"

The biologist stirred about. Then she began to vomit again.

Since none of the guards intervened, even to help her to stand up, Linda Griffith took charge.

Felipe made a discreet gesture to calm one of his men who was preparing to strike a woman who simply wanted to help another.

"Absolute brutes..." Karin thought, without moving her lips.

At that very moment, the sole heiress to the Stockhausen fortune told herself that she and her colleagues had truly fallen into the worst possible hands, with the exception, of course, of terrorists who killed, burned, beheaded and massacred all those who do not share their ideas and their religion.

When Linda was finally able to help her friend to her feet, they stood there for a long time, their backs pressed against the wall of hurriedly braided palms. Haggard, they looked at the men around them for whom life meant little. At that moment, they no doubt recalled reports about the violence of gangs, drug traffickers, garimpeiros, those seeking gold and precious gems who devastated the Amazon.

Images of murder, rape and summary executions danced fleetingly before their eyes.

They shivered.

"And you?" Felipe asked, hitting heels of the logistics manager with the back of his machete.

"Gregory Greensberg. 50 years old. Logistician for this expedition. You and I..."

"Yes?" roared Felipe, squatting very close to Gregory and placing pistol on the temple of the man who dared to defy him.

Silence.

"You were going to say something?"

"When do we eat here?"

CHAPTER 5

A thundering laugh.

Then a grimace. Horrible. Hateful.

"You like to be funny... Gregory! That's it?"

Experienced at dealing with difficult situations and an eternal adventurer who had taken part in countless missions around the globe, Gregory Greensberg said nothing. He attempted to put a mask of impassivity on his face, in an effort to calm the situation.

He was partially successful, since the arrogant hostage taker merely stated, "If you enjoy humor, you'll be spoiled here. But back to the essentials: the rules of life in the camp."

The prisoners all looked at the man who now held their lives in his hands.

"The principle is simple: you listen. Then you obey."

Karin lowered her head a little. The preamble was clear. Its consequences will undoubtedly be painful.

"If everything goes well, we'll stay here. Generally, all you will have to do is wait and sleep. From time to time, and in order to answer our friend," he continued, pointing at Gregory with his machete, "You will be able to as well. There is no real toilet. A hole installed on the other side of this wall between a few trees, with two tarpaulins, will make do."

Some of the hostages swallowed, especially the women. To isolate themselves in the jungle between two tarps quickly put in place and under the unfriendly surveillance of one or two armed guards did not enthuse them. Not at all!

At the same time... what could they do? There would be no point in talking about dignity, the need for privacy and respect with armed brutes. Since regular beatings, blows to their ribs or heads, was not a priority objective for these specialists in ethology, they merely sighed.

"Good. We're only asking you to do one thing: obey orders. If the Stockhausen family is reasonable and cooperates, you'll be released soon and all this will be only a bad memory. Life will go on and you won't suffer and aftereffects. But if Karin's father does not do what I ask in a very short time, things could go wrong...

As he uttered those last words, Felipe Maldorano's expression suddenly hardened. The veins of his neck stood out under his skin and his forehead grew moist. This was not really surprising as it was hot and abominably wet in this makeshift shed stuck under the foliage of gigantic trees. But, this time, his sweating was fueled by an anger that seemed almost inextinguishable on the part of this man who wanted to make one of the most powerful families in the world bend.

"What do you want exactly?" Karin asked cunningly, knowing that no one would dare to hit her or torture her because it was her life that mattered most to Felipe.

"I haven't finished," replied the mustachioed man with blue eyes.

The guards shifted a little. Their leader calmed them with an authoritarian and precise gesture.

"As I said just now, obeying means that there will be no need to repeat the same thing five times. If I say, 'Standing up!', then you stand up. Right away!"

He turned to Luis Urube.

The guard felt an enormous ball invade his stomach and chest.

"You! Stand up!"

Luis stood up with some difficulty because his legs were numb. But he did his utmost to ensure that he complied as quickly as possible.

Felipe watched him, gave the ghost of a smile that looked more like a grimace.

Then he said, "Very good. Sit down now!"

The Venezuelan guide sat down again, his legs resting on the floor littered with leaves and his back leaning against the walls.

Everyone thought that, after this demonstration of forced obedience, they would move on to something else. Error.

"Stand up!"

Felipe had just pointed at Serguei Kucharski with the tip of his machete blade.

The climatologist did not react immediately. It was difficult to know whether this was because he was making a challenge or because his injuries slowed ability to react. Obviously, Felipe viewed it as a challenge. He signaled to the guard closest to the climatologist. The armed man immediately went over to Serguei and struck him in the right shoulder with the butt of his rifle.

Sergei Kucharski shouted once and moaned a little.

As the brute was about to strike again, Sergei raised his left arm and said, "I'm getting up. No point hitting me."

The athletic blond man slowly stood up, using the hand and arm that had not been struck. He finally got up and stared at the man who seemed to take true pleasure in tyrannizing and humiliating his prisoners.

"That's better," said Felipe. "Stay like that bit, you damned climatologist! That will teach you to obey without balking."

Then he turned to the other hostages and stared at them one by one.

"Do you have understood what I mean by obey now?"

A few discreet nods replied to him in silence.

"Good!"

As Felipe Maldorano did not go any further in his puerile demonstration of power, both his men and the prisoners all watched him carefully. It was obvious that this little jungle tyrant took great pleasure in such moments. He imposed his will on all and even his silences took on an unusual pattern. For a kidnapper who had probably spent his childhood in a poverty-stricken suburb of a large South American city, the respect developed out of greed, or fear, symbolized a brilliant revenge on a destiny that must not have been easy during the first twenty years of his life.

The braggart made the most of the power which violence and cruelty conferred upon him for a long moment.

Finally, he continued, saying, "I imagine the reason for your kidnapping is clear to everyone. It is not because you intended to climb Mount Roraima or to strip you of some personal belongings. Nor is it for any stupid ideology. I am my only god!" he summed up, with a great burst of laughter.

He scratched his chin again, which seemed to be either a ritual that helped him think or a simple tic to hide his nervousness and a deeply buried fear that he had continued to hide from himself since his first murders.

"The real and only reason for this mass kidnapping is money. Money of course! The driving force behind all power, the mirror of human infamy and the only thing that really counts in a world where everyone, rich or poor, generous or bastard, winds up eaten by worms a few brief decades after being born. Your foundation is rich. But it was not your Foundation that I took hostage. It's Karin Stockhausen!"

The captives stared at one another. They had been fearing this statement, which marginalized the interest of their own lives, from the moment the person responsible for this immense mess confessed that the ten other prisoners had no real value.

They were, above all, a burden and their life expectancy had just been reduced significantly.

However, Felipe Maldorano said the exact opposite twenty seconds later.

"I have not had your friends executed immediately, for they will all be useful to me. I can even say that, if the Stockhausen family follows my instructions to the letter and obeys without balking, you will all be able to return home in a few days. And in good health. All this will then be nothing but a painful memory. That's all."

As one of his men was starting slip away, he changed his subject, glaring at the guard.

"Where are you going?"

"To piss," replied the guard, who took advantage of the interruption to make a horrible grimace.

"Did I tell you to go away and leave your post?"

"Uh, no. But I really have to..."

Without taking the trouble to answer him, Felipe approached the rebel whose bladder dictated his behavior to him. He quietly put the barrel of his pistol on the man's fly and simply, "You hold on or I'll blow your balls off!"

The image was both strong and eloquent. The unfortunate man grimaced again, sweating. Then he nodded to express his submission. In any case it was too late. The crotch of his trousers grew moist.

Felipe burst out laughing again.

"There you go! Problem solved! You see how simple life can be when you obey orders without racking your brains."

He turned on his heel with disconcerting speed and pointed at the prisoners one by one, saying "The same applies to all of you. You obey and you'll live in peace. Or almost. You disobey... and I cut you up piece by piece like a butcher! That clear?"

The prisoners nodded while wondering about the mental health of the man who held them under his yoke. The shouts, the violence, were all useless, overacted or, and much more disturbing, the almost permanent verbal virulence was the sign of a madman.

Carnage was to be feared.

"The situation is very simple indeed," he said. "Your disappearance must have been reported already. So, the Venezuelan authorities will start looking for you. Rest assured, they won't find us. In New York, the Stockhausen family will move heaven and earth to find out what has happened. Given its influence, one can even imagine that some military satellites are discreetly observing the area around Mount Roraima. They won't find us because we are and will remain invisible under this beneficent forest that hides us. In the jungle, the dense foliage protects us. Thermal and infrared observations, possibly by helicopters or satellites, will remain ineffective because the ambient temperature is close to that of a human body. To find something with a temperature of 37° C in an environment where the ambient temperature between 33° C and 36° C is almost impossible. So..."

He stood there, for once perfectly calm, and left his sentence dangle for a moment so his audience could realize exactly what he meant.

Once Felipe felt that everyone understood, he continued, "Starting tomorrow morning, Karin will have the kindness to give me a little of her precious time so that we can call her family and start negotiations. I almost forgot, the presence of your cameraman, Matt... Matt, is that right?"

"Yes," said Matt Lochner, without trying to say more.

"Perfect. So, Karin and Matt will have a little discussion with me before we call Friedrich Stockhausen and we will be able to show him a little video that will very clearly indicate that my requirements are not negotiable."

When they heard about the telephone call, several captives looked at one another with an expressive pout. How could they remain invisible by calling the family of one of the hostages?

Felipe immediately noticed these chain reactions and smiled.

He stood in front of Gregory Greensberg, whom he had apparently taken a dislike for. He stared intently at the logistician and stared directly into the other man's gray eyes, which caused many women, from adolescents to the most mature adults, to swoon.

"You think I'm a fool?"

"No. Not at all," replied Gregory, trying to look impassive.

"I saw the looks you exchanged. You saying to yourself that in, in this time and day, using a phone when you don't want to be spotted is totally stupid."

The blond logistician remained silent.

"You're right! In principle... That's the best way to be located in a few minutes. But I have an effective way to hamper geolocation. Very effective even. I have a hundred phones that have been stolen from various stores in Venezuela, Brazil and Guyana. They don't have batteries for the time being. I also have more than 1,000 prepaid and unregistered SIM cards. You starting to understand?"

"Yes," Gregory admitted.

"What am I going do? Come on! Don't be afraid to speak up. I won't beat you this time because I'm the one asking you to answer."

Gregory Greensberg ran his tongue over his parched lips. He sighed, and finally started to speak, not without first taking a close look at the guard next to him.

"By speaking very little time each time, removing the batteries immediately to turn off the phone completely and using a different SIM card each time you call, your communications will be virtually untraceable. Especially if you use a different phone and a different SIM card each time."

"That's it!"

The chief of the hostage takers squatted in front of Gregory and tapped the other man's cheek.

Then he stood up and said, "You're perfectly right! I may have been mistaken about you Gregory. In fact, I love you!"

He laughed then, which immediately put the reality of his words into perspective.

"How can my family contact you, then?" asked Karin, staring directly at her enemy with her fascinating amethyst eyes.

"I'll call them. And when they have to give me the information that I ask them, they will use a different means of communication."

Fernando Pinzon sighed heavily.

As he simultaneously shook his head as a sign of denial, Felipe went to him and asked him, in Spanish, if he had anything to say on the subject.

"It won't work," said the Venezuelan guide, as he blinked his eyes, ready for the blow.

"Why not?"

"The Venezuelan army will want to take action immediately before the Americans have any inclination to intervene."

"And what will the Venezuelan army do?" asked Felipe, whose forehead, and cheeks were starting to turn red under the effect of stifled anger.

"It will move into the entire portion of the jungle located at the foot of Mount Roraima."

"The Venezuelan portion."

"Yes. Of course."

"Yes! Of course!" sneered the head of the hostage takers.

At the same moment he grabbed a heavy stick placed vertically just beside the door of the makeshift shed. Live like a jaguar moving in on its prey, he approached the guide who had dared to question his strategy.

With a blow, he struck Fernando on the head. The arch of the man's left eyebrow exploded under the impact. The unfortunate man's eyes and face were immediately flooded with blood.

"Do you think I'm a moron? Some blind and deaf strategist? Why do you think that we're still in Venezuelan territory?"

It was impossible to respond to that remark. It was, indeed, more than likely that the slow and chaotic journey from the place of the abduction and the kidnappers' camp had taken them across the border. No doubt, the hostages and their captors were now at the extreme northern tip of the border between Brazil and Venezuela, probably close to the small village of Laramonta.

Felipe grabbed Fernando by his blood-stained T-shirt and pulled the other man to his feet with one hand. Facing him. No doubt satisfied with this new show of force, he settled for taunting his prisoner.

He spat in Fernando's face and said, "Take a seat! Clown!"

Still flushed with the anger and violence that apparently never left him, he turned to the other members of the Orpheus expedition.

"In less than an hour you will be divided into two groups. And there's one thing I'd like everyone to understand right away. I say right away!"

Since his eyes grew deliriously bright and the veins at his temples bulged as if they were about to burst, everyone looked attentively at this new master of the jungle who viewed himself a wild beast terrorizing his prey. A tacky beast, certainly, but those are often the most dangerous. The most unpredictable!

"This negotiation with the Stockhausen family will be short. But it must be done in keeping with my wishes. If the Venezuelan or Brazilian army tries to intervene, I kill hostages in front of the cameras! If the US special forces attempt a commando operation, I kill hostages! If the Stockhausen family does not pay or tries to confuse me... I kill hostages! Is that clear?"

Silence.

"Is that clear?" he repeated staring at Karin.

"Yes," replied the heiress to the 50th largest fortune in the world.

A macaw made a dreadful noise just then, as it landed heavily on the roof of the building, scraping the woven branches with its giant wings.

CHAPTER 6

Felipe Maldorano kept his promise.

At the first signs of twilight, Paula Cavendish, Martin Physter, Matt Lochner Luis Urube, Fernando Pinzon and Gregory Greensberg were unceremoniously pulled from the first building where they had stayed in unbearable dampness and transferred to a second prison built in the same manner. Located slightly below, it was nestled even deeper in the jungle.

During their brief transfer, the logistician and the two guides noticed that a third building, also built with tree trunks and palms, extended behind the other two. The entire site was discreet and completely invisible from the sky because of the dense foliage that separated the canopy from the ground. And being visible from the road was not a problem. There was no road. Just a muddy trail guarded by armed men in regular relays.

Once the two groups of hostages had been installed and several took up their positions at the corners of each of these makeshift hangars, the tension dropped slightly. After he had reported that one of the buildings had a small infirmary and that Linda Griffith would play a role in the event of illness or injury, Felipe Maldorano departed for the other end of the camp, contributing greatly to this lull.

Karin began talking to Phil Caldwell. But she was almost immediately interrupted by one of Felipe's men, who reminded her that the captives were to be silent. Except when questioned.

Looks and gestures replaced words. But these aphonic exchanges quickly faded in the sediment of daily life in which most of the captives' time was spent watching insects and meticulously counting fan-shaped blades of palm leaves in an effort to avoid lamenting their fate.

It didn't help much.

In the prison of wood and leaves where Karin was held captive, an incident quickly broke the monotony of a painful imprisonment in the middle of the jungle. Alexandra Haffington asked to go to the toilet by addressing the guard closest to her. The man complied without saying a word. But another of Felipe's minions intervened, pointing out that he was the one who should accompany Alexandra. Obviously, the first guard had to be familiar with his colleague's sexual appetites. Felipe's orders were clear: the prisoners were not to be touched without his consent and the four women in the group were not to be harassed!

In this particular context, the first guard did not want the situation to degenerate. For, in that case, the kidnappers' leader would hold him responsible for the possible sexual abuse endured by the young woman. And he would be punished. Obviously, this possibility terrified him.

The two men began to hurl insults in Spanish. Then the second, whose name was Ricardo, grabbed the left arm of the unfortunate biochemist. He immediately began to caress her breasts without any shame. The other man – Pedro apparently because Ricardo had repeated his name several times when mocking his accomplice – grabbed Ricardo by his hand and indicated that he should return to his place.

However, after pretending to release his grip, Ricardo turned back to the young, blonde woman, eyes gleaming explicitly. The crudity of his desire had already created a lump in his trousers covered with oil stains and other dubious spots.

He shoved Alexandra against the wall and began to slip his dirty, damp hands between the legs of the panic-stricken biochemist.

Pedro arrived from behind and grabbed his opponent by the shoulders to shove him aside. Both men fell.

The cries of the altercation, of course, attracted other guards who, at first, were happy just to observe the two men as they struggling and writhed on the ground like cut worms. Then, one of them took the initiative to warn Felipe, who arrived less than a minute later, holding his pistol, a Beretta apparently, in his right hand.

In his left, he held a long combat knife.

"What's all this mess!" he yelled in Spanish.

While the situation was clear, his face, twisted in rage, was even more so.

He immediately went to stand in front of the two men and ordered them to get up. They obeyed immediately.

"Let me repeat my question. What's going on here? What the fuck is this?"

Pedro got in ahead of his new enemy by speaking at once, "Ricardo was bothering the blond girl as she asked to go to the bathroom and I was about to accompany her."

"Is this true?" Felipe barked, looking at Ricardo like a snake trying to hypnotize his prey.

"No. Well, yes, but…"

"But what? What did I say about the women we captured?"

"We are not to touch them."

"Right! So, let me ask you a new question: What don't you understand about *we are not to touch the women*?"

"But,.."

"But what?"

"The urge was too strong."

The gunshot rang out so loudly in the confined space that the insects and bats that had settled on the roof flew off at the speed of lightning.

Ricardo screamed in pain as he looked at his hand. Incredulous.

Blood pissed abundantly on the floor and a piece of bone was clearly visible. Felipe had shot straight at the fingers of his left hand without worrying about where the ball would land after smashing through the bones. The Beretta and its 9 mm parabellum balls caused a great deal of damage to the guard. Not to mention the eardrums of the hostages and the guards located nearby.

"The next time you disobey me, I will shoot you in the head or bleed you like a pig! Is that clear?"

"Yes," whined Ricardo, his eyes bulging and his left hand bleeding.

"Linda! Take care of this asshole. Alfonso will show you where the infirmary is," he said, pointing at the guard who had informed him about the altercation and was standing next to him.

He looked at Ricardo once more and spat black juice of questionable origin on the floor.

"Disinfect the wound and apply dressing. That's enough. Anyway, this rutting asshole... is carrion. Nothing more. If he dies, the jaguars will make an excellent meal of his warm corpse!"

The other guards held their breath. Felipe looked at the careless man who had dared to defy his orders one last time.

"With a broken left wrist, you won't be able to fight with just one hand. So, you're of no use to me any longer. As a result, you'll do the dishes and make the meals. And if you don't, it doesn't matter. You'll play the whore for my men! It's been a long time since they've screwed a woman, a man or a goat. You can satisfy all their desires!"

He burst out laughing and left the building, telling the other three guards, "If anyone is entitled to make the hostages suffer here... it's me! And me alone! Those who don't get this will suffer the same fate as Ricardo."

The message was clear.

Ricardo walked ahead, whining, accompanied by Alfonso and Linda Griffith, who made the most of the opportunity to get a look at the entire camp. First, the trio walked past the other shed where their six ill-fated companions were held. Despite the twilight, the air was still warm and damp. Luckily, there had been no rain for two days. But it was easy to imagine how rapidly the soil, already spongy, could transformed into thick mud with the first storm.

The slightly spicy scents of the jungle were drowned by the smell of damp soil, with the hint of urine and excrement that proved that the group led by Felipe Maldorano's iron fist had been there for some time already.

After walking along the building, they very quickly reached the third and last building. It was built in the same manner. One difference: there were several doors along one side instead of a single one at the end. Alfonso entered straight off through the door at the end of the shed which, because of its multiple openings, had to be partitioned into several spaces.

Felipe had used the word "infirmary". That was an exaggeration.

Linda immediately realized that she could only provide extremely basic care and treatment here. A ramshackle shelf contained a few boxes with dressings, medicines stacked carelessly, and a cardboard box containing syringes, a small pair of scissors, and raveling cotton.

That was all.

Linda's eyes widened and she looked distressed, which did not escape Alfonso.

"There's not much here. But you'll have to make do," he said in very correct English.

"Fine," sighed the young doctor, who, when she had joined the Orpheus team, had not planned to treat gunshot wounds.

She began to clean the wound with alcohol. Ricardo grimaced, moaned a little, but did not shout. Obviously, his manhood and his bearing as a big macho moron had just been ridiculed by his leader. Whining in front of a woman would only add ridicule to his disgrace. He feigned courage, even if his grimaces and the compulsive movements of his lips clearly illustrated his suffering and dismay at the idea of not being able to use his left hand as he had in the past.

Linda was not completely reassuring.

"I'll do my best to prevent infection. But I can't guarantee that you'll still have the use of all your fingers afterwards."

Alfonso translated this into Spanish because the wounded man did not speak a word of English.

Once the wound had been cleaned, Linda gently applied an antibiotic ointment. Her choice was simple: it was the only one.

Using a strip of gauze, she wrapped the guard's hand, making sure to tie it tightly enough to hold the broken bone in place. Healing was by no means assured, but the doctor had done everything humanly possible under such circumstances. Ricardo stammered vague thanks and sat down on a straw chair.

The doctor realized just then that her role could be important in a very isolated place where strangers were unwelcome. After brushing aside her auburn bangs, which had been glued to her forehead with the implicit help of abundant perspiration, she tried to start up a conversation with Alfonso. That man had the double advantage of speaking English and being, apparently in any case, close to Felipe.

"Life must be difficult here?"

"More or less."

The conciseness of the answer made it clear that man did not want to speak.

Linda watched him. Alfonso was quite small. He was about thirty years old. His swarthy skin, dark eyes, and a broad face, covered in several places by several day's growth of beard, indicated without a doubt that he was a native of the region. This was the case of all the guards the prisoners had been able to see so far. He was wearing pants and a shirt of doubtful green that had been coated with brown spots during his many trips into jungle.

She swallowed and stared at Alfonso.

"What will he do with us?"

"Who?"

"Felipe."

"He told you."

"Please, be more specific."

"If Karin Stockhausen's family pays, everything will be fine. If not, I don't know what will happen."

"He could kill us one by one?"

"I have nothing more to say."

Obviously irritated, Alfonso asked Linda to get up with a sharp, precise gesture.

Leaving Ricardo behind to whine in his corner, after giving him one or two recommendations in Spanish and in an unkind tone, he walked Linda toward the exit.

Walking past one of the doors that stood along the side of the only building that did not hold any hostages, Linda glimpsed a man she had not seen before.

He appeared to be in his forties. His skull was completely bald and his face, although hidden in the shade, was obviously not South American. Pale, pallid skin, an elongated and bony face, a gigantic nose and clear blue eyes, all indicated a European origin. Probably Slavic or Scandinavian.

She asked Alfonso a final question. But he did not reply.

CHAPTER 7

"I'm afraid," murmured Alexandra Haffington, looking at Karin.

Immediately after they had eaten a very rough dinner consisting of bananas and an infamous cassava-based brew, the captives' ankles were once again shackled. The guards then dragged them by the feet, forcing them all to lie down on a floor littered with what looked like cattle fodder. A bit of straw, grass and a few leaves served as their mattress. It did not require a fine-tuned sense of hearing, to clearly hear the characteristic crunching of the hundreds of insects that swarmed about in the heart of this carpet of vegetation and its many hiding places.

Alexandra did not know what terrified her the most: the guards with their wily looks or the little creatures that moved about in all directions under her resting place. But the result was obvious: the biochemist was panic-stricken.

Of course, night did not help.

"Don't worry," said Karin, in a very soft voice, so as not to annoy the armed men who were watching them. "It's not in their interests to kill or torture us."

"For the time being," said Phil Caldwell, who was sausaged in between the two women.

"That's true. But you heard Felipe after he had wounded the wretch who attacked Alexandra. He alone has the power of life or death over us. For the time being, he has every interest in keeping us alive and in good shape."

"I wasn't just talking about that," muttered Alexandra, frightened at the sound of her own voice.

"So?"

"At every moment, I expect to see a snake or a monstrous spider move on-to me."

Karin Stockhausen waited a moment before answering.

"The Amazon jungle is a dangerous place. That's for sure. But there is virtually no risk of being attacked here by a snake or a spider with a deadly bite."

"Are you sure?" asked Alexandra.

"The only really dangerous snake in this area is the bothrops, also known as the spearhead. But it's not particularly aggressive and there's no reason for one to slip in here."

"And spiders?"

The Orpheus manager was slow to respond, and this long silence amplified the panic that was gradually invading the young woman's mind.

Karin continued, "Giant tarantulas are sedentary and nocturnal. Since the camp has been here for some time already, there are certainly none in the vicinity. On the other hand..."

"Yes?"

"There is a much more dangerous species. I don't remember the name[6], which is a member of the cteniddae family, a wandering spider. It is quite large and its venom is more toxic than that of black widows."

"Brrr..." shivered Phil Caldwell as he felt the hair on his arms bristle.

"Is that why you say there's no chance of us being attacked?" asked the biochemist, who was already beginning to feel the legs of this hairy crab on her stomach and thighs.

"¡Cállense!" shouted one of the guards, glaring at them.

"What did he say?" Alexandra asked, almost inaudibly.

"He told us to shut up," replied Karin, twisting her mouth with a doubtful air.

Relative silence fell immediately.

It did not last for long. A first shot rang out. Then a second. A third. The guards rose from their seats. One of them, called Guillermo, went out of the building to see what was going on outside.

Several minutes passed.

"What's going on?" asked Phil Caldwell.

It was obvious that the juxtaposition of these dramatic events was upsetting the astrophysicist from Stanford University who was much more at ease sitting in front of his computers than facing executioners. As if, of course, anyone is naturally at with brutes and torturers.

"Intimidation," replied Sergei Kucharski, who had traveled all over the world, and had been involved in crisis situations on many occasions.

"Are you sure?" Karin asked, worried.

"Unless one of our companions has decided to launch a kamikaze operation by throwing himself on one of the guards, there is no reason for them to shoot us."

"A wild animal, perhaps?" Alexandra suggested, in an effort to reassure herself.

"Probably not," replied the climatologist. With a strong human presence, at least forty people if you count the kidnappers and us, I can't imagine a jaguar attacking the camp. Such animals are pragmatic and cautious."

They immediately stopped talking, for Guillermo returned to the building, which served as a dormitory. With his face closed, he whispered a few words to the other three jailers.

---

[6] It is called *Phoneutria fera* and is considered to be one of the most dangerous spiders in the world because its venom is ten times more powerful than that of black widows. Moreover, she is very aggressive.

Then they all sat back down. And silence returned.

Naturally, the six prisoners wanted to ask questions. But since Guillermo had been particularly careful when confiding the information gleaned from outside to the guards who had remained in the prison shed, there was no way to learn more. At best, they would be insulted, at worst, they would be beaten.

So, they decided to be quiet and wait for the morning.

But, with the exception of Serguei Kucharski, who managed to sink into a restless sleep, the three women and Phil Caldwell continued to watch out for the arrival of insects or reptiles.

In the case of the insects, they were not disappointed. The buzzing and squealing were incessant. They had the impression that a whole cohort of little soldiers, outfitted with chitinous exoskeletons, had invaded the ground that served as their bed. At times, Alexandra jumped. She swallowed and sighed. And it started again. Again and again.

Suddenly, she stood up and shouted, "On my leg!"

"What?" asked Phil, under the weary eye of the guard nearest to them.

The four armed men had just been replaced by another team so they could sleep for a few hours. Felipe's orders were clear: the hostages were to watched at all times!

"A beast! A beast climbing up my right leg."

"I'll look," Phil Caldwell reassured her.

The door had remained open. But the light was insufficient because the moon was partially veiled by a few clouds that were skating over the top of the jungle.

The astrophysicist asked for some light in a very rusty Spanish. His message got through and a guard arrived with a torch.

He laughed.

"It's just a cockroach," Phil confirmed, smiling.

He told himself at the same moment that this was the first time he had smiled since the kidnapping.

"I don't like cockroaches!" the biochemist exclaimed, shuddering.

"I'll rescue you," the exoplanet scientist said, wriggling in order to be next to the young woman whose green eyes filled with visceral fear.

He gently took the giant cockroach between his fingers and put it at the bottom of his feet.

"It won't come back?"

"I don't know. There are at least a thousand billion insects per square kilometer here. So, I can't assure you that there won't be any others. But this one looks peaceful. You go back to sleep."

"I wasn't asleep."

"We weren't either!" Karin and Phil chorused.

One of the guards barked an order that could easily be translated as "*Shut up and sleep!*"

The four insomniacs tried to glean a few minutes of rest. They knew very well that tomorrow would be difficult and that the following days would be even more so. It was wise to sleep.

But also impossible.

As soon as the birds quarreling among themselves filled the sound universe with their cries, which were so varied that one had the impression that they were all rehearsing assiduously for a giant symphony, the three women in the group insisted on going to the toilet.

The ritual was always the same. A guard would release the feet of the one who had just made the request. Then he accompanied the hostage to a very primitive place. Hidden simply by three sheets of filthy fabric wrapped around a few tree trunks covered with mosses, lichens and epiphytic plants, the toilets respected nature. That was really their only asset.

Nevertheless, a minimum of privacy was provided. Burt as for anything else... Considering the wind that sometimes lifted one of the sheets, the monkeys and parrots that passed by, the buzzing insects and mosquitoes, and the close observation of the kidnappers' who sometimes took their mission as guards too seriously, the women in the group were not at all comfortable.

This morning the prisoners stood in line in front of these rudimentary toilets while waiting for their breakfast.

Since the meal of the previous day had been basic and ignoble, except for the fruits of course, they hardly expected a feast. Their mediocre hopes were soon quenched, for all there was for everyone was a horrible watery coffee, two cakes softened by the humidity and one very ripe banana.

"What a feast worthy of Sardanapal!" Serguei Kucharski joked.

But none of the climatologists' colleagues seed to have a sense of humor. Sitting directly on the ground, in the dust and on leaves teeming with insects, worms and larvae, no one really felt like joking. They merely chewed their soft, cookies while listening to find out if everything was going well in the second building where their friends were being held.

The lack of noise worried Karin. She finally decided to ask what was behind the shots fired during the night. She selected a guard called Antonio because he seemed less sullen than the others and spoke a little English.

"What were the shots we heard earlier?"

The man hesitated a bit. He looked questioningly at another guard. Since the other man seemed to agree, he replied with a smile, "Nothing."

"Ah. But..."

"Nothing serious!" he interrupted.

"But we heard several shots!" insisted Serguei Kucharski trying to obtain a few more details. "Were our friends hurt?"

Antonio and the man with whom he had just exchanged a wink burst out laughing.

Then Antonio answered in a rather hesitant English, "They shot at bats to prepare lunch!"

The other guard added a few words in Spanish that Antonio translated immediately.

"They had a lot of fun and your companions got a little scared. We like to have a good time here!"

They laughed again.

As they laughed on and on, their eyes flooded with tears. The captives felt that this disappropriate amount of joy, considering the matter, masked obvious fear. A double fear even.

Felipe's henchmen were afraid of their leader, whose reactions were brutal and unpredictable. And what had happened the day before to the unfortunate Ricardo made their fear legitimate. Moreover, they knew perfectly well that, by kidnapping the heiress to the 50th largest fortune on the planet, they were in a very delicate situation and the outcome was very uncertain. For everyone!

This no doubt explained the forced laughter.

Karin rolled her eyes, indicating what she thought of this childish behavior. But the guards did not care. They needed to unwind and all means were good. That is what the head of the Orpheus expedition feared. She dreaded nothing serious for herself because her existence was too precious for the kidnappers. However, Felipe Maldorano's brutality and the lack of professionalism and control of some of the armed men filled her with a deafening anxiety about the fate of her companions. In particular, she thought of their two Venezuelan guides, for Felipe probably regarded them as traitors loyal to Americans with deep pockets. She also thought of Alexandra Haffington. The pretty, young, green-eyed was likely to rouse irrepressible desires in these men deprived of feminine companionship for a long time. Ricardo's recent misadventures corroborated this analysis.

Finally, she was worried about Gregory and Sergei who were not used to letting people walk over them without reacting. Their kind of attitude, which was courageous and healthy in normal times, could turn into a form of suicide in the face of brutes who thought only of money and for whom human life probably had no more value than a package of cigarettes.

Karin had reached that point in her gloomy thinking when a guard emerged from the jungle. His sudden arrival caused several colorful birds, two toucans, and the usual cohort of macaws to fly up over the camp.

"Felipe wants to talk to the redhead!"

The "redhead" was surprised that he was not called by his family name or first name.

This demonstrated that all women who were not dark-haired and dark-skinned enjoyed a special attention which they would have easily dispensed with.

Without answering, the guard nearest Karin placed his hand on the young woman's shoulder.

"Follow me," he said, remaining as brusque as usual.

"I'll be back. Don't worry!" she said to her four colleagues, as they anxiously watched her leave.

A howler monkey hastily confirmed her words. Despite the fact that it was perched at least fifty yards away, one could clearly see its saffron coat and its dark gray face. With his mouth wide open, he howled every morning.

Alexandra gasped. One of the guards looked at her. Amused.

Then his tongue moved explicitly to his lips.

CHAPTER 8

Like Linda Griffith had already done earlier when she had to deal with Ricardo's wound, Karin Stockhausen walked past the second hangar. Then she finally arrived in front of the third, who, besides being an infirmary, served chiefly as headquarters for the kidnappers' leader.

Felipe greeted him with a small smile.

"Did you sleep well?"

"Very badly!"

The kidnappers' leader seemed to be in an excellent mood. Karin decided to curb her anger and put on a nice face to try to find out more about Felipe's real intentions. What she wanted above all to know was the terms, for the goal of their abduction had been evident from the beginning: a demand for ransom. The important thing was to know when and, more important, how?

Karin had reached that point in her thinking when she turned a little and finally saw a man hidden in the darkness.

"Good day," she said, a little taken aback.

"Good day," replied the bald man, in a very calm tone, his English marred by an indefinable accent.

When Felipe noticed that the woman was frankly surprised to discover a man who was obviously not South American and who had so far remained invisible to the prisoners, he immediately added, "Jan Räsänen is my partner."

"Räsänen... Are you of Finnish origin?"

"We can't hide anything from you," said the man, still sitting, a smile cutting across his pale face like a scar.

Silence fell.

Karin took the opportunity to observe the room located at the end of the building. Made of roughly squared trunks, stems and palm leaves, it was as rustic as the other buildings. These sheds were not built to last an eternity. They had only one function: to house the hostages during negotiations. After that, the jungle would reassert its rights.

A ramshackle table and four chairs stood in the middle of the room. To one side, there was a rough wooden cabinet and a small table with three laptops. Helmets, a network of wires feeding on a large battery and various outlets completed the scene. A crate containing cans of beer was carelessly placed on the floor, and leftovers from meals gave the room a pitiful air. Some noise and a few blows against the wall broke the silence. Felipe shouted a few words in Spanish. The noise stopped immediately.

Then he stood up in front of Karin as Jan Räsänen remained sprawled on the fifth chair set off towards the back of the room. In the dark.

Still in the dark.

"Do you know what you and your friends are doing here?"

"No," replied Karin. "But I think you're going to tell me."

"That's right. My commando, *Blue Macaw*, kidnapped you because we're going to ask your family for ransom in exchange for your freedom."

"Who exactly?"

"Jan and I to be precise."

"And your men?"

"They will be paid when everything is over. But don't worry about the fate of those poor wretches who would kill their entire family for a thousand dollars. Worry about your fate and those of your colleagues!"

Felipe's expression immediately hardened. The almost jovial character that he had chosen to show this morning disappeared following the first contradiction, immediately revealing his true character a complex being, probably tortured by inner demons. Karin immediately realized that the man staring at her was dangerous and unstable.

She opted for calm neutrality.

"I'm in charge of the Orpheus mission. As such, I'm concerned above all with my colleagues' fate. You're right to point that out to me."

She was laying it on a little thick. But Felipe pretended to take this thought at face value. He continued in a calmer tone, "Your family is very rich."

"Yes," Karin agreed.

To claim otherwise would have roused Felipe's anger again.

"It is one of the top 50 richest families on our unfortunate planet, which is still in the throes of poverty and misery."

The young redhead did not answer. She settled for staring at her kidnapper with her large amethyst eyes.

She did not blink.

"Would you say otherwise?"

"No. Of course not. But I guess you didn't kidnap us off just to give me a lecture in social economics?"

"No! Of course not!" replied the leader of the *Blue Macaw*, bursting into laughter.

The fact that Karin was not really insolent, but that she did not let herself be pushed around, pleased him.

For the time being...

"Let's get down to brass tacks!"

The Stockhausen heiress raised her eyebrows slightly to indicate that she was waiting.

"We want money!"

"A lot of money," said Jan Räsänen, who had remained silent until then.

Since Karin's expression remained impassive, Felipe warmed up a bit.

"In exchange for your freedom and that of your ten companions, the Stockhausen family will have to pay a small ransom. *Small* must, of course, be interpreted in proportion to your colossal fortune. In fact, we will demand a modest sum of $100 million!"

The jaw of expert in tropical botany dropped and her mouth remained open. Only for a few seconds. But the time seemed very long.

She finally recovered and said, That's impossible."

"Why? Can't your family afford a ransom?" Jan asked with a smirk.

"Yes. Of course..."

"So, everything is fine!" Felipe replied. "As you admitted just now with such disarming simplicity, your family can come up with such a sum without any difficulty. You will still have more than $15 billion! So, as I just said, everything is fine!"

"No."

"What do you mean?" the kidnappers' leader asked, frowning and rubbing his bearded chin nervously.

"For two reasons," Karin said.

"We're listening," Jan whispered, pretending to sharpen the blade of a combat knife on his thigh.

"Unlike some Western countries, the United States never pays ransom."

"You're right!" acknowledged Felipe, pretending to be afflicted by this news, which was not new at all to him.

Karin looked at him questioningly. Her incredible purple eyes, with their golden flecks, were filled with a true lack of understanding. Why kidnap them if it would serve no purpose and no ransom would be paid?

Felipe Maldorano's face lit up suddenly.

"But you're wrong too. The US government does refuse to make any payment when terrorists or organizations related more or less directly to international terrorism are responsible for kidnappings. But in this case, we're strictly in the private sphere. There is no question of terrorism, threats to American soil or major strategic issues. It is simply a matter of money. Just money! Moreover, the financial power of the Stockhausen *empire* is so important, so necessary and provides so many jobs in the United States, that no head of state would ever dare to say "*no*" to Friedrich Stockhausen if he gives the order to release funds to save his beloved daughter. Moreover, we all know that your father is on very familiar terms with Obama and the main political, financial and economic decision-makers in your wonderful country!"

"Granting that's the case," said Karin. "But there is a second problem. How can $100 million in small bills be brought to the heart of the jungle?"

"Who said anything about cash?" Jan Räsänen whispered, as he brought his pale, bony face close to the young woman's.

"But... But..." stuttered Karin. "Honestly, you don't expect my father to write you a check so that you can deposit it in the nearest bank, do you?"

"Don't treat us like idiots!"

The sentence had been uttered in a very dry tone and Felipe suddenly appeared angry. The red blush that washed over his forehead and cheekbones and the veins that bulged at his temples and protruded under his skin were systematic warning signs of an outburst of rage.

But his irritation was short-lived, for the two men took pleasure in playing with their hostage as a cat would do with an unfortunate, breathless, paralyzed mouse. Felipe decided to abandon his stance, which probably gave him the artificial hope of demonstrating that he was the dominant male of that part of the Amazon jungle lost between Venezuela and Brazil, took one of the chairs and sat right in front of Karin.

The young woman noticed the grimace that occasionally distorted Felipe's face. His strange blue eyes were sunk deeply in their sockets. His nose was large. A determined chin with a poorly maintained beard, a hideous scar and brown hair, completed the silhouette of this Robin Hood who had decided to take from the ultra-rich to satisfy his own appetites.

The poor could wait...

He carefully sat down on his chair and leaned against the back as if sitting in an armchair or on a chaise longue. But they were very far away from cozy lounges or comfy setting s. The tumult of the equatorial jungle, the din of the macaws with their constant quarrels, and that subtle blend of the odors soil and urine prevailed in the camp.

"The ransom will be paid in four installments."

At that precise moment Karin realized that Felipe and his partner were not merely brutes thirsty for money and power. They knew how to organize, bribe and manipulate. They probably had a plan B. Perhaps even plans C and D.

Dividing up the ransom when one has the power of life and death over a dozen hostages was a good way to avoid traps. Karin knew that. And the people Felipe would be dealing with in the future would discover it soon as well.

"Four instalments?" she repeated in order to keep the discussion going.

"Yes," Jan replied. "As you will soon be able to see for yourself, we have taken the utmost precautions so as not to be spotted while being able to negotiate with your family. But we're not naive and we know perfectly well that the American special services will try to neutralize us by all means. By dividing the ransom into four equal portions, to be paid as we see fit, we'll avoid certain problems. At least for the first three installments."

"And the fourth?" asked Karin, who knew full well that the two men speaking with her were too proud of their plan to conceal the essentials.

It is true that since the members of the Orpheus expedition were being held, tied up, in a camp, invisible from above and located in the heart of the Amazon jungle, they could hardly communicate such valuable information to just anyone.

"Will we really need a fourth installment?" Jan asked with a sly look.

"I don't know!" laughed Felipe, who was apparently very pleased with the multi-level scenario.

Silence fell.

Karin swallowed. A question was burning on her lips, but she was still afraid of Felipe's passionate outbursts of rage. She made up her mind.

"I see you've planned everything. But how do you plan to let my family know?"

"This is where the fun starts," Felipe rejoiced, suddenly getting up from his chair, nearly toppling it.

The head of Orpheus looked at him with a frown.

Felipe continued, "Your blonde cameraman who looks a bit like a Robert Redford when he was much younger knows how to make a report, I think?"

"Yes. Of course. But..."

Karin Stockhausen let her voice die out. She was starting to imagine scenes that would be extremely traumatic for her family. She immediately thought of her mother, Beatrice, whose health was shaky and who would not be able to bear seeing her daughter held captive and mistreated in a forced video.

"You're not thinking of...?" she replied.

"Yes! Yes. Of course! You and your friends will look gorgeous standing in front of a wall of leaves sweat beading on your foreheads and weapons pointed at your temples."

Felipe stopped for a moment.

Then he raised his arms to heaven and exclaimed, "It's gonna be divine!"

"This man is crazy," thought Karin, without putting her thoughts into words.

Fortunately.

Felipe looked at his prisoner attentively.

Almost immediately, he took on a pleasant, almost playful, air. This amazing switching between anger and good humor seemed to confirm the fact that this arrogant and violent man was suffering from bipolar disorder. This certainly would not facilitate relations with Friedrich Stockhausen.

Jan's face darkened and the man sank a little deeper into his chair. His long, pale face was slashed from the top of his left ear to his chin by a long narrow, prominent scar. Karin had immediately noticed the man's very light gray eyes. Like steel. This pale and metallic shimmering gave his expression the implacability of a machine. Anyone who looked at it immediately felt they were in the presence of a robot. But a robot driven by a characteristic so unique to the human being: cruelty.

She turned away and stood facing Felipe.

"What are you going to do?"

"We're not really in any hurry. We could wait a few days here, without being spotted, in order to increase your relatives' anxiety."

He paused for a moment and twisted his mouth into a mocking grimace.

"But we don't wish to worry your families and loved ones any longer. Everyone knows that the total lack of information is the worst thing under such circumstances. So, we're going to notify your family. And those of all the other hostages."

Felipe Maldorano straightened up, adopting a posture that he probably believed perfectly reflected the haughty and revealing character of his status as a dominant male. He looked ridiculous. A rooster standing on his heap of manure, or in the mud of the jungle to be more precise in this case.

But the tyranny of his own ego dazzled him 24/7. The smug man was so proud of his machete, his bushy mustache, and the dreadful odor of sweat that rolled off him everywhere he went.

Karin waited.

Felipe grabbed her arm unceremoniously and said, "Come with me!"

"Where?"

"Don't argue. Follow me!"

Karin grimaced as her abductor's hand grabbed her right wrist forcefully, partially cutting off the blood flow.

"You're hurting me!"

"Shut up!"

The mask of hypocritical courtesy fell, once again. The man seemed angry yet again. The whites of his eyes filled with blood.

He called Alfonso and ordered him to gather all the prisoners in a group in front of the central building.

The guard obeyed immediately.

CHAPTER 9

Lined up like sheep on their way to a slaughterhouse, the eleven members of the Orpheus expedition were quickly removed from the sheds where they had been lying or sitting almost all day. Alfonso had warned the other guards. Five minutes later, the hostages had been untied.

Now they were all standing along one of the outer walls of the building in the center of the camp. A little rain had fallen less than half an hour earlier and everything was soaked.

Around them: four guards. Very attentive. In front, there were Alfonso and about twenty armed men. In the center, Felipe strutted about. As usual.

He took his time and stared at his hostages one by one. He insisted, in particular, on examining the faces of Serguei Kucharski and Gregory Greensberg. At the outset, his accomplices had pointed out that the climatologist and the logistician had fought their assailants during the attack on the Orpheus camp and Felipe took a certain pleasure in defying the reckless men who attempted to resist him. But today, nobody seemed to be able to oppose the master here. He knew this. And he was jubilant.

Once he had finished this slow and lengthy observation, he asked Karin to settle down among her friends.

By reflex, the leader of the expedition positioned herself near Alexandra Haffington and Martin Physter. The specialist in tropical botany knew that the pair were fragile. Vulnerable. Phil Caldwell was not far away either for, obviously, investigating far-off exoplanets was hardly in the same class as being willing to do battle with armed men. How could he be blamed?

"Listen to me carefully!"

As usual, Felipe Maldorano began to scratch his chin and the short beard that covered it. This reflex indicated how tense he was. The scoundrel knew well that his prisoners would have to listen to him and he could force them to obey him. By fair means or foul. But he always wanted to seduce or, in this case, impress those who looked his way.

He ran his tongue over his lips and waited a moment longer.

Then he said, "You are being held captive in the middle of this impenetrable jungle for one reason: money! Well... Since Karin Stockhausen's family is colossally rich, everything should be fine if everyone does their part."

He paused a second and raised his eyebrows and opened his eyes.

"Starting with you, of course! If you do what I order you without bothering, everything will go well. You'll soon go back to your beloved scientific observations. Otherwise... blood will be shed! Have I made myself clear?"

The hostages nodded discreetly to prove they had understood the message.

The fact that Felipe always felt obliged to point out that he was the one who made all the decisions and would not hesitate to exterminate one or more hostages in case of a problem revealed both his ferocity and his weakness. Ferocity, for no one really doubted that he was capable of carrying out his threats. It was even more than likely that he would take real pleasure in it. But great weakness also, for this visceral need to constantly repeat the horrors he would perform if he were to be driven to the limit, revealed that he needed this fuel of hatred to act. As a result, he was driven by a crude logic that was not compatible with a carefully developed plan. The worm was in the fruit. Permanent and useless, this frantic agitation confirmed this a little more every day.

"To make things perfectly clear, I'll explain what is going to happen and what you are going to do."

At that moment, a furtive shadow appeared behind Felipe. It was of, course, Jan Räsänen who was still unknow to the prisoners, except for Karin Stockhausen.

Still armed with a machete hanging from his belt on the left and his Beretta 92 which never left him, Felipe signaled to his Finnish associate. The other man approached. Then, calmly, almost dramatically, he pulled a paper out of the pocket of his stained, brown shirt.

Felipe smiled. He took Jan's sheet and turned to the hostages.

Pointing his index finger at Karin, he simply said, "The time has come for you to get to work."

The young red-haired woman's expression looked quizzical.

"You're going to read this text in front of our friend Matt's camera... Matt Lochner right?"

"Yes," the reporter replied, frowning.

"Perfect! So, first you will read this statement carefully. It sums up the current state of affairs and also sets out the first steps of the ransom process. We'll practice this two or three times before making the recording that we'll send to the Stockhausen family," Felipe said, staring at Karin.

She grasped the document which her captor gave her with her fingertips.

She paled at once and exclaimed, "But I can't say that!"

"Why not?"

"This message will kill my mother!"

"Let me tell you what I'm thinking right now."

He let his voice fade out, to extend the wait.

He lashed out in anger, "Your mother... I don't care about her! You will read this letter. Without grumbling! You can look sad, dramatic or distraught. I don't care. You will read it. You will memorize this short and powerful text. Then our friend Matt will take this small camera that my men found with your equipment. It will be enough to record a short video to be sent first by MMS to your father."

"Why do you say *first*? Do you intend to send it to other people later? To the media? The social networks?"

"That is none of your business," interrupted Jan Räsänen, barely opening his mouth. "Just obey."

Realizing that she had no power to resist, Friedrich Stockhausen's daughter accepted this demand as a threat.

"I'm ready," she said, sighing.

"Good. Very good!" Felipe rejoiced. "Matt! Pick up that damn camera and get ready to film."

"But it's a simple Handycam camcorder. I use it only to double sequences or in dangerous passages because it's much more manageable than my other cameras. The quality of the video will be..."

"I don't care!" erupted Felipe, copiously spitting on the unfortunate reporter who had linked his fate to that of the Orpheus Foundation. "We're not making an award-winning movie! Just a video showing fear, sweat and tears. That's all! So, stop whining. Turn on your camera and start filming. Is that clear?"

The message was clear, so Matt Lochner picked up his equipment with a trembling hand. He quickly focused the camera.

"Do I stay here?" asked Karin.

"No. You're going to stand in front of the other prisoners so that everyone knows that we have kidnapped all the members of the expedition. Moreover, the text clearly states that the lives of the eleven hostages are at stake."

The guards gathered the captives in front of the wall made of palm leaves. The video shot had to be narrow enough to avoid disclosing any information that could be used to locate them. But, at the same time, a few hastily squared tree trunks and woven palm leaves could scarcely provide a signature. As palms were the most common trees in this part of the jungle, they simply indicated that the group was in the Amazon. The risk was minimal.

Once the group had been positioned in keeping with Felipe's requirements, Karin stood in front of her friends. Realizing that the whole shot looked a little too much like a school photo, the kidnapper's leader asked all the hostages to kneel, except for Karin who had to be clearly visible while she was reading the letter addressed to her family.

Gregory Greensberg and Serguei Kucharski were reluctant to kneel.

Following a blow with a rifle butt to their knees, they quickly followed suit. The two men merely grimaced. They did not want to please their captors by shouting, whining or begging.

"You're nothing but brutes!" shouted Paula Cavendish, glaring at Felipe with her dark, almost black eyes.

Faster than a rattlesnake, Felipe walked over to the biologist who, was apparently, feeling better since this morning. He slowly placed the barrel of his gun against the temple of the captive who had not been able to control her emotions.

"Another remark like that, and Ill decorate the shed with your blood and brains!"

Paula swallowed slowly and was silent.

"Good. That's better. Let's start."

The kidnappers' leader turned to Matt. The cameraman was surrounded by two armed giants who pointed their guns at him, indicating that the slightest prank would be sanctioned immediately.

"We're filming! Karin, you can start reading."

The red-haired woman stiffened a little. She took a deep breath while trying to assume a serious, not too dramatic, expression. At that moment she was thinking of the members of her family, who were going to be terrified when they discovered this scene that recalled some of the atrocities committed each year on hostages in various countries around the world where the value of a human being is worth less than his weight in waste.

"So?" said Felipe, growing patient and wanting to remind Matt Lochner that he had to record everything in order to make a striking and traumatic video for the Stockhausen family.

"My name is Karin Stockhausen," said the botanist, taking care to read every word of the text. "I'm in charge of the Orpheus expedition that the Stockhausen Foundation has organized at the peak of Mount Roraima. The ten members of this expedition and I are being held hostage by a criminal organization that calls itself the *Blue Macaw*."

She paused for a moment because her mouth was dry. Felipe beckoned to her to continue with moving his left index finger in circles.

"The *Blue Macaw* requires payment of a ransom. The amount will be specified in a few moments. If you refuse to pay this ransom, if the police or the army interferes, we shall be executed one by one. These executions will be filmed and broadcast widely in the media. If you do not follow the instructions that will be given to you, we will all be slaughtered or... No! I can't."

Karin burst into tears.

"Keep on filming!" shouted the man with the glacier blue eyes.

"I can't read the rest. It will be too cruel for my mother."

"You'll keep reading, bitch!"

The veneer of gallantry once again melted away like snow in the sun, and the slightly mocking politeness made way for insults.

As Karin did not respond and she had lowered the sheet of paper Felipe turned back to Matt.

"Keep filming!"

He immediately walked over to the group of kneeling captives. He examined them carefully and pointed at Fernando Pinson.

He beckoned to Carlos, a guard with a dark face and an impressive athletic build. The man lifted Fernando up, grabbing him by the left arm. Then he positioned him unceremoniously, just in front of Felipe. The latter smiled sarcastically. He looked attentively at Karin and took his long knife, the metallic blade shining in the equatorial sun, which had finally come out.

"Karin! This should make you realize that I never joke and that nothing and no one will hinder me on my way."

Then he turned to the cameraman and the guards, who were watching him closely, to make sure cameraman was still filming.

"Carlos! Hold him well and place his left hand against the trunk of this tree."

The boss of the *Blue Macaw* had just designated the large ribbed trunk of a strangler fiscus tree that had completely enveloped another tree which it fed on like a parasite. Felipe Maldorano was very fond of the strangler fiscus tree, and felt bound to them by a common thirst for vampirizing others.

Distraught, Fernando Pinzon tried to free himself from this unfriendly and powerful embrace. But he could not face a colossus who found an excellent opportunity to shine before his chief. Carlos placed the hand of the unfortunate guide along the massive trunk.

Felipe told the American reporter to move closer. Matt Lochner felt an uncontrollable nausea was over him. But this was no time to puke. He had to film. Keep on filming. Film until the precise moment when horror would become the norm.

"Check your focus!"

Matt did not answer. But he obeyed, feeling the barrel of the weapon of the guard standing just behind him dig deeper between his kidneys. He knew what a bullet fired at close range into the spine would do. He shivered despite the stifling, damp heat.

Then he framed the whole scene, focusing on Fernando Pinzon who shouted in rage and fear.

Felipe looked at Karin again. He took a falsely calm bearing, stood in front of the camera and said, "The first demonstration of our desire for success. This will prove to you that we are not joking and that all our demands have to be met! Look carefully at this man, one of the expedition guides. His name is Fernando Pinzon and his expression says more than a long speech!"

The brute was not wrong. Fernando's eyes were bulging. Sweat beaded on his forehead. He was trying to twist about. But Carlos held him against the bark of the tree.

Felipe placed his blade over the little finger of the Venezuelan guide's left hand.

"Cut!" he exclaimed, cutting the unfortunate man's finger at the second joint.

The fingertip fell immediately to the ground while Fernando howled with pain and blood flowed over the rest of his hand.

Dramatically, Felipe bent down to pick up the fingertip. He looked at it for a long time, facing the camera. Then he raised it to his mouth and pretended to suck the blood.

"That's good," he said simply.

Then he threw it carelessly towards the jungle.

"Ne next time, it won't be the tip of a finger, but a hand. Then an arm. Then a head!" he yelled, opening his mouth like a divinity ready to spew flames, lava and magma.

Fernando continued to scream and weep. The other captives were stunned and terrified at the same time. This man was crazy! Their lives were in his hands. They had to obey if they did not want to witness a massacre played out in front of Matt's trembling camera. Karin wanted to swallow, but she could not.

Felipe approached her again. Constrained by armed men who did not leave him an inch, Matt Lochner continued to film.

First, Felipe asked Linda Griffith to quickly cauterize Fernando's wound to stop the flow of blood and clean it with a disinfectant. Then she placed a compress on the end the finger from which the tip had just been severed.

Once this procedure had been carried out by the expedition doctor, Felipe turned back to Karin.

"Are you going to continue reading the message for your family or should I cut a hand off the little blonde or redhead?" he said, pointing to Alexandra Haffington and Phil Caldwell.

"It's good. I'll start reading from the beginning."

"And up to the end this time!" he ranted as he pretended to walk over the biochemist brandishing his knife stained with Fernando Pinzon's blood.

Karin nodded. She picked up the sheet of paper and began to read again.

"My name is Karin Stockhausen," the botanist began, taking care to repeat every word of the text. "I'm in charge of the Orpheus expedition that the Stockhausen Foundation has organized at the peak of Mount Roraima. The ten members of this expedition and I are being held hostage by an organization that calls itself the *Blue Macaw*. The *Blue Macaw* requires the payment of a ransom. The amount will be specified in a few moments. If you refuse to pay this ransom, if the police or the army interferes, we shall be executed one by one. These executions will be filmed and broadcast widely in the media. If you do not follow the instructions that will be given to you, we will all be slaughtered or gutted alive!"

She paused for a moment and continued almost immediately:

"Do not abandon us. Please…"

Satisfied, Felipe stepped in front of the camera and stared at the lens in such a way that Karin's parents could really feel that the torturer was looking at them. Them. Just them.

"Friedrich Stockhausen! It is now up to you to make sure that that your only daughter and her companions come back safe and sound. My name is Felipe Maldorano and I'm the leader of *Blue Macaw*. As Karin has just told you, we are not a terrorist organization or a Satanic sect. Our goal is simple: to obtain a ransom. Since your family enjoys the enviable rank of being the 50th wealthiest in the world, the ransom will be proportionate to your fortune. We are demanding $100 million to release Karin and her companions. This ransom will be paid in four installments of $25 million each to offshore accounts located in tax havens in the Pacific Islands, Africa or the British West Indies. I will, of course, give you the account numbers at the last moment. After payment of the first installment, I will release two hostages. Two more following the second transfer. And then two more. The last five prisoners, including your daughter, will be delivered after the fourth and final payment. You will, of course, try to locate us. That will be difficult. You will soon have the opportunity to see that for yourself. I will also contact you by phone. But you will only reply on a page that you will create on Facebook. I'll give you the name for that page tomorrow. Be careful! I know that the American or Venezuelan special services will try to locate us. As you have just seen when I cut a finger off one of the guides of the expedition, we will stop at nothing. The situation is clear. If you try to get the army or the special forces to intervene, I will kill two hostages in front of the camera and the world will be able to feast on their agony! If a drone flies over us, I will kill two prisoners! Once again, in front of the inquisitive, cold eye of the camera. Is that understood?"

Felipe paused for a moment. His eyes were bloodshot and the man sweated, drooled and belched while talking. If he wanted to come across as a determined, cruel and somewhat deranged kidnapper, the result was perfect! He performance would probably even exceed his wildest expectations when the first of the videos would be sent to Friedrich Stockhausen's personal phone.

He turned to Matt Lochner.

"Keep filming! We'll select sequences of 30 to 40 seconds. Each will be sent from a different phone. They will find it very difficult to identify us."

Then he turned back to the camcorder, which the reporter continued to hold under the threat of armed assassins.

"But remain positive," he went on, smiling slyly. "I'm sure everything will be fine because we are reasonable beings. No one wants to take part in a massacre. The next time we contact you, we'll give you details about the Facebook page you can use to respond. Meanwhile…"

Felipe was silent for a moment. Then, with a very theatrical gesture, he positioned himself next to Karin and the other hostages. He gently ran the hand that held his knife along the face of the red-haired woman whose eyes widened at that moment, as she wondered whether the madman was about to do something absurd.

This was not the case. He settled for a fake caress and turned back to face the camera held by Matt:

"Think of Karin when you make the first transfer. It would be a pity if the Stockhausen empire lost its only heiress!"

Then he burst out laughing and asked the cameraman to stop recording.

He turned to Jan Räsänen, pointing his right thumb upwards.

"Fine," said the Finn in a laconic tone, almost detached from the scene.

Then, Carlos and Alfonso walked over to Felipe, who murmured two or three pieces of information to them almost inaudibly.

"You are going to be able to eat," he informed the captives, who were still kneeling.

Some of them stood up quickly. Others took longer because their muscles were heavy and their joints painful.

"Hurry up!" Carlos yelled. "This is no holiday club!"

That much was obvious. But the remark reinforced the kidnappers' natural aggressiveness, even when it was not justified.

Two guards walked over to Alexandra Haffington and Martin Physter, who always seemed the weakest, the most vulnerable. The most dejected. The guards pulled them to their feet unceremoniously and the edaphologist was punished by a masterful kick to the buttocks.

Then they were directed to the two buildings that served as dormitories, places where they took meals and bathrooms. While the captives' privacy was more or less preserved when they asked to go to the toilet, the basin of filthy water they used to wash stood in the middle of dust, cockroaches and the piles of leaves and palms that served as mattresses. In both groups, the men of the Orpheus expedition averted their eyes away when one of the women engaged in very brief ablutions. But the armed guards watched with lustful eyes.

Ricardo misadventure, however, calmed their sexual impulses. For the time being...

As was to be expected, the meal was vile.

CHAPTER 10

Thursday, January 21, 2016 – New York
432 Park Avenue, Stockhausen family apartment

"My God... it's a nightmare!"

Nestled in her husband's arms, Beatrice Stockhausen was looping through the six short videos that had arrived on Friedrich's phone that morning.

Rain fell softly on New York.

Through the immense square windows, three meters high, it was easy to make out the ethereal yet sticky mists that which wove long screens over the city. They frayed and came back together over and over again. But of that orgasm of tenuous light mingled with droplets of water in the atmosphere, all that prevailed at that moment was fear.

Friedrich Stockhausen and his wife were accompanied by four men in the huge living room on the 95th floor of the tower that looks down over New York. Sitting on a soft sofa, made of leather of a light mink color that fit in perfectly with the delicate gray walls, Beatrice and Friedrich were terrified. Distraught. In front of them, another sofa and two comfortable armchairs completed the setting of this part of the L-shaped living room that flowed into a library corner lined with priceless, ancient books.

The area of this space exceeded 1500 square meters. But the huge apartment Stockhausen had just bought at 432 Park Avenue was over 7500 square meters, leaving a little room for the six bedrooms, kitchen, dining room, seven bathrooms and central elevator serving this sumptuous apartment located on the top floor of the most luxurious building in New York.

Brightly lit by 24 windows providing 360° view of New York, it looked like a beacon standing over an ocean of constantly swarming humanity.

But today, the atmosphere was extremely tense and there was no time to admire the scenery.

Friedrich had received the first text message at dawn. The five other short videos, lasting only a few dozen seconds each, soon followed. Beatrice had wept when she saw the defeated face of her daughter as she read the text informing her parents that she had been taken hostage and was being coerced by armed men. But her fear had turned into terror when she saw Felipe Maldorano cut off the finger tip from one of the Orpheus expedition guides.

She fainted. And was revived with carefully measured doses of the medications she took to support a tired and often failing heart. Her caregivers were starting to bring up the possibility of a transplant because her condition was deteriorating. The specialist who had treated her for the past five years had to make a decision in that respect next month. Unfortunately, the horror of her daughter's situation did nothing to improve Beatrice Stockhausen physical condition. Aged 54, she was very beautiful and her long, curly red hair created an immediate complicity between Beatrice and Karin. A complicity that went well beyond a physical resemblance between a mother and her daughter. The two women were linked by a powerful force that sometimes converged in their emotions at the same time. With the same energy.

Today, this energy was suffering and terror. Tempestuous and extremely violent, this flood of emotions overwhelmed Friedrich Stockhausen's wife. He had to fight on two fronts: to save his daughter and protect his wife.

It was for this reason that he immediately called his two closest collaborators in his organization: Dave Williamson and Anicet de Rochechouart. De Rochechouart came from one of the oldest, French noble families. Certain genealogists and historians even claim that the family descends directly from the Merovingian kings who reigned before Charlemagne. But it was not for his ancient and illustrious ancestors that Friedrich Stockhausen had sought to bring Anicet de Rochechouart into his inner circles. It was because of his skills, his address book filled with prestigious names and his clear-sightedness, a quality that was going to be tested now.

The other two men: Chuck Missangro and Paul Travis were part of the NCS[7].

Friedrich knew the CIA's top man, who had immediately commissioned the two men to coordinate research with the appropriate departments within the CIA and their divisions in Latin America where representatives were in place in the American embassies in Venezuela, Brazil and Guyana.

Two laptops, three tablets and several telephones were installed on the huge coffee table that separated the two sofas. The NCS representatives seemed dubious and were talking among themselves as Dave Williamson and Anicet de Rochechouart spoke with their boss.

Once Beatrice had dried her tears, Friedrich kissed her on the forehead and stood up. He walked over to one of the large bay windows that looked down at the city, 400 meters below. This bird's eye view immediately seduced Friedrich who had not hesitated to spend $85 million to acquire this vast apartment that b rushed up against the sky.

Even if the Stockhausen family owned more than a dozen properties located all over the planet, all equally sumptuous and nestled in heavenly places, he had a soft spot for this prestigious address that satisfied his taste for refinement and his need to be close to his main professional activities.

---

[7] The NCS (National Clandestine Service) coordinates all American intelligence activities abroad, including those of the FBI and the Department of Defense.

But this uncluttered approach to a megalopolis seen from above, which could give the illusion of a truly holistic vision of the world, was now confronted with the cruelty of a terrifying reality: his daughter's life was in the hands of madmen ready to torture and kill without any other form of trial.

Paul Travis rose in turn and walked over to Karin's father.

"We can't trace the messages."

"I suspected as much," sighed Friedrich. "They send small pieces of video each time and use different phones with pre-paid, anonymous SIM cards."

"This system, the 'burner', is classic and very effective. A different phone for each call and a short call each time. We may have more luck when you respond to them on the Facebook page that they want you to create. But if they use a battery of proxy servers scattered all over the world along with software that hides their IDs, tracking the exact origin of the transmission will be very difficult."

"Anyway... it won't help!"

"Why?" Paul asked, clenching his jaws as he already knew exactly what Friedrich Stockhausen was about to say.

"We don't care about the precise location! We know that they're close to Mount Roraima, either in Venezuela or in Brazil. With drones and a little information on-site we'll locate them in the next two or three days. But I don't want that!"

As he had raised his voice slightly, his wife and two direct associates turned towards him. At that moment, they saw a peregrine falcon fly very close to the windows facing south. It was always amazing to see raptors who feel at ease in large cities where there are no hunters or toxic products used for intense agriculture. Since the building at 432 Park Avenue, stretching like a slender needle into the sky, the fortunate people living on the top floors sometimes felt like part of the immense crowd of birds free from and hindrance.

Unfortunatelty, today, the hindrances were very real for the Stockhausen family that had just been informed about the tragic situation of Karin and her colleagues.

"What do you mean?" asked Beatrice, growing pale.

"The various messages from these monsters are perfectly clear: if they see a drone they will kill two hostages. If they see soldiers, they will kill more hostages. There is only one possible solution. We have to do what they want and pay the ransom. I can't even consider any other possibility!"

When Friedrich Stockhausen spoke, everyone listened.

Tall, graying hair cut very short and steel blue eyes, the man's very presence was imposing.

Naturally, the fact that he was also the head of a wealthy family increased his power, which combined the charisma, appeal and implacable strength of one who can make and break destinies with a single gesture. Or a single word.

Moreover, Friedrich Stockhausen knew Barack Obama and many other politicians, both Republicans or Democrats, very well. His voice was loud and strong. His power was anything but theoretical.

And this was no usual hostage-taking, either because of the number of captives held by the *Blue Macaw* or because of the immense fortune of one of the prisoners. The two NCS men knew this full well and they had already received specific orders from the highest level of the CIA and the American government. These instructions could be summed up in one sentence: support the Stockhausen family, bearing in mind that the survival of the hostages must take precedence over any other consideration.

The primary consequence of this tactical choice, quite different from the usual attitude in the United States in such cases, gave immense power to Felipe Maldorano. When dealing with a man who seemed prepared to slaughter men and women in front of the camera, calmness was essential. This is exactly what Chuck Missangro recommended when he walked over to stand in front of Friedrich.

Paul Travis's colleague seemed to have been carved out of a tree trunk. He was very tall, very muscular. His neck was as wide as his head. His eyebrows were bushy and his eyes were black. He seemed capable of acting in a James Bond movie and slipping into the role of the villain who gets the upper hand with Agent 007 before finding himself in a difficult situation when the legend of Her Majesty's secret service finally reveals his qualities at the last moment, using some unstoppable, often lethal gadget.

Chuck offered to profile the leader of the hostage takers. This was both childish and perilous. Childish, since man's arrogance came through each word, each attitude. He was very satisfied with himself, with his power and, above all, with the media coverage of his power. In addition, his final intentions were clear. He hid nothing. Karin's father or the NCS men had no reason to doubt that his ultimate goal was money. He wanted a very large ransom and anyone who crossed his path would be eliminated like a mosquito. No more. No less.

"Things will get particularly complicated when people try to establish Felipe's psychological profile," Chuck confessed.

"It's simple!" interrupted Dave Williamson, looking Friedrich straight in the eye. "He's a brute, a killer. A man who would kill father and mother to get what he wants. In short: a very dangerous man who must not be provoked if we want to keep the hostages alive and see the negotiations come to an end."

"Yes," said Paul Travis, in a condescending tone, rubbing his perfectly shaved head with a brief, mechanical gesture. "But there is one disturbing, problematic factor."

"Which is?" asked Friedrich.

"His unpredictability."

The word was out.

"So?" continued Friedrich.

"We are certainly dealing with the worst kind of psychopath."

"The characteristics of psychopaths?" enquired Anicet de Rochechouart, raising his eyebrows to confirm his interrogation.

"Psychopaths are incapable of feeling guilt or shame for what they do. They are unaware of the emotional or physical consequences of their actions. They betray, threaten and kill without remorse."

"Charming," interrupted Anicet. "And how are they different from sociopaths?"

"Sociopaths don't understand the world in which they live. It is this misunderstanding that causes them to do malicious or appalling acts."

Paul Travis continued his brief portrait of psychopaths in general, a description that seemed perfectly suited to the sinister character who had just kidnapped the members of the Orpheus expedition.

"In order to complete this sad picture, we have to realize that psychopaths are manipulative and domineering. They always want to exercise power and are concerned, of course, solely with their own interests. But in this case, the man seems psychologically unstable. As pointed out a few moments ago, he is unpredictable! This complicates our method of analysis."

"Can you be more specific?" asked Friedrich.

"It will be necessary to adjust our analyzes and reactions at any given time, based on his possible outbursts of anger which can very quickly evolve into dementia. In that case..."

"In that case?" interrupted Beatrice, who had just dried her last tears.

"He could attack a hostage physically. Let us not forget that the systematic use of the camera gives him an impression of power. An almost messianic power. At once, he becomes the privileged intermediary of a demanding divinity: money. We must always be prepared to give some pledges of good will in order to allow the pressure to drop. Felipe Maldorano seems irascible. We must always respond calmly. To be precise, you will always have to respond quietly, added Paul Travis turning once again to Friedrich. "Because I don't think he wants to talk to anyone else."

"But there's one thing I don't understand!" insisted Anicet de Rochechouart.

"Yes?"

"Felipe seems to have specified that the answers we will be giving him will not take place live on the phone, but through a social media page. In such a case, how can we customize a message and slip moderation and restraint into his discourse, which is always marked by emphasis and excess?"

Paul Travis thought for a moment.

Then he said, "We'll have to make changes as we go. For now, we don't know what he really wants us to post on that page."

"There is one thing that surprises me with respect to this demand," Dave Williamson said.

"If there were only one demand," sighed Friedrich, looking into the distance in front of him, to dispel the appalling images that filled his mind.

"As we've all noticed, the man who stands in front of the camera and claims to be the head of the kidnappers..."

"Claims?" Beatrice interrupted, pressing her husband's hands tighter still.

"Yes. I know. This Felipe Maldorano seems to be our sole negotiator. But I doubt that."

"Continue..." insisted Chuck Missangro.

"This arrogant and sadistic individual seems to be in the throes of incoercible and brutal fits of anger. So, I doubt that this ambitious project – to kidnap the heiress to the 50th largest fortune in the world... which is no mean feat! – could have been dreamt up by this man alone."

"So?"

"It's most certainly the work of a group. He isn't solely responsible for this kidnapping. When you see the armed men of the *Blue Macaw* threatening the hostages, you realizes at once that they don't have much between the ears. So, there are at least one or two other people in the shadows, pulling the strings. This is certainly our best chance."

"What do you mean?" asked Karin's father.

"If the reactions of the mad man threatening your daughter become too unpredictable, these associates may intervene in order to calm him or even neutralize him," Dave Williamson added. "When you hope to share $100 million, you don't let just anything happen. There is too much at stake."

"Will facial recognition provide information about his true identity?" asked Anicet de Rochechouart, smoothing his thin, blond mustache.

Friedrich Stockhausen's associate was a wise and refined man. Born into a noble family, more than a thousand years old, he had all the bearing of an aristocrat, with a full head of hair, refined elegance and polished speech. He wore only suits costing thousands of dollars, tailored exclusively for him by Ermenegildo Zegna, Brioni, Kiton or Hermes.

Although his apartment was not as large and sumptuous as that of the Stockhausen family, it still looked out on Central Park. For his car, he had abandoned Porsche, Audi and Ferrari in favor of the pure and timeless elegance of an Aston Martin DBS.

But today, it was not the James Bond of finance and acquisitions-mergers that people listened to, but a colleague with marvelous abilities to analyze and draw conclusion. And those two qualities were essential in such a situation.

"No. Not for the moment," acknowledged Paul Travis with a horrible grimace. "But we'll get to that point soon enough."

"That's perfect," replied Anicet. "But it will be pointless, since the fact that this energetic man with his Beretta and his machete ostensibly shows his face proves that he doesn't care that everyone knows who he is. Once he pockets the ransom, he definitely intends to change his look and his identity. No doubt about that. So, knowing that his real name is Luis Fernandez, Pancho Vila or John Smith will be of no help to us. His expressions and all of his gestures will probably be much more instructive."

"Expression?" Friedrich asked, surprised.

"Yes. Did you notice how his mouth twitched when he cut off the tip of the guide's finger?"

"Absolutely," Chuck Missangro acknowledge. "His tension immediately caught our attention."

"Why?" asked Karin's father.

"His grimace demonstrates both the pleasure he takes in making another person suffer, but also the fear that drives him. He is certainly ashamed of this fear and his arrogance and swaggering in front of the camera are attempts to hide that."

Everyone was silent for a moment.

Just then, Friedrich Stockhausen's telephone rang again. Paul Travis plugged in his devices.

Then he made a sign to Beatrice's husband, indicating that he could pick up.

"A new text message," he said simply, in a flat voice.

The number was, of course unknown, but the origin of the video was clear.

Everyone gathered to look at the screen of Friedrich's smartphone. Only Beatrice refused.

She sat back down in the comfortable sofa and stared at the rain that was so consistent with her despair.

CHAPTER 11

The video was clearly filmed in a slightly different location than where the first recordings were made in the kidnappers' camp. The trunks of two large tropical trees stood in the background. The framing was narrower and the other hostages did not appear in the shot.

All that could be seen were Karin, Felipe and two armed guards who pointed their M16s at the young, red-headed captive.

As usual, Felipe Maldorano strutted about, sporting that mocking sneer that seems to be the prerogative of fools. But when fools hold the lives of several human beings in their hands, then stupidity becomes a source of fear.

Karin began to speak, reading from a text. Still under threat.

"This message is for my parents. The *Blue Macaw* requires you to create a Facebook page called 'Karin Stockhausen 2810'. The page type will be the 'entertainment' category. Once it is online, simply post a picture of a blue macaw that you will easily find using any search engine."

The recording stopped immediately.

"So?" asked Friedrich, looking at the two NCS representatives.

"Nothing," replied Chuck Missangro. "The message is too short. In any case, once again it is from an untraceable phone, using a pre-paid and anonymous SIM card."

"Should we obey?"

"Let's give ourselves a little time by agreeing to all his requirements. In any case, this means of dialogue, short and anonymous, is the one he has preferred from the start. It gives him the feeling that he is the absolute master of the game. He will perhaps make a mistake as his confidence grows. Trying to change his mind or procrastinating too long would be very dangerous," Paul Travis added.

"Anyway," said Beatrice Stockhausen, turning to her husband, without daring to look at the screen of his phone, "He is in a position of strength. Our daughter's life is too precious. Let's create this page!"

Friedrich obeyed. With a few clicks he opened an event page on Facebook indicating the strange name including his daughter's name and a number.

"In any case, it's not a date!" Dave Williamson confirmed.

"Yes," Karin's father acknowledged. "But it could be anything!"

Once the page was created, Friedrich chose a panoramic photo of the Amazon for the page header. Then he selected a picture of a hyacinth macaw with beautiful, cobalt blue plumage in keeping with the request of the kidnappers' leader. When typing "blue macaw" on Google, he had immediately realized that this particular parrot is not totally blue, but blue with splashes of yellow and a bit of green on its head.

So, he opted for the hyacinth macaw – which is uniformly blue – in order to avoid further irritating his irascible correspondent. Karin's father created the page, inserted the photo of the hyacinth macaw and waited. They all thought the answer would come quickly.

They were wrong.

Felipe Maldorano seemed to enjoy taking his time like a cat exhausting a mouse without slaying it immediately. He knew perfectly well that the minutes and seconds felt much longer for the Stockhausen couple than for him. This was a real advantage.

Friedrich's phone finally rang an hour later. A new video. Yet another discrete SMS.

This time, all that could be seen was the face of the kidnappers' leader.

"I saw your page. Very good! You've chosen a very beautiful macaw, which means that you're a man of taste and refinement. That's no surprise to me. There's no mystery about the number following your daughter's name. It's simply the height of Mount Roraima where the Orpheus expedition was to work. Nothing more."

He smiled and the video stopped.

"What's this idiot's game?" Friedrich gasped, staring helplessly at the screen of his smartphone, now jet black.

"He's playing with our nerves," replied Anicet de Rochechouart, looking around the immense living room of the Stockhausen apartment.

The decor was minimalist. The bright colors of the walls, ceiling and floor, amplified the gentle light that poured through the gigantic square windows into the top apartments of the 432 Park Avenue tower that stretched into the clouds. Today the clouds were higher, but the rain was very present.

For a moment, Anicet examined the two large paintings by Mark Rothko and Zao Wou-Ki, that enjoyed pride of place on the two inner walls separating the living room from the central space that contained the emergency staircases and the elevators. The Rothko favored saffron and lemon tones while the Zao Wou-ki flowed in an infinity of purple, indigo and the deepest crimsons.

A few minutes earlier, Beatrice had asked, "If we pay, will the hostages be released?"

The fact that the payment of the ransom had been divided into four equal amounts provided real hope for the survival of the first six captives.

But what would happen next? No one knew.

"Let's stay calm!" recommended Chuck Missangro.

"By acting in this way, that is, sending short messages whenever he likes, Felipe is demonstrating the fact that he is in control of everything," added Paul Travis. "He ends his videos quickly to avoid being spotted while demonstrating that he is doing whatever he wants. When he wants. That's the principle behind false, one-way dialogue. We are is obliged to wait for his good will. So, let's wait!"

Friedrich sat down in the sofa next to his wife. He placed his right arm around her shoulders and whispered a few words in her ear.

Discreetly, his colleagues and the NCS men moved away, along the windows or toward the library next to the large living room.

Paul and Chuck continued to communicate with the NCS center. They were able to talk with several people and services at the same time. The results were still the same: no precise identification for the time being.

The most disappointing finding concerned the kidnappers' computer reception. The NCS specialists knew that, in the case of very short videos lasting only a few seconds, they could do nothing to track down the phones, a different one each time, turned off (or even destroyed) after a few seconds, used with anonymous SIM cards. They had become very hopeful on learning that Felipe would connect to the Karin Stockhausen 2810 page. But, once again, it was difficult to track. An unknown source had generated a massive amount of "friends" on the page. What made things even more difficult, a contact that seemed to be Felipe's computer was actually a very long chain of proxy servers, most of which, of course, were in countries that forbid any verification and control.

This dashed their hopes efficiently tracking communications on the one hand and future financial transactions on the other.

"He is using a very sophisticated software somewhat similar to JAP tools..."

"JAP?" Dave Williamson asked, interrupting Paul Travis' explanations.

"JAP is the acronym for Java Anon Proxy," Travis replied. "It's a tool developed in Java, namely a multiplatform, that serves to manage a list of proxies in cascades."

"What's it used for?" asked Beatrice, who did not understand much about proxies.

"This list of servers, more or less long, more or less complicated, serves as an intermediary to guarantee the user's anonymity as he browses."

"So, we'll never know who is behind all this and where they are?"

"We're working on it," Chuck said, reassuringly, although his eyes did not fully support this optimistic approach to the situation.

Friedrich's phone began to vibrate. A new video was available.

Once again, Felipe, Karin and two giants pointing their weapons at the unfortunate botanist. The location, similar to that of the last two videos, and the identical clothing and posture indicated that the recording had certainly been done continuously and that the members of *Blue Macaw* were cutting and editing at their convenience.

Karin spoke again. Her forehead was coated with sweat and their we large, dark circles under her eyes.

"*Blue Macaw* requires a first payment of $25 million tomorrow to a protected account. If the transaction is successful, two hostages will be released immediately. They will be found on the outskirts of Santa Elena de Uairén, near Mount Roraima. Then, a second payment will be required. The same amount. The sum will be transferred to another offshore bank and two new hostages will be released in turn. Dad! Mom! I beseech you... do what they're asking!"

The video ended abruptly. The last image remained frozen on Karin's face, as she begged her parents. Her mouth wide open and eyes almost bulging, she created the image that Felipe wanted to burn into the minds of those watching the video.

The message was twofold. First for Friedrich and Beatrice Stockhausen. This message was crystal clear: help me or we are all going to be tortured and then executed in front of the camera. The second message was of course for the CIA, the NCS and their information networks: do not interfere! Otherwise, the prisoners will be massacred!

A single glance at the faces of the four men and Karin's parents indicated the messages had been transmitted. And understood.

Friedrich had just stood up to paced back and forth in the immense living room and the adjoining library when his telephone vibrated and rang again.

He rushed over to it.

Felipe appeared on screen. Full frame.

"Karin said it all. So, tomorrow I'll give you the details for a specific account that will, of course, be found in a bank located in a country that prefers to guarantee anonymity to its customers. To indicate your approval in principle, simply post a phot of a llama on your daughter's Facebook page. Or an vicuña. Or an alpaca. I don't care! A photo of any one of these friendly camelids will suffice. No comment. No words. Just a picture! It will serve as our agreement. In the meantime, we'll take care of the hostages and feed them well so that they don't lose too much weight!"

A mocking wink ended this short video.

"What do you think?" asked Friedrich, looking at Paul and Chuck.

The two NCS men looked dubious.

"Why do they want us to communicate solely by posting pictures?" Beatrice asked, astonished.

Blonde, elegant and with a luscious figure, Friedrich's wife was still very beautiful. But Beatrice Stockhausen had a porcelain complexion that revealed her failing health. Moreover, their huge apartment contained a well-equipped medical room. A doctor and a nurse lived in the apartment and could intervene at any time in the event of a sudden cardiac complication.

She gazed at her husband, seeking some comfort. But, Friedrich could do nothing more. Except lie. And he did not wish to lie to his wife.

He simply said, "I don't know."

"A smoke-screen!" interrupted Anicet de Rochechouart.

"Meaning?"

"This individual sends multiple brief messages in order to upset. Above all, we can come to the following conclusion: this man is cruel, sadistic and totally unpredictable. So, it is absolutely necessary to follow his recommendations to the letter. Even if they seem odd, futile or absurd. On the other hand, when he gives us a bank account number tomorrow and the terms and conditions for the financial transfer, there will be no question of birds of all colors or hairy lawn mowers!"

"There are other players behind this braggart who brandishes his machete like Zorro waves his sword!" added Dave Williamson, returning to this idea that never left him.

Williamson, an Irish American, was square, stocky, gruff. And a redhead. But he was smart, skilled at maneuvering and, above all, the provided unswerving support to Friedrich Stockhausen since the latter had made his fortune in nanotechnologies and their medical, military, environmental and industrial applications.

His boss looked at him, raising his eyebrows.

He continued, "As I said a moment ago, this brute is not alone. When organizing the transfer of large funds to an offshore account, it's not enough to hide from everyone. It involves creating a tree of accounts that are linked together and disappear very quickly to include five or ten tax havens in a few seconds in a financial chain where prying eyes are never welcome. The process will probably be similar. To attain such a goal, it is not enough to play the role of an exterminator, showing his muscles, his weapons and his scars. It is also necessary to master the mysteries of the gray networks and of the Darknet, namely the 'deep web' where unmeasurable quantities of confidential, criminal and mafia information circulates."

"So, there are several decision-makers in this *Blue Macaw*," said Chuck Missangro. "Your observation corroborates our analysis."

"All this is fine," said Beatrice, flushing slightly. "But what are we going to do?"

"We're going to look for a picture of a lama on the net," her husband concluded, sighing.

Both tired and terrified, Beatrice closed her eyes for a moment.

Then she reopened them and looked carefully at the sumptuous Zao Wu-Ki painting facing her. Starting from the center of the canvas where deep purple and indigo flaky masses were juxtaposed in a strange fractal delirium, long violet, cobalt blue and dark carmine branches branched out toward infinity.

She stared at the starting point of this capricious wandering, analyzing this geyser of color that resembled an estuary soberly poised at the edge of an uncertain world. Without borders, without edges. Limitless.

Beatrice Stockhausen took a deep breath while letting her mind and eyes wander through the imagination of the Chinese painter. At first, she skirted around a few meandering lines that seemed to frolic in this place where the curved lines are frayed and intertwined so intensely that one has the disconcerting impression, both maddening and delightful, that they will penetrate the viewer's brain. Satisfied with this intrusion, the ellipses, spirals and twirls joined the carousel of neurons and synapses.

Karin's mother no longer really knew where she was. She could hear the light hubbub of the discussions between her husband, his colleagues and the two NCS representatives, but her capacity for thought was suddenly overwhelmed by her desire for dreams. So, she dreamed with her eyes wide open.

The meanders and confluences which littered the upper right portion of Zao Wou-Ki's gradually metamorphosed the violet and dark red tones into a chromatic buzzing delineating the whole palette of greens.

She saw the winding Rio Kukenan swell and gradually fill the horizon. Paul Travis had made the most of a quiet moment between the transmission of two videos to explain the geomorphology of the area where the hostages were probably being held. All the credible hypotheses confirmed that the *Blue Macaw* camp was close enough to the watercourse that originated at the foot of the Kukenan tepuy, from which it took its name, and Mount Roraima. This capricious river is fed by numerous waterfalls that tumble from the cliffs of these two gigantic tabular mountains. After heading westwards, the Kukenan flows into the Caroní, a tributary of the Orinoco.

Now informed of the real topology of the terrain, Beatrice Stockhausen could give free rein to her imagination, which was already tyrannized by fear.

She immersed herself in the waves of this tumultuous river, watching for the traces of a camp, here and there. But Zao Wu-Ki's work did not include a village, a camp or a military base. Only the wild irrigation of a stream of violet and vermilion tones brutally striking the right side of the canvas fulfilled her expectations.

And this hope vanished in a cobalt blue and anthracite gray surf.

Beatrice viewed it as a bad sign. A few tears rolled down her cheeks.

"Everything will be alright. We'll pay the ransom and the hostages will be released. Our daughter will be freed," Friedrich murmured in his wife's ear.

He closed his eyes in turn trying to convince himself that he was right. Without success.

The temperature was still high and the humidity level skirted 100% in the jungle and in makeshift buildings set up by the *Blue Macaw*. But the general atmosphere was a little more relaxed in the shed where Karin was held prisoner with her five companions in misfortune.

Obviously satisfied after sending the short videos that Matt Lochner had had to cut into segments not exceeding 40 seconds, Felipe Maldorano was in an almost jovial mood.

He even had a chat with Karin, Alexandra and Linda. Obviously, he preferred the company of women. Since Alexandra Haffington was still terrified, the doctor and the expedition leader took on the duty of answering Felipe.

It was obvious that the blued-eye man with the mustache had a very high opinion of himself. He was so proud of his initiative and the choice of his hostages, that he always gave the impression of waiting for a compliment or some praise. Trained to manage excessive and dangerous behaviors, Linda Griffith sometimes supported this need, while taking care not to overdo things in order to avoid any new outburst of anger. She managed her reactions perfectly and the arrogant personage even provided a few revelations about his past. But it was impossible to discern truth from narcissistic delirium.

Yet, this passed the time and any additional crisis of fury was avoided. Less eager to play the game, Karin paid the man lip service.

Suddenly, she asked a question that had been bothering her for some time, "How will you disappear after you get the ransom? The world is small in 2016. You'll have to change your appearance. Of life."

Felipe bit his lower lip before answering.

"I've got it all planned. But if you think I'm stupid enough to reveal anything to you..."

He left his sentence dangling and picked up his machete with a falsely menacing air. Alexandra and Phil stifled cries. Karin simply stared at her jailor with unfeigned assurance.

This calm seemed to please Felipe, who left the shed, saying, "You definitely are your father's daughter!"

Karin did not know if that was a compliment or an insult, coming from the mouth of this brute. But the danger had passed. For the time being. And that was the only thing that mattered.

The guards were replaced by four new ones. They ate a few pieces of fruit which their guardians continued to distribute sparingly. Phil Caldwell turned to Karin who was sitting next to him. The astrophysicist admired the courage of the young woman who always kept calm and did not hesitate to stand up to the leader of the *Blue Macaw* despite his sick cruelty and total unpredictability.

The Stanford University scientist was quite incapable of reacting in a similar manner. He stared Karin in the eyes, in the hope of acquiring a bit of the indomitable valor that energized the heiress to the empire Stockhausen.

The challenge was probably beyond her strength. He shivered. His eyes gradually grew misty.

"Are you all right, Phil?" asked Karin.

"Yes," snorted the exoplanet specialist.

"Are you sure?"

"No."

"Don't worry. It's a difficult, painful time. The threat is real. But all will end well."

"How can you be sure?"

"They need us too much. Felipe and Jan have been working on this plan for a very long time. They hired these men with one goal: to get a ransom. If they mistreat us, all these efforts will have served no purpose."

"But Felipe is crazy! I have no confidence in the reactions of a man who can cut off another man's finger just to prove that he's telling the truth."

"It's the weapon of the cowards. Effectively. But his accomplice is much calmer and their real goal is to see the ransom paid."

"Yes. But things will get complicated after the payment of the third part of this colossal sum."

Karin sighed, which inflated her sweat-stained blue T-shirt. The result was singularly lacking in elegance. But the vision of breasts swollen under a partially wet cloth immediately attracted the attention of the guard located just opposite Karin and Phil. The brown-haired man with charcoal eyebrows stared at the chest of the red-haired prisoner who, obviously, had inflamed his desire since he had first set eyes on her.

However, the guard – his name was Vinicio apparently – recalled what had happened to the other jailer. As he did not wish to receive a 9mm ball in his hand, or anywhere else, he calmed his ardor by looking suddenly in another direction.

"Be brave!" Friedrich's daughter continued, after making sure that Vinicio was now focusing his attention elsewhere.

"I'm not afraid for myself."

"For who?"

"I'm afraid for my daughter."

"How old is she? What's her name?"

"Six years old. She's called Cymbelline. Along with Vanessa, her mother, she represents everything I love in life. They're what drive me. My life. When I think of Cymbelline's angelic face and my wife's tender, loving gaze, I regain my strength. But…"

"But what?"

"When these crazy people study us with their ferocious, dark eyes, I tell myself that I shall never see Cymbelline and Vanessa again."

Karin Stockhausen stared at the terrified astrophysicist. Then she smiled at him and said simply, "In a few days Cymbelline will see her daddy and will hug him very tightly in her arms."

"Yes. If this nightmare comes to an end."

Two macaws began to quarrel over the roof of the prison shed, making a hell of noise.

The two prisoners nodded, not knowing what this gesture of agreement really meant.

CHAPTER 12

"Be careful!" Felipe Maldorano's face filled the entire screen of Karin's father's smartphone. Behind the *Blue Macaw* leader, there was a palm tree branch that had been cut recently because it was still very green.

Two seconds later, the kidnappers' leader appeared in his entirety, following a slight zoom out. Now, Karin Stockhausen could be seen, her neck held by the wretch's right arm. He was holding a sheet of paper with his left hand.

Felipe spat a spray of brown saliva in the direction of the camera to show that he was not joking and that he required his viewers' attention.

"The first transfer of $25 million will be made at 3:00 pm New York time to an account at the Bank of Marshall Islands which, as the name indicates, is located at Majuro in the Marshall Islands."

The video ended abruptly.

"The bastard!" said Paul Travis.

"A particularly opaque tax haven?" asked Dave Williamson.

"Yes. Some small Pacific states are ideal breeding grounds for such operations."

"All the more so," added Chuck Missangro, "Since this transfer will certainly be rerouted in less than a second to five other banks. The final destination will remain unknown for a very long time. Since they will have already transferred the sums paid into this account to several others as of this evening, all of this money will have evaporated in less than six hours."

"That doesn't matter to me!" said Friedrich. They can pick up the money and choke on it for all I care What I want is to get our daughter and her fellow travelers back."

Silence fell for a moment in the immense living-room, which stood four hundred yards above New York. The human ant-hill was swarming, yellow taxis caught up in the incessant snarls, and the dust from the giant city mingling with a fine mist that surrounded the landscape with a pearly cocoon of batting. Almost protective. Almost loving.

But there was no question of love and protection for the time being in the Stockhausen apartment. Lives were going to be played out with a few clicks on a computer keyboard.

Friedrich, his wife, his two colleagues and the NCS men were waiting until Felipe condescended to send a new video.

The Stockhausen apartment was almost empty. Friedrich categorically refused to allow a team of men from the FBI, the CIA or the NCS to occupy the premises. After a brief appeal to the President, he had made things clear: only Paul Travis and Chuck Missangro were to stay. The rest of the operations were monitored remotely by a host of technicians, advisors, analysts and strategists.

All supposing, of course, that technology and strategy are useful for saving the lives of eleven hostages held prisoner by a very determined psychopath.

Five minutes passed. Then ten.

"That piece of shit really likes playing with our nerves," said Anicet de Rochechouart, who had traded his light beige suit in for a coal gray ensemble more in keeping with the gravity of the situation.

"He's enjoying himself," Chuck Missangro continued. "This is in keeping corresponds with the profile we determined."

"So?" Friedrich asked, raising his eyebrows.

"An extreme psychopath, focused solely on his own life. Completely indifferent to others! When they don't get carried away and don't get drunk on their murderous anger, psychopaths are essentially bored, lacking any internal impetus that makes them want to do something. But, in Felipe's case, it seems that he uses the game to overcome boredom. When he isn't parading about or uttering threats, he plays with us like a cat trying to exhaust its prey."

"A madman!" summed up Beatrice, rubbing her arms vigorously to eliminate a feeling of cold that came from inside her.

"Yes," said Paul Travis. "But he's the only one we're dealing with. If he has accomplices, they are staying in the shadows and leaving him alone on stage. As a result, we must take the excesses of his behavior into account and make sure that our reactions don't harm the hostages."

"The only benefit," Anicet added, "Is that we can only respond in delayed mode, indicating our agreement by means of a photo. There is no more neutral means of communication."

"Perhaps he's afraid of a direct confrontation, man to man, looking one another straight in the eyes" Friedrich suggested without seeming convinced.

"It is very possible that his boasting and arrogance actually hide a cowardice that dates back to his childhood," said Paul Travis. "Like all psychopaths, he must have suffered a lack of affection, even family violence. This quickly led to total intolerance of his social background. His increased violence generated no feeling of guilt, so punishments and sanctions were considered unjust. This fueled his inextinguishable need for challenges, threats and violence. From that moment, on he no longer respected any law and the notions of exchanges with others, self-responsibility and reciprocity of services with others passed into oblivion. This process is well known and generates dangerous and perfectly unpredictable animals. But these beasts are giants with feet of clay. They are often cowardly and conceal their natural cowardice behind the convenient mask of permanent aggressiveness."

"And our daughter is in the hands of such a deranged man?" Beatrice burst out, collapsing into her husband's arms.

"Fortunately," Anicet reassured her, "There is a god that he venerates almost as much as himself: money. And I think that..."

The elegant aristocrat of French origin did not have time to finish his sentence. Friedrich Stockhausen's smartphone vibrated again.

A new SMS. A new video.

The field of the camera was a little broader, showing Felipe who still held Karin by the neck. They were surrounded by two guards armed with their M16s aimed at the unfortunate young woman's chest.

"Good. You certainly had time to look up where the Marshall Islands are located. But we don't care about any of that! What's important is now! I will give you an account number and identification numbers for the Bank of Marshall Islands. If you agree to make the transfer at 3 pm, New York time of course, post a picture of an *Ouroborus cataphractus* biting its tail on the Facebook page reserved for your daughter. You'll find plenty of pictures on the net."

He cut off contact at once.

"Ouroborus cataca what?" said Chuck Missangro.

"It is a girdled lizard that forms a circle and bites its tail when afraid," Anicet told the Stockhausen parents and the NCS men, much to their surprise.

"A weird name."

"Cataphractus means "wearing armor or mail"."

"Thanks for the lesson," Chuck concluded, twisting his nose a little.

"We have four hours to make the transfer," Friedrich stressed, standing up suddenly and pacing about the space between the second sofa and the huge square windows overlooking the city.

As the window measured three meters by three meters and the height of the room was nearly four meters, the apartment was very bright. Normally, this light that washed over the fortunate owners of this prestigious apartment nestled in the sky had a calming effect on body as well as mind.

In the current situation, however, this serenity was frayed by tense anticipation.

"We need to find a picture of this bizarre creature in order to indicate our agreement and prevent the hostages from suffering!" said Beatrice.

"Done!"

Paul Travis turned the screen of one of the digital tablets that were piled on the coffee table that now served as an office for him to Friedrich and his wife. It clearly showed the strange lizard lying on its back. Forming an almost perfect circle, front and back legs crossed, it bit its tail with surprising gluttony.

"Perfect!" Friedrich replied. "You can upload it to the Karin Stockhausen 2810 page."

With three clicks, the transfer was completed.

The smartphone vibrated again. This time the video was very short, lasting less than ten seconds.

"You've responded. That's good."

Paul and Chuck looked at one another.

"Shorter and shorter!"

A new phone ring. Friedrich rushed over again, saying that he had better keep his smartphone in the palm of his hand.

"If everything goes well, that is, if the transfer is made under the right good conditions, we will release two hostages Saturday morning. But don't try anything. Otherwise…"

While talking, Felipe mimed killing Karin with a knife that had just replaced the Beretta that hardly ever left his hand. Beatrice Stockhausen's daughter's expression was explicit. The young red-haired woman was sweating profusely, and the sparks that flashed from the crucible of her large amethyst eyes left no doubt. She was afraid.

Terrified!

"Don't touch my daughter!" Friedrich's wife yelled, forgetting that communication was only one way.

"I can't trace the call. He always uses a different phone and turns it off right after the call. I even think he destroys it every time," Paul Travis confirmed.

The Stockhausens and those who were supporting them during this painful trial looked at one another. Their feelings were particularly confused.

They could be divided into three distinct groups. Friedrich and Beatrice Stockhausen had only one concern: to save their daughter. Their thinking was clear and could be summed up in five words: pay and save the hostages!

Friedrich's collaborators were more divided because, although this was obvious to them – and that was normal – they could not forget that this one-way negotiation presented a dangerous ambiguity. Once the first four hostages were released, what would happen next? After pocketing $75 million, the kidnappers could very well decide to stop there and ignore the fate of the other seven prisoners who would then become a burden. And even a threat because they would be able to reveal information to could be used to find the kidnappers.

Anicet de Rochechouart clearly asked the NSC men, "Wouldn't it be likely that the *Blue Macaw* is planning to recover the first three instalments of the ransom and disappear just after?"

"That's a credible hypothesis," Chuck Missangro simply replied, making a grimace that transformed him into a hairless grizzly.

Dave Williamson and Anicet had some concerns that they did not dare to share with their boss because they knew that the latter had to manage both his anxiety as a father and also support Beatrice whose fragile heart could not bear too many shocks at one time. The Damocles' sword materialized by the uncertainties concerning the last portion of the ransom was a real risk for the last remaining prisoners. Especially for Karin who would, theoretically in any case, be released last once the hostage takers would have secured their escape.

Chuck and Paul had a two-fold mission. First, they had to make sure that everything went well for Friedrich and his daughter who were friends of the President and major players in the economic and political life of the country. But they also had to identify the kidnappers so that they could one day pay for their crimes and be brought to justice. Two-fold and very complex, their mission was impossible because the objectives were too dissimilar.

Looking towards the East River, Brooklyn and the ocean, the five men retreated into a distracted contemplation of a landscape that 99% of New Yorkers envied. But the mist was still there, and the luminous exuberance of billions of billions of droplets of shimmering water stood out in stark contrast to their psychic darkness, in which only a small flickering gleam glittered.

Hope.

Meanwhile, Beatrice Stockhausen sat on the vast sofa, which faced northeast at a horizon lying five meters away in front of the huge Zao Wu-Ki painting.

When she had explored all the meanders, gulfs, archipelagos and purplish and indigo atolls punctuating the painting, Karin's mother threw her head back for a moment, allowing her beautiful blonde hair to cascade over the thick leather of the couch.

Then she suddenly stood up, turned on her heels and asked the group of men who stood with their backs to her, "What are we going to do now?"

"I'll make the necessary arrangements with Charles Bloomberg," Friedrich replied, giving her a wan smile.

"Charles will be diligent and efficient. As always."

"Who is Charles Bloomberg?" asked Chuck Missangro, frowning.

"Charles handles some of our private accounts at Morgan Stanley Bank. He will be able to release the sum requested and make the transfer within the timeframe imposed by this madman."

Friedrich Stockhausen's two closet colleagues remained silent. Chuck and Paul looked at each other with a sigh. Obviously, nothing else was possible. For the time being, anyway.

Karin's father picked up another phone in order to leave the one that regularly received videos from *Blue Macaw* free. He entered Charles Bloomberg's number and left a message asking the man to call him back immediately because the latter was already in communication with another caller.

Less than three minutes later, the Morgan Stanley banker called him back. Friedrich quickly explained the situation.

Then he began to give the coordinates for the Bank of Marshall Islands to Charles.

Suddenly, one of Chuck Missangro's phones rang. The NCS agent immediately took the call that apparently came from an important informant. He blinked and suddenly said, "Stop everything!"

"What's going on here?" asked Friedrich, who did not like to be interrupted while he was making a call for the sole purpose of saving his daughter's life.

"We have a problem! A big problem…"

The second prison shed was as hot, wet and stinky as the first. Paula Cavendish, the two Venezuelan guides, Martin Physter, the journalist and logistician for the expedition, faced the same difficulties as their six other companions. But their situation was even a little more uncomfortable because this hastily-built building was located slightly below the other two. As a result, it received the surplus rain that ran down the adjacent slope. And, since it rained every night, and sometimes during the day, the soil looked more and more like a cesspool.

Since Martin Physter was panic-stricken and Matt Lochner had been given the heavy burden of filming the monomaniacal delusions of Felipe Maldorano when he threatened Karin while dictating his orders to the Stockhausen family, Gregory Greensberg was responsible for making demands.

Generally, the bovine eyes of the four armed men who watched them day and night did not stir when he asked for a dry carpet for Paula or for someone to eliminate the cockroaches that were engaged in a journey of endurance between the leaves that littered the ground. The answer was most often a dreary silence, a growl, a belch or an insult. Sometimes even a loud fart followed by a hearty laugh.

Nevertheless, when he insisted and grew irritated when he saw that the guards were making fun of them, a rifle butt to his chest or his legs put an end to any embryonic and useless discussion. It was easy to see that, without the threat of a brutal reaction from the gang leader, who knew so well how to maintain his authority by shooting anything that moved, these armed brutes would have been happy to mistreat and rape the prisoners. But the memory of the bullet that had shattered the hand of one of their kind checked the natural impulse that gripped them when the logistician demanded improvements to the captive's living conditions.

At the end of the day he had to accept a heart-rending observation: his efforts changed nothing. But things became more complicated when the sad looking brunette biologist asked to go to the bathroom. Gregory Greensberg made the same request, specifying, in Spanish, that this would avoid an unnecessary extra trip. One of the guards looked at his three accomplices with a disturbing smirk. He nodded and untied the feet of the two hostages, releasing the ropes that hampered them.

Since the two prison shacks were always closely guarded night and day, Felipe Maldorano had agreed that only the feet of the captives were to be bound, leaving h left them minimal freedom of movement. Moreover, since the *Blue*

Macaw camp was teeming with at least thirty men armed with M16s, revolvers and machetes, any attempt to escape was pure madness

And which direction would they head?

When Paula Cavendish and the logistician were freed, they could finally follow the smirking guard, whose was called Estéban. The guards' real names were never used in front of the hostages for obvious reasons of security.

So, the trio headed into bit of jungle that separated the prison sheds from the squat toilets made up of three tree trunks and several pieces of filthy cloth. Paula was about to step into the triangular space, which was rudely preserved from prying eyes, when Gregory found that Estéban had an idea in mind and that his most primitive impulses seemed to cause him to forget the punishment that would not be long in coming if he hoped to seduce one of the prisoners. The guard took Paula by the arm while opening his fly with his other free hand. His M16 was held by the strap that lay across his shoulder, but the rutting boor could not reach it immediately since both his hands were occupied.

Gregory immediately took advantage of the situation and jumped on the guard, in an effort to steal his assault rifle. At the same time, he realized that his action was both absurd and very dangerous for the other hostages. And for him too, of course! But he did not have time to analyze the positive and negative consequences of his actions because he was violently tackled to the ground by another guard whom he had not seen coming.

Felipe's were clear: when one man had to accompany the captives to the toilet, another always covered him to avoid any unpleasant surprise.

Mission accomplished.

Gregory found himself sprawling in the greasy, damp soil in the jungle immobilized by a guard while Esteban howled like a pig being slaughtered. The soldier looked pathetic. His fly open and his prisoner held at arm's length struggling as if someone was trying to plunge her into a bath of boiling oil, he stood there. Petrified.

The din naturally alerted other members of *Blue Macaw* who quickly surrounded the two prisoners, Estéban, and the guard who had followed orders, preventing an escape attempt.

Felipe raced out of the building where Jan and he had set up their headquarters like a devil.

"What is this mess?"

"A prisoner tried to escape by seizing Estéban's weapon."

"What were you doing, you fucking asshole?" asked Felipe, glaring at the guard whose fly was still wide open.

"But... I... I was trying..."

"What were you trying?"

"He had taken Paula by the arm while he was opening his fly," summed up the armed man who held Gregory Greensberg on the ground.

"Did you want one of the hostages to give you a blow job?" Felipe yelled, aiming his Beretta at Estéban.

"No. But... if... But..."

He did not have time to finish his sentence. The shot rang out and the bullet pierced his forehead. The wretch fell back, arms crossed.

"Bury this carrion a little further into the jungle to keep the smell of rotting from invading the camp!" was his only epitaph.

Felipe turned on his heels to walk back into the camp.

It was at this precise moment that several violent explosions and detonations rang out. They all came from the east.

CHAPTER 13

Friday January 22, 2016 - Camp of the **Blue Macaw**

"The bastards! They tried after all!" roared Felipe, who, oddly enough, seemed almost satisfied with the hubbub of an attack in the vicinity.

He made a gesture in Alfonso's direction before specifying, "No problem! Those idiots have fallen into the trap we had set for them. Go into the sheds and watch the prisoners. I want ten guards stationed around the camp to sound the alert in case of intrusion!"

Then he froze for a moment and scrutinized his men one by one.

"We have just won the psychological battle. Now they're at our mercy. The money will flow!"

Grimaces of fear metamorphosed into broad smiles. In the eyes of these men who had lived in misery a few years earlier, earning a dollar a day, the prospect of getting a $50,000 fortune each, lit a fire of joy.

All their efforts would finally pay off!

The *Blue Macaw* leader then walked rapidly towards the third building, not without having made an explicit sign in the direction of Gregory who gradually rose from the muck into which he had been propelled unceremoniously. Felipe took his knife in his right hand. He ran it across his throat, as if slashing it. The signal was brief. But clear.

When he reached the door to the room where Jan Räsänen was located, along with several computers and a cabinet filled with inactivated telephones, he said only, "Our miniature version of Operation Fortitude seems to have worked perfectly."

"A few truncated messages, an embryo camp and two imbeciles who have no idea that they are in fact suicide bombers... And Bob's your uncle!"

The two men expressed their joy briefly. Then they hugged for a moment to reinforce their duplicity.

"Now I'll be able to scream and threaten the hostages by saying that the Stockhausen rigged the contract and failed to respect it. This is going to be a magnificent piece of theatre with blood, fury and tears. Everything I love!"

"They're going to eat out of our hands and beg us," Jan continued, his hairless, smooth, bony face splitting with a grin that looked like a grimace in a horror film.

But his faded gray eyes did not lie. He was jubilant.

The trap was slowly closing on the Stockhausen family. In the coming hours, the kidnappers' demands would be inflated significantly.

"It's not possible!" Friedrich said. "They can't have done that!"

"They did..." acknowledged Chuck Missangro.

"But are you sure?" implored Beatrice, taking the NCS man's hands in hers.

They were icy and moist.

Karin's mother had the excruciating feeling of feeling her blood although she had no wounds. All heat had left her. There was nothing left in her but a hard core. Cold. Painful.

"Our correspondents at the US Embassy in Caracas are positive. Two Venezuelan army detachments attacked a camp in the Amazonian jungle located very close to Mount Roraima."

"But why there?" asked Friedrich.

"What were the clues that led them to attack, knowing almost for a fact that it was the *Blue Macaw* camp that was there?" wondered Anicet de Rochechouart, who was just as stunned as his boss when he realized that this astounding risk-taking could well cost the hostages' lives.

"The President has just called his Venezuelan counterpart, Nicolás Maduro," replied Chuck, visibly embarrassed. "Of course, I don't know anything about the content of the discussion between the two heads of state. However, our sources seem to indicate that the attack went badly. But I must immediately temper this because, according to our informants on site, they didn't attack the right camp."

"Your sources are reliable?" Dave Williamson asked, frowning.

"Yes."

Once again, silence fell over the Stockhausens' gigantic apartment. Rain was no longer falling. But the fog had difficulty lifting, which further amplified the strange and surreal atmosphere that enveloped the city. Nestled more than 400 meters over the city, the apartment and its large square windows made the residents feel as if they were alone in the world and partially free from the terrestrial constraints that glue bipeds to the ground.

Unfortunately, that sensation was only illusion. Stresses, anxieties and pain were present. Especially since the news of this stupid attack that jeopardized negotiations that had seemed to be going well.

If Felipe Maldorano, the hostages and their guards were still alive, Friedrich, his wife and friends found it difficult to imagine the angry reactions of this furious fool who cut off people's fingers in front of the camera merely to affirm his virility and his desire for power.

What would happen in a few minutes if he were to call?

By reflex, they all looked in turn at Friedrich Stockhausen's smartphone, fearing a new call from Felipe. Hopefully as well, since the absence of a call would mean that everything was over.

"Fine," said Karin's father, recovering a little. "What exactly do you know about the situation there?"

"What camp did they attack then if it wasn't the right one?" added Dave Williamson, who was obviously very worried.

"We can't be sure of anything," Paul Travis began, nodding his head doubtfully. "What has been confirmed, on the other hand, is that the base they attacked in the jungle was not that of the *Blue Macaw*."

"So, the prisoners are still alive?" asked Beatrice, trying to convince herself that the word that was to follow would be "yes".

"That's almost certain," Paul confirmed. "Once the attack was over, the Venezuelan troops discovered only dummy barracks and two corpses that had been totally burnt and cannot be identified for the time being.

"A fake barracks," thought Anicet aloud. "The establishment of a ghost camp immediately brings to mind Operation Bodyguard. More precisely, the basic principles of Operation Overlord, which played a role in providing disinformation to the Nazis as early as 1943, using material lures, false information and misleading plans. Although the issue is not at all the same, of course, the strategy is similar. This proves…"

"Yes?" Friedrich insisted.

"That Paul Travis has been right from the start! This brute is not alone in this operation. He's pumping his muscles, ranting and raving and scaring everyone. But there are at least one or two other people who pulling the strings of this diabolical with its many levels and traps. Proof!"

"This doesn't make things easier," Chuck Missangro acknowledged, frowning and grimacing.

"So, we have to accept the fact that Felipe and his associates deliberately sacrificed two of their men in order to draw armed forces, be they Venezuelan, Brazilian or American, into a trap?" Friedrich asked, worried.

His wife was distraught and in tears again; he hugged her hoping to give her some warmth and comfort.

But this was all too painful and stressful for Beatrice. She staggered and Friedrich had to grab her to keep her from falling to the floor.

He laid her down gently on one of the two sofas and yelled, Emily!"

Five seconds later, one of the nurses who remained constantly at the side of Beatrice Stockhausen appeared to help her. She sat the other woman up and gave her a pill to take with a little water. Karin's mother opened her eyes.

She looked at Emily. Then her husband.

"Thank you… I'm really sorry. Our daughter and her friends are in a dramatic situation and I faint like a young girl the first time she gets upset. That's unworthy! Please forgive me. I'll pull myself together."

"We understand, madam," Chuck Missangro said, trying to slip a soft and quiet note into his voice.

But he did not really succeed.

Once Beatrice's state of health had stabilized, her husband and the four men resumed their discussion. They all agreed on one point: Felipe's next call would be decisive.

There were two possibilities. Either the gang leader felt in danger despite his diversive tactics. In this case, there was reason to fear the hostages would be seriously abused. Of everything had, in fat, happened just as he had machiavelically planned from the beginning. In that case, he would be delighted, of course, with the provocation and the insult. But the discussion would resume and would likely succeed without too many negative consequences for the members of the Orpheus expedition.

So, they sat around the large glass coffee table on which the phone Felipe called each time stood.

Only Paul Travis remained standing, facing one of the bay windows that looked out over New York.

Friedrich was hypnotizing himself, contemplating the black and lacquered surface of his smartphone. But it remained obstinately mute.

The *Blue Macaw* camp swarmed with activity.

Some armed men appeared very nervous and walked about in all directions to make sure that the enemy's army was not heading for them. They were also watching the fire burning a part of the forest to the east, driving heavy waves of smoke into a cloud-filled sky. But considering the ambient humidity and the heavy rain that fell on the jungle every night, the likelihood that the blaze caused by the explosion of several bombs in the perimeter of the ghost camp would spread was practically nil.

Alfonso was gathering all the prisoners together with the eight guards who watched them day and night.

The atmosphere was truly electric.

The captives suffered from the curses and blows that rained down on them with end. Their khaki-dressed tormentors took care not to hurt the hostages as Felipe had explicitly ordered. But there was no shortage of humiliation. Naturally, Gregory and Serguei were the most frequent targets. As they occasionally rebelled, this latent rebellion got on the nerves of the mercenaries who knew full well that the only person who truly counted was Karin Stockhausen. They itched to brutalize and torture the other prisoners. But for now, at any rate, they controlled their darker designs while waiting for the divine moment when Felipe would finally allow them to have fun.

And they knew exactly what they would do at that moment. The unfortunate Alexandra Haffington would be the first to suffer the assaults of these brutes who had long been deprived of women and who could not truly release their emotions by massacring the men of the expedition.

Felipe stepped out of his barracks, followed by Jan Räsänen and two other guards.

Felipe always dressed the same way. But his weapons had changed slightly. Although he still held his Beretta in his right hand and his combat knife dangled from his belt, he now carried a shinken in his left hand, making sure, as is customary, that the long, sharp blade of this Japanese saber, the modern version of the katana, was directed perfectly vertical, pointing upward.

The saber with a blade measuring 2.5 shakus[8] shone with a silver luster, in which mercury and diamond were tangled in a mad saraband of dazzling bright flashes.

Serguei Kucharski's eyes lit up as he contemplated this formidably effective, traditional weapon. His beautiful, steel gray eyes matched the shine of the shinken blade perfectly. Having spent a few years practicing kendo, the climatologist could not help but be fascinated by this weapon, which was much more formidable than the bamboo and wooden swords, the shinai and bokutō, which he had used at the time.

A weapon for cutting and thrusting, the katana's successor was much more effective than the machete because of its length and the extraordinary power it gave to the warrior who wielded it. Moreover, its cutting edge was incomparable. As the Swedish traveler and botanist Carl Peter Thunberg pointed out at the end of the 18th century, Japanese sword blades were far superior to the Spanish blades so famous in Europe. They could be used to cut a nail easily without harming the edge and, as the Japanese claimed, could slice through a man from top to bottom, with a single stroke.

Even if one could doubt the ability of a Japanese sword to slice through a man, from top to bottom, with a single stroke, its effectiveness was acknowledged and it instilled real fear in men's hearts.

"Will they execute a hostage?" asked Phil Caldwell, staring at Karin, who was stepping out of the shed where they hostages sat in groups of five or six, at the same time he was.

The Stanford astrophysicist seemed panic-stricken.

The crown of his curly red hair was like a flaming diadem that could be compared, with a little imagination of course, to the coronal loops that spring from the solar chromosphere following the powerful magnetic fields of the sun.

But today, the warm sunlight was masked by clouds filled with rain and plumes of dark smoke that reared up about thirty kilometers to the east, where the Venezuelan army had just attacked the wrong target, justifying Felipe

---

[8] An ancient, Japanese unit of measurement, a shaku corresponds to 30.3036 cm. The shaku is divided into ten units (called sun) and 2.5 shaus are equivalent to slightly more than 75 cm.

Maldorano's trickery while exasperating his appetite for domination and vengeance.

A cocktail that was both detestable and explosive.

"I don't think so," murmured Karin. "It's not in their immediate interests. But I dread..."

"What?"

"His fury and the violence that will follow it."

The gang leader held his shinken over his head. He looked at all the haggard prisoners with a long, slow circular movement.

Then he shouted, "Settle in front of the trees over there!"

With his Beretta, he pointed at a group of five or six palm, fiscus and walnut trees. The hostages settled there in a row. But wanted to film a video focused on Karin and himself, Felipe demanded that the eleven prisoners move closer to one another. They squeezed closer.

"Karin! In the center! Next to me."

The daughter of Beatrice and Friedrich took her position the brute with the mustache and the surprising blue eyes with their evil glints.

Jan Räsänen stood in front of the group. With his arms crossed, he wore a smirk revealing the enjoyment he took in these moments. He loved money above all. Of course! But the vision of humiliated captives, hampered and submissive, seemed to satisfy him almost as much.

"Matt! Get to work!"

The journalist, whose skills were in particular demand here, had to take back the camcorder which now immortalized Felipe Maldorano's swagger and challenges.

"Kneel! All except Karin."

As usual, Serguei and Gregory were reluctant. A kick to the knee joint immediately achieved the desired effect. They had to bow to this degrading ritual which had the dual objective of demonstrating that the hostages were entirely at the mercy of the *Blue Macaw* and that this stay in the jungle was no boot camp.

"Good. Matt, you're going to film continuously. We'll make the sound and image cuts right after recording. As for you..." he continued, scrutinizing the prisoners, "I want to see tears of fear in your eyes, terror on your faces and tremors running up and down your bodies. And if one of you pisses his pants... well, don't hold back! It will add an extra touch of realism."

A burst of laughter sanctioned this distressing remark that once again showed that this psychopath, thirsty for money and power, regarded other human beings as objects that are shaken and then thrown away when they have no more use.

The message was the same for the mercenaries at his service. They had had an opportunity to realize that very recently when Estéban was executed without a trial.

Silence returned.

"Film!" he merely said, observing the unfortunate Matt Lochner.

CHAPTER 14

Friday January 22, 2016 – New York
Stockhausen family apartment

Beatrice was hypnotizing herself by looking at the glass rectangle. Friedrich Stockhausen's telephone remained obstinately silent. Black as the extragalactic abysses, this smooth, cold slab symbolized both an opening towards a future without contour and an ignored design. A stolen hope.

For a long time, she examined the inanimate object, which reflected the diffuse lights of the great circular ceiling-light, which compensated for the lack of light caused by the heavy clouds that enveloped New York before finally saying, "He's not calling."

"Let's wait," said Chuck Missangro.

"Are they all dead?"

"No," replied the NCS man. Our people in the field and our intelligence services are now positive: the attack failed. The camp where the hostages are held has still not been spotted by the Venezuelan army."

"Because the *Blue Macaw* camp is not in Venezuela," Anicet de Rochechouart interrupted, smoothing his thin mustache.

"How do you know?" asked Paul Travis.

"If the ghost camp that has just been destroyed is located in Venezuela, it means that the place where the hostages are held is probably on the border with Brazil. The area is wild, difficult to reach. It is the ideal place for holding prisoners without attracting attention."

"It is also the ideal place for preparing an escape under the best possible conditions once the money has all been transferred," added Friedrich, who still clung to the hope of continuing his negotiations with the *Blue Macaw*.

They all took refuge in a silence strangely sublimated by the gray sky. An evanescent, heavy silk hood fell over their shoulders at the same time.

Ten minutes later, the smartphone finally hiccupped. It vibrated and rang with violence accentuated by the surrounding silence.

Friedrich rushed over to it.

"A new video," he said.

All, except Beatrice, of course, gathered around Karin's father.

The first thing he saw was his daughter's silhouette, eyes wide, features drawn, and mouth wide open. Felipe Maldorano held the narrow, gleaming blade of a Japanese sword over the young woman's head.

A grin of hatred split his sweaty face. He immediately began to howl.

"You tried to fuck us! But it didn't work! Now you have to pay for this betrayal. It will cost you!"

Unconsciously, Friedrich closed his eyes for a moment, when he heard the words "It will cost you!" He knew full well that this threat could result the mistreatment of the prisoners. Immediately or in the following minutes.

He shivered and opened his eyes. The scene was similar. Same place, same haggard and distraught faces. However, Matt had zoomed slightly backwards to widen the field. All the captives were now visible, along with Felipe and four guards, still holding their M16s, which they pointed in the direction of the unfortunate captives, still kneeling in the mud.

Felipe grabbed Karin by the hair while slowly and sadistically twirling the blade of his saber over the head of the heiress to the Stockhausen fortune.

Then he stared at the camera that the unfortunate Matt was holding while trying not to tremble.

"Since we knew we could not count on you, we set a trap. And it has worked even better than we expected! A phone that emits a signal from time to time and your henchmen rush at the bait like a mouse attracted by a piece of cheese. How pathetic!"

He paused for a moment, then continued, a grimace of hatred distorting his face, "This is very dangerous for the hostages, in general, and for your delicious daughter in particular!"

Satisfied with his effect and assured that Karin's parents were terrified, he ordered the cameraman to zoom out again. The prisoners could be seen clearly in front of curtain of tress and a dozen armed guards threatening all the members of the Orpheus expedition, their assault rifles aimed at their chests or heads.

Their anxious faces were more eloquent than any long speech or complaints in quivering voices.

Sometimes eyes do not deceive. Today this was the case. Martin Physter, Alexandra Haffington and Luis Urube were frozen with the fear that their last hour had come. However, there was also a fright in the gaze of Sergei Kucharski and Gregory Greensberg, who had shown exemplary courage and had faced brutality, threats and insults.

But, since the failed attack on the ghost camp, the situation had changed and their lives were now in great danger. Only Linda Griffith seemed quite calm. The expedition doctor's chestnut eyes in the direction of the camera in order to embed a message that could be translated as: they would not dare! It was hard to imagine why the woman with the short auburn hair seemed almost serene at such a difficult time. The kidnappers' egos were dilated like a swollen pig's bladder and the slightest incident could cause a massacre. But Linda remained calm.

Perhaps she had gleaned some information from the camp infirmary that led her to believe that Felipe and Jan did not want to go so far as to murder a captive in order to demonstrate their strength and determination.

But, apart from Matt, the other nine hostages faced the lens and were not in a position to observe the quiet assurance of their doctor.

Friedrich, his collaborators and the NCS men were in a position to analyze this attitude that was in contradiction to that of the others. But they concentrated on Karin and Felipe. And this unlikely duo was worrisome. The posture *Blue Macaw* chief demonstrated the man's satisfaction at having thwarted the attack against his trap and rage at having been betrayed.

The first video was already over. But the second arrived quickly and Friedrich's phone did not remain silent for long.

Felipe muttered a little and a stream of drool began to flow down his lower lip. As he made no move to wipe away this unsightly slobber, this indicated that he was probably not in his normal state.

"Is he drugged?" Anicet worried, looking at Chuck and Paul.

"Possibly," Paul Travis said, watching Felipe's eyes carefully.

"In the case of psychopaths, this kind of behavior is not necessarily related to the use of drugs," Chuck Missangro added.

"His rage will feed itself and nothing will appease it?" asked Friedrich

"I'm afraid so..." sighed Paul Travis.

The video came to an end.

Then a silence. Longer than the previous one.

"What are they doing?" murmured Beatrice, holding a little stuffed toy raccoon Karin had played with when she was five or six years old.

"I don't know," her husband confessed, trying to comfort his wife with a look while staying within fifty centimeters of his phone.

"Will they kill a hostage?"

Paul Travis opened his mouth to answer. But the phone began to vibrate. Friedrich rushed over to it.

"This is not an SMS!" he said, looking at his friends.

Since the number was unknown to him, answered the call in a dubious tone, "Hello?"

Nothing.

Suddenly, an immense burst of laughter, deep and coarse at the same time.

"Mr. Stockhausen! What a pleasure to talk to you at last!"

Frightened, Friedrich motioned with his left hand, seeming to indicate "It's him!"

Even before he asked who he was speaking with, the caller introduced himself, saying "Felipe Maldorano at your service!"

The tone was sarcastic. But for once, Karin's father was actually talking with the kidnappers. So, Friedrich played his hand.

"We had nothing to do with this attack. It was an unfortunate initiative on the part of the Venezuelan army. I just want to negotiate so that my daughter and her colleagues can come home safely. That's all!"

"I know."

The simplicity and conciseness of the reply unsettled Karin's father, who was, however, experienced at dealing with the most difficult situations.

He remained silent for a moment. Meanwhile, Paul Travis made a circular gesture with his index finger inviting him to resume the conversation immediately in order to make the chief of the *Blue Macaw* speak as much as possible.

"Fine. Since you know we have nothing to do with this ridiculous assault, we can continue to negotiate."

"..."

"I'm still prepared to transfer $25 million to the account you indicated at Bank of Marshall Islands."

"Too late."

"What do you mean? Too late! What do you mean?"

Silence.

"Hello! Hello! Hello?"

Friedrich turned to his wife and the four men. Their faces were closed.

"He hung up."

"In less than a minute," said Chuck Missangro. "It was to be expected."

"He'll call back," said Paul Travis.

"Are you sure?" Dave Williamson asked, frowning.

"Yes. He's applying pressure. Moreover, this time, exceptionally, he called in person. So, he must turn off, or even destroy, each phone already used before calling with a new device."

"He's irascible and violent. But this man also knows how not to be spotted and how to play with our nerves."

He's succeeded!" acknowledged Friedrich, punctuating his sentence with an enormous sigh.

The smartphone vibrated again.

"Am SMS this time," said Karin's father.

They gathered in front of the screen to watch the short video that the *Blue Macaw* had just sent.

The prisoners could still be seen kneeling. But one of them, Luis Urube had been positioned in front of the group of hostages positioned in a row before the trunks of the trees that circled the camp. The unfortunate man was lying on the ground with his arms crossed and his face facing the camera directly. One of the armed guards held his right arm.

Another held his left arm and threatened him with a machete whose finely sharpened blade could certainly sever his forearm in less than a second. Luis, who had been terrified since their capture, howled with fear and begged his executioners. His face was twisted with fear.

When she heard his cries, Beatrice moved away, toward the back of the vast living room. Emily approached her and led her to one of the many bathrooms in the apartment.

A little younger than Fernando Pinzon, 35 years old and with little experience as a guide, Luis was thinking about his wife and three daughters. He struggled and cried incessantly.

Felipe made a gesture and a third mercenary immobilized his feet. As Felipe had suggested, and hoped, a brownish spot quickly appeared at the crotch of the unfortunate man. The *Blue Macaw* leader then placed himself near the camera while letting Matt film the immobilization of Luis and his immense distress.

"One of the hostages is now pissing himself because he knows full that we are going to cut off his arm. Luis Urube has a wife and three young children. And I will cut him into small pieces in front of you and his friends if you do follow everything I am going to ask you to do tomorrow to the letter!"

The video was interrupted after an explicit shot of the face of the Venezuelan guide who shrieked in while staring at the blade that threatened his arm.

"This madman is a monster! A sadistic and perverse madman!"

Friedrich was wild with rage. His eyes gradually misted.

He began to pace up and down without noticing where his colleagues were. Crimson cheekbones and veins protruding under the skin of his neck, he seemed to be in a state of shock when he realized that a man working for his daughter was going to suffer the worst abuse. Live. And without it being possible to do the slightest thing to stop this horror.

"Above all, Felipe Maldorano is manipulative," said Paul Travis, speaking in a soft voice to calm Friedrich's fury a little.

"But…"

"Listen to me!"

As he spoke, the NCS man stood in front of Karin's father, making sure that the other man could not dodge him.

Then he continued, "This psychopath knows full well that the image of a man about to be tortured and mutilated before our very eyes is truly unbearable."

"We all agree with that!" Added Anicet de Rochechouart, who was as pale as a linen.

"So, he knows that when he's going to call you back to tell you his new requirements, because that's what he's going to do, I'm sure you'll be psychologically a slave to him."

"A slave?"

"Yes. A slave in the usual sense of the term, that is, someone who is in a position of extreme dependence and subject to the will of others."

Friedrich first shook his head.

Then he sighed and finally said, "You're right. I'm so scared…"

He stopped for a moment and big tears ran down his cheeks.

"I'm so afraid for Karin that, of course, I'll do everything this monster requires."

"So," Chuck Missangro add "Luis Urube will be threatened, humiliated, maybe even jostled a little in front of the camera. But he will certainly not be mutilated or killed. Not for now anyway."

"What?"

"Let's be clear. Felipe's interest is in frightening, even terrorizing people. But he now has no reason to torture or kill his prisoners. On the other hand, if things were to go wrong in future negotiations, with respect to the discussions or in the practicality of fulfilling requirements, he would be obliged to set an example."

"Obliged?"

"In front of his men, and on account of the image which he must incessantly give to the mercenaries whom he pays handsomely. In this pitiless universe where brute force and immediate cruelty are the only two laws, the leader must always be implacable and fierce. Otherwise, he will be cast to the wolves for the slightest decision, or failure to make a decision, which can be seen as a weakness!"

"So," concluded Anicet, "There's no room for error."

"Exact!" confirmed Paul Travis. "We will pay cash for each error. To be paid immediately."

"When you say 'cash', what exactly do you mean?" asked Friedrich.

"I mean that a hostage, perhaps Luis, perhaps another member of the expedition, will be killed if the slightest false step interferes with the plan he has carefully prepared. A plan he will not fail to reveal to you in a few minutes, I think."

Karin's father looked out through the window next to him again.

The fog refused to leave New York and the feeling of being on a sea of cloud reminded him of the cover of Pink Floyd's last album: *The Endless River*. But in his case there was no man rowing in a yellow boat wearing a beautiful white shirt wide open on his chest. Just desperate parents.

Beatrice returned quickly with Emily and put her arms around her husband's waist. They exchanged a furtive kiss. Then she took Friedrich by the hand and they sat down in front of the large glass table where a desperately silent phone pontificated.

Each person there held his breath while waiting for the call from the chief of the *Blue Macaw*.

As had often been the case since the kidnapping, Felipe once again toyed with the wealthy man so that his emotions grew stormy. And the storm transformed into a tsunami.

He did not call back at once. In such cases, every second drags on and a single minute lasts longer than a desert crossing. With the discussions interrupted, the sound of a heartbeat becomes almost as obsessive and maddening as in a soundproof room that absorbs 99.90% of the sounds and where anyone goes crazy in less than an hour.

Boiling with impatience, Karin's father grabbed his phone. He shook it a little as if simply waving it like a child's toy would make the bell ring. But it did not.

He put it back down. Watched it. Then picked it up again.

Nothing happened.

Suddenly, a new vibration stirred the table and the smartphone. He rushed over to it.

"Another SMS…"

The video was almost frozen. Just an image of Luis Urube still stretched out, his arms crossed, a machete positioned above his left arm. The view grew a little wider, showing the other hostages, Felipe still holding Karin Stockhausen by the hair and amusing himself, sliding the hyper-sharp blade of his Japanese sword along the young woman's neck.

The video ended very quickly. Friedrich did not have time to put his phone back down, as he grumbled. The bell rang again.

"He's calling me," said Beatrice's husband simply, signaling to the two NCS men that Felipe wanted to speak to him directly.

They worked at their computers trying to see if the signal could finally be identified.

CHAPTER 15

Friday, January 22, 2016 – New York
Stockhausen family apartment

"Friedrich! I hope you'll let me call you? As a result of inflation caused by this unpardonable betrayal, the ransom has suddenly increased from $100 million to... $200 million!"

A brief silence.

Karin's father spoke immediately.

"Ok! The ransom will be paid in four installments of $50 million each?"

"Yes. Your sense of analysis and your pragmatism are delightful."

Felipe let his voice fade and waited a moment.

He continued, "I wish, as you can imagine, for things to go quickly. So the first transfer will be made not to the Marshall Islands, but to Botswana, which, as you know, is one of the many states that are not too finicky when it comes to the source of the funds that feed the accounts in their banks. Or their subsequent use elsewhere!"

The transmission ended immediately. Friedrich looked at Paul Travis questioningly.

"Not enough time. This jackal is clever. He always disconnects too soon."

The phone vibrated and rang again. Of course, the number that was displayed was unknown and different from the previous one.

"The transfer must be made tomorrow at noon New York time to an account of the First National Bank located in Gaborone, the capital of Botswana. I'm sure you know that Botswana is often called *Switzerland of Africa*. But don't tire yourself trying to follow this cash flow because, a few milliseconds later, the funds will have already transited through other countries in Africa, Azerbaijan, certain Micronesian states and, perhaps, Delaware or some Asian country whose name is as difficult to pronounce as it is to write!"

Satisfied with what was supposed to have been a joke, he went on to repeat the number of this anonymous account in the First National Bank of Gaborone twice.

After Friedrich had carefully noted it down, he realized that the communication had been cut off. He sighed and looked at his friends.

"Let's wait," Williamson said.

And they did not wait long, in fact. A new number appeared a few seconds later. Unknown. Different again.

"Let's be clear! If this transfer is made on time and without problem, Blue Macaw will free two hostages of our choice as agreed. In this case, I would remind you shortly after verifying that the initial installment has indeed been transferred and that the sum is exact. Even though I have few doubts about this last point! Once you have collected the funds and are ready to transfer them to the account I indicated, post a photo of an orangutan on the Karin Stockhausen 2810 Facebook page."

"An orangutan?" Friedrich asked, surprised.

"Yes. I'll call you back in a moment to give you some essential information."

The communication cut off abruptly. Karin's father clenched his jaws and waited.

Another call.

"It is essential for you, for your colleagues and also all the CIA people, the President of the United States and the President of Brazil to understand that if there is any problem, the least deceit, I will kill a hostage. A new attack and I will execute a hostage in front of the camera, cutting him into bits. Any delay or any error in the payment of the ransom... I will kill a hostage before your very eyes! Of course, it won't be Karin. I'm saving her for the last. She's our life insurance policy in a way! But I'm prepared to massacre a hostage every minute if necessary. And in front of the camera, of course, so that the video of the execution will immediately flood the social networks and video sharing sites!"

He paused for a moment before concluding, "I'm impatiently waiting to see the picture of a red orangutan with his big eyes and his so strangely human smile posting. Otherwise..."

Silence.

The five men and Beatrice looked at one another, stunned.

"The threat is clear..." Friedrich muttered, standing up as if he had been bitten by a scorpion.

"It's always hard to believe 100% in the reality of such a threat," said Chuck Missangro. "When members of ISIS make threats, in Iraq or Syria, everyone knows that they are realistic. They regularly broadcast videos and images of executions that can only make their hate speech and their total lack of scrupulousness credible when it comes to massacring and decapitating men, women or children. In the case of the *Blue Macaw*, we've essentially witnessed posturing, bragging. There has been a lot of staging, cutting off the finger of the unfortunate guide. But, since the ultimate goal is to obtain a colossal ransom, it is obvious that they will not begin to torture and slaughter their prisoners in order to give substance to their requests. This is a criminal organization in which ideology and terrorism have no place. Their goal is simple: to have an impact and to be as efficient as possible in a very short time. They have succeeded and we can hope they will stop there."

"Hope?" asked Beatrice, worried.

"Yes. For if everything goes according to plan, I'm convinced that they will release two hostages. But if an unexpected event interrupts the process, there is a legitimate fear of a very violent reaction. Very spectacular."

"What do you mean by 'very spectacular'?" added Friedrich Stockhausen.

Chuck Missangro took a deep breath before answering. He avoided looking at Karin's mother and simply said, "Seriously injure, torture or kill a hostage in front of the camera."

"My God!" exclaimed Beatrice, blinking and covering her mouth with her hands.

"Are you sure?" asked Anicet de Rochechouart, who was as pale as his shirt.

"Sure? No. But based on what we now know about Felipe Maldorano and the unpredictability of his behavior, we cannot eliminate this tragic hypothesis."

The colossus with the neck of a bull was silent for a moment and then continued, trying to smile a little, "But everything should be fine if everyone does what he has to."

"I'm looking for a picture of an orangutan right now," Dave Williamson said.

"I'm preparing the transfer with Charles Bloomberg," Friedrich concluded.

In the distance, big black clouds continued to roll in the sky over New York and the horns of the yellow taxis honked constantly, the hubbub rising in vertical sound waves.

A guard finally freed Luis Urube's wrists and ankles.

Without a word he pulled the man upright. The unfortunate guard wobbled, for anguish had paralyzed his muscles. The armed man, who was apparently called Jorge, caught him with a strong grip and forced him to stand.

With his usual smirk, Felipe finally let go of Karin's hair and walked over to the unfortunate guide. At the same moment, Alfonso asked the botanist to join the other captives.

Thinking that the recording was finally finished, Matt Lochner put the camcorder on the ground after turning it off.

"It's not over!"

"But..." said the reporter before realizing that this was no time to ask questions.

He bent down and picked up the little camera.

"Film everything that happens here. Don't forget to record the sound. Otherwise, you'll find yourself in the same situation as Luis."

Matt stifled his urge to say what he thought and resumed recording.

Felipe then made a precise gesture to the attention of six guards who began to beat Phil, Serguei, Martin, Gregory and Fernando. At first the pantomime looked much like an idiotic, playground game. The captives were still on their knees and the armed men settled for slapping them on the head, back, shoulders and kicking them in the buttocks.

Martin Physter fell forward and began to whine. It was at this precise moment that everything degenerated.

The man who had been mistreating him for a minute seemed to release his worst instincts. He began to beat the unfortunate edaphologist, who writhed like a cut worm, imploring his executioners. Joining in the fray, two other guards immediately began to beat him. The brutes took turns in keeping with an infernal, perfectly regular rhythm. As the punishment increasingly resembled a lynching, Karin and Serguei Kucharski yelled, demanding that it stop immediately.

As a result, the blonde climatologist took a serious blow to the right eyebrow, which exploded like a ripe fruit. Karin who, along with the other Venezuelan guide, was not on her knees, was violently slapped by the man who was closest to her.

The three brutes continued to beat Martin Physter, Jan intervened suddenly, yelling "Stop! That's enough!"

They all stopped, looking alternately at Felipe and his accomplice with the long, bony face.

Felipe looked intently at Jan Räsänen. He knew full well that his reaction was likely to have a dangerous impact on his authority over this motley band, which was only motivated by money.

He burst out, therefore, with an enormous, probably forced laugh, then said, "Jan is right, you band of morons! There is a lot of money to be made this week. Our hostages are worth gold. Heaps of gold! So... we stop!"

He then turned to Linda Griffith while pointing to Serguei Kucharski and Martin Physter, saying "Take them to the infirmary and take care of them. For tomorrow, I want them to be as beautiful as gods and as clean as corrupt politicians facing their constituents!"

The mission was impossible since the climatologist's face was covered with blood after the blow that had shattered her eyebrow. Martin's condition was even worse and the man was almost unconscious. He whimpered from time to time. But his glassy eyes indicated that he was not well at all. He had several wounds on his face, his arms and his legs. In addition, his breathing was painful and hissing after the many blows that rained down on his chest, back and kidneys.

Two of his torturers grabbed him by the arms. They had to carry him to the infirmary because the wounded man was unable to walk. Serguei was able to move on his own, not without having first spoken his mind in Spanish to the brute who had hit him in the face with the butt of his M16.

The man sneered and spat at his feet as a sign of defiance.

Meanwhile, Alfonso asked the jailers to gather their prisoners and lock them back up in the two damp sheds where the strong smell of soil mixed with urine always reigned.

Felipe told Matt that he could finally end the recording that he would certainly edit into three or four sequences to give Friedrich and the American authorities an opportunity to witness the violence and savagery of this group of renegades with the almost lovely name.

But in this place, the *Blue Macaw* was above all an Angel from Hell.

Two minutes later, Karin found herself in the shed where they had been staying since they arrived at the camp. She found herself with three of her colleagues.

Linda Griffith was absent for the moment because she had to treat the wounded who had been tortured by the brutes. Sergei was just one of those wounded

"I'm really scared..." said Phil Caldwell, looking in Karin's eyes for the flame and courage that were sorely lacking at the moment.

The astrophysicist had taken a few blows of course, like the others, but the results were not serious. Nevertheless, the image of Serguei Kucharski's bloody face and Martin Physter's huddled still occupied his mind. Filling him with fear.

Karin carefully observed the guards at the four corners of the shed before beginning to whisper. Apparently, they did not speak English, which made discussion between the prisoners a bit easier. Moreover, they all seemed concentrated on one mission: to prevent a hostage from escaping. So, discussions in English among the prisoners did not seem to bother them so long as they did not try to free themselves from the ties that bound their feet.

Reassured, Friedrich's daughter was finally able to answer the exoplanet specialist.

"Our kidnappers are brutes. We know that now. But Jan and Felipe know what they want. They will make sure that our lives are not in danger as long as the ransom is transferred according to their requirements."

"And if a problem occurs?"

The red-haired botanist widened her large amethyst eyes a little before answering.

"I don't have the answer to that question," she said, shaking her head lightly.

The shed grew silent for a moment. Phil Caldwell once again observed this equatorial prison, which he was now thoroughly familiar with. The air was still heavy, damp. Almost greasy. His skin was perpetually moist with sweat and the smells of musty, rotting vegetation and various excrements, created an olfactory symphony, that was both sickening and gentle. Covered with palm leaves, giant leaves of alocasias and banana trees, the ceiling regularly allowed in insects, small amphibians and a particular gecko species that Paula Cavendish had identified as a *Chatogekko amazonicus*. With its wide head and large yellow eyes, this brown and rusty gecko ran about everywhere. Alexandra Haffington had been very scared at first. But Paula had reassured her by telling her that this tireless animal was absolutely harmless. Of course, it had the detestable habit of slipping into people's clothes during the day and scratch near their heads at night. This frenzied activity was sometimes irritating, especially when twilight fell, but it also brought moments of distraction into a sinister and repetitive daily routine.

"Here. Here's the meal!" said Alexandra, seeing three mercenaries arrive, each carrying two plates.

A fourth came back with the climatologist whose forehead was now covered with a large bandage already stained with blood.

He reassured his friends and sat down near them.

"A piece of fruit and a disgusting soup," said Serguei Kucharski, making a horrible grimace, "They're watching our weight!"

"Talk for yourself!" replied Karin Stockhausen, with a faint smile. "Alexandra, Phil and I are getting thinner. For you, on the other hand, this sad and austere regime is not entirely useless."

"Very funny!"

Despite the mediocrity of the feast, the five hostages began to drink their broth, in which a few small saffron yellow leaves of uncertain origin floated.

Karin had just finished her soup when Alfonso entered the building, pointing at her.

"You! You come."

One of the guards removed the ties that bound the botanist's ankles. Then he helped her to stand up with an effort of gallantry that was difficult to picture in this universe where violence prevailed.

But as Karin Stockhausen was the most valuable hostage for the leaders of the *Blue Macaw*, she enjoyed, against her will, certain attentions which she would have done well without.

The young red-haired woman stepped out of her prison. The sun had returned partially, shining between two giant altocumulus clouds and she blinked in the strong light, as she left the perpetual shadow of the dark shed where they spent 23 hours a day.

She walked past Laura Griffith, who was returning from the infirmary where she had cared for Serguei and the edaphologist.

"How's Martin doing?"

"He's suffering a lot because he has many bruises. But nothing broken. Martin is solid. He'll be back on his feet soon".

"So much the better!"

The doctor and the person in charge of the Orpheus expedition did not have time to continue since Alfonso pulled Karin by the arm with a force that brooked no rebellion or even inertia.

They walked for a few moments. Then Alfonso went directly to the third building, which served as an infirmary, a command post, and probably a weapons room.

He pushed Karin in the back to make her enter the office where Felipe and Jan were working. The two men sat at a tipsy table. Three glasses and a bottle of beer sat on the dust-coated surface. Along the wall opposite the entrance, a wooden shelf was cluttered with computers and mobile phones with open casings. Apparently, none was plugged in at the moment.

"Sit down. We need to talk!" Felipe began, pointing to a third empty chair.

His face was torn with an almost honey-like smile. But his little, intense blue eyes and his thin mustache, which rose slightly at the two ends invalidated this almost grotesque courtesy in such a place under such circumstances. Karin was not fooled.

She simply said, "I have nothing to say to you."

"She's got guts!" said Felipe, laughing and looking at Jan Räsänen, who was still little talkative.

Beatrice and Friedrich's daughter did not answer, Felipe offered her a glass.

"A beer?"

"No. Thank you."

Felipe pouted as he slid his lower lip over his upper lip. He let it pass for a moment and then continued, "Will your father pay?"

"Certainly."

"Can you expand on that?"

"The transfer will be made as agreed."

"We hope so anyway," Jan said. "Your Facebook page has just been decorated with a beautiful photo of an orangutan. Look!"

As he spoke, he rolled back a little on his wheeled chair and turned a computer screen to face her. The screen was already lit and the slightly boring face of a reddish monkey from Borneo appeared in the center.

Felipe burst out laughing.

"Very well," said Karin. "That is what I just told you. Good. Can I join my friends now?"

"Not right away."

Felipe stepped toward her while still holding the glass in his hand. His eyes sparkled with an evil gleam, and his breath smelled of alcohol. The heiress of the Stockhausen Empire turned away a little.

"How do you think things will end? Honestly?"

"Why should I tell you?"

"Shut up!"

As the courtesy was swept away by a perfectly predictable tsunami, the botanist did not blink. Despite being from one of the richest families in the world, Karin Stockhausen was not part of this tribe of little madmen who spend their time drinking alcohol and sniffing cocaine to forget the fact that time is passing, that their youth will wither and that the outcome common to all human beings is already waiting for them at a turn in the road, at any time, any place.

She adapted to this radical change.

"Fine! To answer your question, it will depend only on your ability to channel the savagery and imbecility of your henchmen."

Felipe's eyes fluttered as he heard the words "imbecility" and "henchmen". But he said nothing, leaving the floor to Jan Räsänen. The man with almost monastic impassivity looked attentively at the young woman who could earn them at least $150 million over the next few days.

"That's our business. These men are brutes. Certainly. But we pay them handsomely. And if one of them goes too far... You know the fate that we reserve for them when they don't respect our orders. Don't you?"

"Sure."

"Things will be settled tomorrow. If the first payment arrives at the First National Bank of Gaborone, that is to say without delay and without interference, the situation will clear up for you."

"Otherwise?"

"Blood will flow!" shouted Felipe Maldorano.

CHAPTER 16

Saturday, January 23, 2016 – New York
Stockhausen Family Apartment

The tension was still high.

"It's almost noon and he still hasn't called," Beatrice murmured, nervously clutching her hands.

Karin's mother had been wringing her hands, turning her bracelets and rings in all directions. As if that could provide some sort of protection. Reassurance. But no comfort was possible until the first two captives were released by the kidnappers.

"Anicet? Is everything ready?" asked Friedrich, staring at one of his two most faithful colleagues.

"Yes. Charles Bloomberg has confirmed it. The funds were transferred to one of your private accounts at Morgan Stanley. Normally, there will be no problems for the transfer to Botswana."

"Normally... I don't like that word!"

"We've prepared everything upstream so that this transfer takes place without a hitch."

"Let's accept it."

Exceptionally, the two NCS men were accompanied today by their leader: Robert Pol-Jackson. A tall man with a shaved head, strangely light eyes and a slightly arched back that revealed that he spent more time in front of his computers than in the field. Generally, Robert Pol-Jackson never moved. He received direct instructions from John O. Brennan, the Director of the CIA, or that man's Deputy Director. Afterwards, he issued his orders and made sure they were followed in the field.

But Friedrich Stockhausen's personality, his financial weight and political influence had significantly altered his recurring pattern.

Friedrich was in direct contact with Barack Obama. It was the President himself who had approved this operation, circumventing the sacrosanct rule of "no ransom is paid to hostage takers". The management of the CIA and its active branch, the National Clandestine Service, provided support to the Stockhausen family while leaving them free to deal with the *Blue Macaw*.

In any case, except for making the immediate and irrevocable decision to sacrifice the eleven captives, there was nothing else to be done, since Felipe Maldorano generally spoke alone in front of the camera. And when he called Friedrich directly, he only wanted to talk to him!

Robert, Paul and Chuck were talking to each other in low voices so as not to disturb the Stockhausen family, who watched the fatal moment approaching with terror.

The sky was still foggy over New York. However, the huge square bay windows that looked down over the city today drew in a light which, under other circumstances, would rather have invited a certain serenity. It must be said that the minimalist Zen decoration of the Stockhausen's living room reaffirmed this desire for peace stripped of the material constraints and hardness of everyday life.

But this morning, in any case, the daily routine was singularly brutalized. Everyone was watching the time on their smartphone, except for Beatrice who starred at a wristwatch adorned with diamonds, never taking her eyes from it.

Friedrich stood up, keeping his phone in his hand.

He approached the three NCS men.

"You still haven't been able to pinpoint the exact location of the *Blue Macaw* camp?"

"The only time a tracer is possible is when they connect to the internet to go to Karin Stockhausen 2810," replied Robert Pol-Jackson, his face closed.

"So?"

"Nothing."

"They are using a staggering number of proxy servers around the world," said Paul Travis.

"Anyway," Dave Williamson said, "We all know that knowing where the hostages are being held will only be useful after the last installment of the ransom has been paid. Any intervention ahead of that moment will result in a massacre. No one will make the decision to take such a risk."

"Not in the United States, anyway," murmured Chuck Missangro in a surprisingly discreet voice for a colossus.

"What do you mean?" Friedrich asked, worried.

"Despite the assurances Dilma Rousseff gave our President, we cannot be 100% sure of the reactions of a sovereign country."

On hearing this, Beatrice took refuge in her husband's arms.

"I'm afraid," she said simply, sniffling a little.

"Gather all the hostages again in front of building No. 2!"

"Right away!" replied Alfonso, looking Felipe straight in the eyes.

In less than two minutes the prisoners were freed from the ropes that bound their ankles and took them out of the sheds where they had been languishing for hours after a very agitated night.

Jan Räsänen looked at his watch.

"Ten to one for us, so it's ten to twelve New York time."

"Perfect! In a few minutes we'll either be rich or covered with blood," replied Felipe, in an almost joking tone.

Then he turned to a group of about fifteen mercenaries. Most of them were former Colombian FARC members who had decided to make a lot of quick cash. However, there were also some Venezuelans and Ecuadorians who had known Felipe for a long time.

With a few words he organized the staging, which had to be able to be adapted to two possible scenarios: the transfer would be made in time and time or there would be no transfer.

It was essential for the positioning of the hostages and the threats made against them to be dramatized, while giving the impression that the lives of the members of the Orpheus expedition were not in danger if the Stockhausen family followed the instructions scrupulously.

The gang leader hesitated a bit.

Then he decided to stand all the prisoners in a line in front of one of the two sheds where they had been locked up. Once they were all standing in a row, he asked Matt Lochner to take the small camera and adjust it to take a short that was wide enough to show the captives and their jailers who could become their torturers. Or their tormentors.

When the cameraman was in place, Felipe checked the setting and the focus for himself. He seemed satisfied.

He then called Jan Räsänen, who in turn checked at length.

Felipe asked twelve mercenaries to stand just behind the hostages who were visible in the field of the camera. The image gave an impression of strength, due to the number of gunmen, while also looking somewhat like a school photo. But this was one of the cruelest schools of life: one that focused on submission, alienation, and total deprivation of freedom.

"It's good like this!" he said, strutting about.

Standing firmly, like a warlord about to order the start of hostilities, he examined the group. Then he smelled that sweaty, dampness so characteristics of the jungle when it rains or has just rained. That was the case today. A heavy shower had drenched the camp. The sound of drops falling from the leaves and of the surrounding trees continued their slow equatorial oratorio. People floundered. Boots and shoes made obscene sucking noises. Clothing stuck to skin, o the skin by intimately mixing the sweat of the bodies and the rain of the sky.

But Felipe cared very little about this discomfort. No doubt he saw hundreds of bundles of hundred-dollar bills already gathering over the forest, while the sound of coins tinkled in his ears like a waterfall sprouting from the cornucopia adorning, according to mythology, the forehead of the goat Amalthea.

With a mechanical gesture he swept aside the mist of his dreams to complete his preparations for this moment which was to culminate the audacious plan he had worked on so long with Jan. He stared at Karin, who never lowered her eyes under such circumstances.

"My dear Karin, come over here, next to me!"

On hearing this sly friendliness, Friedrich's daughter could not help but smile. Or, rather, grin.

"What an asshole..." she thought, comparing him to a cock strutting about in its own excrement, puffing up its chest, singing and trying to look handsome in front of his chickens.

Of course, her thoughts did not cross the barrier of her lips. The red-haired botanist settled for walking slowly towards the man she hated most in the world.

She stood in front of him and waited.

While using his right hand to hold his long Japanese sword, its blade glistening with droplets of water, he grabbed her by the waist as if they were a couple in love. Karin felt like vomiting. But she held back her disgust for later.

Felipe turned about to face the camera with Karin at his side. The other prisoners and the guards who were watching them stood two meters behind. Behind them all, the dirty, muddy wall served as a very mediocre backdrop. But since the objective was precisely to show that the prisoners' living conditions were deplorable, this dilapidated and filthy setting was perfect.

Felipe looked carefully at Matt and said, "Is the shot good?"

"Yes," replied the unfortunate blond man, with blue eyes, feeling the barrel of a weapon pointed at his back.

"Perfect! So, you shoot everything from now on. If you stop, Francisco will immediately shoot one of your knees."

Then he paused before specifying, "You'll see that life is much less entertaining with a damaged knee."

Probably satisfied with this remark that once again highlighted the fact that the lives of others had no value for him, with the excepting of Karin Stockhausen, he picked up a phone and turned it on after checking that it held a SIM card.

"It's ringing!" Friedrich yelled, raising his smartphone over his head.

He looked at Robert Pol-Jackson, who immediately nodded.

"Hello?"

"This is your best friend calling. Are you ready to make the transfer?"

"It will be done in two minutes as you requested."

"Perfect! I'll hang up now to send you a short video."

The screen darkened at once.

"He's sending a video," said Beatrice's husband, who had once more moved away from the phone and the horrible images it showed.

Felipe kept his word. The phone rang again after only a few seconds.

"A SMS!" Friedrich commented.

The five men immediately joined him to watch the new, brief video sent by the leader of the *Blue Macaw*. The scene was traditional, with the hostages standing in a row, armed guards watching them and Karin and Felipe positioned in the center, slightly in front of the others.

Felipe Maldorano held his long saber above the young woman. The blade was vertical and you could see his Beretta hanging from his belt. Ready for use.

"Karin, say hello to your relatives and CIA friends!"

"Everything's fine, Dad. But follow the instructions. Otherwise…"

She paused. A few tears formed on her eyelids.

"Otherwise," she went on, "They'll kill us all!"

"Fine," said Felipe. "It's not that I find your company boring, but I don't want to delay you because you have something important to do in less than thirty seconds. I'll call you back to give you a kiss if the transfer goes gone well. Otherwise… I'll slice up one of your daughter's colleagues while you watch! You know what's at stake. Do your best! Goodbye!"

He concluded with a gesture of his hand that could be viewed as humorous or disturbing. Everything depended on the feeling of the moment. Friedrich and Anicet sighed in unison.

"It's time," Dave Williamson confirmed.

Anicet de Rochechouart took his place in front of one of the computers. He typed the keys after entering a secret code that Friedrich had given him five minutes earlier and now allowed him to validate the transfers. He dutifully entered the sum: $50 million. Then he clicked again on some items drowned in a labyrinth of lines in a computer table that pulsated like a jellyfish, where the name of the Morgan Stanley Bank shone like a sun. One final click and sign lit light up in the center of the screen.

Anicet straightened up and looked at Friedrich, saying "It's done!"

They were all enveloped in a thick silence. Almost painful. Friedrich got up and looked out the window. In the distance, a large carrier took off from JFK Airport. Karin's father closed his eyes for a few moments.

Suddenly, Anicet intervened in a wan voice, "We have a huge problem…"

CHAPTER 17

Saturday, January 23, 2016 – New York
Stockhausen Family Apartment

"What?" Friedrich yelled, turning suddenly pale as if all his blood were flowing back to his heart.

"The transfer did not go through!"

"But…"

"The transfer did not go through."

"Some computer bug?"

"Probably. The entire transfer procedure was carried out normally. But once the transmission had been completed, the acknowledgement of receipt remained blocked as if the information disappeared suddenly within a virtual labyrinth. I'll immediately ask John Donohue, our best expert in this field, to analyze the problem and tell us what can be done quickly. Very quickly."

"Very quickly will probably be insufficient," Friedrich answered, slumping down on a corner of the sofa beside his wife, who was petrified with fear.

The three NCS men did not move. Did not speak. But it was easy to read in their eyes what consequences this computer glitch, which had really happened at the very worst moment, would be.

Anicet's phone rang. Everyone held their breath.

The conversation lasted only twenty seconds.

"So?" Friedrich Stockhausen asked with a disturbing gleam in his eyes.

"It was John. He tells me that there seems to be some sort of lock or interference on the encrypted line. He's working on it and it should be repaired in less than two minutes."

"Phew…" Karin's father whispered, his face some color flowing back into his pale face.

Not for long, since his smartphone also rang. The number was unknown.

"It's surely Felipe. He's not sending a video this time," Friedrich said, looking at his wife, who leaned back against the sofa, her arms tightly closed around her chest.

He took a deep breath and said simply, "Hello?"

"Are you making fun of me!" Felipe yelled.

Even without video, it was very easy to imagine that the face of the *Blue Macaw* leader was flushed, dripping with sweat. His shrieks and bellows of rage were as loud as the cries of the howling monkeys in the jungle.

"Not at all..." Friedrich started to say, knowing that he would find it very hard to explain the inexplicable to a brute who only dreamed of spraying blood in order to demonstrate his intransigence and determination.

"Shut up and listen! I'm giving you two minutes to make this fucking transfer to our account in Botswana. After that, I will kill a hostage in front of the camera. Is that clear?"

"Perfectly clear. But we did all that was necessary. The transfer went well..."

"We have not received anything!"

"There was a computer glitch. But everything should normally be settled in less than two minutes."

"We agree! Everything must be settled in less than two minutes. If not, I'll send a video of the execution of the first hostage. Then I'll kill one every five minutes! Every five minutes! Understood?"

"Yes," Friedrich answered in a dull voice, although he noticed that the other man had already cut off the communication.

He remained motionless for a moment. Karin's father struggled to stay standing. Upright. As he had always been throughout his life. But, at this moment, he was carrying on his shoulders all the sufferings of a renegade century, which would be burned in horror in humanity's memory.

Provided, of course, that humanity still has the leisure to recall the history of men in the twentieth century...

"The fate of the prisoners is now in the hands of John Donohue," he sighed, looking at Beatrice, his two colleagues and the NCS men, one by one. They all seemed hopeless and helpless.

But they had all been helpless from the outset in the face of the ferocity of a man who was ready to sacrifice the lives of the eleven hostages and almost all of his men to satisfy his appetites for money and power. A man like so many others on Earth in 2016.

The sumptuous apartment of the Stockhausen family, its 7,500 square meters, its eight spacious rooms and its 360° panoramic view of New York and its surroundings, seemed lugubrious. Dark. Dirty. Covered with all the filth of the world and its worst accomplice: cruelty.

The time had come. One of great beauty or great tragedy.

For the time being, the tray of the Dantean scale on which the Stockhausen family had been floundering for three days seemed to be shifting towards tragedy.

Beatrice began to choke. She clasped her throat and her face turned purple. Her husband walked over to her, while shouting, "Emily!"

The nurse rushed over.

Using a small inhaler, she gradually cleared the airway of Karin's mother. Then she made her drink a little water and take a medication prescribed by the doctor who had been treating her for years. Chuck Missangro and Friedrich

Stockhausen picked her up and carried her to the library next to the living room. They placed her on a chaise longue with cushions under her back and neck to keep her head raised.

"Thank you," she said in a breathless voice.

Then she stared at Friedrich and simply said, "Save our daughter. If anything were to happen to her, I would not survive."

"Everything will be fine," replied Friedrich, knowing full well that he had no control over the future.

This was the first time in his life that total impotence governed his thoughts and actions. A snub that cruelly slapped his ego, this feeling of mental impotence reached a peak, when the life of his daughter and her ten companions was in peril.

The worst-case scenario!

Dave Williamson turned to Anicet and said, "No news?"

"No."

"Time is passing. Be quick about it!" Robert Pol-Jackson insisted, boring his light gray eyes into those of the descendant of one of the oldest French noble families.

"I know. I know!" Anicet said, irritated with himself. "John is doing his best to fix this glitch. If he can't, no one can."

Everyone scowled, then, in fear and doubt. In one of his autobiographical essays, combining parody and philosophy, *Ecce homo*, Nietzsche said: "Not doubt, certainty is what drives one insane". In the case at hand, it was the narrow and nauseating border between doubt and certainty that, little by little, was driving Friedrich Stockhausen and his wife insane.

Powerless, their friends and the NCS men could only wait. And wait some more.

Anicet's phone rang.

"Yes?"

Silence.

"So?"

Friedrich's collaborator remained silent while he listened to the person on the other end of the line. His elegant gray pearl suit suddenly blended with the color of his skin. His smartphone still in his hand he turned to his boss.

"John still can't fix the problem. Not for now, anyway."

"But what's going on?"

"The transaction went well at the start. The transfer left from Morgan Stanley, but it does not arrive at the other end and is not credited to Felipe's account in Botswana. Looks like..."

"Yes?"

"Some unknown element has grabbed the information and us blocking it between the transmission and reception."

"But that's not possible!" Friedrich yelled.

Suddenly, he turned to Chuck, Paul and Robert.

"Unless... No. It's not possible! You didn't do that, did you?"

"Do what?" asked Robert Pol-Jackson, his eyes growing as round as golf balls.

"Did the CIA hack the account?"

"No! I assure you we didn't. The instructions are clear and come directly from the President. No one would be crazy enough to contradict Obama's orders and jeopardize your daughter's life."

"Where's the problem coming from then?"

"We don't know," replied Anicet and Paul Travis in chorus, with disgruntled expressions indicating they would probably prefer to work in a salt mine in Siberia than to be in the Stockhausen apartment right then.

"And what do I tell Felipe when this crazy guy calls me back, holding a knife to the throat of one of the hostages?"

"That we are working on solving this problem and that everything will return to normal in a very short time," replied Robert, mechanically rubbing his bald head with the back of his hand.

"But he only gave me two minutes!"

"It's been two minutes," Dave Williamson concluded as he looked at the clock on the screen of his smartphone.

Friedrich's phone rang five seconds later...

"So?" Felipe shouted.

"We're working on this little computer problem. It should not take much longer."

"A small computer problem? I don't give a fuck about your little computer problems! I want the first ransom payment. Now! But..."

The *Blue Macaw* leader let his voice fade for a moment so that the other man would focus on what he was going to say in the following seconds.

"But... as I have the very unpleasant impression that I am considered a fool, or that your CIA henchmen want to trap me, I suggest you look very carefully at the video I will send you live in less than a minute."

He hung up without giving Friedrich time to answer.

But what could Karin's father say except: we wait, things will be arranged... soon! All phrases that the head of the hostage takers clearly did not want to hear. Since Felipe's patience had been exhausted, Friedrich must now fear the worst.

Friedrich forwarded the message to the five men who surrounded him.

Anicet and Dave sat on the sofa facing him. The NCS men stood, leaning against one of the giant windows which looked out on a dark azure sky.

Close to darkness.

Border between Brazil and Venezuela – **Blue Macaw** *camp*

The rain was once again drizzling down on insistently on the camp nestled in the Amazonian jungle at the extreme northern tip of Brazil. But it the caprices of the weather were not really of concern at the moment. The focus was elsewhere. In the center of the camp.

The important thing was the Felipe Maldorano's burning rage.

Mad with anger and convinced that he had been betrayed by the Stockhausen family after first thinking that his threats had been effective and were yielding results, the *Blue Macaw* leader paced like a caged beast.

His men watched him, anxious. The hostages also watched him. They were all terrified. They felt that the hour of the great massacre was approaching. Quickly. Very quickly.

Felipe walked over to Karin again and, with his eyes wide open as if he were now possessed by a demon, he said, "Your father and the CIA have betrayed me! I will kill you all. One by one!"

It was at this precise moment that Serguei Kucharski shifted a little closer to the astrophysicist.

He whispered a few words in his ear. They stared at the pistol which the guard, standing between them, wore at his waist. Either in a moment of distraction or because he focused on the outburst of anger and rage that now invaded the camp, the mercenary had dropped his hand along his right thigh. This meant that it was no longer on the handle of the Glock 18 he always wore with him in the same way as all the men in the *Blue Macaw*. It was only Felipe who favored his Beretta.

The eyes of the two captives wavered between the weapon, almost within their reach, and the gang leader, who was threatening to execute them all in the next few minutes.

Sergei made a sign. Phil Caldwell immediately frowned, as violence and struggle did not course through his veins. He thought of his wife. Of his daughter.

"Let's make a break for it!" murmured Serguei, grabbing the Glock with one hand and the exoplanet specialist with the other.

The two men began to run as if all the demons of Hell were following them. Screams rang out immediately. But, since the clearing was small, the fugitives soon found themselves hidden from the eyes of their executioners by a thick row of tangled tree trunks.

"Catch them or kill them!" shouted Felipe, grabbing Karin by the hair to keep his most precious hostage next to him.

The Stockhausen daughter howled with pain. But she could not move. A dozen armed men immediately rushed after the escapees. A shot. Then another.

Frightened, Sergei Kucharski turned back and shot in turn. One of the kidnappers fell to the ground.

A blast of M16 bullets tore through the usual hubbub of the jungle. Birds and monkeys fled at full speed, realizing that the madness of men was still there. Always there. Anchored in us as the most insidious and the deadliest of cancers.

Sergei collapsed in turn. His legs were bleeding profusely and he could not run. Or walk.

Terrified, Phil Caldwell stood still. He raised his arms in the air and said piteously, "I surrender!"

Four heavily-armed guards seized the two prisoners who had dared to defy Felipe. Dragging them unceremoniously, they threw them down in front of the blue-eyed man with the mustache grimaced horribly.

He pointed his finger at the climatologist with the gray steel eyes faded by pain.

"I'll reserve you for a little later. You disobeyed and you wounded one of my men seriously. I'll gut you alive in front of the camera!"

Matt Lochner gasped in horror and nearly dropped the camcorder he was still holding in his hand when he heard this terrible sentence.

Then, Felipe turned to the Stanford astrophysicist.

"You there..."

He stopped for a moment as if he were looking for his words, then went on, "You're going to die in the next minute if this transfer does not go through immediately to our account in Botswana!"

Phil fell to his knees and simply found the strength to say, "Pity!"

Felipe picked up a new phone and dialed Friedrich Stockhausen's number.

New York – Stockhausen Family Apartment

When the bell rang, Friedrich clenched his teeth and jaws. Then he simply said to the five men who accompanied him, "It's time."

He picked it up.

"Bastard! You and your entire clan have tried to trick me. Enough! I have only one question. Has the transfer gone through or not?"

"Uh no. Not yet," Karin's father said, trying to make his voice sound a little friendly so that the monster would not hang up right away. "But we're working on the problem and it will soon be..."

"Shut up! I don't believe you anymore! The time has come for me to keep my promises. In a few seconds I'll kill a first hostage in front of the camera and you can watch it live because I'll send you the video right away. This time, there will be no delayed. The man you have just sacrificed is one of your daughter's colleagues. His name is Phil Caldwell. He has a wife like you. He has a daughter, like you. And he will die as you watch! If the transfer does go through within five minutes after this first execution, I will sacrifice a second hostage. And so on, every five minutes!"

"Don't do that!" Friedrich yelled.

But it was too late. Felipe had hung up.

Karin's father's heart sank so deeply that he felt for a moment that he was going to collapse.

He did not have time. The phone rang again.

"A video..." he said in a quiet voice, looking at his friends, whose powerlessness was total at that moment.

Without warning Beatrice, who was resting in the library located just behind a book covered wall, they all clustered around Friedrich. The palms of their hands were moist. Cold.

No. Icy.

The scene was simple and terrifying. First, the camera showed all the of hostages and their guards. There were only eight because Matt was filming, Serguei was lying on the ground with a mercenary who was pointing his M16 at his head. And the unfortunate Phil Caldwell was in the middle of an open area.

Next to him, Felipe Maldorano picked up his Japanese sword, which he now held vertically, respecting samurai tradition on the use of katana.

The weapon was modern, of course, but the enraged brute obviously wanted to make a dramatic gesture in order to emphasize the horror of the scene.

"Turn around!" he said so that the redhaired man would face the camera.

"Pity!" Phil Caldwell begged again. "I have a little girl. You can't!"

"Too late!"

As he uttered those last two words, Felipe raised his arms and rotated the sword blade horizontally.

Karin and Alexandra shrieked with terror. Their cries undoubtedly exacerbated the psychopath's barbarous enjoyment. Felipe took a swing and with a precise and very powerful blow he cut off the unfortunate captive's head.

Under the force of the blow, the head spun about for two to three seconds. Small geysers of blood gushed from the monstrous wound, forming a crimson halo that moved slower than Phil Caldwell's head.

After many gyrations, it landed on the back of the skull and settled there, in the soil and in the rain. The victim's green eyes continued to stare at the sky, searching perhaps for a new light before finding eternal rest. Then the head tilted a little to the side, to stare at the headless body lying ten meters away.

"My God!" howled Friedrich Stockhausen, putting his left hand over his eyes to avoid seeing the terrible death throes.

Paul, Chuck, and Robert continued to observe this macabre execution, which illustrated the determination of the *Blue Macaw* leader. They saw Phil Caldwell's body sprawled on the muddy ground. His friends tried to approach. They were driven back, beaten with rifle butts.

Then Felipe Maldorano strutted about, still holding Karin by the hair.

Anicet slipped out to vomit, Dave Williamson walked over to one of the bay windows. The sun was finally beginning to cut through the heavy clouds that had covered New York City for a few days. But it was too late. Far too late.

"What's going on?"

Beatrice's frail voice brought Friedrich face to face with his.

"They've just executed Phil Caldwell," he said as he walked over to his wife to take her tightly in his arms.

CHAPTER 18

The space is white. Uniformly white.

The space is white. And immense.

The space is white. Quiet.

The space is white. And empty.

Within this petrification with soft surfaces, iridescent, translucent in places, a form begins to stir.

The white being in a universe where the *outre-blanc*[9] reigns seems to snap. It breathes.

Slowly.

Flat and embedded in the vertical wall that seems to be made of a material similar in all respects to it, the creature tries to open its eyes. But it cannot. Tired, it waits a little.

Then starts again. But its dazzling eyelids remain obstinately closed. It tries again. Persists. Suffers.

The creature that seems to be the only living organism in this titanic, petrified universe also tries to move its arms a little. Its legs.

But are they really arms and legs? It's difficult to say at this precise moment because the shimmering of billions of reflections that are all well beyond white is still crystallized in the wall that envelopes and attracts it.

It stops moving because the ties that weave around his body and hold him to the wall seem to be stronger than it is.

It pants. Then calms down. A new trial. Unsuccessful. Another.

Yet another.

Suddenly, the light begins to filter along the thin slit that separates deep inner night from the dazzling surrounding light. A sweet and fragile radiance at first, it gradually invades visual space.

The sudden arrival of raw light makes the being locked in the wall. But, despite the force of this cry, the creature utters no sound through its wide-open

---

[9] In January 1979, French painter Pierre Soulages invented a black that is beyond black, which he first called "noir-lumière" before giving it its definitive name: "*outrenoir*". It is actually a black transmuted and magnified by light. At the same time, in this work we evoke a magnificent white that is beyond white: "*outre-blanc*". So, we use the French word *outre-blanc* in the English version instead of *hyper-white* or *beyond white*. But the meaning is always the same, it is an immaculate white that lies beyond white and highlights our intimate darkness.

mouth. White hole in an *outre-blanc* world it polarizes all fears. All anxieties. All terrors.

The creature hurriedly closed its eyelids, which it had taken so long to open. Cruel paradox. But, for now at any rate, it cannot bear the virulent light which terrifies it and seems to simultaneously burn its retina and its soul.

But what is a white soul in a white silhouette lost in an *outre-blanc* universe? A ghost.

A dream? A divinity in the making?

Or a being lost in the most dazzling and sinister of prisons: itself?

The creature lurking in the wall, of which it has always been one element among others, finally decides to face this blinding light that tears its eyeballs and riddles them with needles of ice and grains of sand.

After a long breath it tried again. Slowly. The effort is painful, but less so than before. It blinks, frowns. Persists.

Little by little, this immaculate whiteness that seems to shine like a thousand stars gathered together in the same place grows less virulent. Almost friendly. The embedded creature then realizes that it is starting to tame the light. It smiles. The simple, slight lifting raising of the corners of its mouth gives it much satisfaction.

Immobilized vertically in a wall that seems made of the same flesh as it, the flat creature tries to look at its immediate environment. Since it cannot move its body and even less turn its head, this effort is frustrating. What it sees is cruelly lacking in precision because, in an oversized space that seems to consist of a single material, volumes fade and depths are juxtaposed in a disconcerting visual maelstrom.

In front of it, the being filled with light sees another wall. White as well.

"Well, I'm making good progress," it thought, after realizing that the support of the word and the comfort of sounds were denied him for the time being.

Understanding that this situation will not evolve unless it makes a great deal of effort, the being tries to extract itself from the wall that envelopes it.

Its first attempts are pathetic. And unsuccessful.

It starts again, resting on its lower limbs. Then it realizes that the only way to detach itself from this vertical flatness will be to use its arms twisting and forcing violently on one side. Then on the other.

Its tries. Strains. Runs out of breath. Suddenly, the bonds stretch. Bit by bit.

The tearing is not painful. Silent, it settles for making a little sucking sound. Unappealing. But effective.

Haggard, the creature finally separates from its support. It stays there. Standing. Seeking a very fragile balance in a monochromatic world where distances lose their meaning and simple notions of high and low become uncertain. Fluctuating like a mirage.

Reassured by this effort which finally bore fruit, the white creature begins to feel itself.

Two immediate surprises. Its limbs and its skull are extended with long filaments. Naturally, they are white and pearly. Second source of astonishment: its body is relatively flat, like those of some fish that live at the bottom of the ocean. But the iridescent being of pale light does not know what a fish is yet. Or an ocean.

In fact, it has no idea what it is. And where it is.

"Not easy..." it soliloquies, knowing that being alone, unable to speak and not knowing who it is, its internal monologues will quickly confine themselves to the analysis of all the shades of white that line this incongruous space.

Annoyed, it looks around. Detached from the wall at this point, its body, head and eyes allow it to investigate more fully. Complete, but disappointing for now.

In front of it, another wall looms. Very far away.

It looks over and realizes that this space-universe is expanding. In the immobile firmament of a world dominated by the tyranny of an all-powerful overseer, it finally notices translucent spheres. Shimmering. Almost immodest, their transparencies reveal other spheres intertwined in one another like the tiny bubbles of a virginal foam drifting at the edge of an endless surf.

Endless... Why does this expression suddenly acquire so great an intensity and acuity? So devastating?

It does not know.

The only sensible development: by feeling its body with the long hairs that stretch from its hands, it realizes that its arms, torso and legs are not as flat. They are gradually taking on a volume that seems more normal to it.

But normal compared to what? Once again, it still does not know. How frustrating!

Gently walking on its feet covered with filaments like the delicate and thin tentacles of sea anemones or the long filaments of spirographs, he looks down.

Of course, this pale creature with the wild expression does not know what spirographs and sea anemones are. It does not even know that it is a human being.

But what would a human being be doing in such a place?

For a long time, the pale creature observes the abyss that opens beneath it, the almost infinite gap resembling a white cesspool. The *outre blanc* is everywhere and this omnipresence grows almost sickening. The being holds back retching at the last moment. It calms the chaos in its stomach and forces itself to a make a slow and conscientious examination.

The environment grows more understandable as well. This gigantic cliff-shaped wall climbing the Empyrean is in fact a titanic, truncated cone, with the narrowest part at the bottom. A white, volcanic chimney flaring up in a still whiter world.

"A giant funnel the size of the most powerful gods," it suddenly thinks, not knowing yet why these words flow into its mind because it does not know what a funnel is.

And the notion of gods is blurred in its mind.

Whatever! If these words spring naturally into its head, that is because there is a good reason for this. No doubt a distant reminiscence of another world. Of another life.

Of another time.

This immaculate truncated cone extends far downwards and continues even further upwards. Spiraling in a lamination of innumerable rings that rise in narrow, white, lustrous terraces, and watery lights in a hundred thousand million shades of white, this universe resembles Dante's *Inferno* a little

But an ultra-white hell of cosmic dimensions.

Another notable difference is that the being is alone. It sees neither the three dangerous beasts that bar the way – the lynx, the lion and the wolf – nor its companions. The iridescent creature of dazzling lights perceives neither Virgil nor Beatrice. It is alone. Totally alone.

After heaving a sigh, widening its rib cage, which had been flattened up to that point, the being with filaments and tentacles flowing from the ends of its limbs and the top of its head looks at the infinite vertical surface and asks a single question, "Why?"

Since this simple question has titillated the universe for nearly 14 billion years, there is very little chance that this white and mute creature will be able to answer it in a few minutes.

As the silence grows more and more oppressive, the being finally decides to turn. The wall in which it was embedded a few minutes earlier still bears the signs of its time there. But they disappear little by little as if the wall is digesting them with unfeigned delight.

It is at this precise moment that the being begins to compare the structure of its arms with that of the ground, the giant funnel and the wall. The observation is maddening: they are all the same!

This world... is itself!

It is, moreover, possible to reverse the observation and state that the creature itself is the white, smooth, shining and living world that surrounds it.

Extending its observation, it notices that some portions of the cliff-shaped wall are less white and almost totally translucent. In these flat spaces that ostensibly refer to a geometry of chaos it discovers some slightly colored shadows. It is the only touch, diaphanous and very discreet, that creates a watermark on this universe tyrannized by the *outre-blanc*.

But, unlike the funnel that flares upward, seemingly ruled by calm and immutability, the furtive shadows perceived in the translucent areas seem agitated with a frenzy tiring for the eye.

They don't move, they run. They no longer run, they race at full tilt, twirling, panicking and evaporating.

The movement accelerates. Keeps accelerating.

Exhausted by this galloping hysteria, the vaguely colored forms gradually fade.

Then disappear.

The translucent areas then act as mirrors, allowing the sole survivor of an odyssey whose causes and conditions are unknown to it to finally see itself completely. Its heads, topped with filaments that move in all directions is totally surprising. Its eyes bulge.

The white outgrowths, slender and crazy, form a baroque helmet or the crown of a barbarous monarch. Thus adorned, the creature looks like a gorgon[10], hallucinated and petrified in a monochromatic world. Quiet. Motionless. Eternal.

An unnamed shipwreck in an off-white desert, the being is scared. Then it conceals its panic and moves closer to a particularly flat and translucent area that reveals its image in front of a few billion leaves of an unsettling transparency.

Its face reminds it of a buried memory. Deeply buried. Far too deeply.

It blinks and realizes that its eyes are made of a matter substantially different from the rest of its body and the wall from which it has just extricated itself. Its eyeballs are gorgeously faceted and almost infinite in number, resembling an almost perfect sphere.

Delicately, it attempts to brush its eyes with the long pale filaments that extend from its hands, replacing its fingers. The contact is gentle despite their apparent minerality. This experience confirms at least one thing: it can still experience certain sensations.

Yet, the lack of precise memories limits the scope of this satisfaction. At this very moment, it recalls neither its name nor its life.

Or its death.

Its death? How could it be here if it is already dead? What is death?

It has no idea.

As the permanent reiteration of all that the creatures does not know overwhelms it with contradictory feelings, out of harmony with this white, hushed, silky, silent universe, it move off a little way.

Staying here would be pointless. Because nothing is happening.

A little clumsy, since walking on filaments and tentacles is apparently not very convenient, the creature begins to advance towards the edge of the abyss. Since each terrace forming a new stratum is very narrow, it must remain attentive and prudent.

---

[10] In Greek mythology, the gorgons were evil creatures who turned any person careless enough to look at them to stone. There were three Medusa was mortal, while the other two, Stheno and Euryale, were immortal.

Good news. Finally! The only possible path swirls around the central well located at the very heart of the giant truncated cone. This means that climbing or descending will be very easy. No bold climb. No dangerous or slippery descent.

"Let's explore this world that is now my world," it thinks, recalling that the speech is forbidden to him.

Forbidden? That's not sure. But it is certainly impossible. Any and all efforts to speak, shout, whisper or sing remain ineffective and vain.

When it arrives at the edge of the abyss, it looks up at the top first. The slope of the cliff-shaped wall flares out very slowly. But the angle of inclination remains imposing. Above all, the eye gets lost within a firmament that is very distant, almost infinite.

"What is at the top of this giant funnel that would dwarf the dimensions of a giant planet?"

No answer is credible since this slope extends far beyond the firmament.

Once again, the flat, white creature finds itself mentally using words it does not know and which it does not really understand, such giant planet.

It's confusing. And nerve-racking. Yet, since the creature can do nothing to change the situation, it decides to set asides its questions. They will all be carefully locked up in a corner of its brain to be brought up later. When a few elements finally allow it to understand where and who it is.

So, what is a *brain*?

The silent and almost blissful contemplation of the horizon above the abyss finally comes to an end. After titillating its mind by staring at long clusters of spheres which themselves form clusters of bubbles extending to infinity, the human-shaped creature with its shaggy filaments decides to look towards the abyss.

It is at this precise moment that it discovers a silhouette similar to its own, a silhouette that, turn, is trying to break free from the nurturing wall that seems to be both mother and prison.

The newcomer is five rings lower. In order to reach it, the creature would have to either walk five times around the gaping chasm, which would take weeks, walking without stopping, or to take the small crossings that connect the rings along a gentle slope.

The pearly being of light is stunned. It opens its diamond eyes. Then it opens its mouth to call out to this new companion. But, no sound comes out of its throat.

For the first time since emerging in this strange world, the creature feels an unprecedented emotion, an unfamiliar emotion, one it cannot define.

But two sparkling tears begin to flow down its cheeks.

CHAPTER 19

Mute, the creature tries to attract the attention of the other being just below. But that being is facing the same problem. Embedded in the white cliff, it makes a lot of effort to extricate itself from this vertical matrix which is both welcoming and constraining.

The first creature looks around, trying to find a means to communicate. Or at least to signal its presence. This gloomy, shining, desperately white world is actually a desert in the form of a giant chasm, communication between the only two living beings there would be wonderful.

Alas, there is nothing apart from a wall that is soft and smooth at the same time, narrow terraces and a bottomless abyss.

The being who had awakened first looks at the other which finally manages to free itself from the thread-like outgrowths that hold it to the cliff like a limpet clinging to its rock, waiting for the next tide.

Its reactions are similar. It moves slowly, looks around. Then behind him. The one who is located a few terraces higher realizes that its will not be able to warn the newcomer without making a great effort. But what should it do?

Feeling desperate, it begins to tap along the vertical wall located less than a meter away. This *outre-blanc* universe appears to be a unique, perfectly coherent entity, and it imagines that its tapping may generate vibrations that its companion in misfortune may feel through the filaments that adorn its feet.

So, he taps once. Nothing.

It starts again, tapping several times at regular intervals. Nothing.

Its continues its attempts at communication, alternating short and long taps. Still nothing.

The second white creature with its long pale filaments devotes less time to the slow examination of its environment. Does it know who it is and where it comes from? Hard to say. But reality is imperative: it begins to walk slowly along the narrow terrace overlooked by the titanic cliff opening up toward a sky dotted with billions of translucent and white spheres.

The being who regained consciousness first realizes that its only companion is in the process of beginning the slow and almost infinite descent to the bottom of the abyss glazed with light.

"Why doesn't it head up?" it laments.

Then, realizing that whining will not solve anything, it decides to make the same descent, using the small paths that connect the terraces to one another and cutting the distances considerably.

The only problem is that the paths, while not steep, slope gently, and the terraces that stratify this astonishing cliff in the millions are almost horizontal.

The slope is very real and the surface of this white and glossy material proves very quickly to be slippery.

The creature understands at this moment why its feet and hands are equipped with fine tentacles and a dense network of filaments that move about in all directions.

"A sucker or paws like those geckos have would be better still," it tells itself without astonishment because it talks about *suckers* and *geckos* without knowing the real meaning of these words, the slap of the second one sounding like an onomatopoeia.

The descent starts without hindrance. But, a few minutes later, the being with the gorgon-like head falls heavily to the ground. It does not get hurt because the gravity seems a little lighter here. Its body weighs less, movement is easier and the consequences of falls are less serious.

"Good news at last!" it thinks, knowing that it would prefer to know much more about this universe that has welcomed it into its bosom.

But every bit of information, however tenuous and insignificant, is always good.

He stands up, grumbling about its awkwardness. The being continues along its way, taking make sure that each step on the slightly sloping surface, which is a bit too silky for racing, cautiously. In any case, the tentacles that swarm at the ends of its legs and under the soles of its feet do not facilitate speed, even as they make walking possible.

The creature reassures itself that its companion below is facing the same challenges. As the distance between the only two representatives of an active form of life in this truncated cone of stellar dimensions does not decrease, the immaculate wanderer darts its sparkling eyes in the direction of the white silhouette that seems to be a double of itself. It decides to accelerate.

Bad idea. It slips and falls more heavily to the ground. The impact, while not very violent, spreads a new sensation throughout its body. Almost unprecedented. A dazzling pain in its pelvis!

The result is unpleasant. But new. This demonstrates that certain emotions and sensations are finally starting to appear at the edges of this monochromatic body with its plumes, protrusions and filaments. It is no longer a robot but a being of flesh. And blood.

And blood?

This foolish remark evokes strange feelings. Without knowing why, it bites its right forearm in order to verify the color of the liquid that would normally flow.

He is not disappointed. A few drops percolate at the opening of the small wound. They are white, iridescent. Shimmering. As everything else in this world-universe governed by the omnipotence of the *outre-blanc* that Pierre Soulages would have celebrated with the same artistic ease as the *outre-noir* had he been able to know this space in the form of a cosmic volcanic chimney.

"My body is modeled in the image of this world," it says to itself, comparing the infinite depths and multiple variations of the pure white of the cliff with those that lie in the hollow of each of these droplets of a precious nectar.

Life. His life.

After this biting experience, the being with the diamond eyes once again worries about its companion, which seems more skillful than it because it is continuing its descent and increasing the distance separating them. It stops and tries to scream again. The echoes of a penetrating, almost sticky silence respond to this totally silent call.

It tries to grumble, by making its vocal cords vibrate in a different way. But the result is the same. Nothing!

Annoyed, it sits down and looks at the other pale silhouette continuing its long journey down into the abyss.

"I can't do it," he laments.

Again, a few tears slide over its sparkling, silky skin.

The shipwrecked man remains standing in this white and endless Thebaid for a long time.

Well after its tears have dried, it continues to examine the other side of the strange, motionless vortex. Motionless vortex? The image initially brings a vague smile to the creature's lips because the word *vortex* pleases it. But that's all. Yet, scraps of memories gradually return to the edges of its memory. Not actually memories. It is still unable to recall a scene from its life, focusing its attention on a moment, a face. A feeling.

No. The sensation is more discreet. Deeper as well.

When it says and repeats the word *vortex*, it does not visualize a memory, or even a precise image. The very structure of a vortex rises in it rather like an ideal figure, an archetype that develops in a part of its body. Whatever!

In the case of a vortex, this emotional and visual assimilation is transcribed and materializes on its left thigh...

"My brain is in my thigh?" it wonders before bursting into a deep inner laugh.

The first laugh. Fantastic. Colossal. Saving. Painful. And mute.

It makes another effort and strives to imagine the general form of the gigantic truncated cone that opens onto a starless infinity.

"That's a word that pleases me!"

The traveler, its head crowned with tentacles, endeavors to embody the perfect figure of a star in the heavens. This effort is more difficult and perilous than it seems. It frowns, closes its eyes and slowly covers itself with an insidious moisture that beads on the surface of its skin. The creature wipes its face and finds that this liquid is translucent and white. This no longer comes as a surprise. But it also remembers the word for this delicate secretion that is gently exuded by the pores of its skin: sweat!

Delighted by the fact that it can finally give a name to certain phenomena, it focuses again on the symbol of the star. The image forms very gradually in its mind. It immediately seeks to see the image materialize on its naked body. The creature discovers it almost immediately on its left forearm.

As the image slowly appears on a uniformly white background, it softly touches the twelve-pointed star with some of the filaments of its right hand.

The result is surprising. A part of the star is modified by contact with the fine, light-glazed filaments. The design then loses shape, a little like the surface of water into which a pebble has been thrown. The wave spreads in concentric circles. But if the end of a wooden stick were to be placed against these circular wavelets, the process would be disrupted and chaos would appear.

The star imprinted on the skin of the *outre-blanc* castaway's arm twists. Then it scatters in all directions as if a cold and fatal wind had decided to annihilate it and disperse all its components in the distance.

Distraught, the shaggy being tries to recreate the star with one of its filaments which is simultaneously fine, supple and precise. The result exceeds its expectations because it manages to reconstruct the beautiful twelve-pointed star with a luxury of details that surprises it.

"I can draw on my body..." it marvels, continuing with several other simple drawings.

Then he tries another experiment and begins writing S, T, A, R.

He straightens up, delighted.

"Star!"

While speech is forbidden to him, he can now draw and write. So, he can communicate.

Delighted with this discovery, it does not immediately realize the strangeness of the situation: its skin is a magic slate on which it can draw signs, erase them. Start all over again.

After many attempts and several doodles on its arm and thigh, the creature realizes that the result is much better on its forearm than on other parts of its body which it used as a parchment that can be used over and over again. A palimpsest!

This word, which finds a place at the zenith of its memory also pleases the creature. It endeavors to write it forthwith. After a few hesitations, it spells the word out properly and observes the result. Satisfied with this discovery, it looks down and realizes that the creature that resembles it strangely is now very far away.

Aware of its inability to catch up with the other being, the first creature then focusses its attention upwards.

The top of the giant funnel stratified with its millions of successive terraces is still as far away. Inaccessible. Beyond it, the firmament is riddled with millions of spheres that sparkle and are adorned with iridescent reflections. But instead of breaking down into all the colors of the rainbow, these pearls pile up and compile the infinite palette of the shades of the *outre-blanc* which this universe begets without ceasing.

The being with the pale, thread-like limbs stands there. For a long time.

Standing, it tries to find the breath of this world. Its breath. But the exploration is difficult. Yet, after spending a long time distinguishing the rhythms of a thick silence that seems to be coordinated with the demands of its innards, it suddenly notices distant music. Weak, almost imperceptible, the music swirls and gradually invades this immense chasm that resembles the tail of a comet streaking towards its protective star.

Very fragile sound layers mingle with gurgling, ringing bells and very deep sounds close to infrasound. This minimalist, hypnotic and mesmerizing symphony worries him at first.

Emerging almost unrealistically in totally silent universe, this irruption of music in a white space streaming with light brings with it a touch of life of unknown origin.

"And what if I am the source?" the creature wonders.

The question will certainly remain without an immediate answer since the great architect of this crazy universe seems to be absent for the time being. But the question makes sense because the presence of two immaculately white creatures here may symbolize the beginning of a new story. A new cosmic breath.

A new world.

Overjoyed by this observation, the creature immediately makes a scrupulous and complete examination of the top of the truncated cone, flaring out towards the infinite.

The being with the diamond eyes decides to take its time because the space is immense. And it is very difficult to distinguish something white from a uniformly white background. It scans each zone. One by one.

It sees nothing special, apart from the terraces that look a little like the terraced rice paddies found in Asia. But they are very steep. And white. Fearfully white!

"What's Asia?" he wonders.

It writes the word on its forearm. After it initially writes "azi," the word is diluted almost immediately. Two attempts later, it finally finds the right spelling. This reassures the creature a little, because this process of automatically erasing of errors strengthens its feeling that it is headed in the right direction and that it will one day find the key to this gigantic puzzle of the pearly, white cliff.

However, it does not discover any other form of life. And it persists.

Suddenly, it turns towards the cliff which is still mosaic of irregular parts in which the *outre-blanc* makes way for milky transparencies. Acting like a mirror.

He looks and grows afraid because the tentacles and filaments that extend from his head seem stranger and stranger. Yet it extricated itself from the flesh of the wall in this form. No further additions. No cosmetic contribution. He was born so!

But that intrigues the creature.

While facing the most transparent part, he makes an effort to observe the vaguely colored and very agitated shapes that it has been able to see since waking. But they have disappeared. There is only a kind of chromatic vibration – a pulsing to be more precise – that hurts the creature's eyes. A mad, frightening whirlwind that seems to want to drag the creature into a dance with strobe effects.

After rubbing its eyelids with some very soft filaments, it resumes its slow scrutiny of the upper portion of the white volcanic chimney designed to house titans.

This lasts a very long time.

Suddenly, the creature freezes. Its heart beats louder.

"Another! Another creature. Like me…"

CHAPTER 20

The creature festooned with hairy filaments is taken aback.

It does not know why this discovery has stunned it so point because it has already seen a being similar to it in this chasm textured in the very flesh of a material common to the rest of this monochromatic universe.

"I was not able to catch the first traveler of this great white ship. Perhaps I could catch up with the second one?"

This remark is not groundless since the walker climbing from terrace to terrace above the creature is closer. It will be able to catch up if it picks up its pace.

As it begins to climb, the pale creature wonders where this idea of a *great white ship* comes from. It knows what *white* means. But *ship*?

It concentrates, frowning. Immediately, the round shape of an old galleon shaped like a walnut shell appears just beneath the surface of the skin of the inside of its right forearm. The wanderer looks at this fragile sketch and smiles. Its memories and reminiscences are buried deep within it. But with great effort and the unexpected help of the palimpsest of it skin, it has finally managed to exhume scraps of images, sensations. Emotions.

The only problem is that these precious relics from its his past life arrive in spurts. Without any consistency. However, the being that is slowly starting to climb up the countless terraces that separate it from the top of the well is nourished by the intimate conviction that it has all the time necessary for this slow, complex and perilous anamnesis[11].

Perhaps an eternity.

It surveys the upper part of the gigantic truncated cone and tries to count the number of terraces that separate him from his companion. Four.

However, the steep paths that connect each stratum can be used to considerably shorten a journey that would take weeks if the creature were to walk completely around the abyss each time. Just one problem. It has to climb steep slopes. Feet covered with tentacles and filaments do not make this task any easier. But there is less risk of falling than if the creature were to climb down. The climber with its pale, velvety skin nibbles its lower lip. Impatient now, it urges itself to go faster.

---

[11] In psychology, *anamnesis* is the compilation of information about the patient's past that is collected by the psychologist. In esoterism, anamnesis is the act of recovering the total knowledge of one's own previous existences.

Since gravity is quite low in this place, less effort is required. Of course, the castaway climbing ahead of it in this great desert enjoys the same advantage. The creature must move faster. Faster!

After a few minutes, it stops. Out of breath.

The exhausted walker bends over, placing its hands on its knees. It stands up. Breathes deeply two or three times. It sets off again.

The path is safer as he climbs up, so it takes the liberty of looking at the infinite palette of whites that lie in a tangle along the flanked cliff of terraces. It is even more exuberant in the sky of this world dominated by gigantic, iridescent, sparkling spheres that attract its gaze and invite it to harmonize with a cosmic entity that surpasses understanding.

At this precise moment, the creature climbing heavily, despite the crystalline, almost ethereal atmosphere remembers a sentence. No. Three sentences. Subjugated by the music of its own thoughts, it incessantly repeats: "*There, on the peak that is sharper than the finest needle, stands only the one that fills all the space. Up there, in the most subtle air where everything freezes, only the incandescent perpetual remains. There, in the center of everything, is the one who sees everything accomplished, from its beginning to its end.*"[12] It knows perfectly well that this vision of a beatific and incandescent world is not its own. It knows full well that these words were written by another. It does not know who. But this allegory suits it well.

Cheered up, the creature continues on its way. Then, the climber realizes a curious fact. Apart from the strange repetitive music that seems to be flowing up from the bottom of the abyss, the silence is total. It is in a good position to observe this because its vocal cords are inoperative.

But it also realizes that its footsteps on the lustrous and almost living surface that forms the giant funnel, the terraced cliff and the paths connecting the various strata of this cosmic mille-feuille make absolutely no sound.

"Noises and rackets are banned here," it says to itself, without really knowing what a racket is.

But, again, the sound of the word seduces him. Moreover, the context in which certain words which tear through the surface of his memory much like gas bubbles emerging from the bottom of a lake, usually gives him sufficient understanding.

"*Up there, in the most subtle air where everything freezes, only the incandescent perpetual remains...*" An incandescent perpetual! In a white universe. Only white, thinks the castaway of the abyss, while observing its companion in front of it and this mad horizon haloed with sparkling lights.

Incandescence may be white. Can the primordial fire be white?

---

[12] Translation of an extract from an unfinished philosophical and allegorical tale, *Mount Analogue*, written by René Daumal (1908-1944). *Mount Analogue* was published in 1952, eight years after Daumal's death.

It stops for a second and asks itself the only question that matters here at this moment, "And if this fire were in me? And if this fire... were me!"

Quickly realizing quickly that it risks losing its mind if it gets caught up in the meanders of a labyrinthine of thoughts turned in on itself, the creature chases away these wicked thoughts and focuses again on the essential: making the legs of its muscles work so it can join the light silhouette walking ahead.

It sighs, and plods on.

The effort is challenging. Droplets of sweat gradually flood over its forehead. It wipes them away, grumbles and continues on its way.

To shore up its courage, it focuses on the shape walking at a good pace, two terraces higher. The being the creature pursues is also taking the crossroads that connect the strata to one another and seems to have decided to climb to the top with an impressive boldness.

The creature tries again to call the other being. But its throat remains frozen and only the throbbing music, highlighted with layers of infrasound, sharp chimes and dull hammerings echoes its despair.

Suddenly it wavers. Not really dizzy. Tingling assaults its eyeballs and white flames dance before its eyes. He freezes and waits.

Gradually, space vibrates and spins before it. The sensation is quite similar to that produced in superheated deserts when the atmosphere generates mirages, caused by the deflection of the light beams by the superposition of layers of air of different temperatures. However, in this case, this atmospheric hysteria does not just deform or duplicate images. It creates new ones.

For a brief hallucinatory moment, the traveler with its head covered with white tentacles and filaments, sees two shapes that seem familiar appear. They are strangely positioned on an odd tool made up of two large wheels connected by a strange jumble of tubes. This ephemeral image is surprising and incongruous. Yet, the creature feels that the image is strongly anchored within itself. Moreover, this brief psychic suggestion is not totally monochromatic. A few pastel tones enrich this vision which seems to be veiled by gauze or very fine muslin.

The hallucination disappears as quickly as it came, leaving the wanderer distraught and worried.

"Where do these crazy images come from? From what world?"

Since the creature is unable to provide any answer to these legitimate questions, it continues on its way, courageously and stubbornly. It scans the upper levels and realizes that its fellow traveler has once again taken off. The creature must walk even faster.

The hours that follow are difficult as the vibrating, quivering mirages besiege the creature's mind with an unpleasant regularity.

First, it observed a room with a table and several guests. They seem to laugh but no sound comes out of their wide-open mouths. Then it sees a boat with an elegant sail, floating the ocean, accompanied only by the sun and a few flying fish.

Then it watches in surprise as two completely naked beings, lie on top of one another in a meadow next to a basket, food, a colored piece of cloth. A short while later, the angelic face of a girl with curly, red hair appears at the edges of its mind. She calls the creature. Unconsciously, the prisoner in the *outre-blanc* desert extends its arms with their many filaments towards this little girl with the radiant eyes. But the image is blurry. And disappears. It cannot help but cry.

Finally, a frightening image tears through the translucent screen of its memories. A long gleaming blade appears above its head. Twirling. Twirling again. Twirling yet again. Frightened, the creature falls to its knees and covers its eyes with its hands covered with pale filaments.

When it finally uncovers its eyes, made of the purest of diamonds, the menacing blade has disappeared.

The mirages seem to stop their visual assault at this moment because peace finally washes over the climber. It sighs, releasing a great blow of breath, without producing the slightest sound. Standing up, firmly suppor5ted on its legs, it looks up. The firmament with its billions of translucent spheres is still there. The cliff with its millions of terraces is still a dazzling *outre-blanc*.

But its future acolyte has moved far away during this time. The creature will have to walk faster to catch up. Almost run. It takes off at a frenzied pace forced to strive even harder on feet unsuited for this kind of activity.

"I'm not a gazelle!" it says, shaking its head.

At the same moment, the graceful silhouette of an impala appears on its left arm. The being smiles and continues its effort. Unfortunately, it quickly realizes that it will not be able to run this way for long. Out of breath, chest heaving, it must slow down and walk at a more steady pace.

Even this easier rhythm is tiring. It berates itself.

"If I can't catch up with that shape that is just above me, what am I going to do in this white desert? Alone?"

Just as it asks this question, some elements of the cliff next to it change.

The smooth, lustrous surface is suddenly adorned with small horizontal extensions like tangled branches, followed by forks, globes or hands, drawn roughly. By reflex, he seizes the first branch stretching towards it. As soon as its own filaments brush against the extremities created by the cliff, it feels a beneficial heat wash over it. An inner light that transforms into energy. In the will to conquer. In strong power. Almost titanic.

Renewed by this transfer of new potentialities, the creature resumes its march with increased vigor. Gradually, the distance separating it from the other white being decreases. It persists. Continues to strive. At last, it runs. Only ten meters left. Five.

Exhausted, but happy, the creature finally arrives just behind the other being which continues to walk and does not seem to have heard it coming. But as everything is silent here, apart from the repetitive and hypnotic music that flows up from the depths of the abyss, this is not really surprising.

The creature slips behind his companion of misfortune and places the filaments of its right hand on the shoulder of the other survivor. The contact is soft, warm, almost luminous.

Surprised, the traveler jumps. Then it turns around and their eyes meet. Millions of turbulent emotions, vortices of light, and whirlwinds of foam are exchanged in their eyes like shining gems.

They both open their mouths. At the same time. But they remain mute. The one that has just been caught is naturally more stunned than its new companion because it had not yet discovered that other beings live here.

It makes an effort and says clearly, "But who are you"

"Phil Caldwell! My name is Phil Caldwell."

"Me too!" replied the other, bursting into tears.

CHAPTER 21

From an article in the daily *Guyana Chronicle* this morning.
Title: "The End of the *Blue Macaw*".
Followed by an enigmatic subtitle: "Geysers of inexplicable light of an un known origin following the attack on the *Blue Macaw* camp".

The coordinated attack yesterday by the Brazilian army and American special forces to free American hostages was a total success, but the losses were heavy.

Two hostages were killed: a Venezuelan guide and the member of the Orpheus expedition in charge of logistics. A female doctor has been seriously injured, but her condition is no longer critical. The Brazilian forces suffered one dead and four wounded.

The kidnappers suffered much heavier damages because the *Blue Macaw* mercenaries resisted the attack with the energy of despair. Since the kidnappers were heavily armed, the assault troops had to deploy heavy weapons. Twelve of the kidnappers were killed, including their leader, Felipe Maldorano, an Ecuadorian who has been involved in drug trafficking with well-known Colombian cartels.

The exact conditions of the attack are not fully known at the moment. But one of the representatives of the Brazilian Ministry of Defense, Manoel Alves, confirmed that the decision to conduct a joint attack with American special forces was made at the highest levels of the two countries concerned.

The element that triggered the attack was the payment of the second part of the colossal ransom demanded by *Blue Macaw* to release Karin Stockhausen and the members of the Orpheus expedition who had gone to Mount Roraima to conduct scientific experiments.

Four hostages had already been released. But the Brazilian and American authorities feared that the blackmail would result in tragedy.

Indeed, the behavior of the leader of the kidnappers, a psychopath apparently, became uncontrollable and very disturbing. His outbursts of anger, which he had a reporter, who was also a member of the expedition, filming under duress gave increased media coverage of his demands as he posted them immediately on the internet.

Cruel, blood-thirsty, and remorseless, Felipe Maldorano placed the captives in extreme danger.

Analysts from the CIA and the Brazilian special services quickly confirmed that no more prisoners would be released after the payment of the third part of the ransom.

A bloodbath and the widespread massacre of the six remaining hostages – the first prisoner, Phil Caldwell had already been beheaded by the bloodthirsty monster when the first ransom payment failed – was conceivable. Worse, it was predictable.

As soon as the precise location of the *Blue Macaw* camp was obtained from a source that the Brazilian authorities have not disclosed for the moment, the intervention was carried out rapidly. It is easy to imagine that the fact that the heiress to the world's fifth largest fortune is one of the prisoners whose life was now clearly in danger accelerated the process leading to this decision, which has had far-reaching consequences.

The airborne troops intervened in record time. The surprise was almost total. This made it possible to save the lives of four hostages because the *Blue Macaw* leader and his mercenaries did not have time to execute the captives as they tried to escape into the jungle. But the area was already sealed off. The neutralization of the criminals was quite easy, although there were several victims.

Unfortunately, experience shows that this type of intervention usually results in significant human losses. As the kidnappers were very determined and very well armed, the attack could not be carried out without collateral damage.

The bodies of the two hostages killed, Fernando Pinzon and Gregory Greensberg, have already been returned to their relatives who live in the suburbs of Caracas and Portland (Oregon), respectively.

Our local correspondents in the province of Cuyuni Mazaruni[13] have also pointed out a strange phenomenon that occurred three days earlier, only a few hours after the execution of the first hostage.

Many inhabitants living in three small villages close to Mount Roraima: Amokokopai, Akar and Kokadai, observed a burst of white light, very bright, intense and fleeting, which they all instinctively referred to as a "ball of white light".

One of the journalists for the *Guyana Chronicle*, Edmundo Parras, was on site to question those who had witnessed this strange phenomenon.

Their statements are surprisingly consistent. They all say that this geyser of light came from the southwest, in the middle of a dense part of the jungle.

Curiously, it seems that this extraordinary phenomenon took place shortly after the murder of the American hostage that certain networks broadcast in full before the transmission was cut off just before the decapitation.

---

[13] Cuyuni Mazaruni is the westernmost province of Guyana. It has a common border with Venezuela and Brazil. The Mazaruni River flows through it into the Atlantic Ocean just north of Georgetown, the capital of Guyana.

The opinions of the witnesses diverge somewhat with respect to theduration of the phenomenon – from a few milliseconds to one or two seconds – and its intensity.

Some people described a column somewhat similar to a tornado extending very high in the sky. Others mentioned an immense white ball that rose very quickly and disappeared at once.

Since then, the craziest hypotheses have been circulating: a concealed military test, a collective hallucination, an extraterrestrial attack...

Since our newspaper is serious and we wish to check all our sources, we will stick to the facts for the time being.

There is no point in focusing on assumptions, hypotheses and wild fantasies, which are the usual lot of commentators as soon as an unknown and inexplicable phenomenon is brought to light.

Perhaps scientists will be able to tell us more in the weeks to come.

Alvaro Jimenez - Georgetown - January 19, 2016

Manaus - Brazil – Tuesday, January 19, 2016

Extract from an article published in the *Amazonas en Tempo* daily newspaper this morning.

Title: *"Tragedy and unexplained phenomenon in the province of Roraima"*.

We return this morning to the attack on the *Blue Macaw*, which our army managed perfectly, while striving to limit human losses on the part of the hostages. Two were killed by the kidnappers, but the other prisoners were released after several days of captivity in appalling conditions.

The Office of the President of the Federal Republic has informed us that President Barack Obama personally called Dilma Rousseff to thank her for the effective intervention of our elite troops who worked in perfect harmony with special American forces specially commissioned by the President of the United States.

Our correspondent in New York has informed us that Karin Stockhausen and her three companions were initially taken to the New York-Presbyterian University Hospital of Columbia and Cornell Hospital where they were examined and treated for their injuries.

Yesterday evening, Karin's father, Friedrich Stockhausen, made a very important and particularly moving statement accompanied by his wife.

Conducted in their New York apartment, this interview was broadcast by CBS, NBC and ABC.

Friedrich Stockhausen thanked all those who worked for the release of the hostages. He also addressed the families of Fernando Pinzon and Gregory Greensberg, both of whom perished during the assault. He expressed his compassion to them and all the viewers felt at that moment that these words were not mere polite statements. The Karin Stockhausen's father was both delighted to recover his daughter in good health and distressed that this delicate recovery cost the lives of two innocent victims.

During the interview, no details were provided for obvious reasons of confidentiality, but it was immediately understood that the Stockhausen family will do everything in their power to help the victims' families. This macabre list also includes the unfortunate astrophysicist Phil Caldwell who was executed in a particularly atrocious manner.

The Stanford University researcher leaves behind a widow and a little girl who will never see her father again. It is legitimate to imagine that Friedrich Stockhausen and his family will see to it that the mourning of this wife, overwhelmed by grief, takes place under conditions that are the least worse possible. Of course, we cannot use the expression "best possible conditions" because it is easy to imagine what a woman must feel when her husband has been beheaded by a psychopath hungry for money and power. It must be pointed out that the body of the unfortunate scientist was found by our troops at the edge of the *Blue Macaw* camp. The corpse had already been partly shredded by the predators that swarm in the jungle. Unfortunately, the soldiers have not found Phil Caldwell's head.

It was probably devoured by a jaguar.

But the mystery remains unresolved because, shortly after her release, Karin Stockhausen stated that she had walked past the site just hours after the terrible public execution of her associate.

The headless body was still there – one of the executioners was pulling it by the feet away from the camp – but the victim's head had already disappeared...

The Brazilian and American governments have little to say about the consequences of this hostage incident. All we know is that the sums transferred for the ransom were identified and blocked in tax havens before they could evaporate without leaving any trace.

But the tragic character of this incident which highlighted the tortured and barbaric personality of Felipe Maldorano is complicated by an event that some unscrupulous commentators have referred to as the "mystery of Mount Roraima".

The information that has reached us from this very dense area of our country's northernmost province is both consistent and ludicrous.

Consistent because all the inhabitants of western Guyana, the province of Bolívar in the south of Venezuela and the province of Roraima, are saying roughly the same thing.

The observations were particularly detailed and accurate in the small towns and villages of Santa Elena de Uairén and Icabarù (Bolívar Province) and Boa Vista, Amajari and Pacaraima (Roraima Province).

All describe a gigantic ball of white light, almost dazzling, which suddenly emerged from the jungle and which almost immediately disappeared into the sky. This amazing, unique physical event took place shortly after the American hostage was decapitated, on Saturday, January 16, in the early afternoon.

Here is the testimony received by one of our correspondents on site.

The person who describes what he saw in Boa Vista is trustworthy because he is a doctor: Dr. Juarez Barzon. This rheumatologist mentioned *"an immense ball of white fire that rose in the sky at a speed exceeding that of terrestrial rockets. The ball of light was followed by a plume resembling the tail of a comet. The speed was impressive. The sphere disappeared at once. And very quickly. Very fast!"*

When our reporter asked him whether this burst of light had been *preceded by another event or if it had made a particular noise, his answer was clear: "No. Nothing special before. Moreover, this burst of dazzling, perfectly white lights took place in absolute silence."*

When we speak of ludicrous information, we are naturally evoking all the speculation and various rumors that have been spreading over the last two days on the Internet and, more particularly, on social networks.

The social media are on fire and Twitter is "tweeting" more and more!

Everything is possible, from a military experiment carried out by North Korea, the Americans or the Iranians to the emergence of extraterrestrials previously hidden in the earth's crust for millions of years.

Particularly inspired and anxious to make a buzz, a Filipino singer has already posted a piece on YouTube that has been viewed several tens of millions of times....

Sung to a basic rhythm like Christmas balls on an artificial tree, the words are immensely stupid: *"Let us welcome, welcome, our friends who come from the depths of space. Let us welcome, welcome those who will help us and save us!"*

What can we say when faced with this flood of absurdities whose din drowns out actual research conducted by scientists who have been able to retrieve several photos and very brief videos of the phenomenon filmed with smartphones.

Once the specialists have analyzed this data, we will finally be able to determine the origin of this flash of light unlike anything that is known.

Unfortunately, in the meantime, the planet will be singing: *"Let us welcome, welcome, our friends who come from the depths of space. Let us welcome, welcome those who will help us and save us!"*

Ludicrous and also grotesque!

Gilberto Carvalho - Manaus - January 19, 2016

CHAPTER 22

"It can't be!" murmurs Phil Caldwell, staring at the being who calls him-self Phil Caldwell.

But his voice breaks again.

The other white man tries to speak in turn. But silence prevails. It seems that creatures wandering in this bottomless pit that is lost in the delusions of an *outre-blanc* firmament are again deprived of the ability to express themselves orally.

The two men who claim to be Phil Caldwell are dumbfounded.

Mouths wide open, bewildered looks, they do not understand what is going on. Or what is happening to them.

After a long moment of silent scrutiny, they try to speak again. Without success. Phil Caldwell 2 grows a little nervous. His eyes shine and he raised his head and his eyebrows. But all these attempts do not allow them to find speech. And words.

And the emotions that words sometimes sublimate.

Disappointed by this omnipresent silence after such a brief verbal ex-change, they observe one another. Probably in order to determine in the other a real part of humanity that could give the sensation, here in any case, of having been brutally cloned. Or to stammer.

They endeavor to appropriate this name, which constantly returns to the confluence of their respective memories: Phil Caldwell. But this is not easy be-cause this quest immediately comes up against this simple question: who is Phil Caldwell?

They do not know. They know strictly nothing.

Noticing that the pale man who is facing him does not really resemble his own shape as he was able to perceive it in the slightly deformed mirrors embed-ded in the translucent part of the cliff, Phil Caldwell 1 began to write on his arm in the only language he knows. His!

"Who are you really, Phil Caldwell?"

"I don't know. I don't know," replies the other man, who seems less agile with his filaments than his new companion.

Noting the negative response that confirms the immense feeling of frustra-tion that is washing over him, Phil Caldwell 1 insists.

"Where are we?"

No answer.

The other man simply shrugs, while making an explicit sign with his lips that could be interpreted as: "I don't have the slightest idea."

After a few quick, abortive mime s, Phil Caldwell 2 starts to write a longer text on his right arm, clearly indicating that he is left-handed. One more difference with his counterpart. Indeed, the two men do not really resemble each other despite their naked bodies, entirely white, slightly flatter than those of humans, with their extensions, fine tentacles and countless filaments. Phil Caldwell 2 is smaller, fatter too. Moreover, his face is almost emaciated while that of his new companion wandering in the middle of this *outre-blanc* funnel without beginning and end is rather babyish. Conversely, their eyes – sumptuous diamonds embedded in the eye sockets – are the same shape and the same uniformly white color and they irradiate with an inner light similar to tiny stars.

After a good minute he finally stretched the inside of his forearm with its hastily scribbled inscription towards the other: "This multi-terraced laminated well reminds you of nothing?"

"Dante's Inferno."

"Exactly."

"The only difference: there are not nine concentric circles here, but... millions!"

In perfect time, the two men then look at the sky dazzling with countless transparent spheres that rebound, jostle, bounce away, and collide again.

They try to mentally count the stack of white terraces that shape this cliff, likely to dwarf the deepest canyons of Mars. But they give up quickly because that feat is almost impossible. Their eyes grow tired in the midst of this monochromatic *outre-blanc*. Thought is engulfed. Wavers. And finally sinks.

After two heavy sighs, Phil Caldwell decides to verify a point that has bothered him since he encountered another Phil Caldwell whom he could see and touch without needing to constantly run. He gently raises his arms in the direction of his new friend so that the other man does not interpret his gesture negatively.

Then, gently, he brushes the arms and hands of the other man with the lightest of his filaments.

This contact should be gentle. Silky maybe. It is not. A slight electric shock flicks their tentacles, which immediately retract.

The two men move away.

Phil Caldwell 1 writes quickly on his arm: "It's better for us to avoid touching."

The other agrees. Then he turns on his heels, covered with pale filaments, and carefully looks at the chasm that lies at their feet. He seems lost in this serene and tiring contemplation both because of the rather dazzling character of the material which seems to be common to living beings, to the terraces that structure the space and to the titanic cliff that rises up to the sky dotted with translucent bubbles.

Suddenly, he freezes. Opening his eyes, he stretches his left arm towards the center of the well. Phil Caldwell 1 looks in turn.

The two men are stunned.

Two immense structures, both as white as the rest of this monochromatic world, have arisen from the bottom of the abyss.

They wind upwards in a strange ballet dancing around an imaginary axis. The two immense creepers, lined with translucent eyes, form regular curls that wind along the elegant geometry of an infinite helix.

The term "infinite" is perfectly justified here because these silky cords that evoke the structure of DNA[14] start from the bottom of the titanic volcanic chimney and extend well beyond its summit. Difficult to discern in this uniformly white horizon cluttered with billions of mutinous and quarrelsome spheres, these two structures gradually diverge. They follow the topography of the site and the steep slope of the cliffs with their millions of narrow terraces.

The two castaways in this mysterious world closely observe this architecture which oscillates slowly while maneuvering, ever more slowly, these two immense, erect totems. The surface is as white as the rest of the giant well, but constantly irradiated. Continuous shimmerings dot the twin structures. More surprisingly, these fragments are not immobile as if they were embedded and perfectly fixed in the dazzling material that makes up these DNA strands in XXXXL version. On the contrary, they constantly climb to the top and are replaced by others.

This permanent elevation provides a visual sensation of a pulse. An almost devilish that nothing can stop.

But, for the moment in any case, there are no reasons for this luminous rush towards the highest heavens of an outre-blanc world.

The two Phil Caldwells look at one another.

They question each other and must quickly admit their inability to explain this luminous carousel of almost Dionysian vivacity. This shimmering cavalcade immediately evokes a parade of fiery maenads during the Dionysia which, every year since the time of Pisistratus, celebrated the god Dionysus. But in the Greek time, the maenads wore a large stick decorated with ivy leaves and topped by a pine cone: the thyrsus. Besides, they were dressed in the skins of wild beasts. Running through the streets of Athens and the other great Greek cities with satyrs feverish with alcohol and unbridled sensuality, they did indeed form shimmering and very frenetic processions.

Along the helical structures which climb to the top of the heavens, frenzied activity prevails, as in the Dionysies. However, monochromatic white here replaces the clashing colors and the orgiastic excesses that, in the Greek time as in the twenty-first century, ended too often in mud, urine and vomit.

---

[14] Deoxyribonucleic acid (DNA) is a molecule, present in all living cells and constituting the genome of living beings. Its structure is a straight double helix, composed of two complementary strands.

Within this *serene hell* as Phil Caldwell 1 has decided to call this strange funnel with its cosmic dimensions, excesses of this type do not exist. Exuberance is banished in favor of an almost oppressive tranquility.

Satisfied with luminous fulgurances dancing a crazy farandole, the two men stand face to face.

"What should we do?" writes Phil Caldwell 2.

"We climb up together," replies his friend.

After nodding, they begin to climb the dazzling cliff again.

However, Phil Caldwell 2 stops very quickly. He walks over to the edge of the abyss and his companion does not know what to do. If he tries to touch him, to grab him, the electric shock may surprise the other man and cause him to fall. Yet, if he does nothing, he risks having the death of his only friend on his conscience.

He stands there a good time.

Then, just as he is about to grab one of the other man's arms in order to pull him towards a less dangerous and less slippery part of the terrace, Phil Caldwell turns to him. His eyes are wild and his eyebrows curve upward in pale arches.

He stretches his left arm towards the center of the well. This time, he does not point at the two structures that roll into a hieratic, almost petrified dance. He motions toward a specific point on the other side of the abyss. Just in front of them!

Phil Caldwell 1 blinks a little to see better. Apparently seeing nothing, he pouts in disappointment. His companion grows excited. He stretches his arm in a very precise direction. Since the other does not seem to see anything precise, he finally decides to write on his skin.

"A woman. I saw a woman!"

"Where?"

"Just in front."

Since Phil Caldwell 1 still sees no feminine shape within the white cliff, the other man resumes writing.

"She's trying to get out of the very flesh of the wall. As we did a while ago."

Phil Caldwell 1 silently screams an abortive sentence.

Unnerved by this frustrating constraint, he overcomes his impatience and finally writes, "I see her. She is trying to free herself from the wall of the cliff!"

"She will succeed in freeing herself from her bonds in a short while. Let's wave at her."

Immediately, the two companions began wave their arms with their long filaments.

At first, the woman does not see them. She is totally absorbed by the efforts she needs to make to extricate herself from the matrix of white and translucent material that makes up the wall of the cliff where she has been enshrined for a very long time. Maybe even millennia. A millennium? This word resonates in the head of Phil Caldwell 1 like the sound of a bell ringing nearby. However, he is totally incapable of giving it real meaning. Yet the word pleases him. It seems to awaken in him reminiscences that surface at the edge of his consciousness, then lose themselves, evaporating little by little. Like the water of some rivers that never reach the ocean.

After countless efforts, the woman finally manages to free herself completely from the bonds that had held in a vertical position along this bewildering cliff several million floors high. She falls to her knees and remains there for a long time. Haggard. Lost. The two Phil Caldwell continue to wave, jumping up and down on the spot and windmilling their arms.

The woman finally stands up, and they clearly see her hair shaped like an albino sea anemone. Apart from this detail, which seems characteristic of all the creatures that awaken in the heart of this *outre-blanc* abyss, she seems very beautiful.

Systematically in a virginally white, almost immaculate place, her nudity reveals two beautiful, round breasts and very sensual forms that leave no doubt as to her gender.

Nevertheless, at this moment, the priority of the two men is to gorge themselves with voluptuous and sensual images. They want at all costs to attract the attention of this woman who has just awakened at the edge of a wall worthy of Titan mythology and who, of course, does not understand who she is, where she comes from or where is she.

The problem is exactly the same for her companions because, apart from the name that resonates in their heads without them knowing why – Phil Caldwell – they know nothing of this titanic, white universe.

At first, the young woman seems hypnotized by the two oscillating structures that spring from the bottom of the abyss and extend to the heaven dotted with transparent spheres. She eagerly scrutinizes these strands of light, which are equivalent to a human body in diameter yet strength to the stars in length.

Then she turns around suddenly to look at the strange wall from which she has just extricated herself. This simple gesture allows both Phil Caldwells to realize that the tentacles and filaments that make up her hair do not merely stand up on her head like the hysterical serpents that haloed the heads of Medusa and the other two Gorgons. In the case of this young, panicked woman, they continue backward, covering her shoulders and the upper part of her back.

She turns again and faces the chasm. It is at this moment that she finally sees the two pale men waving at her from the other side of this gigantic, luminous volcanic chimney. The woman freezes.

Frightened at first, she finally decides to make a timid waving. The two men respond by waving broadly.

Then they stop and start to make a slow half-rotation with their right arms to signal that they will join her. She seems to understand and sits gently along this cliff with its eternally warm, silky surface.

Almost alive.

Almost alive? The question is embarrassing because the feeling that prevails here is that everything is alive. All is One... But why?

The two Phil Caldwells hurriedly leave the terrace on which they find themselves, in order to take the little path that ascends to the upper stratum. There they will all be at exactly the same level as the woman.

Then they begin to walk the few kilometers that separate them from the young woman. The diameter of the giant funnel is not considerable at this level. Less than a thousand meters, even if it is difficult to assess distances in a monochrome, very bright environment. As they are able to distinguish the silhouette of the young woman without much difficulty, the distance must be of this order of magnitude. Of course, the more one climbs the more this diameter increases. For, if the slope of the cliff is abrupt and forms an angle of at least 75° with the horizontal, the overall height of this Dante's Inferno in the white, cosmic version is simply prodigious.

At the top of the immense cliff, the diameter of the abyss must exceed one hundred kilometers. It is possible to imagine that a well as deep as this one would be perpetually dark. However, the dazzling luminosity that reigns here, whether it comes from the heavens or the very flesh of the mountain into which this funnel has been dug, is so powerful, so wonderfully distributed, that this inverted truncated cone radiates like an immaculately white star.

And this light is strength. And this light is cruelty. Omnipresent, it provides no rest.

Obstinately, they continue their walk, making sure to stay near the cliff so as not to fall because the width of the terrace they are walking along rarely exceeds three or four meters. Sometimes it is much narrower, like a mountain road hanging at the edge of a mad peak that would tear the clouds apart.

The only difference is that there are no clouds here. Just two long structures twirling on themselves, a white sky and mother-of-pearl spheres.

They continue to walk, although the distance seems to grow with every passing moment. An optical effect no doubt. Sometimes they stop for a few seconds and wave at the young woman who remains there. Seated.

Sometimes she clasps her head with her hands. She must be asking the same question as these two companions: what am I doing here?

Finally, after long minutes of effort, muscles burning, skin covered with sweat that dissipates quickly in this universe where the temperature is constant and almost ideal, they finally approach the position of young woman.

They can see her features, her cheerful face, her cheekbones. Her breasts. Her breasts...

Phil Caldwell 1 tries tear his eyes away from the chest of the woman they will join in less than a minute. But they automatically slip towards her navel. Then her pubis. Completely hairless.

He swallows and forces himself to look her in the eyes. Only the eyes.

The two men finally stand in front of her, putting on their most beautiful smiles. The woman then opens her mouth and simply says, "Who are you?"

They remain motionless. As still as statues, silent.

"My name is Phil Caldwell."

"That's our name too!" they say, strangling.

CHAPTER 23

Phil Caldwell 2 wants to go on and say, "But... how can this be?"

Alas, the few words they have just exchanged are the last. For the time being.

They are silent again. All three of them!

The young woman grows excited because this frustration is new for her while the two men have already suffered this blow of fate that dashes their hopes as a violent wind could do.

But there is no north wind or blizzard here. Only a gentle breeze that carries a few notes of music throughout the complex structure. Similar to the music of the spheres defined by Philolaos and the Pythagoreans as early as the 5th century BCE, this mesmerizing and sublime harmony weaves its plots and arpeggios, replacing human speech. This is probably too crude. Too brutal.

The first two Phil Caldwells try to appease the woman with a wraparound gesture inspired by yoga or tai chi-chuan. They smile and try to show her that this inability to speak voice is not an insurmountable handicap.

As these tests prove to be unsuccessful, Phil Caldwell 1 quickly writes on his forearm,

"We can communicate with our skin."

The young woman is stunned. First, she opens her eyes. Then her beautiful face finally lights up with a smile.

With an almost childish joy, she endeavors to write on her left arm. The first results are disappointing. But, after a few abortive attempts, she finally succeeds, writing "That's wonderful!"

"We can swap easily," says Phil Caldwell 1, smiling broadly.

He then looks at his two companions and continues, saying "This system is slower than speech. But we take the time to think before speaking."

The young woman then engages in a strange pantomime. Her aim is apparently to restore some order to her long albino hair that is inextricably tangled with tentacles and filaments some of which fall back in front of her eyes. She simply forgets that she has no fingers and that her hands end in fine filaments. While appendages are very practical for writing on one's own skin, they are most unsuitable for disciplining an unruly mane.

After a few twirls that give the impression that she has as many arms as Shiva, she stops her hairstyling and stands facing the other two Phil Caldwells.

She immediately begins to write in a frantic manner. She has so many questions to ask!

The first is obvious "Why are we all called Phil Caldwell?" The men spread their arms indicating that they do not know.

She begins again, "But who is Phil Caldwell?"

Same sign of impotence.

She persists, "Where are we?"

This time, Phil Caldwell 2 decides to respond by writing on the skin of his right arm.

"We don't know. In fact, we've only been awake here for a few hours."

"What's an hour?"

Her two companions merely look at her.

After a few moments, Phil Caldwell 1 writes on his arm whose skin becomes smooth, white and pearly once the information conveyed has been read.

"We often use words whose meanings escape us. Perhaps we will find the solution when we reach the summit of this gigantic chasm shaped like a volcanic chimney."

"But we shall have died of hunger before that!" the young woman snaps, comically arching her eyebrows.

"No. And that is one of the most astonishing singularities of this world in which we emerge without knowing where we come from or why we are here."

Since this sentence is longer than usual, Phil Caldwell 1 must divide his message into two parts.

"Why?"

"If we can rely on our brief experience in this immaculate chasm, we are not subject to any material requirements."

"So," says the young woman, "We no longer need to drink, eat, or go to the toilet?"

"There's no restaurant or toilet here," replies Phil Caldwell 2 with a broad smile.

"One less constraint..." sighs the young woman who, gradually takes on a new name: Phil Caldwell 3.

As a direct result of this terse remark, the three companions who have joined forces out of necessity begin a short discussion about a very simple and crucial theme: what are they to do?

They reach a conclusion.

"We absolutely must stay together and climb to the top of this cliff," says Phil Caldwell with visual encouragement – mimes and nods – from his two new friends.

They all look up at this moment. The realization is frightening. It will be impossible to reach the top of the enormous wall. A lifetime would not be enough!

A lifetime? Yes. Countless lifetimes?

"We'll need an infinite amount of time to cross these thousands or millions of floors!" says Phil Caldwell 3.

One of the two men stands in front of her. He looks at the young woman for a long time. The gems that have replaced their eyes shine even brighter.

Then he writes on his arm, "An infinite amount of time? Yes. Probably. All the more reason to start right away."

That's obvious.

Phil Caldwell 1 then writes, "Let's start climbing."

He concludes his remarks with a great gesture for his two companions. The trio immediately starts walking along the gentle slopes of the paths that connect all the terraces, and thus avoid the need to make a complete circle of the abyss to climb up a single additional floor.

They stop regularly to look at either the abyss where the two structures that mimic the DNA helix, or at the top of the impressive white cliff that looks out onto a *outre-blanc* heaven. As they are totally mute, the ubiquitous and hypnotic *music of the spheres* that accompanies them sets the pace for their progress.

As an undeniable sign of the fact that material weights are excluded from this universe which continually transforms all the shades of white, their footsteps are inaudible. They do not know if this is a result of the structure of their feet, the very special material that forms both the cliff and their bodies, or harmonics specific to this place that alleviate disturbances likely to affect the inhabitants of this world without beginning or end.

They stop for a moment to clarify this point. Phil Caldwell thinks that it is the filaments cushioning and extending from the soles of their feet that are responsible for this deafening silence, to use an oxymoron dear to poets. Phil Caldwell 2, for his part, evokes the very peculiar qualities of the shiny, pearly matter on which they walk, similar to that of their own bodies.

Have they not been born from this cliff that streams with light?

The young woman with the full breasts states that this universe is governed by very particular laws that eliminate the superfluous elements of life in favor of the deep meaning of things. Naturally, when Phil Caldwell 1 asks her what she means by the deep meaning of things, she cannot answer.

But, as they still do not know who they are, where they are and why they find themselves here, this lack of response is by no means out of place. They continue climbing up the cliff with the obstinacy of Sisyphus.

After a long time, they start to feel tired. This indicates that this abyss does not free them from all physical constraints, even though this fatigue is healthy, natural, and incites them to stop in an effort to find understanding. And it is precisely by trying to understand that Phil Caldwell 1 stops dead in front of the wall. The vaguely luminous forms he had noticed shortly after his awakening had disappeared a long time ago. They have now been replaced by a luminous vibration. A photonic mist which enters into resonance with a beat that accelerates unceasingly.

His two companions had not noticed anything at all, for they had extracted themselves later from the immaculate silk, both soft and constraining, of the cliff overlooking the abyss. Born after Phil Caldwell 1, they had not seen the luminous pulses that followed this carousel of materials, colors and shapes that had gradually faded. Then disappeared. Them too.

The shimmering, partially translucent parts continue to cut through the almost vertical wall forming absurd giant mosaics, without any order. But what can sometimes be discerned behind these windows that look out onto a strange and unknown world reveals nothing specific.

Sometimes, a shadow appears, a fragile filigree seeding a reality that is no longer one within a titanic, almost empty universe. But these giant, lanky silhouettes are merely cold ghosts. Pale and undefended emanations from a beyond that chokes blood and crushes the heart.

This world, if it still exists, shares nothing in common with this giant abyss that rises like an angry serpent towards an empyrean in which the power of the *outre-blanc* and its billions of transparent spheres millions is displayed in majesty. Transparent spheres in which other universes are mirrored in an abyss.

All of a sudden, Phil Caldwell 1 freezes.

He opens his mouth and tries to speak. Without success, of course.

He then points to the nearest translucent mosaic. His two friends approach and look at the wall just opposite them with him.

The orange light – totally incongruous here – is at first only a weak and almost impalpable glow that seems to dig into the wall under the effect of a different energy. Deaf. Dense. Unsettling.

Then, this bubble of saffron light gradually swells. Swells again. Brutally, it becomes monstrous and seems ready to swallow up the part of the cliff where the three Phil Caldwells walk.

One last start. A dantesque spasm that consumes color, light and life all at once.

Then calm returns. The wall is white again, translucent, the peculiar mother-of-pearl giving it an unheard-of depth.

Phil Caldwell looks attentively at his two companions. Slowly, almost theatrically, he writes two sentences on his arm, concluding a story that is over ten billion years old.

He then indicates what he has just expressed with the long filaments of his right hand: "The sun has just died. Before our eyes!"

CHAPTER 24

The young woman seems devastated.

"The sun?" she writes.

"Yes."

"But why? How is this possible?"

Phil Caldwell 2 thinks for a moment. He frowns, then relaxes.

He scribbles quickly on his arm, "Our time is no longer that of the sun".[15]

"But what is the... sun?" asks Phil Caldwell 3.

"I don't know exactly," admits the man who described the death of the sun with a perfect economy of words. But it was a familiar object, indispensable. Beneficent.

"But when?"

"Before."

"Before what?" insists the young woman who writes on her arm with remarkable dexterity for someone so new to the exercise.

"Before," Phil Caldwell repeats. "I can't say more. I simply know that it was very far from this universe where we were born."

"Reborn," interrupts his friend, shaking his head.

---

[15] Since Einstein, we know that space and time are closely linked. Restricted Relativity specifies that time slows down sharply when moving at a speed close to that of light. Einstein completed his theory by integrating gravity. Since it is impossible for an observer to say precisely whether he is undergoing a uniform accelerated motion or is located in a gravitational field, there is no difference between gravitation and acceleration. It was the principle of equivalence that brought Einstein to the concept of general relativity. If speed slows time, acceleration (and therefore gravity) also slows time. The denser the material, the slower time is. Imagine the representatives of a technologically advanced civilization that send two ships to the periphery of a stellar black hole. One of the rockets would remain in orbit around the event horizon, namely the zone where the light coming from the black hole can no longer escape. The ship that would continue to orbit around the black hole would see the other ship moving towards that event horizon. The descent would take place more and more slowly. For the occupants of the rocket that would arrive near the event horizon, their personal time would remain identical. But it is everything they would observe looking out from the black hole that would accelerate more and more. As they approach this invisible border, they would be looking at a bewildering spectacle. The life of the surrounding stars would accelerate and would soon unfold in a fraction of a second. This is what happens for Phil Caldwell within the *outre-blanc*...

Since all the living beings that suddenly appear in the abyss are pale and their skin is silky and iridescent, each particular movement generates streaks of light similar to a luminous object rapidly crossing through the space behind a fogged glass. But there is no mist here.

No night either. Apparently.

When Phil Caldwell stopped moving his head, his two companions watched him. The remark he had just made them appealed to them: reborn?

Yes. But to be reborn one must have already lived and died. But they had no memory of their death.

"Some sort of metempsychosis?" suggests the young woman, opening her mouth mechanically as if the sound of her voice could comfort what she writes with almost enjoyable eagerness.

"Perhaps," admits Phil Caldwell 1 who does not really know what metempsychosis is, but who feels its symbolic value in certain fibers of his body.

The man who emerged first out of this cliff of cyclopean dimensions immediately tempers his observation.

"Anyway, we don't remember anything. These speculations will remain mere hypotheses until we know more about ourselves."

"And about this white world that seems to have taken a fork and is completely different from the one which we had undoubtedly known," adds the other man.

"The one that belonged to the sun that has just exploded and died?" asks the young woman with large white eyes.

"Without a doubt…"

The flow of questions is considerably more powerful than that of answers and certitudes, so the trio returns to climbing, glancing from time to time at the unlikely summit of this giant volcanic chimney.

The temperature is uniform and they climb without difficulty at a regular pace. Running would be useless since the number of terraces to be crossed is so bewildering that any haste would be pointless. Even dangerous.

Several hours later, the small group stops for a moment to make a detailed examination of their environment. Ahead of them, regular strata punctuated with narrow terraces and small connecting paths. Below, the abyss gapes, like the mouth of a large, white fish. The comparison is not absurd because this bottomless well irresistibly calls to mind the esophagus of giant fish such as a whale shark or, at the end of the Oligocene[16] period, the huge and formidable megalodon.

Overhead, the *outre-blanc* sky is still studded with billions of jostling translucent spheres. Some flow into one another like the fine bubbles of the

---

[16] The Oligocene is a part of the Cenozoic era that extends from 34 to 23 million years before our era. It followed the Eocene and preceded the Miocene. Certain fish and mammals were really gigantic during that remote time.

foam of a tempestuous sea that finally calms, leaving myriads of shimmering spheres greedily awaiting the sun's caress on the shore.

But for the moment, the trio is observing the few strata located vertically on the immaculate wall.

This quest proves very fertile because they discover, a few minutes later, another woman walking painfully along a terrace just two floors above them. Her back is stooped.

"She's old!" confirms Phil Caldwell 2, wide-eyed.

Up to now, the "rebirths" – if that term is accurate, which is by no means certain – affected beings of about the same age. Between 25 and 40 years old. But this unfortunate woman, bowed to the ground, is certainly much older. The slowness with which she climbs the path before her confirms her difficulty in moving.

By reflex, Phil Caldwell 3 tries to scream at the old woman.

Noting that her efforts are vain because she is still desperately mute, she tries to pound the floor to warn the old woman of their presence. But, as was the case in the past when one Phil Caldwell tried to warn his counterpart using the same means, the material texturing this strange world seems inert. In any case, it does not transmit vibrations. Or too weakly for them to be detected by the filaments that adorn the feet of the inhabitants of this titanic and silky version of Dante's Inferno.

Eager to reach this woman quickly in order to reassure and help her, the trio of climbers pick up their pace. The effort is arduous and their skin gradually grows wet.

Sweat first shimmers. Then a few pearly drops begin to roll down their foreheads, over their chest and under their arms. The fine filaments that extend from their hands are very useful, evacuating these direct consequences of the effort with the same ease as a handkerchief. The three Phil Caldwells indulge in these intimate movements without shame. The total absence of clothes does not seem to pose any problem in this immense and hushed place. The notion of desire seems unknown here, even if sensuality still exists. The two men do hesitate to observe the generous breasts and round buttocks of their new companion. As for Phil Caldwell 3, she observes and compares, also without shame, the penises of her new friends and their respective dimensions.

She has already noticed with some amusement that Phil Caldwell 2 was much more generously endowed by nature than the man who had the honor of first escaping from the white, shimmering sheath that held them prisoners on the flank of the cliffs.

But this affirmed and claimed sensuality is just a game. For the time being.

Two hours later, and after spending a lot of energy in a short time, they finally reach the stooped woman who continues to walk with a courage and energy close to despair. In order not to frighten her, they wave, trying to make a noise that will eventually catch her attention and make her turn around. They want to avoid tapping her on the shoulder, which could traumatize her, even if the electrical sparks of earlier have gradually disappeared.

Alas, Phil Caldwell 4 seems to be a little hard of hearing. Their jumps, just behind her, do not move her at all. Phil Caldwell 1 decides to brush her left shoulder with his filaments.

The effect is immediate. The old woman jumps. She brings her hands to her mouth while turning partially about. She seems astounded when she discovers a woman and two men as white as she is, and with the same astonishing filaments extending from their heads, hands, and feet.

She finally opens her mouth and says clearly, "But... but who are you?"

"We are called Phil Caldwell," they chorus.

"Me too!" croaks the old woman whose wrinkled face grows beautiful under the effects of that luminous and radiant *outre-blanc* which exhales from each being, each wall, each abyss.

Her amazement is total. Phil Caldwell 3 hastens to write on his arm:

"We are with you now and we will remain together."

This first remark seems to relieve the old woman somewhat. But she still tries to talk.

"It's useless," says Phil Caldwell 1. "We must communicate by writing on our arms. Or any other part of our skin."

"Where are we?" asks Phil Caldwell 4 with a trembling hand.

"We don't know," admits the first man to have awakened in the place.

Then he erases his sentence by adding, "We will have to climb up all the terraces in order to finally discover who we are and why we are here."

"But... we all have the same name?"

"Yes."

"Why?"

A great scriptural silence follows this question.

Then the young woman finally decides to answer, "All is One."

Since this luminous yet maddening remark does not really require comments, each one takes refuge for a moment in an almost stiff immobility. This statue-like posture could create the feeling that these beings who are born in the cliff will fossilize there forever. But the word forever has no meaning here.

After a while, they decide to pursue their vertical odyssey within this white matrix that surrounds, protects and oppresses them. Phil Caldwell 1 moves ahead. The two women follow him and the other man closes up behind. Since the paths and terraces are often narrow and the peak is very impressive, they walk in single file.

Soon, they stop to observe the strata located a little higher. Then they continue on their way. In the beginning, the process is frustrating because this immense white thebaid provokes a crushing sensation in their minds, further amplified by a flood of disorderly emotions. A few bits of advice, hastily written on pale forearms, confirm the larval fear creeping into their hearts and slowing the efforts they need to make to complete this inhuman climb.

Suddenly, the head Phil Caldwell stops and crosses his arms to signal to his friends that a new event is occurring.

And what an event!

The roads connecting the terraces suddenly look blurred because of white masses emerging from all parts. They are all born from the cliff, of course, but their number is growing constantly. Soon, there are a dozen men and women scattered along the upper strata or on the other side of the abyss.

The change in the environment is also noteworthy, for the two immense strands of shiny, pearly matter in the center of the abyss are moving faster and faster. The upper part of these giant strings that mimic the helical structure of DNA is vibrating intensely. They gradually move closer to the translucent spheres that hang in clusters at the top of this world ruled by the gentle tyranny of the *outre-blanc*.

"But where do they come from?" asks the young woman, pointing at the shapes just above them along the huge cliff.

"From the same place we come from", Phil Caldwell 1 replies.

After a brief pause, he continues, "The same white matrix that lines this well, this cliff and the whole of this universe in which we are only fragile trinkets."

Since this sentence is a little long, he must write it in two parts. But his friends immediately understand what he means.

"Let's join them!" proposes Phil Caldwell 2.

He immediately sets out for the upper terraces where several men and women as pale as they are begin extricating themselves from the cliff. Some stagger as if drunk. Others fall to their knees. Some remain stuck to the wall as if dreading the discovery of an unknown world whose visual images are mind-boggling for those who are born or reborn here. But, since they are also strangers to themselves, knowing nothing of their past, this additional incongruity is simply grafted into a long rosary of immaculate quirks and streams of light.

The four Phil Caldwells, who have been climbing for several hours, wave at the newcomers. Initially these efforts are pointless because the new arrivals are looking every which way. Their eyes seem dazzled by the light that radiates from each patch of white, supple, almost living material.

Suddenly, one of the women who has just emerged from the cliff finally discovers the quartet standing below. Humans speak to each other. Or at least they try. But, after a first wave of words, speech fossilizes and making way for silence. Mime replaces words and attempts at communication become infinitely more complicated until each being has discovered the astonishing property of their own skin to act as a palimpsest.

Four men and two women gather near the edge of the terrace from which they were just born. They respond to the friendly signs of those located a little lower.

Then they sit down and wait for travelers from the depths of the abyss to arrive.

An hour later, the first four Phil Caldwells arrive at the same terrace. Another few hundred meters and they meet face to face.

"Are you all Phil Caldwells?" asks the first man who awoke, speaking in a loud and perfectly audible voice.

"Yes!" respond the six humans who discover that all the other beings living in this abyss are uniformly *outre-blanc* and countless tentacles and filaments extend from their limbs and heads.

"But why?" insists one of the two women who is significantly smaller than the others.

Her question is the last one to be heard since silence once again becomes the norm.

Immediately, Phil Caldwell starts to write on his arm, "We don't know. But let's stay together and everything will go well."

He stops for a moment and continues, "It's the best way to communicate with one another."

The six new Phil Caldwells look at one another. Stunned. Then they frantically begin to draw and write on their arms. Some even try their thighs.

They seem delighted, even if this technique is slow and sometimes frustrating.

Since the terrace they are all standing on is quite narrow, they move off a little to settle in a more comfortable, less dangerous area. Even though gravity seems rather weak here, no one is tempted to leap into the abyss where the background is perfectly indistinguishable.

When they finally discover a large overhang that looks over the vertical wall of the abyss, they settle down a few moments in order to exchange their impressions. Since they number ten now, this takes a while. But since the discussions always revolve around the same subjects, they take place without any real loss of time. In addition, some responses form a pattern, always coming back to: *"We don't know! and the solution is probably at the top of the gigantic, dazzling funnel."*

The rather trivial questions about food and basic physical needs are handled by Phil Caldwell 1 who most often takes the initiative. He evokes the fact that he woke here first and that this timing may have meaning.

No one can disprove this hypothesis. Or confirm it.

He quickly explains to the six newcomers in this monochromatic, borderless universe that material contingencies do not affect them.

"We don't need to sleep either?" asks one of the men from the last group, astonished.

"Apparently not."

"It's never night here?" he continues, widening his eyes because he finds this linearity of daytime a little frightening.

"I don't know," admits Phil Caldwell 1. "In any case, I've never detected the embryo of twilight since emerging here."

Phil Caldwell 1 preferred to replace birth by emergence. This way of hiding reality from himself surprised him. But he did nothing to fight against this psychic self-censorship.

"How long ago?" asks the young woman from the last group whose elegant shape drew the looks of the men present on this cornice overlooking the abyss.

"I don't know. The notion of time is very strange here..."

"We have witnessed the death of the sun!" writes the young woman whom the first two Phil Caldwells met at the beginning of their climb.

This comment generates much discussion. The most relevant focuses on a question asked by one of the men, "How could you have witnessed the death of the sun?"

Phil Caldwell 1 is dumbfounded. Just then, he realizes that some of his new companions probably have more memories than he does because the sun and normal life seem customary to them, while this notion remains blurry for the first four members of this rather motley group.

Beyond the obvious physical differences that exist between them, it seems that each individual's level of knowledge differs significantly according to whether he or she emerged some time ago or very recently. However, this does not change their overall problem: they must climb to the top to discover, perhaps, the truth about this universe, its purpose and its reasons for being.

Phil Caldwell 1 finally replies, "We saw a huge ball of fire swell, explode and disappear inside the cliff."

"But how are you sure it was the sun? It should die in seven billion years!"

"Time does not flow at the same pace here," replies Phil Caldwell 1.

The man speaking to him continued writing a sentence on his arm, trembling with emotion, upon hearing that their life cycle had nothing to do with what they might have known before when the first young woman with firm, round breasts pointed her right arm straight in front of them.

They all turn around.

Their faces grow haggard. Their legs begin to shake. On the same stratum, on the opposite side of the inverted truncated cone, a silhouette stands out. Clearly. Without any ambiguity.

A massive, feline silhouette. An impressive head with round ears and a slightly open mouth showing teeth about ten centimeters long. A long tail, flicking constantly. An immaculate coat of thick hair. The animal is just over three meters long.

A tiger!

The difference between it and Siberian tigers or white tigers is that its fur is as white as the skin of the Phil Caldwells who scrutinize him, incredulous, and its clawed feet are abundantly covered by filaments resembling those of the humans. But, strangely, its head is devoid of such appendages.

The ten humans are stunned. Up to this point, they had imagined that this monochromatic universe was dedicated to humans all called Phil Caldwell.

"What is that tiger doing here?" asks Phil Caldwell 6, the largest of the two women of the group that has just joined the quartet.

"It's incredible!" Phil Caldwell 2 simply says.

"It's exciting. Wonderful!" exclaims Phil Caldwell 1.

"I'm afraid," says the old woman.

"There's no reason to be afraid. The presence of this white tiger in an immaculate universe demonstrates that the world in which we have just been born or reborn is fundamentally different from others."

"Others!" says the young woman with the round breasts and long hair, astonished.

"Yes. It is possible that we all came from the same world. But…"

He leaves his sentence dangling to give other Phil Caldwells to complete his observation. It does not take long. Phil Caldwell 8, a strong, very muscular man whose square head looks like that of a cartoon hero, begins to write. As he is part of the group of those who have just emerged from the very flesh of the cliff, his writing skill is limited. His layout is uncertain. But his companions still manage to read.

"So, we're not all from the same universe?"

"I don't know," acknowledges Phil Caldwell 1, biting his lower lip. "But the fact that we are all Phil Caldwell, without us knowing who that character, someone who can appear as male or female, really is, demonstrates that we are not from the same world."

"Or the same time," Phil Caldwell 6 intervenes, shoving her bosom almost under the nose of Phil Caldwell 1.

And Phil Caldwell 1 cannot help but look at the two white nipples challenging him. Then he looks away to avoid developing an erection that would be inappropriate under the circumstances.

"Indeed," he replies, "we may all come from different ages."

"From times when women could also be called Phil Caldwell?" insists the colossus with the jaws carved in marble.

"Perhaps…"

The discussion stops immediately as Phil Caldwell 3 waves broadly. The young woman had moved away to better observe the splendid animal which is about a kilometer from them, just opposite.

She turns back to the other nine and hastily writes:

"The tiger is coming!"

171

They all turn around and realize that the white animal is starting to move in their direction. It is incredibly powerful and supple, and walks much faster than humans do. Moreover, the long filaments that extend from its paws do not seem to bother it at all, unlike the humans who always feel like they are walking on a carpet covered with dozens of balls of wool.

"Are we heading up?" asks the old woman, still worried.

"No," replies Phil Caldwell 1. "I don't think it's aggressive. Anyway, if it wants to catch up with us, it can do so without any difficulty."

"You must never run away from a wild beast," the colossus confirms, while ostensibly rippling the muscles of which he seems very proud.

Two of them wave at the feline. Then they sit down, leaning against the cliff, to wait for the tiger to join them.

Less than an hour later, the impressive animal finally comes to a stop about ten meters away. With very serious, perfectly audible sounds it asks, "Who are you?"

The humans grow even paler, if that is possible, of course.

Understanding that it is up to him to speak in order to justify his dominant male status that he has assumed despite the fact that no one has asked him to, Phil Caldwell 8 responds in a stentorian voice, "We are called Phil Caldwell!"

"Me too," replies the tiger.

CHAPTER 25

Faces freeze. First. The mouths open. Next.

Everyone tries to speak, which immediately creates a hubbub.

"Welcome!" says Phil Caldwell 1 simply.

Then he hastens to continue, "We shall soon be all mute. But we communicate by writing with our filaments. Do you know how to write?"

"No," replies the tiger in his warm, cavernous voice.

The man is surprised because the feline with its coat in all the deep shades of the *outre-blanc* seems to be able to continue expressing itself without problem whereas the humans no longer can.

His companions are dumbfounded. The old woman is still frightened and slips cautiously behind the colossus with the prominent jaws.

"That's wonderful," Phil Caldwell 3 writes, kneeling down right in front of the wild beast.

She feels its warm breath on her cheeks and forehead.

This is followed by a surreal dialogue that have thrilled Hieronymus Bosch and titillated his imagination as he created his paintings and triptychs. The young woman with the pearly hair from the abyss asks the wild beast, which has slipped its two large front legs near her knees, many questions. The great white cat is perfectly able to read the questions on the left forearm of Phil Caldwell 3. It responds to her by sprinkling her words with grunts and growls that may impress the humans around it, but are devoid of any aggressiveness.

Naturally, the tiger asks the question that all the inhabitants of this immaculate version of Dante's Inferno are asking themselves, "Where are we?"

The young woman cannot answer.

Phil Caldwell 1, who has also settled down in front of the impressive predator, simply says, "This world is... out of the world!"

This remark does not seem to satisfy the wild beast which, unlike the mute humans, is able to gather some memories of his previous life.

Since the animal is still able to talk, it monopolizes everyone's attention. Gradually, all the humans gather around him. Only the old woman stays cautiously back, even though she seems calmer.

"If so, why are we here? Is it a punishment? A reward?"

Their complete lack of unknowledge of the motivations of the being that brought them together does not facilitate analysis. Phil Caldwell 1 focuses on the only elements that are tangible, predictable or at least probable.

The tiger asks him, "Where are we going?"

He answers, "We must climb to the top of this gigantic cliff."

At that moment, Phil Caldwell 7, a man of small stature, wrinkled, with a large scar that tears across his right cheek and gets lost in the confusion of his tentacles and filaments, stands up,

"Why do we have to go up? This wall is as high as ten planets! It might be simpler to go down."

"True," admits the colossus, "The solution to this enigma of cosmic dimensions may just as well be at the bottom of the abyss. And we would probably have less distance to cover."

"There are only bad answers in the depths of the chasms," retorts the tiger, roaring and showing its teeth, the largest of which measure about ten centimeters and are made of pure white diamonds.

Regardless of the relevance of the brute force of an animal that can kill two men in less than a second, its conclusion is steeped in common sense. This is what Phil Caldwell 1 strives to emphasize, looking at all of his friends one by one.

"The tiger is right. The firmament is littered with billions of translucent spheres in which are reflected as many sparkling universes as there are atoms in the universe that we have left. Moreover, the titanic strands of DNA that gently oscillate in the center of the well unfold and extend to the sky. The solution is up there!"

Since his sentence is long, he has to break it up into three parts.

Once everyone has finished reading, he continues, "But if some of us want to get down, they can try that. ButI... I'm going up!"

Most of the others nod in agreement. Only Phil Caldwell 7 insists once again.

But as all the others reject his analysis, he decides to follow the group. Meanwhile, the young woman with the breasts and the tiger continue to converse as if they have always known one another.

Two hours later, the group finally starts on their way up. Naturally, the beast walks in the lead, followed by the young woman with whom he has become friends and Phil Caldwell 1.

A few minutes pass. Suddenly, the tiger crouches down and observes. Its friends hang back behind him, looking for the source of a possible threat.

But there is no threat, just a strange animal standing in front of them. Since the is still very narrow, it cannot escape. Strangely, it does not try to dodge the strange group led by a tiger measuring more than three meters in length, from nose to tail, and weighing around 280 kilos.

Equipped with a shell made of boney plates covered with horns, the newcomer is easily recognizable. It is an armadillo with 9 bands similar to those that dwell in the southern United States, Central America and much of South America. Its elongated muzzle, erect, pointed ears and long, ringed tail are reminiscent of a familiar and rather sympathetic silhouette, despite its resemblance to a battle tank. But this creature is much larger than the traditional 9-banded armadillo that can gobble up close to 40,000 ants a day. It is white, of course.

The armadillo that is often seen in Texas measures about 40 centimeters long and its tail is almost as long as its body. The one blocking the way ahead of the tiger and the ten humans is almost two meters long and its tail is every bit as gigantic as well. Its short legs, which would usually be hairy are covered with an exuberant forest of filaments that give the comic illusion that the creature moves about on an ocean of white woolen threads that envelope it like a cocoon.

The armadillo's little eyes are gleaming gems that reflect all the light of this universe that stretches towards a dazzling sky.

"What are you called?" asks the tiger, who already knows the answer.

It replies, "Phil Caldwell. And you?"

"Me too. And my human companions are all called Phil Caldwell."

"But who is Phil Caldwell?" asks the armadillo pointing its muzzle in the direction of the humans whose heads are much higher than its own.

"We don't know," reply three of them, before sinking again into the silence that affects the women and men of this universe as soon as they utter two or three sentences.

"Where are you going?" asks the albino armadillo gently stirring its tail which is partially covered with uniformly white hair.

"We are climbing to the top of this gigantic cliff," says Phil Caldwell 1, pointing his arm at the dasypus[17].

"I don't understand," says the animal, which obviously knows how to speak but does read yet.

"Humans must write in order to communicate with one another," says the tiger. "Our friend is simply pointing out that we are beginning to climb this cliff that has just given us life."

"Why?"

"It is probably the only way in which we can find out who we are and why we have been reborn here."

"That wall is immense! Impassable…"

"Nothing is impassable!" says the beast, opening its mouth wide, revealing fangs that could shred any living being in less than five seconds.

The armadillo is not impressed. It simply steps back a little and says, "Perfect. I will follow you."

Still led by the majestic feline with its immaculate coat, the ten humans and the armadillo continue to climb the millions of terraces that form an astonishing box around this chasm without beginning or end.

---

[17] The armadillos are part of the Dasypodinae family, which is itself included in the Xenarthres super-order which also includes the anteater and the sloth. They were formerly included in the edentulous order along with pangolins and aardvaks, which, unlike the xenarthra, are devoid of teeth.

They have been walking for several hours when the young woman who first extracted herself from the white and luminous sheathe of the cliff suddenly stops. Phil Caldwell 8 bumps into her. The man with the muscular stature apologizes, writing a single word on his arm: sorry!

Phil Caldwell 3 then approaches the edge. For a long time, she observes the gigantic gaping well whose center plunges towards an unknown nadir and seems to defy the sky. She looks and nods.

Suddenly, she writes a message quickly on her skin for the tiger who sits and scrutinizes the text. Its mustache bristles and his mouth opens wide. With the suddenness of lightning it straightens up and says in a thundering voice, "Our friend has just given me a curious piece of information."

"Yes?" asks Phil Caldwell 1.

"Space expands very quickly. More precisely, the width of the well increases as we climb."

All the Phil Caldwells then position themselves facing the part of the terrace that runs alongside the abyss. They look on the other side of the well where the giant DNA strands quietly nod as if caressed by a light breeze.

The remark made by Phil Caldwell 3 is relevant. When the first man emerged here, the breadth of the abyss was almost the same. It grew only as they climbed, since each stratum is bordered by a terrace, whereas the wall encircling the abyss remained at an angle of about 80° with the vertical.

Now, the highly changeable character of the environment becomes unquestionably clear. As the young woman pointed out, the diameter of the gap that the cliff is now more than four or five kilometers. And the phenomenon is accelerating. The outre-blanc material that shapes this universe seems to be as malleable as modeling clay. It stretches without jags, without tears Similar to Einstein's space-time, which changes shape near a very strong gravity, the pearly material that composes the large structures of this vertical world designed for Titans adapts to all situations. To all constraints.

Phil Caldwell 2 approaches the feline and the young woman, points his arm at both, and says:

"Will this world die like the sun did?"

No answer.

The tiger looks once again at the young woman with the full breasts and the long, albino in which thousands of filaments are woven into strange braids, curls and rings. It then observes the group of humans and the armadillo, still impassive.

"We have no way of knowing. But it would be absurd for this universe to give us life and then take it away again afterwards. So, we have to keep climbing, even if this gaping hole becomes as large as an ocean."

Phil Caldwell seems to appreciate the comparison.

He stands there in front of before his companions and simply writes simply on his forearm:

"We go up!"

And they immediately start to climb, while wondering whether this space is going to continue expanding infinitely.

Phil Caldwell 3 suddenly feels notions arise in her mind that she does not really understand even if the general meaning seems relatively clear to her. She thinks of accelerated expansion. She also imagines eternal inflation.

The young woman decides to raise this matter with Phil Caldwell 1. The latter is stunned. These notions remind him immediately of other places, other times. Knowledge familiar to him and now buried in him. Or even within this smooth, monochromatic universe.

Another life perhaps. Distant. And yet so close. Yes. But what?

He doesn't know. But he thanks the young woman with a broad smile while shuddering at the touch of her skin, iridescent with light and silky like a piece of fabric gently placed on a body. Naked. Another reminiscence?

After conversing a little with the young woman, incessantly erasing and writing on his left arm, which has become an indispensable notepad that he uses all the time, he walks over to the tiger as he continues to scribble on his skin.

"What is the purpose of these vaults under the terraces?"

Phil Caldwell 1 focuses on an additional oddity that they have all been able to observe for less than two hours now. Up to this point, the wall of the cliff was smooth and the stratifications structuring this gigantic white funnel materialized in the form of terraces. More precisely, as an almost greedy accumulation of millions of floors stacked up on one another, reaching up to the immaculate sky of a world adorned with sparkling pearls and filled with pale beings who all call themselves Phil Caldwell. These terraces slope gently and intermediate ramps make it possible to go from one to another without making a complete circuit of the abyss each time. This structure is a blessing because, as the circumference of the abyss is growing with every passing second, it would take a week to cross a single level.

But, starting just a short while ago, the very structure of the wall has grown surprising.

Now, the vertical, white walls are filled with regular vaults measuring about ten meters high and about thirty meters wide. Their peaks are marked by a lowered arch[18] forming a half-ellipse. The wall under this vault is smooth and glazed like the rest of the cliff. But their very recent appearance here and especially their geometrical regularity intrigues some of the members of the group.

"I have no idea," admits the tiger, expanding the range of its vocalizations, all of which are deep, cavernous sounds.

---

[18] I architecture, this type of arch is called a "basket-handle arch". Such arches are very often usedf to build the archs of bridges, for example.

"Maybe they are exits? Passageways?" intervenes the armadillo, making the plates of its white shell shine with little hairs and filaments that vibrate unceasingly.

The other watch it. Stunned.

The armadillo's comment is not irrelevant. The humans are astonished.

"Did I say something stupid?"

"No," replies the tiger, opening its eyes a little wider, the two translucent gems shining unusually bright. "But our companions are certainly delighted with your intervention. Even if they remain obstinately mute. Unlike us!"

While uttering this last sentence in a somewhat mocking tone, the feline opens its mouth wide, revealing, once again, the impressive row of teeth.

The ten humans remain petrified for a moment. Then Phil Caldwell 1 walks over to the nearest arch. He feels the smooth wall with his filaments in order to determine if there is a hidden opening. Or a device for tilting this surface. His efforts are unsuccessful as the surface is a single piece. The arch is sculpted in the ubiquitous outre-blanc material, and no weakness is noted in the structure, and there is no indication of an opening device.

Moreover, since the abyss started expanding regularly, the crystalline incrustations in the cliff have disappeared. There are no windows, no opening through which someone could fleetingly glimpse all that is beyond this pale world. The material that makes up this giant funnel with floors is thickening more and more.

The version of Dante's Inferno recreated here is disconnected from the usual time and space and is no longer connected to any paradise. It is. It remains. Forever.

Disappointed, the first man to have awakened here steps back. Then he walks over to the tiger and writes on his forearm:

"We continue to climb up the cliff."

The group sets out immediately.

They walk for several hours. They proceed at a regular pace and do not grow tired. At the same time, they do not feel a need to eat or drink. The sensation is strange because this absolute tranquility is both a deliverance and a source of anxiety. Since there is neither night nor fatigue here, they be able to keep climbing, without stopping, for centuries. For millennia!

Astonishing, this incredible idea does not really seem to bother the argonauts in this white universe where the only really relevant objective is steeped in a vertical logic: climb. Climb again. Keep climbing.

Climb until they reach the divine, yet very distant, moment when they reach the top of this colossal cliff. At this magical moment, crystallized and almost deified by such a long wait, the horizon of a new and unheard-of universe will finally unfold for them.

Suddenly the tiger stops. Still a little distracted, Phil Caldwell 3 steps on its tail. The young woman is not heavy and the filaments that wind under her feet cushion the pressure, but the beast knows that someone has just trampled its tail. It turns and grumbles a little.

The young woman walks over to the powerful animal and caresses its head by way of atonement.

"Look!" says the feline.

The spectacle is very amazing. A little further up, an unexpected quartet is walking along a path that connects to the terrace just above the group led by the feline who also claims to be Phil Caldwell.

The first two members of this small expedition within the white desert are two men who are not alike at all. This is the case with the six male Phil Caldwells who vary in size and build. But in the case of the foursome, the disparity is almost comic, for one is very tall and very thin, while the other looks like a nativity figurine who has lived for a very long time on a planet with strong gravity. But figurines are generally colorful, while this round character is uniformly white.

In reality, it is not these two men who fascinate the ten humans, the tiger and the armadillo. They are amazed by the two other creatures who, very likely, will claim to be called Phil Caldwell.

The first animal is quite easy to recognize. Just dive into a book about dinosaurs. A small head with a long muzzle, very massive hind legs, an imposing body and a long tail with four long pikes that serve as a formidable weapon, the animal has a comical look. But the most characteristic element of this dinosaur, which lived at the end of the Jurassic period is on its back. Seventeen large plates stand there almost vertically.

A stegosaurus!

Significantly smaller than its cousins of the secondary era, measuring less than four meters, this reptile with the thick, coarse skin holds its head rather low while its tail remains almost horizontal. Always ready to strike, it seems.

Of course, this miniature stegosaurus is totally white and clusters of undisciplined filaments swarm between its paws.

The other creature is totally unknown to the Phil Caldwells.

"What is that?" asks the armadillo with its customary candor.

Since the group is still too far from the quartet, the humans cannot take advantage of the brief opportunity given to them at each encounter to communicate orally and not by scribbling on their arms.

The Phil Caldwells think.

Suddenly, Phil Caldwell 3 puffs up her his chest with some pride. This simple gesture naturally highlights her pretty breasts that the men of the group often look at with mixed feelings, sometimes confused, unaware of their actual power.

The young woman writes a name on her arm. Then she shows it to the tiger so that the feline can read it with his powerful voice that always seeks to dig up the infrasounds lost for millennia in this abyss that plunges below their feet.

"Apparently, it's an anomomo... Excuse me. It's an anomalocaris."

The other members of the group remain speechless, except for Phil Caldwell 3 of course. The young woman continues to write, leaving her friend to read her messages out loud.

"This animal lived in the oceans more than 500 million years ago. It was..."

The tiger stops, for Phil Caldwell 3 must erase her previous sentence to write the next, a constraint that always annoys the courageous few who try to inform their companions about sudden observations or recollections.

"It was the first major predator."

The humans look at one another. A little surprised.

A major predator? The animal is hardly impressive, measuring barely a meter long. However, after reflection, they decide that the notion of predator is always closely related to the size of the prey. In its world, the praying mantis is a formidable killer, but does not impress a calf...

They continue to observe this strange creature that Phil Caldwell 3 apparently knows but it does not evoke anything for them. Describing an anomalocaris is an exhilarating exercise for the mind because this giant arthropod gives the impression of having been conceived by a mad scientist anxious to create a new being by rummaging through a toy box or near the odoriferous stall of a fishmonger. Its head is rather small and is extended at the front by two growths which resemble the bodies of shrimps with their heads cut off. As another touch of whimsy, if one is really necessary of course, its almost round mouth looks strangely like a slice of pineapple finely cut and hollowed out in the center. On the sides of its head, two stalk-like are covered with more than 15,000 facets called ommatidia, which are receptors that are very sensitive to light. The body is armored, as is often the case for animals that lived in the Cambrian era. Its flanks are decorated with numerous swim lobes which act somewhat like the lateral fins of certain fish. The tail ends with two long, whip-like filaments.

Strangely enough, the anomalocaris is white and its armor drips with light, but its form is rigorously identical to that which paleontologists regularly dig out of sedimentary rocks. There are no incongruous tentacles or exuberant filaments vibrating in all directions.

For a moment, the group located slightly below continues to observe the strange crew composed of two very dissimilar humans and two archaic animals that are even more dissimilar still. Then they begin to wave in their in their direction. Naturally, the quartet does not see them.

The tiger decides to roar with an astonishing force in this place where only ethereal music is audible in white, vertical and silent thebaid.

The silence is broken. The two men, the stegosaurus and the anomalocaris, freeze.

They turn around to find out what astonishing creature can utter such a thundering sound. The being with the stalk-like eyes is very agile and does not slip on the surface of the terrace where they stand. It flies and levitates! For the dinosaur with the boney plates, the process is longer, given its size. But, above all, as a result of its nature as a placid herbivore.

Phil Caldwell 1 waves to catch their attention. As they do not really seem to understand, the tiger roars very loudly "Wait for us! We're heading up."

CHAPTER 26

The four Phil Caldwells positioned on one of the upper terraces wait for the others who start climbing once again. The tiger is still leading. It seems anxious to reach the foursome quickly because this animal from the depths of time with the mind-boggling name intrigues it to the utmost.

As usual, the elderly woman and the armadillo bring up the rear struggling to keep up.

Phil Caldwell 1 looks at the central gap that continues to expand. The phenomenon is almost frightening as the diameter of the abyss is now close to thirty or forty kilometers. On the other side of the abyss it is now difficult to make out anything other than a colossal heap of white horizontal streaks at the base of a gigantic cliff.

But this continuous expansion has one valuable advantage: the laminated, almost lamellar structure of this giant funnel, which widens unceasingly, is much easier to see, with the top of the wall brushing against the transparent spheres that calmly bob back and forth a few million floors above. This expansion also makes it possible to better understand the ominous odyssey that awaits him and all the other Phil Caldwells who emerge in a random and perfectly erratic way from the flanks of this volcanic chimney inspired by Dante's Inferno.

Three hours later, they finally join the motley quartet which had climbed down a bit towards them to hasten their encounter.

The thin, very tall man walks towards the tiger, Phil Caldwell 1 and the young woman who is able to talk to the feline so easily. His forehead is high, clear, which increases his almost sickly leanness. He is emaciated and his slender limbs give the illusory impression of being able to be broken with a glance. Fortunately, this is not the case.

He smiled a little and said, looking first at the great white cat, "Your name is probably Phil Caldwell?"

"Absolutely!" responds the tiger using a maximum of deep tones.

The two humans and the stegosaurus remain motionless, dumbfounded by the experience of meeting twelve more Phil Caldwells, all very different from one another.

In contrast to this almost generalized mute amazement, the anomalocaris stirs. It takes advantage of the strange possibilities that are given to it in this world to rise above his climbing companions.

The strange animal with its stalk-like eyes and two long shrimp-like tail outgrowths moves to stand just in front of the feline and Phil Caldwell 1.

"What are we to?" it asks in a shrill voice.

This sound is astonishing, much like hearing the voices of people who have amused themselves by breathing in helium and sound like Donald Duck or a castrato singer for a few seconds. In the case of humans, this change is caused by the fact that helium is much less dense than air. Sound propagates much faster,[19] and the vocal cords vibrate faster and at a higher frequency.

But in the case of this creature whose ancestors lived on Earth half a billion years ago, this very high-pitched voice seems natural.

"We will continue to climb so we can finally discover who we really are and why we have just been reborn here," says Phil Caldwell 1, taking advantage of the brief moment when humans can express themselves other than by scribbling on their arms.

"This cliff is huge," says the creature with the incredibly faceted eyes. "Are you climbing in groups?"

"Yes," replies the man, whose voice once again dies.

A little irritated, he starts to write on his forearm. But the tiger takes the lead.

"We are all climbing these terraces and the roads that connect them. As we are all feeling confused because we share the same name, without knowing what it means, we must admit that we are connected by a powerful bond. Breaking it would probably be absurd. Maybe even dangerous."

"You're right," says the stegosaurus, replacing the two humans who are once again mute.

In the group of four that has just been joined by the rest of the troupe, the chubby little man nods to confirm this common-sense statement.

"Follow me!" then says the anomalocaris, gently fluttering over the tiger.

The creature's companions look at him with envy.

Being able to fly quietly over the white paths and terraces that stratify this ever-expanding world is a considerable advantage. But the strange animal is not proud of this ability. It merely proposes to pursue this mind-boggling quest with the very uncertain outcome.

Phil Caldwell 1 wonders how the anomalocaris was able to escape from the cliff safely because, with the two long filaments that extend from its tail like whips, it could have torn various delicate parts from its tousled body. But, at the same time he looks at his human companions, all of whom carry countless tufts of filaments and fine tentacles strangely placed on their heads, at the ends of their hands and under their feet.

He then realizes the absurdity of his questioning.

Astonishing and baroque, the white procession resumes its foolish journey under the guidance of the creature gently fluttering over the group that now includes fifteen Phil Caldwells, in addition to the anomalocaris with the high voice. Since fatigue is almost non-existent here, the group finally settles for the

---

[19] Sound spreads at about 340 m/s in air and 1000 m/s in helium.

pace set by the old woman and the armadillo. When those two lag slightly behind, the archaic creature fluttering impudently overhead, giggles and says,
"Stop!"

At first, both the tiger and Phil Caldwell 1 were a little offended by the
friendly take-charge attitude of their new friend whose faceted eyes saw everything with a maddening insight. But they now seem to have adapted to the verbal exuberance envied by all the humans.

After crossing at least thirty successive terraces, using the crossroads that
join them, making incessant zigzags somewhat similar to the stairs of the Mesopotamian ziqquats, Phil Caldwell 1 and his companions feel the need to stop to
take stock.

A first question is asked. It comes from the colossus who writes on his
muscular biceps in order to demonstrate, no doubt, that he fears nothing and nobody except the jaws of the tiger and the powerfully armed tail of the stegosaurus, of course.

"If we don't need to eat, drink or sleep, do we have to climb constantly?"
asks Phil Caldwell 8.

Although seemingly trivial, this question is meaningful, for climbing millions of successive strata may take several centuries, and it is not a bad idea to
wonder what pace should be set for this fantastic climb above the abyss.

"We can stop whenever one of us wishes to," replies the feline, in its deep
voice which now serves as a counterpoint to the falsetto tones of the
anomalocaris.

"Good idea!" responds Phil Caldwell 3 enthusiastically, writing on the skin
of her forearm with a speed that the others envy more and more.

But in silence, of course.

"There must be another solution," says Phil Caldwell 1, positioning himself very close to the abyss and looking at the other side of the well.

It is now possible to speak of a *shore* rather than a *side* since the distance
that separates the two edges far exceeds one hundred kilometers. The opposite
cliff opposite still consists of a stack of narrow terraces that give it the appearance of an albino mille-feuille. But the horizon is moving farther and farther
ahead. Obviously, it is the same when looking up.

The sky is still so far away and the hieratic, translucent spheres continue to
jostle and interpenetrate without shame. The two helical structures oscillating in
the center of the abyss are growing brighter and brighter. The long luminous
strands rise, brushing against the sky in a dance that is strangely erotic and monastic at the same time. Despite the colossal expansion of the central well, the
two helical structures are still visible. The only possible explanation is that they
are growing in unison with the abyss.

Phil Caldwell 1 stands there. Like a statue.

A few seconds later, he kneels down and raises his arms, as if imploring the bubbles, but the countless, unusual shades of irradiating from them crucify his hopes.

His eyes bathed in tears, he suddenly says in a loud and perfectly audible voice, surprising all his friends after so long a silence, "Why? Why this void? Why this void?"

The repetition of this word demonstrates that he can no longer bear not knowing who he is. What he has experienced and done. And what he will do. This notion of total emptiness gnaws at him. He suddenly feels like an empty shell. A useless trinket tossed onto the surface of a crazy ocean.

He bends a bit, placing his hands on the ground.

Just then, night falls.

This is no dark night, splashed with the cold, pale lights of a moon in its first quarter. No. This is a bright night. A night in which twilight and darkness come alive from inside and shine with a black sun that explodes all certainties.

Terrified, the other Phil Caldwells stick cling to the wall.

Phil Caldwell alone remains at the edge of the abyss. Petrified. Frightened.

Then he calms. Abruptly.

He closes his eyes.

A part of his past rises up suddenly from the murk in which his memory has been mired since he detached himself from the pearly, supple and lukewarm cliff.

He sees a room. Students. He is speaking. He points at stars, galaxies. He mentioned hidden stars which he calls *black holes*. He also describes strange, multi-colored planets in distant systems where bewildering beings live on silica, phosphorus. Arsenic!

He sees...

The astrophysicist remains there for a long time. Phil Caldwell 3 and the tiger walk over to him.

The young woman gently caresses his head, trying to restore some order in the confusion of tentacles and filaments that cling together, forming a weird helmet with extremely gothic looking horns, forks and outgrowths.

The man remains prostrate.

The tiger moves closer. Its nose is now almost at the same level as one of the ears of the man who just lifted a very small piece of the veil. A tiny part of an immense veil capable of covering an entire galaxy: the web of a human soul in all its frightful complexity!

"Did the night answer your request?"

Feeling the feline's breath in his ear and on his cheek, Phil Caldwell 1 finally stands up.

He looks at the tiger and the young woman with the full breasts. He smiles at them.

Then he tries to speak out loud. But this privilege is taken away once again.

He writes, "It's not really night."

"What is it then?" writes Phil Caldwell 3.

"A special moment. Sorry. A particular breath in the middle of this monochromatic universe."

"What is so particular about this breath?" asks the tiger, frowning and opening his mouth as if to bite.

"I don't know. But I think we're going to find out soon."

Phil Caldwell 1 is not wrong.

A few seconds later, the wall in one of the arches supporting the terrace just above them gradually changes appearance. At the center of the half-ellipse formed by the basket-handle arch, the smooth, *outre-blanc* wall begins to vibrate. It gradually irradiates lights and transparencies that implies that it is metamorphosing. Imperceptibly.

The old woman, the colossus, and the stegosaurus, who had positioned themselves along the arcade, immediately leave. Contrary to them, the astrophysicist approaches. While the tiger and the young woman remain three or four meters behind him, he places his filaments on the still lukewarm surface. Almost lovingly.

Suddenly, he catches his breath and blinks. A point appears.

This point becomes a bubble. The bubble becomes a sphere.

A luminous drop slowly advances towards him along a horizontal plane in contradiction to the omnipresent verticality of this giant funnel worthy of Dante's imagination and sublimated by a divinity with disproportionate ambitions.

Phil Caldwell 1 opens his eyes wide. He seems hypnotized by this luminous sphere that grows, like a gas pocket rising from the depths of the sea and preparing to break through the surface of the water.

It is at this precise moment that he realizes that this iridescent ball is only one element of a substantially more complex process. The part that emerges in his direction is actually spherical. But it is only the end of an umbilical tube. A gallery, rather, which comes towards him and is about to swallow him up. He should flee. But he does not.

Staggered and delighted, he shifts his gaze in the direction of that shimmering and sparkling surface that irresistibly evokes the elegance of a drop of mercury vibrating with a thousand fires. A mirror of all the labyrinths of life, space and the human soul, this luminous worm twists a little before exploding on the surface of the cliff, which is now plunged into a radiant night.

The sphere continues to grow. It becomes enormous and even seems to extend well beyond the top of the arch in front of which Phil Caldwell 1 stands. His body twitches.

For a moment, he closes his hard eyes that sparkle like the most precious of diamonds. Then he opens his eye again and allows himself to be filled with this confused feeling that inextricably combines immediate enjoyment and imminent pain.

The enormous marble of mercury approaches. Only ten meters away. Five.

It finally rises to the surface of the cliff wall.

The night is still as luminous within the well. His companions watch him. Stunned. Frozen.

Abruptly, the thin film still separating him from this maddening, shiny, shimmering universe, cracks. Explodes.

The astrophysicist is caught by the monster adorned with disturbing mercurial reflections.

CHAPTER 27

Cold. Intense cold, petrifying.

The cold that breaks bodies, molecules, atoms.

Absolute cold.

"I don't want to die!" screams Phil Caldwell.

But he no longer has a mouth. No body either. He is simply pain.

An obscene remorse invades his mind. The sound of a cesspool, a sink that is suddenly unplugged. The swallowing of an enormous prehistoric reptile that gulps down everything and then spits out the superfluous and useless.

Phil Caldwell is rejected as useless debris on a shore where the fires of a slow hell are blazing. Patient. Infinite.

Then he explodes. And dies.

The wind blows hard and the smell is dreadful.

Lying on a heap of ropes, Phil Caldwell finally wakes up. Bewildered, he notices that he is wearing a dirty shirt, trousers full of holes and held up by a string and shoes. A filthy cap is screwed on his head despite the tropical heat that reigns here.

Sailors around him speak in Portuguese. But he understands what they say perfectly.

The air is hot. Wet. Sticky.

"Are we near the equator?" he wonders.

His head is heavy but he immediately realizes that he is no longer in the *outre-blanc* world where shared his life with a dozen humans who all bear the same name, along with some strange animals that are the only beings able to speak.

"Who am I?" he yells in order to clear his lungs still blocked with mucus.

"Joaõ Serrão. You're drunk again. As usual!" answers one of the sailors.

The sailor moves over to him and gives him a good kick, reminding him that he must take his watch and hoist the sail that is just above him.

Phil Caldwell is delighted to discover that he can speak normally again, that this world is full of beautiful colors and that he understands everything that is said to him, although he does not normally know a word of Portuguese.

But, as he rises, these three pieces of good news are veiled with anxiety. Clasping a moist bulwark, soiled with fluids of which he does not want to know the origin, he immediately realizes that he is on board a rocking caravel. Fortunately, the ocean is calm. The sun burns in a sky dotted with chubby, little, white clouds. Two other ships accompany the one on which he has just awakened without understanding why he is there.

Again, he knows that these carracks, with their high forecastle and aftercastle are very high, are called the *Concepción* and the *Victoria*. He is on board the *Trinidad*, the flagship of Fernão de Magalhães, better known as Fernand Magellan. He has no idea why he knows all this information since he just woke up.

But he does... That's all!

"We are approaching the island of Mactan!"[20] shouts Antonio Pigafetta one of the Magellan's assistants.

"So, it's April 1521," says Phil Caldwell, who is called Joaõ Serrão and seems to have a strong inclination for strong and possibly adulterated spirits.

The heavy, capricious ship slowly turns to starboard to head for a sandy coast where the Trinidad will be able to anchor so that part of the crew will meet Lapu-Lapu, the formidable lord of Mactan. For his part, Juan Sebastián Elcano, the new captain of the *Victoria* following the death of Luis de Mendoza, will remain a little behind in order to protect the expedition if Lapu-Lapu's warriors prove to be so irascible as that petty little king who constantly defies the powerful King Humabon, Magellan's new friend.

Since the hull of the *Concepción* had suffered much after such a long journey, the third ship cautiously stays offshore.

With a slow circular look, Joaõ Serrão counts the number of men on board the *Trinidad*. With Magellan, Antonio Pigafetta and Duarte Barbosa, the helmsman, there are about sixty. Then he scans the two masts which are now wrapped in their slumped sails. The caravel slides slowly over the waves and the sound of burbling water replaces the chatter of the sailors who have accompanied Magellan for nearly two years now. Twenty months of trials, dramas and efforts.

He walks over to the rail on the port side to observe the *Victoria* which is less than two hundred meters from *Trinidad*.

The beautiful carrack commanded by Juan Sebastián Elcano is nearly thirty meters long. Its round hull is reminiscent of the silhouettes of the boats seen on some Persian miniatures, sailing amidst thousands of raging waves driven by the wind. A large central mast dominates while the mast at the rear is significantly smaller. As for *Trinidad*, its sails sag and the carrack remains almost motionless off shore of this small island whose lord has a reputation for being a bloodthirsty brute. Lapu-Lapu's sinister reputation precedes him because he refuses to pledge allegiance to King Humabon.

Naturally, the fact that Humabon quickly converted to Christianity, along with a part of his people, further increases the visceral hatred between the two

---

[20] The small island of Mactan is located in Bohol Strait, very close to the island of Cebu. Cebu International Airport is also located on Mactan. Cebu and Bohol are located in the southern Philippines between the two large islands of Palawan (west) and Mindanao (southeast).

sovereigns. Magellan accepted without reluctance to carry out a goodwill mission between the kings of Cebu and Mactan.

But, turning to starboard, Phil Caldwell immediately realizes that this peaceful, ambassadorial initiative will not go as well as Magellan could hope for.

The captain of the expedition soon becomes aware of this. He looks at his men, one by one, and simply says, "Be prepared to fight!"

His proud face hardens.

Magellan is large enough. His build imposes respect. His face does too. A full-bodied nose, sparkling eyes and a dark beard give the man a grave expression. But this inner strength is by no means austere. One can almost presume that he does not shrink from anything.

His journey proves this. His determination is unflagging. When necessary, he can be ruthless and brutal so that no one questions his legitimacy and authority during this long, perilous expedition.

A year earlier, he had subdued a mutiny that broke out on three of his five ships. It was during this rebellion that the rebel captain of the *Victoria*, Luis de Mendoza, was killed. Anxious to maintain his authority and not to hinder the success of the expedition, Magellan had beheaded another mutineer, Gaspar de Quesada, captain of the *Concepción*. Yet, he had abandoned Juan de Cartagena, the former captain of the *San Antonio*, a great Spaniard and nephew of the Bishop of Burgos, as well as the priest Pedro Sánchez de la Reina, who had very imprudently taken the mutinous party, in southern Brazil.

This man has the stuff of a great conqueror, thinks of Phil Caldwell, still hiding behind the identity of a simple sailor: Joaõ Serrão.

Magellan observes his men, trying to see if he can count on them.

Apparently, the lights shining in their eyes reassure him. Leaving the approach maneuver in the hands of Duarte Barbosa, he gives his orders.

"There are too many rocky outcrops and corals near the beach for us to approach closer. We're going to anchor here."

He stops for a moment, makes a precise gesture to the helmsman and attentively watches a crowd of almost naked men arriving at this part of the island from a village nestled in a coconut forest.

Their intentions are obviously warlike, as they all carry arches, spears and a weapon specific to the Filipino warriors: the kampilan. This long, tapered sword is formidable. Lapu-Lapu's warriors seem perfectly capable of wielding it.

After analyzing the situation and assessing the enemy, Magellan once again addresses the 49 soldiers on the *Trinidad*

"I want to see your weapons before we board the launches. Lapu-Lapu is a dangerous warrior king and, as you can see for yourselves, he has more than a thousand men. Since our caravel cannot get closer because of the reefs, our guns are useless. If these ruffians do not want to hear reason and swear allegiance to King Humabon, my friends, we will have to fight."

"Fifty against a thousand!" says Phil Caldwell, choking and widening his eyes in terror. "He's crazy! That's suicide!"

Magellan seems unconcerned by this numerical asymmetry which would make even the most courageous warriors quail. Now lined up in two rows on the bridge of the *Trinidad*, the soldiers proudly display their swords, axes, crossbows, shields and harquebuses. Some wear light armor to protect themselves from arrows and various projectiles that the small army of the renegade king is prepared to use. But most do not because of the stifling heat in the southern Philippines.

Since Duarte Barbosa has totally immobilized the caravel after a long creaking sound caused by the anchor clinging to the rocks and coral that line the bottom of this very shallow arm of the sea, it is now possible to lower the boats.

Orders ring out. Dry like the sound of the blade of a dagger cutting into a piece of wood.

"Eight men per boat!"

Four sailors will remain on board rush to launch the *Trinidad's* canoes and launches.

The boats are heavy and not very maneuverable. But the crew us used to them after the many stopovers they have made since their departure from Sanlúcar de Barrameda on September 20, 1519. The small boats rock from side to side, but finally they pull away from the hull of the large vessel as the sailors man their oars vigorously and howl encouragement in time.

The sea is of a blue that hesitates somewhere between sapphire and emerald because of the white sand of the sea floor and the intense light that reigns under the benevolent auspices of a burning sun.

Phil Caldwell is in a canoe. The smallest. It skims quite close to the launch where Magellan stands, his right foot resting on the bow to monitor the immediate environment with utmost attention. Lapu-Lapu's soldiers stand to the left of the long beach lined with palm trees and barringtonias – large trees covered with flowers with long pink stamens – in clear view.

They are dressed in simple loincloths, but their determination is obvious. They scream and wave their lances, while protecting their bodies with shields made of very hard wood.

In the center, a curtain of trees. On the right, there are some rather rudimentary houses built with coconut trees and covered with palm leaves.

"Let us show our strength right away!" yells Magellan, pointing at the small village.

Immediately, his longboat turns to the right and the other boats from the *Trinidad* follow its wake. The distance is short, only a few hundred meters, but the canoes are sluggish. This brief journey seems extremely long. Phil Caldwell grows more and more worried because he fears that the army of the king of Mactan will take advantage of the opportunity to attack them when they land.

Strangely, the King's men are not really moving about and are content to continue shouting and cursing those men who have come from the other side of the earth and presume to dictate a law they do not even want to hear about. Obviously, the conflict between the King of Cebu and Lapu-Lapu is an ancient one.

There is a flood of hatred here.

And it is not the Eden-like character of the place that will change this antagonism which has its roots in a distant past whose deadly traces always present.

King Humabon warned Magellan: "This small village, called Bulaia, is a den of brigands. We must burn everything to make ourselves understood and, above all to earn the respect of these savages who totally dependent on Lapu-Lapu."

Burn everything... Phil Caldwell is not sure that this is the best way to enter into a fruitful dialogue with the Mactan people. But Magellan seems determined to follow the advice of his new friend, who has entrusted him with a delicate mission: to settle the dispute that has pitted the enemies against one another for once and for all.

Probably intoxicated with his past successes, Magellan is determined to go to the end of a logic that carries within it the fumes of his future failures. He harangues the fifty soldiers rowing the heavy skiffs.

"Let us get to the sandy coast quickly!"

The waves are choppy, driven by the current in the strait separating the islands of Cebu and Bohol. Mactan lies like a modest piece of ocher and green confetti in this arm of the sea. The current is always strong, making it difficult to land.

Their arrival is tumultuous. But the canoes do not capsize. Seconds later, Magellan's soldiers finally set foot on the damp sand littered with shells and pieces of coral carried there by the waves and the surf.

They immediately pull the boats high enough up on the sand to ensure that they will not be carried away by the current. A man armed with a harquebus stands guard at each boat in order to ensure a safe withdrawal in case of a problem.

Magellan then divides his group into two. Fifteen soldiers armed with torches and will set fire to the first houses in the village while the others will position themselves to shoot Lapu-Lapu's warriors if they attack.

The men charged with burning Bulaia set out immediately for the village.

As soon as they are within a few meters of the first house, the flaming torch they had cautiously taken with them is used to set the others on fire. They pass the torches about, setting fire to each dwelling.

It seems that Lapu-Lapu had foreseen this eventuality because the village is deserted.

In less than three minutes, flames rise amidst dense plumes of smoke, created by the dampness of the lumber and the palm leaves, which are regularly drenched by the frequent rains that pour down on this coast located less than 800 kilometers north of the equator.

Magellan yells an order. The fifteen soldiers immediately join the rest of the troop.

Terrified, Phil Caldwell remains a little behind. Apparently, he shares his cowardice with Joaõ Serrão because no one is surprised to see the man in the tattered pants hiding behind the double row of soldiers armed with their harquebuses, axes and spears.

"What should we do?" asks one of the sailors from the *Trinidad*, staring at his chief.

Magellan's gloomy gaze hardens again. He frowns.

"We wait."

Another soldier is about to speak but the words freeze in his mouth.

An immense clamor. Followed by an attack.

The group of Filipino warriors is impressive because in addition to their curses and insults, they have a formidable asset: poisoned arrows! They are for the most part skillful archers and formidable warriors. But it is, above all, the poison with which they coat the tips of their arrows that destabilizes Magellan's men, causing them to waver. They fire at the enemy and manage to wound and kill a large number of the men in Lapu-Lapu's army. But they their shields and the thick, hard wood deflects the bullets.

Moreover, Magellan's soldiers have difficulty reloading their arms. Most of their harquebuses are old and equipped with flash pans, like muskets. The rate at which they can fire is very slow, one bullet per minute at most, and the weapon gets very hot. Magellan's men have only a dozen harquebuses with a wheellock, a system described by Leonardo da Vinci, which creates a spark.

The result is substantially more satisfactory. But firing such guns is still much slower than the regular flow of arrows that rain down on them causing nasty wounds. The combination of a very effective assault, obvious numerical superiority, and the use of poisoned arrows considerably complicates the task of Magellan and his men.

Understanding that they are about to be routed, he orders an immediate withdrawal.

Just then, the captain of the most fabulous maritime expedition of the time was struck in the chest by an arrow. He collapses. Almost immediately, a long lance cleverly thrown by one of Lapu-Lapu's warriors strikes his right thigh.

Magellan howls with pain. His eyes bulge.

Without knowing where this strange spurt of heroism and boldness comes from, Phil Caldwell seizes Magellan and tries to drag him to the nearest boat. But the captain's is a large man and Phil Caldwell is anything but an athlete.

He pulls, pants, sweats and suffers.

"Leave me," whispers Magellan.

"But…"

"Leave me. Continue my work and tell the king that…"

Magellan's eyes glaze over suddenly, and the few rounded clouds that float in the sky are reflected in the convex mirrors, now deprived of life.

Terrified, Phil Caldwell rushes towards one of the canoes. He immediately sees the bloodied corpses of six other soldiers. He runs. Keeps running.

But the boats manned by the sailors from the *Trinidad* are already heading towards the ship, its cannons thundering to cover the flight of the vanquished.

Haggard, he turns and sees the horde of Lapu-Lapu's warriors running towards, gesticulating. They all hold daggers, spears, or kampilans.

He falls into the water. His legs no longer hold him up. Suddenly, a dazzling vortex of mercurial and pearly reflections opens beneath him.

He dives into it, closing his eyes.

CHAPTER 28

Cold. Again.

Surreal sensations. Unusual. Tingling. Caresses. A lukewarm, almost sickening fluid suddenly flows into his mouth, floods his belly and his veins, popping out through his rectum like a burning fountain.

Then the stretching. And finally, the spreading. Painful. Infinitely painful. Atrocious.

A moment of calm. Darkness. Thick. Slimy.

Then a machine arrives. Monstrous. As large as a pyramid of the pharaohs of the ancient Egyptian empire and haloed with metallic reflections, it moves Each extremity is equipped with arms. Each arm ends with a scalpel, a miniature saw, pliers or a hook.

The evisceration begins.

Totally!

"Argh!" he yells.

Phil Caldwell 1 remains there for a long time. Nose to the ground.

Then he finally decides to get up. On his elbows first. He looks in front of him. Everything is white. He pats his eyes; they are as hard as carefully cut diamonds.

The fog and luminous haloes that hampered the astrophysicist's vision finally dissipate. A woman is standing in front of him. Her skin, filaments, tentacles and face are white, almost pearly. Her breasts are radiant, her face angelic and her smile endearing.

He avoids looking at the pubic triangle that is located level with his head and seems oddly benevolent. Embarrassed, he finally stands up, his legs still trembling a little after such an experience. A majestic tiger observes him. It is albino too.

Just above the feline with long tousled mustaches, a strange creature gently floats. A bizarre head with two large stalk-like eyes and two outgrowths shaped like a shrimp. Scales and two long filaments shaped like whips complete this Luciferian silhouette, which seems to have been born from the feverish imagination of a painter.

Phil Caldwell scans his three friends. Then he smiles at them.

"I was very scared," he says.

Then he grows mute.

He then takes up an old reflex and writes what he meant to say before his vocal chords failed him on his forearm.

"You scared us too!" grumbles the tiger, once again using his deep, thundering.

"Where were you?" asks Phil Caldwell 3 as she writes on the pale skin of her left forearm as if a pack of devils were on her heels.

The young woman scribbles her letters with a haste that is in total contrast to the cold, monochromatic serenity of this truncated cone, the dimensions of which increased even more during the tropical escapade of Phil Caldwell 1.

"In the Philippines."

"In the Philippines!" says the anomalocaris with its inimitable falsetto voice, laughing.

"Yes. I was with Fernand Magellan at the moment of his death."

"Magellan!" the young woman repeats, comically raising her eyebrows.

"Yes. I don't know why I found myself there. Moreover, the colors were brilliant under the tropical sun and I could speak without having to communicate by writing on my arm."

The quartet remains mute for a moment.

The astrophysicist takes the opportunity to glance around this terrace whose wall is again white, smooth, soft and warm.

"Was the night long?" he asks, staring at his three companions in turn.

As usual, it is the creature from the shadows of the Cambrian era that responds with its natural propensity to chatter.

"It lasted quite a long time indeed. You also emerged from the cliff..."

"Expelled would be more like it," interrupted the tiger thinking of the inelegant trajectory of their friend when the wall vomited him up, much like a fish bone caught in one's throat.

"Expelled if you like," says the anomalocaris, projecting its shrimp-like outgrowths in all directions at once. "So, you were expelled from the wall only moments after the night had faded, replaced by that dazzling light that radiates simultaneously from the well, the cliff and the sky."

The creature stops for a moment, then continues its inexhaustible babbling: "So, you found yourself with Magellan on his trip around the world?"

"Yes. In April 1521."

"What was he like?" asked Phil Caldwell 3, quivering at the thought of discovering an explorer she had always secretly admired.

These partial memories indicate that the various Phil Caldwells all remember certain bits of memories, but they remain scattered and they can only increase their mutual knowledge through incessant dialogue.

The astrophysicist begins to tell about waking up on board the *Trinidad* and his discovery of the crew as they arrived near the coast of Mactan Island. As he can only scribble on his left forearm, this takes quite a long time.

Just before describing the attack of Lapu-Lapu's troops armed with bows, poisoned arrows, spears and kampilans, he freezes suddenly.

Phil Caldwell 1 looks at the tiger and asks, "But where are the others?"

Curiously, and probably still somewhat affected by this astonishing journey into a past that does not really belong to him, he had not immediately noticed that his three friends were alone on the terrace overlooking the abyss.

He looks around and realizes that the narrow area on which he is standing is empty. In the distance, much higher, he sees a few white silhouettes.

The feline looks at his friend with his large faceted eyes and answers, "They left."

"But…"

"They decided to continue climbing because some thought you wouldn't come back."

"Or would take a few million centuries!" says the unrepentant chatterer whipping the air with his tail.

"That's it, that's it," says the tiger, growling. "In fact, most of our companions decided to continue on their way when the crowd swept over us."

"The crowd?" asks the astrophysicist, astonished.

"The term is a bit exaggerated," the young woman writes. "But we were suddenly overtaken by 80 or 100 Phil Caldwells who all looked very much like you."

"They were males," adds the tiger. "They seemed in a hurry. They came in talking a little. Then, when they were silent again, one of them simply scrawled on his arm: we will continue on our way because the bubbles are waiting for us."

On hearing this, Phil Caldwell 1 raises his head to the *outre-blanc* sky where billions of translucent spheres jostle. Like gigantic soap bubbles!

"Yes," continues the tiger, placing his large forelegs very close to Phil Caldwell 1 "I don't know if they hope to reach the spheres that clutter the sky quickly, but I have the impression that they did not understand the scope of the task to be accomplished."

"They're crazy! They're crazy!" repeats the anomalocaris, initiating a bizarre dance that makes its swim lobes vibrate.

In this posture, it looks like a large carpet with crumpled edges, stirring in the wind. But a carpet with a tail with two whip-like filaments.

The Cambrian-era animal continues, "Climbing this immense cliff with its millions of terraces is not at all a speed race."

"You're right," the tiger admits. "There will be no rewards to the winner."

"This immense journey is no race at all," says the young woman, who consciously or not, always positions her generous, bouncing bosom in the astrophysicist's. "It is, I believe, a quest of initiation."

Whenever she writes a text of more than one line, she must, like all the silenced Caldwell humans, make two attempts to finish her sentence. This is a bit annoying, but there are no other solutions.

Phil Caldwell 3 accepts this, though she sometimes grumbles. Silently of course.

"That's right," conceded the man with the pale. An initiation. And each time one is immersed within this wall from which a giant bubble of giant mercury suddenly emerges corresponds no doubt to a stage. There will likely be many!"

"If that's the case," says the feline, "It's time for you to finish your story and tell us what happened when Magellan, his soldiers and you were attacked!"

The astrophysicist from Stanford University returns gracefully to his narration. As he must write, then erase, and then write again, he disciplines his imagination in order to describe the essentials without losing himself in the details.

But even in doing so, this simple account of the attack that was decisive and put an end to Magellan's odyssey takes a long time.[21]

When the description of Magellan's and Phil Caldwell's flight in the vortex adorned with luminous mother-of-pearl finally ends, the tiger looks at the motionless traveler and simply says, "What an adventure!"

"What does it mean?" asks the young woman.

"It's a first milestone."

The trio turns towards the anomalocaris with the ridiculous voice.

"Can you... be more specific?" asks the tiger, raising its eyebrows.

"Our friend must undoubtedly go through different phases of a life that is simultaneously in him and outside him."

"That's nonsense!"

"No," replies Phil Caldwell 1, writing very quickly because his emotions suddenly overwhelm him. "It is possible that this process is repeated. Who knows what really lies in our hearts?"

"We do!" replies the young woman, thinking that her answer is absolutely logical.

"Not at all!" retorts the astrophysicist whose eyes shine brighter and brighter. "We know only the periphery of ourselves."

"So," retorts the feline, "no one really knows who he is deep down. This immense cliff with its millions of terraces symbolizes a slow journey towards this unknown reality that lies within each sensitive creature?"

"Yes. I think so. Really!"

"This means," the anomalocaris intervenes, "That this immersion at the time of Magellan's death was only the first of a long series."

"A very long series, no doubt," writes Phil Caldwell 1 sighing.

The young woman looks at him, a little incredulous.

---

[21] After Magellan's death, only the *Victoria* returned to Sanlúcar de Barrameda on September 6, 1522, almost three years after the departure of Magellan's fleet. The captain of the *Victoria* was Juan Sebastián Elcano. Only 18 crew members were still on board. The *Victoria* was the first ship to complete the circumnavigation of the globe.

Then she asks, "But then what is the role of that sudden night that arrived after such a long stroll in the midst of an eternal, white and luminous day?"

The man remains silent.

Once again, the exuberant anomalocaris intervenes under the angry gaze of the tiger.

"Each nocturnal episode no doubt brings about a pause. A breath. This radiant night makes strange worlds emerge, along with reminiscences of a global past that our friend must appropriate in order to finally know, one day, who he really is!"

The companions of the strange creature born more than half a billion years ago in the oceans of the Cambrian era are amazed.

"You're perfectly right," writes the astrophysicist.

Then, on impulse, he takes the long creature covered with shining carapaces, scales and white lateral fins in his arms. The scene is confusing. But the other two Phil Caldwells are moved. A few sparkling tears quickly bead along their lower eyelids.

The tiger sneezes, blows his nose noisily and says, "When you've finished hugging, maybe we could get back to climbing?"

The two humans smile because they know that the tiger has a grumpy heart of gold. Even if his impressive white silhouette, armed with powerful teeth and sharp claws, contradicts this new-found generosity.

The anomalocaris finally extricates himself from the arms of Phil Caldwell 1 and snorts.

Then, the quartet begins to climb the countless terraces that loom overhead.

The environment has changed a bit. The overall architecture is the same, of course. However, the central opening has widened further. The opposite edge is less and less visible. Since the structure is a titanic funnel, it is still possible to see the part of the cliff which located in front and along the sides because it rises so high that it is almost like the surface of a giant planet seen from a satellite orbiting too near its protective star.

The only difference, an important one, the satellite is white, the giant planet is white and the sky is *outre-blanc*.

Phil Caldwell 1 raises his head and looks above himself. For a moment, he watches incessant reel of the giant spheres that bob above abyss.

He seems lost in his thoughts. The tiger asks him, "Are we going?"

"Yes," he whispers, forgetting for a moment that speech is pointless.

He writes "Yes" on his arm.

Then he turns towards the two long luminous braids that extend from the bottom of the well, following the elegant helical curve of DNA. Although they are still at the center of a circle that now exceeds one hundred kilometers in diameter, they are still clearly visible.

"The central structures grew larger during my brief journey alongside Magellan?" he asks his three companions.

"Yes," the anomalocaris hastens to reply, waving its stalk-like eyes in all directions. "We always have the impression that the luminous strands have the same diameter while they are much further away from us. Thus, their thickness always increases at the same rate!"

Apparently satisfied with its analysis, the disheveled creature begins one of the ridiculous dances known only to it.

The astrophysicist observes the creature for a moment. Then he writes, "I also have the impression that the luminous pulses that rise from the bottom of the abyss are faster and faster. Am I wrong?"

"No," rumbles the tiger knowingly using the deepest tones its throat can emit. "The pace is accelerating. One can even say it is racing."

"Do you have an explanation for that?"

"None."

The feeling of impotence question and validated, the time has come to resume climbing.

The feline takes charge and starts to climb quietly along the slightly steep path that will allow them to reach the terrace located just above.

Apart from the snorting of the tiger and the incongruous noises that the anomalocaris emits with its strange mouth that looks like a slice of pineapple with several layers of sharp teeth in the middle, silence reigns. The monochromatic material that makes up the wall of the truncated cone and the millions of strata is still soft and warm. But the quartet moves forward without difficulty because the young woman and the scientist from Stanford walk on feet equipped with a precious mattress of filaments that give them irreproachable stability and grip.

As for the extravagant creature from the depths of time, it flies over them with an unfeigned delight.

"I see a group a little higher up," it cries, whipping its tail.

"It's some of our former companions," says the tiger. "I see Phil Caldwell 8, the two men with such dissimilar silhouettes, two women and the stegosaurus."

"Well," scribbles Phil Caldwell 1. "Let's join them!"

The young woman mechanically wipes the sweat from her forehead. Then she nods.

The group then begins a long climb to join the other group walking ten terraces above them.

The tiger roars with unheard-of strength to catch the attention of their friends. Upon hearing this terrifying roar, they immediately stop and look down. Noting the return of the quartet, Phil Caldwell 8 immediately signals that they have seen them and will wait for them.

The climb resumes. It will take more than three hours.

CHAPTER 29

"Nice to see you again!" says the stegosaurus, in his deep voice, sounding like a bear with a cold.

"Likewise!" writes Phil Caldwell 1 approaching his old companions, who had sat down to wait for them.

"You shook us... but we still caught up with you!" says the tiger who takes time to catch its breath since it had travelled the last few meters at high speed.

"Where did you go?" asks the stegosaurus in order to satisfy its personal curiosity and that of all the Phil Caldwells present.

The astrophysicist indicates that the tiger should describe his journey in words, which will be infinitely faster than writing.

The feline does so, with frequent interruptions from the resident gossip which slides its sharp voice into the discussion with the regularity of metronome.

Once the account of Phil Caldwell's brief participation in the Magellan expedition has been completed, a short discussion begins. But, once again, the constraints of systematically writing, then erasing and starting again, alters the natural exuberance of some of the humans. So, the stegosaurus speaks and translates, more or less reluctantly, the questions asked by its companions.

When the barrage of questions has is finally subsided, the ten argonauts in a universe without beginning or end continue their climb.

As always, the tiger leads and the anomalocaris, who believes it is useful to chatter without stopping for a second, flies overhead. Phil Caldwell 8 immediately follows to prove, no doubt, that he is an athlete and that he can follow a formidable feline without running out of steam. Just behind, the astrophysicist and the young woman with the full bosom follow accompanied by the other two women and the tall, lean man who says little.

The stegosaurus and the little Phil Caldwell, which resembles a tobacco pot, bring up the rear.

After a discussion between Phil Caldwell 1, the colossus and the tiger, they decide to stop at every third terrace to give stragglers time to catch up with them.

As the creature with the falsetto voice frequently says, "This is a marathon, not a sprint!"

Each Phil Caldwell knows perfectly well that arriving at the peak of this gigantic funnel, like something out of Dante's Inferno, remains a distant objective. It is nothing like traveling the 42 kilometers of a marathon. The distance is immeasurably larger. Several thousand kilometers in any case. Maybe millions.

While climbing, they observe their environment regularly.

They quickly realize that the pack of "hasty Phil Caldwells" is now much higher. Moreover, this strangely rushed group quickly turned right. Phil Caldwell 1 and his companions are climbing almost vertically, taking care to take trails that connect to the upper terrace, turning this way and that. This allows them to maintain a strictly vertical climb.

In contrast to this approach, the others have systematically taken the steep paths as they appear. They are now out of step with the small group accompanying the astrophysicist.

The tiger then asks his companions, "Do we do as they are doing or continue as close as possible to the vertical?"

"We continue!" replies Phil Caldwell, and the other eight approve.

Once this matter has been settled, they continue to climb.

From time to time, one of them examines the sky trying to determine when a new night will temporarily darken this *outre-blanc* abyss that radiates from within. But the light is constant.

More and more, this progression resembles a procession whose initiatory character dissolves in the constantly expanding mother-of-pearl abyss undermining certainties with a mad energy.

So, they climb. Again.

They stop at regular intervals. Then start climbing again. All the Phil Caldwells have grown accustomed to this comfortable, yet maddening situation, which exonerates the body from all material constraints. Sometimes jubilant. Sometimes scary. However, Phil Caldwell 1 and the young woman who accompanies him readily acknowledge that jubilation is far more prevalent.

After a very long series of periods of climbing, followed by breaks, they finally stop near one of the smooth walls marked by an arch hanging over it. Like all these structures that fit into the cliff, this giant niche is about thirty meters long and ten meters high.

Night falls. Immediately. Without warning. Without twilight. Frozen, the members of the small group look at one another. Once again, just by chance, the astrophysicist is next to the wall. Phil Caldwell 3 is less than a meter away. Without realizing it, the young woman begins to shiver although the ambient temperature is still uniformly 30°.

By reflex, the eight others shift a little, moving close to the tiny parapet that separates them from the abyss.

In the center of the wall, forming a horizontally elongated semi-circle, a sphere of mercury appears again. It grows larger. Quickly. Very quickly.

Hypnotized by the light that slices through the darkness, Phil Caldwell 1 mechanically places his right arm on the left shoulder of the young woman standing next to him.

The bubble adorned with mercurial reflections expands. Stretches.

Then it explodes drawing the man and woman into an immensely powerful surf.

Cold. Still.

Banks of frost and broken icebergs. Splashes of petrified lights clashing against a symphony enclosed for centuries in a deep cave. A cavern wrapped in seaweed and gold.

Then the fall.

Immense. Terrifying.

Muscles numb and tongues pasty, Phil Caldwell and his companion find themselves lying flat on their stomachs. The grass is sweet. Green and indigo blue, it looks nothing they know.

The landscape is unknown as well. The sky is orange and immense mountains circle a parade filled with the chirping of a stream chiseled from changing reflections that explore all the color palettes before immediately destroying them. Then takes them back. Again, and again. The autodafé of the colors is permanent, but the rebirth is immediate. Fruitful.

The man and the woman look up. They see each other at last. They're naked.

In front of them stands a large dark rock, its rough surface littered with small clumps of scarlet plants. Phil Caldwell 3 is very surprised because this symphony of colors unsettles her after such a long spent in a universe exclusively devoted to the *outre-blanc* and its infinite nuances in the abyss.

She straightens up and says, "Where are we?"

"I have no idea."

The young woman is about to write a new sentence on her arm, but the astrophysicist reassures her, saying "Here you can talk as long as you want"

She seems delighted and then opens her mouth, "We could…"

But she falls silent at once, for she hears a strange sound coming from behind the big rock, which conceals a part of the narrow valley below.

"Did you hear that?" asks the scientist with the curly, red hair.

"Yes. It sounds like moaning".

Without consulting one another, they start to walk around this large rocky block covered with hundreds of bouquets of exuberant plants. A few seconds later, they finally discover the landscape that plunges towards the valley through which a river splashed with light winds. A small, lush forest is surrounded by tall grass that bends obediently under the caress of a light wind. The grasses constantly bend and stand back up, in keeping with a rhythm imposed by a capricious divinity.

The groans the pair had heard seem to come from a precise point at the edge of the forest, where the grasses are the highest, the most abundant. The most welcoming as well.

"Those are not cries of pain," says the red-haired man, casting an appreciate glance at the young woman who was swallowed up with him in this serene, colorful world.

"No. That's for sure. Sounds more like groans of pleasure."

Driven by curiosity, they approach, making sure to make as little noise as possible.

When they reach a point a couple of meters from the couple, they understand that their discretion has been useless since the man and the woman who embrace one another are focused on their mutual pleasure and the sound of rustling grass will not attract their attention.

The scientist is fascinated by both what he sees and the fact that he is observing this couple without the slightest. He does not really have the temperament of a voyeur. But in this Edenic place located near the gardens of Arcadia, observing a woman and a man making love is no longer voyeurism. It's... The problem is that both Phil Caldwells do not know how to define what drives them to look at this instant of intimacy without any sense of immodesty. Without reservation. Without shame.

The man turns over and settles on his back. The two sets of prying eyes immediately notice the size of his erection. But they do not have time to perform a precise anatomical analysis because the woman settles on her lover and caresses male's penis as his eyes fill with pleasure. Then she impales herself on the erect limb, initiating the regular swell of a movement of the pelvis which will generate, in a few times, the gradual rise of a volcanic orgasm.

She begins to groan. Her skin is sweaty and her nipples harden. She shouts once. Twice.

The astrophysicist then moves his mouth closer to that of Phil Caldwell 3. She stops him.

"It's not possible."

"Why not?" asks the red-haired man, astonished, as he too beings to sweat.

"It would be almost incest!"

The woman screams a third time. In pleasure.

Phil Caldwell 1 is about to reply to the young woman with whom he has been climbing the millions of terraces of the abyss for a long time when a great cry rings out from the plain below. This cry is no moan of pleasure or the chirping of a torrid orgasm.

This howl is a cry of hate. The cry of the hallali!

Bewildered, the two lost in the infinite, monochromatic universe suddenly see a small band of about ten men. They are naked too. And armed with axes and long spears with metal tips.

The woman screaming in enjoyment turns around. Powerless. As she is still closely united with her lover and the powerful shaft that penetrates her belly, she cannot flee just then. And since her lover is still lying on his back, he cannot run away from this shrieking, furious horde either.

The spectacle is brief. But horrible. The couple begs for an unlikely pity, an impossible forgiveness. An insult in an unknown language rings out like a shot.

One word stands out in this guttural litany: Lyrixianna! It is perhaps the name of the unfaithful wife surprised by her husband and some men of the family or the village. It is impossible to learn more. But the sentence is immediate. A very muscular man with a bull-like neck and long black hair stands in front of the two lovers, their bodies still entwined. His scarlet face expresses the intensity of his rage.

He raises his long javelin.

One more word. Only one.

Then he throws his powerful weapon at the couple of star-crossed lovers, piercing the two lovebirds through and through.

Phil Caldwell 3 is terrified as she hears the sound of the ribs shattering as if she were standing next to the two unfortunate victims from whose mouths some sinister pinkish liquid flows. Moments later, blood flows abundantly from wounds that torn in their backs and chests.

Nailed to the ground like insects pierced by the needles of an entomologist, they continue to try to speak. But it's impossible. One last rattle and their eyes grow glassy.

Both Phil Caldwells are petrified with fear. Petrified with horror too. They hold hands, unable to look away from the atrocious scene that unfolds near them.

The man with the long, jet black hair bursts into a thundering laugh. He stops and takes the big ax that one of his acolytes has been holding firmly until now. Taking the weapon with both hands, he raises it high. The gleaming blade is immediately adorned with the strange apricot and apple green reflections that dominate the atmosphere of this world confined to the very edge of the customary madness of men.

Then he throws the heavy ax at his rival's chest.

His torso explodes under the blow and blood gushes out in powerful waves that form an abject orb before flooding over the skin of the unfortunate victim and the surrounding grass. The executioner rises, repeats his gesture, shattering the chest of his adulterous wife this time.

First, he places his fingers on the two bodies and collects some blood which he carries to his mouth with a delight in which obscenity rivals the barbaric.

Suddenly, his eyes come alive with mad reflections. He immediately plunges his right hand into the man's gaping wound. He grumbles for a moment, screams and finally shouts in victory. Straightening up like a wild beast, he lifts his rival's heart, which he has just plucked from the rib cage, high above his head.

Scared, Phil Caldwell 3 is racked with spasms. Then she vomits on her knees a lukewarm liquid that reminds her that she is still a human being.

As the monster holding the victim's heart starts to lift it to his mouth, intending to bite into it as the ultimate defilement, the hiccups, sobs and spasms of Phil Caldwell 3 attract the attention of one of the colleagues of the character intending to feed on the still warm remains of his enemy.

He screams, pointing to the little grove of grass where the two wanderers have hidden themselves.

Terrified, the astrophysicist pulls the girl's arm and says, "Let's go!"

They immediately start running away from the site of the tragedy.

"Will they kill us?" asks the young woman whose long blonde hair is flying over her shoulders.

"Without a doubt. Let's run!"

Both Phil Caldwells accelerate.

But the cries and the curses that ring out behind them fill their hearts with terror.

They run in a zigzag fashion to avoid the spears that start raining down in their direction. Since both the pack of pursuers and the two preys are moving, the shots are inaccurate. The companions of the hunter drunk on vengeance even pitch a few axes in their direction. But these weapons are heavy and ill-suited for throwing over long distances. As their attempts are unsuccessful, they prefer the spears.

The whistles are getting closer and closer.

Suddenly, the young blonde woman falls. The scientist stops. He pulls her up unceremoniously and they resume their disheveled flight. They head towards a slight hollow, almost circular, cut in the hillside. The screams are coming closer and the light wind brings carries a strong odor of sweat to the fugitives, indicating that their pursuers are now on their heels. Both Phil Caldwells are out of breath. Their muscles are knotted.

Suddenly, a white, silvery pond suddenly shimmers in front of them. Five seconds earlier it was invisible. But now it is there. Clear to see.

Their salvation?

"Dive!" yells the red-haired man, pulling his friend by the arm.

They are injured in this pool, the consistency of which is close to a molten white metal or to a swamp dotted with droplets of mercury.

They are consumed there. And die.

CHAPTER 30

"You frightened us," says the creature from the Cambrian period, with its helium voice.

Phil Caldwell 1 and 3 find themselves slumped on the ground. By reflex, they look behind them, frightened as if they still had all the demons of Hell on their heels.

"Calm down!" roars the tiger, baring its teeth. "There is no risk."

"But what did you see?" insists the anomalocaris, as curious as a magpie.

"An unspeakable atrocity," replies the young woman, who knows she will soon have to replace speech with writing.

"So?" insists the big cat.

"A double murder and inhuman barbarity," summarizes Phil Caldwell 1.

"All too human, on the contrary!" insists his companion in the odyssey, transcribing her thought on her forearm with nervous tremors that make the filaments of her hand vibrate.

The astrophysicist realizes just then that they are surrounded by a crowd of Phil Caldwells. There are at least thirty men, seven or eight women, the stegosaurus, as well as a giant snail, a groundhog, a porcupine, several insects, and big cats and reptiles, all of measure between one and two meters long.

"Where has this crowd come from?" asks the worried Stanford scientist, widening his faceted eyes that sparkle like diamonds.

"They joined us during the night," said the twirling twirling, whipping its tail.

"There are more and more Phil Caldwells here," adds the tiger. "They have all climbed up from the lower terraces. But..."

"But what?" asks the astrophysicist who knows well that the feline appreciates those moments of silence that create a sense of expectation in its listeners.

"Apparently they have recently been extracted from the part of the cliff where we are. If this phenomenon is widespread, and if it is similar all around the well which is constantly expanding in diameter, there will soon be millions of us!"

Phil Caldwell 1 and the young woman who was immersed with him in the abominable world where murder is the only law seem to be frozen on the spot. They are no longer moving. Only a few filaments and tentacles on their heads move.

"But this is not a problem," continues the anomalocaris while fiddling as if it has been bitten by a scorpion. "This crowd and, above all, the energy that drives it, will push us to climb this titanic cliff in order to finally find the answers to our questions."

"If there is an answer," the wild beast grumbles, revealing, once again, the almost painful shine of its teeth that glitter like gems on the threshold of an explosion.

"So?" says the creature from Cambrian, impatiently. "Are you going to tell us about your journey or not!"

Phil Caldwell 1 does so, summarizing as much as possible to make it easier to read the modest text that he writes on his arm with his filaments.

He carefully refrains from mentioning the kiss that could have united him with the young blond woman who avoided the situation at the last moment raising the issue of possible incest. He also eliminated two or three particularly atrocious details such as when the executioner assaulted the bodies of the two victims. But he did describe the atrocious wound, and the impious gestures that followed: the tearing out of the heart and the cannibalism.

As the sentences move, the faces of humans and the animals are frozen, in horror or indignation.

"How awful!" simply says the tiger.

The tiger is silent, looking at his companions and then back again at Phil Caldwell 1.

"What creature could indulge in such martyrdom and humiliation?"

"Man," replies Phil Caldwell 8 sneaking his athletic figure into the crowd of beings who had appeared during the night, pulling themselves out of the warm, pearly matrix of the giant cliff.

"You're right," says the astrophysicist. "This abject singularity is perhaps at the origin of this painful ordeal which is reserved for me."

"You mean," says the stegosaurus, beating its tail with its long, sharp darts, "That you are the only Phil Caldwell who can sink into the universes concealed within the mercury bubbles that burst on the surface when the fake night falls?"

"Fake?" the colossus asks, astonished.

"Yes," replies the dinosaur, whose back is studded with bony plates. "There is no sun here. The brightness comes from the wall, from the firmament. From US! So, this night is artificial."

"But I was also absorbed in this maelstrom when the sphere with the silvery reflections exploded on the surface of the wall!" says the young woman who was with the astrophysicist in the valley where the massacre took place.

"Maybe because you were right next to me at the precise moment when it brushed against our world."

Silence falls for a moment. The ubiquitous and discreet *music of the spheres* that wove its intricate plots resumes.

The first Phil Caldwells who awoke vertically from the abyss have become accustomed to this background music. They do not pay much attention to it. However, newcomers are always very attentive to these hypnotic sounds that keep rhythm with a pulsation coming from a different world. A universe where light and music mingle and tangle in one and the same embrace. A world where executioners do not exist.

A world of illusion no doubt.

"I don't know if these terrifying falls in spaces that are so different are and will remain my exclusive privilege," says Phil Caldwell. "But I would willingly relinquish my place to others!"

"We understand you," concludes the tiger. "But, while waiting for the next night and its exuberances, which often take the appearance of nightmares, we must our climb to the top this cliff that defies the sky. We still have several million levels to cross through."

Adding movement to its rumblings, the tiger immediately begins to climb towards a new terrace just above them. The anomalocaris hovers close overhead. And it starts talking again in its shrill voice.

Without ever stopping!

Since the crowd of Phil Caldwells is dense and silent, apart from some animal versions of the astrophysicist who roar, whistle or screech, organizing the climb is rather complex. Since the narrowness of the terraces barely changes despite the considerable widening of the well, the opposite edge of which is visible only because of the incredible height of the wall that hangs over the abyss, climbing here becomes difficult for nearly one hundred individuals. And dangerous.

With its keen sense of organization and the proven power of its claws that immediately calms all potential recriminations, the tiger takes control of operations. It organizes the horde of Phil Caldwells in single file. It suggests that the stegosaurus and the athletic Phil Caldwell 8 stay at the back so as to intervene immediately if there is a risk that anyone will fall.

The procession is burlesque. Extravagant even. Gathered up in the same effort and in the same quest, humans and animals try to rise above the limits of what is said. They direct their steps and their eyes towards a place without frontiers, without limits. A vast and crazy horizon where billions of translucent spheres, each the size of a planet, bob and clash.

This universe is fascinating, baroque.

Inexplicable.

Under a light that sublimates all the colors of the rainbow into an *outre-blanc* shine that focuses the eye and symbolizes a majestic river of light rising upright from the sky, this hymn to verticality upsets, crushes and metamorphoses the meaning of life.

It connects the exterior and interior.

It reconciles all the disparate demands that animate the human mind so that a crazy hope finally settles in response to the question that everyone asks himself at least once when observing the inanity of his own life: WHY?

But this answer is far away. A few million white, pearly layers separate the Phil Caldwells from this moment when everything may be cleared up. But there seems to be no end to the climb with its highly initiatory character.

The astrophysicist walks over to the tiger and its chatty companion. He simply asks, "Does this make sense?"

The feline and anomalocaris look at one another.

Then the archaic creature darts the 16,000 facets of its stalk-like eyes in the direction of its friend and says, just as simply, "We don't know. But, it's definitely worth a try."

Phil Caldwell 1 shares this feeling. He just makes a small sign to his two friends, which are so different, but whose presence he so thoroughly enjoys at his side.

A few hours later, the problem of climbing in such a large crowd gathered in the same place gradually fades because some of the newcomers, the majority in fact, rapidly scatter in several different directions. Instead of respecting the alternation of the access ramps to the terraces, going once to the left, then once to the right, they renounce absolute verticality, following various paths as they see fit.

Most Phil Caldwells fan out, scattering all along the wall and breaking up into several small groups.

The tiger and the astrophysicist are disappointed at first.

Then, the anomalocaris sums up the situation perfectly, saying "Each one chooses his way in life."

It is difficult to contradict this analysis mingled with common sense.

A few minutes later, the young woman whom the scientist had almost kissed in the paradisiacal valley, which was transformed into a bloody tragedy, stops suddenly. Frozen, she blocks the way of her six other companions who remained with Phil Caldwell 1, the tiger and the eternal chatterer.

Stopped, the stegosaurus begins to grumble.

"Why are we stopping?"

All of a sudden, Phil Caldwell 3 climbs up the path to join the astrophysicist walking about a dozen meters away. She places her filaments on his shoulder in order to attract his attention. He turns.

She is worried. Her eyes are bulging.

"What is going on"?" he writes.

"Faces!"

"What?" roars the tiger.

"Faces in the abyss. Lots of faces!"

"There are apparently faces that have just appeared in the abyss!" translates the big white cat so that the rest of the troop understands what is going on.

They all head towards the edge, taking care not to fall.

The young woman with the full breasts and the radiant smile is right. The two long oscillating sculptures that rise from the abyss and towards the sky resembling the strange and delicate helical appearance of DNA that contains all the information necessary for the development and functioning of each living organism. But these strands, which pulsated in corteges of dazzling lights, are now the seat of a very strange procession.

As Phil Caldwell 3 just defined it, these are faces. Thousands of faces.

Soon to be millions.

"Looks like human faces," the tiger begins, continuing to widen its eyes. "But faces quite different from yours."

"Their traits are indeed simian," concludes the astrophysicist who remains standing there, his arms dangling and his mouth wide open.

The spectacle is almost magical.

The women and men whose heads rise from the abyss of this well, which is apparently the matrix of a new world, parade at a frantic pace. Now, time gives the fascinating impression that it is two-fold. The set of physiognomies rises very quickly, but the moment potentially devoted to the observation of each face seems much longer. This temporal distortion implies that the carousel of the beings exhumed from the mists of an archaic past is fast, almost unbridled. But, at the same time, the various Phil Caldwells standing at the edge of the immense central gap can observe these distant ancestors one by one.

Even more strange, these faces, which pass through these two luminous elevators, that grow incessantly, intertwine and extend over millions of floors, express only one emotion as they rise towards the sky. This expression fixed for eternity symbolizes perhaps the most ardent shudder, the cruelest also, which has embraced them at the zenith of their brief existence?

But these faces almost all express suffering. Some still seem calm, even devastated by a distressful and beneficent enjoyment at the same time. But, generally speaking, inextinguishable fright prevails.

Anguish, terror, suffering and hatred prevail.

"Is the world only fury and pain?" thinks the Stanford scientist, not knowing whether this is true for him and for all the Phil Caldwells who accompany him.

"It's wonderful!" says the anomalocaris, his castrato voice even higher.

"It's especially tragic," says the young woman who accompanies the astrophysicist.

"Why?" insists the twirling creature.

"The vast majority of these human beings eternalize a terror or anguish that seems to have been the hallmark of humanity for seven million years," replies the white big cat, opening its predatory mouth thirsty for light.

Within the small group of ten Phil Caldwells who remain there, petrified by this aesthetically beautiful and humanly distressing spectacle, no one is really surprised that a white tiger can synthesize like this.

Normal... they're all Phil Caldwell!

Since it is difficult to contest the tiger's analysis, its companions remain silent. They observe, fascinated. Others count. Or try to count because they realize very quickly that that mission is impossible. The parade of lives is immense. Colossal.

"Humanity," writes Phil Caldwell, 1 showing his arm to the tiger and the stegosaurus, so that they translate into words what he scribbles with unbearable slowness.

He grows annoyed, erases what he has just scribbled and starts over. Struggling.

"It is simply the caravan of all the human beings born on Earth from Toumaï[22], more than seven million years ago."

"How many individuals?" asks the tiger stressing the word *individuals*.

"Probably more than 200 billion," replies Phil Caldwell 1 without taking his eyes from the hallucinating luminous and vertical saraband.

His attention focuses quickly on a woman. She lived at the end of the Pliocene or at the beginning of the Pleistocene because her head is still small, her cheeks are hairy and her distracted eyes are embedded in deep sockets under voluminous supraorbital ridges.

But it is especially the intensity of this frightened, fragile look that moves him. Without being overly imaginative, he discerns a web of bereavements, tragedies.

Perhaps the loss of a child?

The scientist shudders and takes the hand of Phil Caldwell 3. Their filaments entangle. The young woman does not shy away.

They stay that way. For a long time. A long time.

The procession of the temporarily resurrected humans, rising towards a sky cluttered with innumerable translucent spheres, continues.

Observing that the seven humans who accompany them seem hypnotized by this crazy spectacle, the tiger, the stegosaurus and the creature from the Cambrian period begin to move. They talk to one another in low voices. They quickly reach a conclusion.

"Are you planning to count 200 billion human beings one by one? Or are we going back to climbing?" asks the feline frankly, making sure that the deepness of his voice finally stirs up the neurons of his bipedal companions.

Phil Caldwell 8 is the first to answer, "We can resume climbing."

Phil Caldwell 1 the young woman whose hand he has just released, and the two men of differing sizes who have not parted since their arrival here, all nod.

---

[22] Discovered in Chad, Toumaï (Sahelanthropus tchadensis) is generally considered to be our most distant ancestor. He lived in the Miocene, about 7 million years ago.

"So, let's go!" concludes the tiger and the group once again sets out on their usual long, zigzag walk in order to respect a strictly vertical slope of the cliff.

As always, the feline and talkative anomalocaris take the lead. The stegosaurus brings up the rear. It climbs, panting a little, because the big white tiger has accelerated its pace after this very long stop.

The astrophysicist approaches, walking a little faster. He wipes his forehead, which is once again covered with a few drops of sweat.

Then he stands himself in front of his friend with the long teeth and writes, "Why?"

"Why what?" growls the tiger.

At the same moment, the anomalocaris floats gently down towards Phil Caldwell 1.

Its appendages, shaped like shrimp tails, touch the scientist's forearm. Its large faceted eyes stare at the man as if it wants to engulf the thoughts of his friend by this artifice alone.

The astrophysicist writes a message for the beast:

"What is the meaning of these multitudes of humans rising from the darkness of prehistory?"

"A resurrection? A redemption? A new army?"

"It's ridiculous!" the creature then utters in its falsetto voice. "The answer is not outside!"

"It comes from the depths of the abyss!" roars the tiger, obviously unhappy about the interruption of the impenitent chatterer. "I know. We are not blind!"

"I believe that these beings, on the contrary, come from deep within us," insists Phil Caldwell 1 taking care to write each word distinctly.

"So, they would be a part of ourselves?" asks the young woman moving very close to the man she accompanied during the frightful massacre of the star-crossed lovers.

"Not exactly. I think…"

"That this horde of humans having lived on Earth is part of a global process whose final meaning we will understand only when we reach the top of this cliff!" concludes the tiger, interrupting the astrophysicist in the process of writing.

"You're right!" says the twirling creature enthusiastically, spinning on itself like a 13th-century whirling dervish.

"Indeed," acknowledges Phil Caldwell 1 who readily agrees with his two companions. "The key to this mystery is at the top of the cliff. But I'm also convinced now, that it is also in us."

"Then hurry!" concludes the anomalocaris, heading in the direction of the small group advancing in single file along the slightly sloping paths that connect the various terraces.

As the diameter of the abyss has increased, the true structure of this cosmic funnel shaped like an inverted truncated cone is better understood.

It is enough to stop for a moment and observe the opposite side. The slope is still steep – about 75° – but the careful arrangement of the countless white terraces, that extend up to stratospheric heights, immediately evokes a mythical monument symbolizing human arrogance and its lack of discernment: the Tower of Babel.

The impossibility of reaching the heavens and the disorder associated with the brutal multiplication of different languages reminds us cruelly that human beings have hardly ever managed to live truly together throughout their long history.

Here, the process is reversed. This cliff brushes against the sky and its billions of shimmering spheres that bob lazily in an incomprehensible, majestic ballet. Moreover, the confusion, incomprehension and hatred that arose out of the difficulty of not speaking the same language are outdated here. Everyone is using the same language and the animals have a crucial advantage over humans: they can talk all the time.

Conversely, since man has superabundantly abused language so far, he must say little and well by committing himself to writing. And on his own flesh!

The lesson is clear, authoritative. Bearing hope. Demanding too.

After once again contemplating the parade of all the human lives clustering along the two giant DNA strands, they get back to climbing while observing the other side of the abyss from time to time. This allows them assess the effort to be made. And it is colossal!

After two good hours of walking at a relatively fast pace. Phil Caldwell 1 suddenly stops. He does not seem to be doing very well. He leans against a part of the wall located under a protruding arch. The white material is warm and smooth.

The astrophysicist tries to continue breathing. It looks as if an enormous weight is oppressing his chest.

At this precise moment, the anomalocaris yelps, "Listen!"

"But... listen to what?" the tiger asks, irritated.

"A strange sound. Like scraping."

"Scraping?" asks the young woman. "Where is it coming from?"

"From the abyss," answers the creature with two long whips that elegantly flow from its tail.

As it speaks, it flies softly towards the edge of the abyss to identify the source of this noise that has nothing to do with the *music of the spheres* that is regularly heard here. It rises again a little.

Then it turns back.

Terrified, it takes refuge between the tiger's legs.

"How awful!" he yells.

"But what?" roars the tiger.

Without getting flustered, Phil Caldwell 8 walks over to the edge of the chasm in turn. He looks for a moment. Horrified, he recoils precipitately and falls back, hitting one of the large back legs back of the stegosaurus.

"Run!" he tries to say.

His word is silent, of course. Nevertheless, the terror that is can be seen on his face is sufficiently explicit. But it's too late!

Before their bewildered eyes, a monster rises from the giant well.

The creature is grotesque. Terrifying. An absolute caricature of a man on a titanic scale, the being who has just climbed up from the terraces located just under theirs is already singular because its trunk is almost as large as that of a thousand-year-old oak. Two enormous legs, twisted as if they had been forged around a barrel support a being capable of feeding nightmares for several centuries. But its most terrifying feature is in the upper part of its hairy chest.

This creature from the underworld has... 50 heads and 100 arms!

"One of the three Hecatoncheires!" the astrophysicist immediately thinks, positioning himself in front of Phil Caldwell 3 to provide a fragile barrier with his body.

Brothers of the Titans, Cyclops and sons of Ouranos and Gaia, these three monsters helped Zeus defeat the Titans.

Since that time, they have been the guardians of Tartarus, the deepest and most sinister place in hell.

Almost four meters high, the creature resulting from the union of Heaven and Earth is structured in a very effective way. Its 50 heads are positioned in a hierarchy, all extending from a neck whose width would make a bull turn pale. Some are positioned centrally with the smaller ones in front and the larger ones behind. Others are positioned diagonally to the left and to the right. They bear the most horrific, hateful grimaces.

The most horrifying also.

The arms are arranged in the same manner. The smaller ones are located in front and the longer, muscular ones extend from the creature's back. They are all armed with daggers, swords, axes, or short scythes. The Hecatoncheire is a frightful war machine in the service of the most infernal and evil Chthonic divinities. An angel of death with 50 screaming heads, capable of the most absolute ferocity.

From the first few seconds, Briareos's intentions are totally unambiguous[23]. He starts windmilling his longest arms. Located too close, the stegosaurus must immediately retreat because despite its thick skin and the bony plates that

---

[23] Briareos, sometimes called Aegaeon, is the most formidable of the Hecatoncheires. He has two brothers: Kottos and Gyges. Briareos is one of the five giants mentioned by Dante in the *Divine Comedy*. He is depicted as being particularly harmful.

protect its back could be cruelly wounded by the weapons that Briareos spins with an astonishing vivacity for a being hampered with so many arms.

But, like some centipedes that coordinate their movements perfectly to advance smoothly, the movements of the Hecatoncheire grow fluid, to the gyration of a sophisticated chopper blade.

The stegosaurus turns and strikes the monstrous creature with its spiked tail. Briareos is destabilized for a moment. Then he steadies himself on his two large, hairy legs and Attacks again.

Like all the Phil Caldwells who live here, the Hecatoncheire is white.

Yet his paleness does not lie within the infinite palette of radiant *outreblanc* that prevails here. In his case, the paleness of his skin, hair, heads and arms, is adorned with innumerable shades of dirty gray that seem to symbolize all the defilements of the world. An immense river, without borders, without beginning or end.

Briareos howls sometimes. He belches and shrieks above all.

But, unlike the humans and animals that climb up these millions of carefully stacked terraces, he does not really speak. His cries are raucous, feverish. They give the maddening impression of being the audible emanations of a cosmic sewer that would translate the stench of the universe into sounds.

This very selective synesthesia[24] revives the Phil Caldwells, who feel the miasma emanating from the monster penetrate their ears and invade their brains.

Adding even more horror to terror, most of the Hecatoncheire's heads are frozen in grimaces of hatred. The faces are scarred, the eyes seem mad and the wide-open mouths spew a whitish liquid through sharp teeth likely to frighten a Tyrannosaurus Rex. The snapping of jaws further amplifies this nightmare vision multiplied by fifty.

The proliferation of heads and the abundance of arms which form almost a fan-shaped forest unsettle any possible opponents of this monster who has exited brutally from the foul-smelling, marshy moors of Tartarus.

At the same time, it is impossible to follow all these manifestations of anger arising from the most archaic times. Vision is blurred, the mind wanders, and terror is insinuated into every muscle, every nerve, every cell of the body of those that are to be crushed.

Realizing that the Hecatoncheire will kill them all if no one reacts, Phil Caldwell 8 stands in front of Briareos and challenges him. Unfortunately, the colossus is no match for the monstrous war creature that is twice his size and

---

[24] Synesthesia is a neurological phenomenon whereby two or more senses are associated, and sometimes crossed. This synesthesia also has a metaphorical value in ordinary language. For example, when we evoke a "gaudy color", we also associate the senses of sight and hearing in a single expression in order to better the sensation experienced.

powerfully armed. After a few quick abortive attempts, he receives a violent blow to his head and falls back.

Briareos walks over to the unfortunate man and raises one of his largest arms to finish him by chopping him with a sword that gleams under the light of an impassive sky.

At that precise moment the tiger chooses to leap.

Accompanying his movement with a terrifying roar, he attacks the Hecatoncheire, biting him cruelly on the throat of one of his central heads. The monster pauses for a moment.

He raises several hands to the wound and remains motionless for a long time.

It had been millions of centuries since such a misfortune had happened to him. Probably only during his ancient and enormous struggles alongside his two brothers and the cyclops when they fought against the Titans, which they then threw into the sulfur lakes and boiling pitch of Tartarus. Girded by the muddy waters of the Phlegethon and isolated from the rest of the universe by thick, brass walls, this prison in the heart of hell became their world. A world of darkness and suffering where they served at the guardians legitimized by the will of Zeus himself.

But here, Zeus is nothing and the *outre-blanc* abyss where only Phil Caldwells live is omnipresent. Its pre-eminence is total. Perfect. Unique.

And this universe is not that of Briareos. It will never be.

Determined and driven by mad rage, the big white cat is determined to teach Briareos a lesson with claws and teeth.

He leaps on the brother of Kottos and Gyges again. The tiger bites another head, shredding the front of the face puffed up with the hatred, ferocity and inextinguishable cruelty of creatures born to exterminate. Skillful and prompt, the wild beast escapes immediately, avoiding the blows of dozens of arms which become tangled when speed must take precedence over power.

The hecatoncheire roars. Bellows. The beast is wounded, but not dead.

Intoxicated by his own power and his reputation of invincibility, Briareos rushes towards the frightened group huddling along the cliff wall.

The tiger springs again after having supported itself along the smooth and welcoming verticality of this reverse Tower of Babel which draws its reason for being from the confluence of an endless chasm and an endless sky.

The tiger leaps, targeting one of the central heads which it shreds with a swipe of its claws that is even more powerful and furious than all the others it has already used on the ogre with the 100 arms. Surprised, the creature of darkness wavers at the edge of the abyss. The wound is horrible. The creature is bleeding heavily.

At this very moment, the other Phil Caldwells realize that an unheard-of event is going on.

"But his blood is red!" howls the anomalocaris, hurting his friends' ear drums.

The exuberant and gossiping creature from Cambrian era is right.

This is totally incongruous in a world devoted to the *outre-blanc* and the gentle tyranny of an absolute monochrome. But that is the reality. Visible. Glaring.

The Hecatoncheire sees its blood flowing and this blood is a beautiful vermilion red that seems almost surreal on these lustrous, white, pearly surfaces.

Strengthened by this first victory, the great tiger jumps on Briareos once again and bites him at the base of one of his necks. Cruelly wounded, the monster now howls and vomits rivers of blood. Oceans of blood.

Red. Red!

He moans again. At this precise moment, the anomalocaris rushes towards the brother of Kottos and Gyges. The maneuver may seem suicidal if one simply takes into account the difference in size between the two belligerents. But the most archaic version of Phil Caldwell pivots at the last moment and violently flagellates the Hecatoncheire with the whip-shaped filaments that extend from its tortoiseshell tail.

Sparks spray on this mass of muscles hardened by the effort, electrocuting the sentinel of Tartarus. Briareos' skin and hair start to burn. Almost all his heads grimace, their features are convulsed and Briareos howls with pain

Then he topples into the abyss with a dreadful crash.

His roars and bellows continue to be heard for a few seconds. Then, silence returns to the depths of this volcanic chimney of cosmic dimensions.

The human faces that float up and up, towards the sky, along the two DNS strands continue their endless ascent. They are still disfigured by suffering, sadness or the urge to kill. Some smile. A little. But they are so rare.

For a moment, the tiger looks in the direction of the abyss which engulfed the emanation from a pestilential, cruel hell. Alas, this hell has been inscribed in our genes in letters of horror and suffering. For seven million years!

Both elegant and unbearable, the incessant parade of faces is undoubtedly the most vibrant and terrifying demonstration of this.

A few seconds of pure silence.

Then, the carmine and ruby blood of the nightmare with 50 heads quickly fades, returning its white virginity to an immaculate universe.

CHAPTER 31

"You saved us!" trumpeted stegosaurus, approaching the tiger whose fur is still bristling.

The young woman rushes over and immediately takes the head of the great wild animal in her arms. She remains like. Long time.

Phil Caldwell 1 does the same immediately with the anomalocaris, squeezing the creature that overcame the monster from the abyss in his arms without worrying about its tail filaments. The animal stirs a little in order to free itself. But it does not succeed and simply says, "

"This is all very nice, but ... you're choking me!"

Phil Caldwell 8 and the small man approach in turn. The beanpole who had accompanied him up to now has fled with the other two women in the group. It is possible to see his lanky silhouette at least five terraces higher. And he is still running.

"I don't know where that monster came from."

"From the abyss!" sums up exuberant creature with a conciseness that is unusual for it, interrupting the tiger.

Too happy with the outcome of the fight to be offended, the big white cat continues, "Thank you. I had noticed that. I did! What I mean is: why did this infernal being who lived in the early ages of the World and who fought the Titans appear here? And why did it want to kill us?"

"Perhaps we are in the early ages of this New World," writes Phil Caldwell 1 taking care to capitalize the first letter of New and World.

"In that case," the stegosaurus intervenes with his big cavernous voice, "Our road may be very long."

"A few million terraces to climb..." sighs the tiger.

"What's with this red blood?" asks the young woman after finally freeing the tiger from her friendly embrace and once again taking refuge near the astrophysicist.

"This sudden, fleeting appearance of color in the middle of this *outre-blanc* universe is very surprising," Phil Caldwell 1scribblesing, splitting his sentence into two parts because it is too large for his forearm still covered with goose bumps.

"The red that characterizes blood is not a color like the others," intervenes the tiger.

"Its symbolic value is very strong," concludes the young woman without knowing how she is able to define and analyze this symbol.

Not for now anyway.

She then approaches the scientist and takes him in her arms.

Phil Caldwell 1 is moved when he feels the young woman's firm, round breasts pressing against his chest. But he does not insist on embracing her. He knows she does not want him. Her name too is Phil Caldwell. The number that follows each of the beings resurrected here highlights a difference in form, not a difference in substance.

The astrophysicist stands there for a long time. The man and woman feel their hearts beating in unison. Their skin moistens slightly. A sweet sensation invades them. Somewhere between peace and ecstasy.

As the anomalocaris continues to chat tirelessly over their heads, they finally disengage. The scientist walks over to the tiger. He takes its big round head in his hands, then makes a friendly sign with some of his filaments. He then walks over to the wall and writes a few words for the big white cat.

The latter approaches, reads the text and roars. It is obviously a roar of pleasure.

But he does not have time to reply to the thanks of Phil Caldwell 1 thanks because night falls. Abruptly. With the suddenness so peculiar within this universe dedicated to eternal whiteness. To the constantly renewed wonder of tender and dazzling lights radiating from everywhere at once. All the time.

Except, of course, when this radiant night falls, paralyzing the bodies and clouding minds with a passing solitude. Beneficent. Indispensable in a world where everyone is himself and the other at the same time.

The astrophysicist looks at the wall and immediately notices the sphere of iridescent mercury growing at a crazy speed. He would like to leave, to flee. But he cannot move. The filaments of his feet seem suddenly anchored to the ground.

The shimmering bubble explodes and engulfs him. With the tiger!

Still cold.

The eyes of the man and the wild beast turn to stone. Then explode.

Long needles of ice brush against their cells. Slowly, sadistically, they penetrate inside. The liquids of the body freeze and become weapons too.

They would like to cry, but their sockets are empty. Cradles of their atomized eyeballs, they are no more than cold receptacles.

In the distance, lights stoned by ice splatter a crazy horizon that curves extravagantly and ends up devouring itself. Lungs are no more than ashes. Limbs, atrophied at first, split in turn into thousands of compressed leaflets that shimmer and suffer. Twist and thin again.

Finally getting drunk on a cold so cold, so absolute that the electrons stop their crazy race around atomic nuclei. Mute, impotent, motionless, they freeze at the zenith of a dismembered body that denies its own existence.

Ghosts pass. Then run away.

The man wants to say something to the big cat. But his mouth, crystallized, crushed, emits only a raucous noise. Cracks. Crumbles.

And they die. Finally.

The plain is ocher. Powder. Windy.

Phil Caldwell and the tiger lie on the ground. They are motionless. The desert dust accumulates rapidly on their bodies. In front of them, a tall man weeps near his friend's grave. Just behind, stands a gold and lazulite statue bearing the effigy of the deceased. His name is engraved in cuneiform characters: Enkidu.

In the distance, the brick walls of a city that is sleeping under the implacable sun of this arid part of Mesopotamia is visible.

The red-haired man wakes up at once.

He lifts himself up on his elbows. He sees the big cat, lying on its side. The tiger does not seem hurt. Just asleep. He turns his head and immediately sees the colossus, who is clad in the skin of a beast. His only attire in this austere and disinherited place. The man who weeps for his dead friend does not look at the astrophysicist who has appeared behind him in absolute silence. In any case, the sound of the wind masks any sound weaker than a strong clamor or an explosion.

Phil Caldwell gently wakes the tiger, instructing not to roar. The two friends remain there, motionless and mute. But they still hear the tears and groans of the man in the animal skin, screaming the name of his lost friend.

"Enkidu! Enkidu! I too weep for you! Here a cruel fate has snatched you from me! For you, I will plunge the most glorious of my subjects in mourning. I will now take on a disheveled appearance. Simply clothed in the hide of a lion, I shall wander the steppe!"

"Is he wearing the skin of a lion?" says the tiger, choking. "That guy's crazy!"

"He's a king."

"A king! Dressed like that?"

"His name is Gilgamesh. He's the ruler of Uruk. He reigned in Mesopotamia nearly five millennia ago."

"Ouf..."

The red-haired man sits down for a moment next to his friend who has accompanied him to this almost deserted steppe strewn with pitfalls, which separates him from the immortal sage who can usefully advise him: Utnapishtim.

He then recalls a few fragments from the epic of Gilgamesh which he had discovered thanks to a student of Ancient Eastern history who had seduced him by his intellectual qualities as well as by her passion in bed. He collects some scattered memories and whispers them to the tiger who remains amazed.

"*Exceptional monarch,* began the tribute that the narrator of the epic placed at the head of the story, *famous, prestigious, proud offshoot of Uruk, buffalo with the terrible horn!*

Phil Caldwell recalls that, at that moment, he had asked Linda – his mistress expert in Sumerian, Akkadian, and shameful caresses – why he was compared to a terrible buffalo.

The young woman with auburn hair and splendid green eyes, spoke of a complex mythology and the role played by the celestial bull that Enkidu and Gilgamesh had defeated. This provoked Ishtar's anger and, much later, was also the cause of the fatal disease that killed Enkidu.

He brings up other elements of this epic labyrinth that was the first in the history of mankind, well before the Iliad and the Mahabharata.

He suddenly recalls the end of this ode to the ruler of Uruk, the son of King Lugalbanda and the goddess Ninsun, whose name also means "lady of the wild cows", which explains the affiliation of Gilgamesh with buffalo and large bovids. This particular characteristic comes back again in another part of this epic that the scientist of Stanford University finally recalls:

"Such was the son of Lugalbanda, Gilgamesh with accomplished force, the child of the sublime Cow: Ninsun Lady Wild Cow. Such was Gilgamesh, perfect, dazzling! He who opened the passes of the mountains, dug wells on the nape of the mountains, crossed the sea, the immense sea up to that point from which the Sun emerged, and explored the whole universe in search of life without end!"

Realizing that the feline is annoyed, he puts an end to these memories which faithfully transcribed this passage of the epic whose hieratic and panegyric character was evident.

Suddenly Gilgamesh turns around.

He, too, seems astounded when he sees a majestic tiger, and a man rather frail and red-haired, whose white skin and green eyes stand out in the midst of a desert that chisels the complexions of its courageous inhabitants.

"Who are you?" he yells, lifting a war ax that never leaves his side.

The astrophysicist thinks quickly. To claim to the King of Uruk that he is called Phil Caldwell could well complicate their situation because this name is nothing like the names of the time. He quickly drags a name up from his memory: Lugal-Balih.

"My name is Lugal-Balih and this great tiger is my faithful companion. My friend."

Gilgamesh then pulls himself up to his full height, which has always impressed his subjects and especially his opponents in combat. He stares at the two intruders who have just appeared out of nowhere at the very moment he is making his last farewells to his friend Enkidu. As a wise warrior, he examines the impressive musculature of the beast, the size of its claws, its teeth.

Then he raises his eyes and contemplates the sleepy city that the winds of the desert shade slightly with ocher and sand.

Gilgamesh turns back to Phil Caldwell and the tiger. He stands in front of them. Holding his great ax with his right hand, he adjusts the lion's skin covering his shoulders, his chest and his belly.

He simply says, "I'm Gilgamesh. King of Uruk!"

The red-haired man realizes that it is time to utter the sentence that will, perhaps, facilitate their later relations.

"We are your servants and we would like to accompany you for some time in order to bring you a little comfort at this time when your best friend has just died."

Since this declaration could be interpreted in different ways, Phil Caldwell scrutinizes the large bearded face of the colossus that reigns over the kingdom of Uruk, one of the oldest in Sumer. Gilgamesh's jaws contract, his gaze hardens and his heavy ax swings in a disturbing manner. The tiger begins to growl. Slowly. Deeply.

The astrophysicist finally decides to make a small prayer to Anu, Enlil, Shamash and Enki, asking the most powerful deities of the Mesopotamian pantheon to come to their aid at this crucial moment.

The King of Uruk seems to hesitate. An inner volcano rises to the surface of his dark eyes, revealing contradictory and violent emotions.

He suddenly calms, takes a last look at the great gold and lazulite statue erected in memory of Enkidu, and simply pronounces these few words laden with consequences, "I will continue my quest to join the man who can teach me how to defy and conquer death."

"Utnapishtim!" says Phil Caldwell, without immediately realizing that he has just interrupted a powerful sovereign.

Sorry and worried about the possible reaction of Gilgamesh, he places his hand over his mouth as a sign of apology. The king does not seem to be offended. He simply asks, "You too, Lugal-Balih, you know Utnapishtim?"[25]

"Yes, lord. I know that this man was the only one to have survived a deluge orchestrated by Enlil in order to punish the swarms of men whose din unsettled the gods. As a reward, he received the gift of mortality from these same gods, whereas all other humans must now live only a few decades because of the debilitating illnesses and the effects early aging."

"Perfect! I see that you know of this wise man who impressed Enki and Enlil and who was justly rewarded for his intelligence. Enkidu died, and his death has caused me so great and so violent a grief that I have decided, for myself and my people, to go in search of immortality."

"O Gilgamesh?"

"Yes?"

"We would you like to accompany you a little during this quest that will take you to the remote abode of Utnanapishtim?"

"We?"

---

[25] In the Babylonian version of the Deluge, Utnapishtim is called Atrahasis. In earlier versions in the Sumerian language, he is called Ziusudra, which means: *days to prolonged life.*

"My tiger and me."

The ruler of Uruk pauses to think for a moment.

Then, his face lights up with a slight smile, the first since the death of Enkidu.

He says, "Lugal-Balih, I agree!"

"Thank you, O great king," adds the great beast, whose fur, shimmering with all the shades from yellow to orange, fits in so well with the ocher and red of the desert.

Enkidu's friend is stunned. He never heard a tiger speak. He has never seen one either, for the only cats found in this part of Mesopotamia in the twenty-seventh century BCE are lions and panthers.[26] But the animal's strength and presence command. In addition, this formidable feline with the ability of speech seems to be a longtime companion of Lugal-Balih who, since he also knows of Utnapishtim and his fabulous powers, may be very valuable in this long quest for immortality.

"Then follow me!" he says in a loud voice that resonates as far as the mountains that can be seen far to the east.

The ruler of Uruk looks at the statue with the effigy of Enkidu one last time. Then he turns on his heels, followed by the astrophysicist and the tiger.

The walk quickly grows difficult, even trying, because the wind is constant and the heat unbearable. Sometimes large rocks scattered in a perfectly erratic manner provide a minimum of shade and coolness.

The great king has taken his precautions. Equipped with a bag filled with food and water bags made from goatskins, mean that they can hold out for a good time before finding water. In the evening, they gather a few twigs from xerophilous shrubs to make a tiny fire. With a warrior as formidable as Gilgamesh and a feline measuring more than three meters long, the trio has little chance of being attacked by any predator.

At dawn, they set out again. Always walking east.

For the King of Uruk, their goal is clear: they must quickly reach two very large mountains whose cloud-topped peaks and twin silhouettes fully justify their name: the Twin Mountains.

The home of the Scorpion Men!

Four days later, after a long and exhausting trek through the arid desert, they finally arrive at the feet of those two titanic mountains which touch the

---

[26] Panthers were found in a very wide area ranging from Egypt to the country of Akkad and to the Turkey of the future Hittites. The pardalide or panther pelt (traditional element of the sacerdotal costume of ancient Egyptian priests) and the nebris (skins worn for the Cult of Dionysus by the menaeds, satyrs, sileni and centaurs worshipping Dionysius) were made from panther hides.

heavens and scratch the Empyrean. High and fairly narrow, they surround and protect a gigantic dark gap which can be likened to an opening to Chthonian abysses or a new entrance to the Hells, Irkalla, where Nergal and Erehkigal reign undivided.

"What's this hole?" asks the tiger with a certain candor.

"The entrance to a tunnel," replies Lugal-Balih.

"It is the passage through which the sun goes in and out every day during the dark period called night," Gilgamesh says. "Praise be Shamash!"

The great beast seems circumspect. But since the ruler of Uruk and Phil Caldwell seem certain, he agrees, beating his tail in rhythm.

The piedmont of these gigantic Twin Mountains is dotted with small bushes whose branches, leaves, thorns and needles are covered with sand and dust. This powdery sheath gives them a ghostly, disturbing look that fits in perfectly with the general atmosphere of the place.

Because of the canyon that separates the two mountains and the call of the air flowing through the entrance of this black tunnel that opens a demonic mouth to the unwary who dare to venture into these nightmares, the wind snores, scolds, moans and roars.

The noise quickly becomes unbearable.

"What should we do?" shouts Lugal-Balih.

"We keep going," Gilgamesh screams.

He stops for a moment and finally says, "The Scorpion Men!"

"What are the Scorpion Men?" roars the tiger who, at the same time, ingests several puffs of sand that cause him to cough and spit.

His eyes grow moisten. The beast grows annoyed because this place seems dangerous to him. Malicious even. He is not wrong because, a few seconds later, two Luciferian silhouettes suddenly appear in front of them.

"Is that the... Scorpion men?" asks the red-headed man, imploring the King of Uruk with his eyes.

"Yes."

The answer is short. But enough. Indeed, there is no doubt as to their belonging to the order of arachnids. The pair of hybrid creatures is an impressive size, standing more than three meters tall. Facing the newcomers, the trio freezes. Gilgamesh and the astrophysicist veil their eyes for a moment because of the intense light diffused by the shells of the Scorpion men.

The upper part of their erect bodies is actually a cephalothorax, the back covered by a thick shell, with two median eyes and five pairs of smaller lateral eyes. Four pairs of legs move in all directions. Finally, their mouths, hideous and shining, are surrounded by a pair of chelicerae, the last two parts of which form powerful forceps.

Even though they are covered with iridescent shining scales, their torsos are human, making it easy to see that one of the Scorpion men is male and the other female.

Their legs are powerful and structured like those of the terrestrial scorpions. A long tail, also covered with powerful scales, contains a venomous dart while allowing them to remain vertical when these guardians of the *sun tunnel* wish to mimic the human biped.

Phil Caldwell swallows painfully, thinking that a single puncture would probably be fatal in a few minutes. Conversely, the King of Uruk and the tiger plant themselves in front of the pair who click their claws under the fiery light of a sun turned almost crazy.

"There is something supernatural about the one who comes here," scolds the male, pointing at Gilgamesh.

The female replies that he is the son of a goddess and the very powerful King Lugalbanda.

"Why did you walk so long with your friends?" asks the gigantic Scorpion man. "I want to know the reasons for your quest!"

The sovereign of Uruk looks at the monstrous creature who stands more than a meter taller than he does. He adjusts the lion's skin on his shoulders and immediately confesses: "The sole objective of this immense journey is to finally meet Utnapishtim, the venerable one who was admitted to the Great Council of the Gods after having survived the Deluge. The wise among the wise who obtained life-without-end. I want to ask him about Death and Life!"

The Scorpion man motions to his female. Then he stands for a long time in front of the day star and its divinity: Shamash. He then pivots on his tail and finds himself facing the trio who remains motionless, worried. And silent.

Opening his arms as a sign of appeasement, he finally replies while slamming his jaws. Phil Caldwell realizes at this moment that the hysterical moaning of the wind has been quiet since the Scorpion man has spoken...

"We will not block your way. We will not block you or your two strange companions. But no one has entered these Mountains. Shadows cover twelve bêrus[27]. The darkness is deep in this long tunnel where the sun penetrates and leaves before flooding the earth."

He pauses for a moment and continues, "Leave, Gilgamesh! Enter the Twin Mountains. Cross through the mountains, and let your steps take you to your goal. Safe and sound! The Great Gate of these Mountains is wide open for you and your companions!"

The ruler of Uruk starts to thank him, but the gigantic armored creature is already leaving with his companion.

"What now?" asks Lugal-Balih, pulling on his short hemp tunic as if this banal piece of clothing were choking him.

"We go into the tunnel!" says Gilgamesh, loudly.

"And if the sun penetrates through this immense tunnel during our crossing?" asks the tiger, realizing that it will be difficult to face a giant fireball.

---

[27] 120 kilometers.

226

"It's a purely symbolic journey," says Phil Caldwell, the Stanford astrophysicist, who feels a world nearly 4,700 years old being reborn within him.

"Fortunately," says the feline, retracting his claws after this brief fright.

Five minutes later, the trio heads for the entrance to this ghastly abyss which continues for more than a hundred kilometers before coming out on the other side of the Twin Mountains.

When they come to the edge of this immense vertical gap which tears through the central part linking the two peaks erected like lithic prayers defying a menacing sky, the two men and the tiger look attentively at the environment. The black disc is higher than three Gothic cathedrals. It seems able to engulf any human construction, however arrogant.

Some plants, mainly moss and ferns, festoon the edges. But when one truly penetrates into the bowels of the mountain along a gentle slope, all trace of life disappears.

"This is the vestibule of the kingdom of Ereshkigal!" exclaims Gilgamesh, mechanically wiping the sweat covering his forehead.

"Let's hope that our trip avoids the Irkalla[28]," says Lugal-Balih.

The sovereign does not answer. But his face darkens, his features harden and he rummages through his shaggy beard.

"How can we go in the dark?" asks the tiger with his customary sense of practicality.

Gilgamesh scans the few groves of coniferous shrubs which form a very fragile barrier in front of the vertical, black gap.

"Let's take these branches where the resin pearls on the surface of the bark. I'll light a first torch with two large flints. The others will serve us all along the way."

The red-haired man is dubious. But he still accompanies the King of Uruk to gather enough pieces of wood, with resin on them to make five long torches.

Gilgamesh then picks up two stone chips. In less than five minutes – and without crushing his fingers – he creates a few sparks that ignite the twigs. These in turn transmit this beneficent and magical fire to the end of the first improvised torch.

"Let's go!" cries the sovereign, adjusting the lion's skin which had started to fray after all his adventures in the cedar forest and his fight against the demon Humbaba and his conflict with the Celestial Bull.

---

[28] In their symbolic and mythological organization of the world, the Mesopotamians placed Heaven at the top, then the Earth (the world of the living), followed by the Apzu (a vast underground ocean) and the other world below: the Underworld. The place where the devils and the dead lived under the domination of the infernal gods. It was sometimes called Irkalla, the name also given to Ereshkigal, the Queen of Hell.

The tiger immediately follows the sovereign. Phil Caldwell remains doubtful for a moment. Nevertheless, he decides to follow his companions in this quest for a very improbable immortality.

The ground is cold and dark, but dry. This last point reassures the trio because a wet and slippery surface would have made their progress nightmarish. So, they are making good progress.

Naturally, as they progress, the opulent sunlight flooding the desert declines. It becomes a simple, almost white circle. A dim light. Then a weak and almost impalpable light. Finally, darkness completely fills this huge tunnel which continues to slope gently in a straight line.

The low light cast by the torch is veiled by the acrid smoke generated by the burning resin. The King of Uruk leads the way, Lugal-Balih follows closely behind him, carrying the other four torches in a shapeless sack. The big cat brings up the rear.

After a few hours, and after a very brief rest, shadows suddenly rise before them. They are hardly discernible because it is the very faint glow cast by the flickering torch that that makes it possible to discern forms scattered in the depths of the darkness. Proteanous clouds, they creep everywhere. Abruptly, they vanish, leave only a very thin coat of moisture on the skin. Five minutes later, they come back. Always as discreet, as sly. Impalpable.

But a cavernous sound gradually emerges. It gives the astonishing impression of coming from everywhere: fog with changing shapes, the ground, the walls of this immense tunnel that the sun symbolically crosses over before being reborn every morning. This sound is serious. This sound is frightening.

This sound is terror.

Terrified, Phil Caldwell tries to turn back. Having no lit torch in his hand, he quickly stumbles and falls.

"We continue!" Gilgamesh orders in an icy tone.

Sheepishly, Lugal-Balih joins the sovereign and the tiger. He blocks his ears and waits until this macabre *Te Deum* finally stops.

Three hours. Three hours of cavernous sounds carried by bronze drums and the beating of the hardest, darkest stones. Perhaps diorite. Three hours of choking. Glaucous splashes and screams that could easily be attributed to the damned being thrown into lakes of boiling oil.

Finally, silence returns. Heavy. The astrophysicist stops for a moment. He bends over the back of the powerful animal and floods his fur with profuse, tepid tears.

"Weeping is sometimes indispensable," says the King of Uruk who himself has long mourned his friend Enkidu. "It's healthy. This proves that you're a man and that your weaknesses can become the bronze of new strengths."

Cheered by these words, the red-haired man approaches Gilgamesh and takes him in his arms. The monarch does not reject him. He waits for Lugal-Balih to calm his terror caused by the long journey in the darkness.

Then he sits down and says, "Let's eat a little."

Four days later, gaunt, exhausted, but delighted, they finally see a small circular, pale glow that grows over time. They do not actually run, but they hasten their pace. Faster and faster.

In just a few more strides, they are all stand at the edge of a vertical gap that is similar in all respects to that at the base of the Twin Mountains.

But here the scene is really different!

The three find themselves at the edge of a forest. But the trees that grow here have no leaves, fruits or flowers. They are covered with gems.

"The forest of gems!" says Phil Caldwell, amazed.

The astrophysicist knows perfectly well that this magical place, the Garden of the gods, marks the boundary of the known world. The vast circumterrestrial sea with its turquoise and tourmaline water that opens before them marks the final frontier before finding the wise and immortal Utnapishtim.

He also knows that it is here that their paths will separate. Quickly. But he waits a while to enjoy this hallucinating spectacle with the King of Uruk: trees decorated with precious stones, branches bending under their weight!

Amazed, Gilgamesh starts to advance into the middle of these gold and ivory trunks, which are totally covered with sparkling stones. Magical, vibrant with an inner life enclosed in this adamantine hardness that gives them a unique beauty, they all cast a very particular glow which pulsates in keeping with an archaic rhythm

Fascinated, the astrophysicist names the trees covered with millions of shiny gems in the place of fruits. He immediately recognizes cornalines, garnets, onyxes and peridots. Moving a little further into the forest, composed solely of chryselephantine trunks and colored stones that capture, amplify and sublimate every ray of the sun, the trio also sees chrysoprases, citrines, abraxas and sumptuous amethysts.

The wind is light. Harmless. Stiffened by tightly entwined ivory and gold, the branches do not move. But some gems sometimes brush against the caress of the breeze coming from the sea. Crystalline sounds build into a soft symphony that stops immediately. It continues, a short while later, at the whim of the fantasies and jokes of a mutineous breeze.

The King of Uruk and the Stanford scientist walk very quickly, heads up, trying to count all those gems that have metamorphosed into masterpieces. They look like children, discovering an infinite number of toys, each more beautiful than the last.

More pragmatic, and probably less fascinated by precious and semi-precious stones, the tiger sits down and observes his companions who walk in all directions like ants moving their eggs to protect them from danger.

When his eyes are finally sated with beauty, brilliance and light, Gilgamesh stops for a moment. Then he sits down, leaning back against the gnarled trunk of a majestic tree whose branches gleam with a thousand amethysts. The slightly purplish light that this strange foliage casts invites quiet. Meditation.

It is this moment that Lugal-Balih chooses to warn the ruler of Uruk.

"Great King?"

"Yes?"

"I am going to leave."

"Me, too," says the tiger, placing his head against his friend's torso.

"Why?" asks Gilgamesh, astonished. "We still have to cross this sea with the ferryman we see in the distance, whose boat is lying on the shore."

"UrSanabi. I know," murmurs Phil Caldwell, sighing.

"You know his name?"

"Yes."

"There's a lot of things you know in advance about my quest. Would you be a soothsayer, Lugal-Balih?"

"No. It's hard to say. Impossible even, because I still don't understand who I really am, why I'm here and the meaning that one can give to this strange contact that binds us for a moment. And that will release us now."

"All this is very mysterious."

"What's important, O Great King, is the future encounter with Utnapishtim. That interview will give rise to decisions that will change the course of your life and will have beneficial consequences for your people. The time has come to go our separate ways."

The feline scrutinizes the monarch and notices that a few tears are rolling down his cheeks. His punishment is incomparably less severe than the death of Enkidu, of course. But it is very real.

The tiger approaches Gilgamesh and simply says, "Great King!"

He rubs his head against the legs and pelvis of the King of Uruk and begins to move away. Slowly. Phil Caldwell is moved as well.

He does not know what attitude to adopt at this precise moment. He hesitates again.

Then, suddenly, he goes over to the king who is still wearing his lion's skin. He stands in front of Gilgamesh and hugs him. Tightly.

For a moment, the two men share their heat, their emotions. Their sadness, too.

"Go in peace," says the son of Lugalbanda.

Lugal-Balih sniffs. He stands there. Motionless. Then he turns on his heels and joins the great tiger, not daring to turn around.

"That's better," whispers the tiger, growling very quietly.

As soon as they move away from the forest of gems, a shimmering lake appears before them. Mercury apparently.

They plunge into this deadly liquid and drown immediately.

CHAPTER 32

The giant abyss and the sky are still immaculately white.

But some details are fundamentally different.

Having been expelled from the sphere of mercury, which deposited them on the terrace where they were at the time of the attack of the Hecatonchire, Phil Caldwell 1 and the tiger remain stunned for a moment. Their eyes flutter and they are surprised that they no longer see trees with chryselephantine bark and branches bearing thousands of dazzling gems.

Here light reigns. Even more so than in the world of Gilgamesh located beyond the Twin Mountains. But this light is *outre-blanc*. The cliff is *outre-blanc* and the sky is *outre-blanc*.

This ubiquitous monochrome makes them feel nauseous at first. But the two companions quickly manage to curb these inappropriate gastric flows.

It is at this moment that they finally observe their surroundings. Their three main friends are still there. The stegosaurus stirs its head supported by a massive neck in one direction, while its tail with the four long spikes swishes rhythmically in the opposite direction. The young woman with the full breasts flourishes and the irreproachable figure observes them, with a broad, inquisitive smile. Finally, the exuberant anomalocaris chatters incessantly. It can even be said that is what it does best. But that caustic remark is unfair because its playful character and falsetto voice bring a little joy to this world whose origin and end remain totally mysterious.

"Where are the others?" asks the astrophysicist, taking advantage of the brief moment when he can speak without having to write and write again on his forearm.

"Gone!" replies Phil Caldwell 3, who seems delighted to see her friend in good health.

"This journey with the King of Uruk was very long," sighs the tiger, stretching its muscles a little.

"Long!" chorus the stegosaurus and the creature from the Cambrian era.

"More than a week in any case," says the big white cat.

The other three Phil Caldwells seem stunned and totally incredulous.

The tiger insists, saying "What is going on?"

"For us," says the stegosaurus, in its deep, bass voice, "Your immersion in the mercury bubble lasted the time of a normal night."

The two Phil Caldwells who have just shared Gilgamesh's quest for immortality for several days are somewhat surprised.

However, the time reported by the stegosaurus confirms that time does not flow the same way everywhere.

Generally, at the end of meal where drink flowed freely, the astrophysicist's friends would ask him: *what time is it*? He would then systematically evoke the great discoveries made by Einstein at the beginning of the last century. One theory states that time slows when one goes very fast, and especially that it slows considerably when one approaches the speed of light. The red-haired scientist also confirmed that since time is inextricably linked to space, any massive deformation of space – near a massive star or a black hole for example – generates a slowdown of time which, when one penetrates within the *event horizon* of a stellar black hole, petrifies everything for the incautious who would cross this barrier of brass that no superhero would ever dare cross!

In these cases, questions were raised and the alcohol fumes rapidly diluted the explanations given by Phil Caldwell, which would be eagerly forgotten by his friends the next morning.

But here, Phil Caldwell and his companions have already witnessed the cataclysmic death of our sun. It is by no means incongruous to imagine that time does not flow at the same speed in the gulf of Dante's Inferno and in the adjacent universes – the mercury worlds as Phil Caldwell calls them – into which the unfortunate scientist plunges regularly when this strange radiant night invades the well and its millions of stratified terraces on the side of a cliff.

Phil Caldwell 1 writes a brief message for the tiger who hastens to communicate it to their three friends while adding his personal touch.

"It is clear that time does not have the same value here and in the worlds of mercury that explode every night under the arches decorating the wall. I would also like to say that this expedition with the King of Uruk was exciting and... tiring!"

The exoplanetary specialist stands up in front of the girl whose breath he feels close to his mouth and cheeks.

"Why have all the others gone?"

"Look!" she says, pointing at the terraces below.

The sight is almost maddening. Hordes of Phil Caldwells are climbing the different levels and rushing to the very distant peak of this mountain whose circular cliffs have reached cosmic proportions.

There are hundreds of them. Men above all. Essentially quite young. But some are significantly older. There are also dozens of women climbing with the same speed and energy as the men. There are also some very disparate animals. It is almost a simplified Noah's Ark simplified, both comical and pathetic at the same time.

"Where are they going?" asks the tiger, opening its eyes wide.

"To the same place we are," answers the anomalocaris with a brevity very rare for it.

The astrophysicist remains motionless. Almost frozen. This crowd scares him. Afraid of its number, of course. Afraid because all these beings seem to be rushing without thinking. At this moment, he tells himself that this crazy race is usual for human beings. They rarely take the time to pause and examine their situation, to ask themselves the right questions. Given the context, this crazy race towards the peak seems to him to be a vain caricature.

"I want to go down," he writes on his arm.

After a brief moment, he adds, "Right now!"

"Why?" asks the creature with the two shrimp tails on its nose and a pair whips at the tip of its tail.

"The journey we took with Gilgamesh made me understand that the search for immortality is a fake one."

"But that of the King of Uruk does not end in the legend," the feline objects, beating its tai angrily. "You've made it clear: after meeting Utnapishtim, Gilgamesh realizes that this appetite for immortality would force him to isolate himself from the world, like the wise man who lives eternally beyond a circumterrestrial sea, completely detached from real life."

"So?" asks the stegosaurus who does not understand all the subtleties of this search for eternal life.

"The son of Lugalbanda returned to his people and reigned over Uruk, until his death. So, this vain quest does not apply to you or to him."

Phil Caldwell 1 nods. Apparently, he does not want to hear reason anymore and the remarks, however judicious, made by the tiger do not convince him. He walks over to the girl. Stands in front of her. Then, with a sudden movement, he kisses her on the forehead and heads off at full speed towards the lower terraces.

His friends are stunned and stand there, without reacting. They seem to be frozen, waiting for a possible change of heart on his part. This does not happen and his pale silhouette disappears very quickly drowning in the crowd that rises from the lower levels.

Like a mob in the subway or on a station platform, this sheepish mass, pale and almost bloodless, is frightening. The Phil Caldwells climbing the paths connecting the various terraces are almost mad. They do not speak and make very little noise when walking on the innumerable filaments that pad their feet. Cautious, the tiger, the anomalocaris, the young woman and the dinosaur press against the wall without really knowing what to do. Going down is almost impossible. And pointless. Riding along with the horde of the new Phil Caldwells would be tantamount to purely and simply abandoning their friend who has just made a detestable decision.

Since they cannot bring themselves to make the same cowardly choice, they wait.

In front of them, thousands and thousands of human beings who lived before Phil Caldwell continue to scroll through the two giant DNA strands. The silhouettes and facies are still prehistoric, but it is already possible to discern some representatives of *Homo sapiens* in the midst of a crowd of *Homo neanderthalensis*. This double ascent is haloed with light and the walls of the two helical structures shine intensely. Almost fiercely! For their part, the human beings who take this titanic tube-shaped elevator shine like diamonds. Or stars.

But this luminous euphoria is denied by the faces, most of which are frozen in pain, hatred or apathy. Smiling faces are the exception.

"Few men are responsible and happy..." thinks Phil Caldwell, 3 while mechanically smoothing the anomalocaris's scales, as the little creature continues to chirp with its shrill voice.

A few hundred meters lower, Phil Caldwell 1 is stuck. The rising pack of uniformly *outre-blanc* women and men continues to grow denser. They are in such a hurry that they occasionally jostle him. Without looking. Without smiling. Pale faces of an ordinary life that flows at the ordinary rhythm of an ordinary ambition, they walk on. That's all.

The astrophysicist tries to catch their attention by waving his arms, staring at them. But all his efforts at communication fail. The horde climbs the slopes and paths with a gluttony that shows no logic. Only a powerful, unspeakable, even visceral appeal can justify this grouping of beings who come together when they have nothing to share. Nothing to love.

"Gregarity edified as a norm," he thinks.

Lucid and cruel, this phrase immediately evokes memorable memories in him. The Stanford University scientist brutally recalls entire sections of his dead existence. His confusion grows , for he suddenly sees the reactions of some of his friends in the banal circumstances of an ordinary life. Then his. He wants to vomit while discovering the abject bond that connects him to those soulless lemurs that pass before him and ignore him. For they love only themselves. Themselves...

Terrified and sad, he sits down. And cries. He remains there a long time.

Suddenly, a strange sensation. People look at him. Scrutinize him.

Observe him.

He raises his head and sees a young woman and a girl about 6 or 7 years old. They are of course white and have tentacles and filaments instead of hair and thin strips that extend from their hands and feet. Moreover, they are naked, like everyone else here. But he quickly recognizes their faces. Recognition is painful. Very painful. The verifications and confirmations are made at the edge of his consciousness like the top of a giant jellyfish emerging slowly from the waves.

Suddenly he realizes and stammers, "Vanessa! Cymbelline!"

Phil Caldwell 1 has just recognized his wife and daughter!

Under the blow of emotion, silence, which is the absolute rule for the human Phil Caldwell, vanishes for a moment. All of a sudden, he can actually talk. This does him good. A stream of honey flows down his throat.

He exults, jumps in the air, fidgets.

But, Vanessa and Cymbelline do not seem to recognize him.

"It's me!"

As the crowd of Phil Caldwells continues to climb along the trails, the young woman and her daughter remain silent. They look attentively at this man who calls them by unknown names. Obviously, and the slightly panicky gleams dancing in the depths of their irises confirms this, they do not recognize him at all.

The little girl opens her mouth. But no sound comes out of her throat. Her vocal cords are paralyzed. She can simply make a gesture of incomprehension by spreading her arms. Her mother remains motionless for a moment. Then she writes a short sentence on her forearm. Cymbelline reads it. She then merely waves her hand in the direction of the astrophysicist who still does not understand why his wife and daughter treat him like a stranger.

Vanessa takes her daughter by the hand. They continue their climb from where they had stopped when they had seen the man and froze before him. The astrophysicist's wife realizes at the same moment that her own reaction is strange because she has no reason to stop in front of a Phil Caldwell whom she knows no more than the thousands of others who make up this dense crowd that seems afflicted with a severe herd mentality.

But while she stopped and observed him until he lifted his head and seemed to have recognized them, why is this man unknown to them?

Who is he? A name immediately comes to mind: Phil Caldwell! But the thousands of beings who move about here and climb up like Sisyphus to the top of this endless cliff are all called Phil Caldwell.

But then, who is Phil Caldwell? A God? An architect?

Perhaps it is simply the name of this titanic wall with its millions of terraces, which touch the sky, scratching against the translucent spheres that jostle at the top, extending boldly from a bottomless chasm where two giant strands of DNA flow? A wall that must be climbed. Ceaselessly. Climbing again. Without rest.

All this makes no sense. It is, moreover, the only fact that unites the astrophysicist, Vanessa and Cymbelline. Nevertheless, coming together solely around an aporia of this type is a little short. Frustrating even.

Without really knowing why she stopped in front of this man and why she flees, Vanessa Caldwell leaves, taking care to take her daughter with her. Error. She's not called Vanessa Caldwell, but Phil Caldwell. Like the little girl.

By the way... who is Phil Caldwell?

The astrophysicist finds himself in a very different state. He is overwhelmed. Devastated. He has just found Vanessa and Cymbelline. Yet, they are leaving. Heading off in the distance.

His reaction should be to run immediately behind them. To catch up with them. To force them to look him straight in the eyes. Above all this should be the ideal and magical moment to pronounce these three simple words, "I love you!"

Yet, he remains there. Sitting on the ground. Completely unable to react.

Haggard, he looks away from Vanessa and Cymbelline. Their white silhouettes gradually fade in this ambient luminosity, both soft and cruel, which pricks his eyes. He rubs his eyelids. A moment.

When he opens his eyes again, Phil Caldwell 1 realizes that his wife and daughter have completely disappeared from his field of vision. He curses himself. Calls himself a coward. Then he begs a long litany of regrets.

But his contrition and his repentance add only fear to shame, disarray to misunderstanding.

"Why? Why?" he repeats incessantly.

The answer lies perhaps at the top of this gigantic cliff. It probably also lies in him. Is that the same thing?

This reflection completely overwhelms him. It brings to light a total, paralyzing anguish that envelopes him every time he emerges from the mercury sphere and from the patchwork of its embedded universes. Disjointed. Inconsistent. Useless and crazy.

"The puzzle is still empty...". he suddenly tells himself.

That sentence came of its own volition. He has no idea what puzzle it refers to.

Other questions immediately gather at the edges of his feverish imagination: what is its size? What is its real shape? What is the purpose of this crazy puzzle designed by some mad deity?

He has no idea.

He knows nothing about it. And this irritates him to the highest point. But his powerlessness is total. For the time being, anyway.

Having stupidly given up following Vanessa and Cymbelline, he remains stuck to the ground and in a state of shock close to a coma. Thousands of Phil Caldwells continue to march past him. But he does not see them. He does not hear them. He does not smell them either, for the sense of smell seems to be the most diminished sense within this expanding volcanic chimney, with its dimensions.

A strange silhouette stands in front of him. He recognizes a camel.

This immediately awakens some memories in him. He sees temples in ruins, sand, dust and a burning sun. On the walls of these temples, innumerable shapes have been sculpted. These men, these women, these divinities dance brutally before his eyes.

The lines vibrate, overlap and link. And disappear.

One of the musicians gently rejects the harp that she held until now in her hands. She turns to him and smiles at him while gently tilting her head on the left side. Then she gives him a sign, which allows Phil Caldwell to see her long, elegant fingers and the bracelets that jangle at her wrists.

It is at this precise moment that the astrophysicist realizes that he has gone completely mad. Crazy?

But by what yardstick?

CHAPTER 33

Frustrating and tiring, the climb is difficult.

The astrophysicist suddenly feels all the weight of his own contradictions and mysteries on his shoulders. Sometimes he has to stop to catch his breath. He leans against one side of the wall. Then he continues to climb again, making sure to use the paths connecting the terraces. His goal is to join his friends. His real friends. For the other Phil Caldwells who climb these slopes with disconcerting haste and vacant eyes scare him.

He does not recognize himself in them.

But why should he recognize himself in other beings?

Because they're all called Phil Caldwell? Because they are all pale in a universe dominated by the *outre-blanc*? Because they all aspire to climb this cliff and finally lose themselves in the chaos of the sky?

That's ridiculous. Just as ridiculous as discovering that an Egyptian musician from the Middle Empire can wave to you and invite you to join her. Just as ridiculous as finally finding his wife and daughter and letting them go. Without trying to hold them back. Without trying to join them.

When the peculiarities of the external world become attached to those of the private world, the boundaries of the sensitive world explode. The exoplanetary specialist has the exhilarating and painful feeling that this moment is approaching.

He clenches his jaws, curses himself and continues his long climb.

"Here you are!"

Panting, he rushes into the arms of Phil Caldwell 3. The tiger and anomalocaris are there, too.

Apparently, the stegosaurus grew tired of waiting and joined Phil Caldwell 8 and the chubby little man. It is true that the somewhat crazy idea of turning back and walking down the abyss against the flow of other Phil Caldwells was confusing for many of his companions.

"We thought you wouldn't come back," said the creature from the Cambrian period, without forcing his natural talent to investigate the specter of the sharpest sounds.

"You scared us," said the white big cat. "We truly believed that you had gone completely mad!"

While hugging the young woman, the astrophysicist looks at his two non-human friends with whom he feels a very strong bond. Since the tiger's last remark fits in perfectly with his own feelings, he does not hesitate and replies, "That's what I think sometimes. Indeed. But the finding you, my friends, gives me strength to continue this endless climb with you. I only hope that it will finally bring answers to all the questions that arise and for which, for the moment in any case, we have only received baroque, confused and vain answers."

"Bravo!" replies the anomalocaris enthusiastically, initiating one of its twirling dances.

Phil Caldwell 1 is amazed because he has just uttered several sentences in a row without having to write them on his forearm.

Delighted with this discovery, he tries to answer his companion whose two large faceted eyes shine with a thousand lights. Alas, reality returns implacably. He is mute again and must therefore settle for scribbling on his pale skin:

"Let's go!"

Cheered by their reunion, the unusual quartet starts to climb.

Just before leaving, the astrophysicist looks at the faces that float through the abyss following the two soft and constantly moving strands of DNA that rise to the sky. Most of the faces are still terrifying.

Phil Caldwell 1 says to himself that, if the history of mankind were to be summed up in one word, it would certainly be: fear!

Fear of dying. Fear of suffering. Fear of others. Fear of the omniscient divinities that perhaps instrumentalize the destiny of a fragile two-legged creature who proclaimed himself master of the universe. Fear of the unleashed elements. Fear of nature. Fear of predators. Fear, above all, of the most terrifying of enemies: ourselves.

Fear of that hydra which rumbles in us and of which we discern, throughout our lives, only a fragment.

Phil Caldwell 1 recalls a discussion he had had with several of his colleagues at Stanford a few months before undertaking a great adventure that he cannot remember for now. The discussion was part of the famous sentence engraved on the front wall of the temple of Delphi and which Plato summed up in three of his dialogues: *know thyself*.[29]

This emblematic sentence quickly drifted to the relentless weight of others' eyes at a time when social networks are forging, often very artificially, the personality of disoriented human beings lacking other benchmarks.

The astrophysicist then expressed his vision of personality, spirit and the human soul, stratifying it into four successive layers, like onion peels.

He said at that time, "In my opinion, the human being is a four-layered mille-feuille."

Naturally, his colleagues had laughed a little at him, pointing out that a four-layered mille-feuille was, by definition, an impostor.

Once the purely gastronomic and mocking considerations had been exhausted, he was able to resume.

---

[29] The Charmides, the Philebus, and the first Alcibiades.

"The outer layer is a fragile film that corresponds to the need to present a valuing self-image to a world in which appearance takes precedence over the true. It is therefore the synthesis of the postures that one takes in order to define an image that one deems true to our hopes. In fact, this is what others know about us when they do not really know us."

There was no real debate about this. He could continue without running the risk of being interrupted at any moment.

"The second layer corresponds to a small part of what we really are: our emotions, our feelings, our addictions, some of our shortcomings and the concretization of our main interests. These elements of our personality are generally known by our relatives, our family, our friends. The third layer corresponds to the private. It is our 'secret garden' where we store, carefully enclosed, our impulses, our affects, our fragilities, our hidden vices, our ultimate ambitions. This third layer is a zone where the mud and the purest diamonds reign simultaneously. It is generally known only to us. Sometimes, with a keen sense of risk, we invite some people to come down with us into these shadowy caves. But never for very long. That would hurt too much. This would be far too dangerous for our ego and our mental cohesion."

"And the fourth layer?" asked John Thorne, a galactic cluster specialist.

"That is what we ourselves do not know. That of which we are only faintly able to catch a few parcels under very particular circumstances."

"What?"

"Torrential emotions, terror, taking of hallucinogenic drugs. These fragments, nestled in the depths of our minds, can also be exhumed brutally when we come very close to death. But, again, the principle of the iceberg plays a role."

"We only know about 10%?" asked John, worried.

"No doubt much less. The heart of our innermost being is a place more unknown, hermetic and distant, than the billions of galaxies that only appear as ghostly points on the photos taken by the Hubble telescope. This concentration of impulses in which chemistry and brainwaves conceal even more mysterious marriages than those which unite the great forces of nature remains forever indistinguishable, indescribable and unknowable."

His colleagues had been left dumbfounded.

Obviously, this radical approach to lack of knowledge one has of oneself unsettled them too much. They returned to their equations and stellar observations.

But today, the astrophysicist gradually discovers the deep meaning that one can give to this fear. He knows perfectly well that he is only at the onset of future discoveries that will either amaze him or terrify him. He looks at the young woman, the tiger and the anomalocaris. Then he smiles.

The trio does not really know the reason for that smile, but they take note and decide to continue climbing.

The hordes of Phil Caldwells rushing up the cliff and its millions of carefully stacked terraces is no more than a memory. The flow has dried up. The space is gradually becoming almost virgin.

The walls broke into blisters a few minutes ago, constantly expelling livid lemurs with dull looks, finally regain their natural flatness.

Reassured when he realizes that the maddening effervescence that reigned here has disappeared, the astrophysicist asks his friends to stop for a moment to contemplate the incessant parade of human faces rising towards the sky, . Stuck in a tube of dazzling lights that creates as many sparkling plumes as there are spheres in the sky of this hollow world, these faces are connected and continue to rise with a maddening regularity. There seems to be slightly more women than men, although the proportions change as the faces rise. There are also many faces of children who bring a touch of candor to this linear universe where hate and suffering prevail.

Sometimes, a tranquil face pops up from nowhere.

The scientist recalls a memory from five years ago when his father-in-law died prematurely and tragically. The family was devastated because the unfortunate had died in an absurd traffic accident caused by a drunk driving without a license. As he accompanied Vanessa to vehicle his eye was caught by a modest tombstone located only a few meters from his in-laws' vault.

A single inscription. An epitaph.

But the simplest and most beautiful of all.

Engraved in the marble, were these five words: *Here lies a good man.*

Phil Caldwell stood in front of the grave for a long time. His sister and daughter-in-law pulled him by the arm. But he stayed there. Motionless.

Returning home, he devoted himself to his wife and sought at length the phrases that were likely to portray his immense compassion. His immense distress too.

But this phrase – *Here lies a good man* – remained buried in his memory. Very often, he wondered what memories he would leave to his family. And at that moment he said to himself that this very simple epitaph represented the quintessence of his hopes.

Then time passed. But this inscription was firmly embedded in him. He appropriated it by trying to give meaning to his life.

Today, surrounded by his three strange friends, as he watches the parade of the past lives of the billions of human beings who lived before him, he observes that this objective is still current. Certainly, the peaceful faces are rare. Certainly, the faces disfigured by fear are very predominant. But as long as he watches the silhouettes of some women and some happy and good men, this hope will remain pegged in the depths of his heart.

For a moment, he examines this uninterrupted stream of lights that are shaped around skin, a nose, a mouth and that try to translate all the diversity of humanity. Of course, this gigantic kaleidoscope is not as shiny, variegated and happy as he could legitimately hope for.

But he also knows perfectly well that dirty gray has reigned on Earth for seven million years. Not color.

"Now we go on to the *outre-blanc*," he says to himself. "This is already progress!"

He dares not write this somewhat facile thought on his forearm.

They head on and walk. Walk and walk...

CHAPTER 198

The astrophysicist no longer knows how long he has been walking with his three inseparable friends. But it's been several years. That's certain.

The environment has changed little. Nevertheless, the abyss has increased greatly, making the magnitude of the task that remains to be accomplished obvious.

"Millions of terraces," said the tiger a long time ago.

Phil Caldwell 1 now wonders if it is a matter of hundreds of millions of levels, strata, floors. But the luxuriance of words is useless. The conclusion is there. Brutal. It will be necessary to walk for several centuries!

The brutal, luminous night sets the pace for the course of the climb. Each time, a giant umbilicus of iridescent lights, with a tip that resembles a ball of liquid mercury, crosses the abyss of this cliff whose Cyclopean dimensions defy Ouranos and Gaia. The bubble approaches, vibrates and explodes on the surface, engulfing the astrophysicist. Sometimes one of his friends.

Today he is alone.

He docilely watches the sphere with its icy cold approach. A cold that shatters bones, tears flesh and distorts time.

Phil Caldwell 3 and the creature with two long whips at the end of its tail are chatting softly. The sharp voice of the anomalocaris dominates the abyss as the girl writes, now at full speed, on the pearly, white skin of her left forearm. The tiger is resting, a few meters away.

The bubble of mercury brushes against the wall topped by a small arch, standing out in relief.

Then it explodes.

While the cliff is governed by the tyranny of the *outre-blanc*, the passage that the astrophysicist takes each night is governed by the cold. Extreme cold. The body cracks. Splits. Breaks.

It finally shatters into as many pieces as there are atoms in the universe. A vortex of raw light then carries it off, scattering all the sparse bits.

The plain is black. And indigo.

Monoliths stand. Some curl like an adult leaning tenderly towards a very young child. But there is no tenderness in this petrified universe where the fragments of a tortured and crushed body are spread like the seeds of certain tropical corals during gigantic synchronous, nocturnal laying sessions to mitigate the effects of predation. The remnants of a body, once whole, clump together, forming translucent shells.

Then they join in a shape that is monstrous and beautiful at the same time. This new being, a hybridized echinoderm with a fractal structure, is quick to metamorphose, changing color, appearance, smell.

Then it climbs the highest of the monoliths and utters a powerful, inaudible cry.

And throws himself into the void.

Campo de 'Fiori square is crowded despite the cold weather this morning of February 17 in Rome. The year is 1600 and a remarkable man will perish. Burned live!

Emerging suddenly from a void that remains mysterious to him, Phil Caldwell is caught between two guards of the papal army of Clement VIII and a matron whose arms are bigger than his own thighs. The guards are armed. Their short uniforms allow the gagging stench of sweat to escape.

Without having to implement the delicate workings of a memory mistreated by immersion in the liquid mercury sphere, the astrophysicist knows where he is. He also knows exactly why he is at that place, on that day.

Phil Caldwell is horrified.

He knows the harsh reputation of Pope Clement VIII, who, despite the fact that he legitimized the consumption and marketing of coffee in the West, showed utter intransigence towards those who did not literally respect instructions issued by the church at the end of the 16th century. He took strict measures against the Jews and forbade Talmudist and cabalistic literature. He also showed extreme severity towards Beatrice Cenci[30], who killed her father after he had abused all his family by openly practicing incest.

But today, the naked, gagged man who is being taken to the stake is not a murderer, brigand or plotter endangering the Vatican and the haughty Catholic hierarchy. Clement VIII ordered the Inquisition tribunal to pronounce judgment on a Dominican monk, declaring him a heretic and condemning him to be handed over to the executioner in accordance with the usual formula: *with as much clemency as possible and without bloodshed.*

Namely, to be burned alive at the stake!

This man who changed our vision of the world and is to perish here in a few minutes is Giordano Bruno.

The astrophysicist stands on tiptoe. The crowd is dense. All he sees for the moment is the horrible pile of wood surrounding a pole which, in our unconscious minds, immediately symbolizes one of the most appalling of punish-

---

[30] The frightful fate of Beatrice Cenci inspired various painters. Caravaggio, for example, used it for the decapitation scene in his painting of Judith decapitating Holopherne. She also appeared in numerous literary works by Stendhal, Alexandre Dumas, Shelley, Alberto Moravia and Antonin Artaud.

ments: to perish in flames, to feel one's skin sizzle and internal organs melt until the fatal moment when the eyeballs explode and the brain begins to boil.

Phil Caldwell, like any self-respecting scientist, had studied the life of this Dominican friar who, drawing inspiration from the works of Nicolas Copernicus and Nicolas de Cues, affirmed the relevance of an infinite universe filled with a countless number of stars and worlds more or less identical to ours. Shortly before the discoveries of Galileo, these remarks were naturally considered blasphemous and heretical.

After a trial lasting many years, the sentence was rendered: death!

The red-haired astrophysicist recalls this detail that Paul Harrison, his professor in the History of Science at the University of California, San Diego, had given them in order to give a little humanity to this tragedy. Paul quoted the phrase attributed to Giordano Bruno after his sentencing. He addressed the judges of the Inquisition and simply said: "*Perhaps you pronounce this sentence against me with greater fear than I receive it.*"

On hearing this remark, Phil Caldwell simply said, "That man had balls!"

The comment was a bit audacious. But it perfectly summed up the admiration that the future exoplanetary specialist felt for this philosopher who suddenly expanded our approach to the world by transforming a narrow, reductionist and sclerotic vision into a truly holistic vision of our universe.

The only superior psychic and philosophical threshold that has been crossed since Giordano Bruno is that we now feel that our universe is merely a trinket within an even more vast and complex whole called the Multiverse. That's all!

But the Dominican friar paid the highest price for this prescience, which was iconoclastic for the time. And today, he has to satisfy the cruel requirements of the papacy.

Phil Caldwell cranes his neck to see the arrival of the cart carrying the unfortunate man to the scene of his torment. Unable to see anything, he decides to move a bit closer.

What he observes then terrifies him even more.

Indeed, there is a very large stack of wood, which will guarantee a particularly intense fire with high flames that will lick the head of the unfortunate man very quickly. But, above all, the wood is very dry. Death will be all the more horrible because, when the wood is wet, the victim dies rapidly of asphyxiation. When the wood is dry, burning is total. Total, appalling and long enough for each nerve to be pain.

Phil Caldwell swallows. He approaches a richly dressed man whose cobalt blue, satin doublet indicates his aristocratic rank. He settles beside him and, with a feigned silliness, asks "Who is being burned?"

The smug man looks at him with disdain, for the astrophysicist is dressed in a mantle, a wide-open shirt, breeches made of coarse cloth, and leather gaiters. His attire indicates the modesty of his condition.

But the richly dressed man, answers him anyway, "I don't know. A heretic no doubt."

Phil Caldwell recalls that the Inquisition had not wished to place any particular importance to this execution, perhaps in order to avoid making Giordano Bruno a martyr from the day of his death.

Suddenly, a commotion breaks out. Cheering, heckling and drum rolling wash over Campo de' Fiori square, which is still overshadowed by the impressive fortresses of the Orsini family and surrounded by beautiful houses with colorful facades. A heavy wagon struggles to make its way through the crowd, which closes in around it like a greedy oyster.

Phil Caldwell continues to move closer.

Suddenly, the cart appears just in front of him. He trembles a little. Then feels ashamed by closing his eyes in an effort to overcome this cowardice.

He opens his eyes and finds himself suddenly facing Giordano Bruno who is standing, in this modest cart that grinds frightfully with every turn of the wheel.

The philosopher is completely naked despite the biting cold that prevails here in this fateful month of February. His arms are tied behind his back and a thick wooden bit fills his mouth, preventing him from haranguing the crowd.

"Is the Inquisition so afraid of this man?" Caldwell asks, without his words crossing the threshold of his lips.

As is usual in the case of a public execution, the crowd shoots and boos. Insults rain and some spoiled vegetables are pelted at the cart. The unfortunate man's eyes are wide open and gleam with a strange filigree, with a celestial message that will not be perfectly understood until a few years later, when Johannes Kepler will define the physical laws that bear his name and define the movements of planets in their respective orbits.

But today these laws are still unknown and the relevant observations made by Giordano Bruno are considered heresy and blasphemy.

Phil Caldwell tries to catch the attention of the Dominican friar whom he has admired since his studies gave him an understanding of the man's role and the qualities of his analysis which, however, was only philosophical. But the earliest Greek thinkers were both researchers and metaphysicians, and in 2016 metaphysics and cosmology are sometimes united in theories that were astonishing, confusing and magical at the same time.

He stares at him. But the mind of the unfortunate Giordano is probably already setting off for a beyond that he imagines dotted with infinite worlds and insolently beautiful celestial lights.

The carts passes by and stops fifty meters away. A papal guard and an assistant of the executioner move Giordano Bruno ahead after untying his legs. He wobbles and falls. Once. Twice. A strong crack of the whip and an unfriendly wrist movement quickly straightened him up.

Finally, he climbs onto the pyre, which is about two meters high. The enormous wooden pillar, wrapped with chains, stands upright, a rectilinear figure with a striking symbolism: an elevator to Heaven. Or Hell!

The guard moves away and the executioner and his assistant immediately work around the philosopher.

Twice, they check that the metal rings that tie his legs, pelvis and arms to the central post are installed properly and that the tortured man cannot try to escape.

Phil Caldwell is horrified. He feels like vomiting. But he still wants to see whether or not the executioner will shorten the sufferings of Giordano Bruno. Indeed, the executioner, when handsomely paid by the condemned man's family, sometimes strangles the victim before the fire burns the entire pyre.

Alas, this is not the case today.

It is easy to imagine that the Inquisition wishes to set an example, by maximizing the sufferings of one who has dared to defy Aristotle and the restrictive interpretations of Catholic Church at that time.

One torch. Then two.

A few guards move about at the foot of the pile of wood that is already beginning to crackle.

And just then Phil Caldwell does something crazy.

He rushes towards the empty cart. He jostles the men and women who continue to scream and insult a man they do not know. The search for a scapegoat is always the best cement of a society when it begins to doubt itself. This abject reaction does not surprise the scientist who for the time being has only one objective: to finally reach the damned cart!

He steps over a child playing between the legs of two women, excited by the imminence of the execution. While wondering what kind of disgraceful mindset can lead a mother to take her child to such a spectacle, he finally reaches the cart. A single guard is standing next to the ox that had been pulling the vehicle until now. He then climbs rapidly onto the rear of the cart, and stands before the crowd, which stops for a cursing and haranguing the condemned man for a moment.

He glances behind him and realizes that the fire is gaining ground. The lower parts of the pyre are burning, some flames already rising very high. Only the lack of wind has slowed the rapid spread of the fire.

He pivots on his heels, ardently stares at the front rows of spectators and begins to speak in a loud voice, "People of Rome! Do not rejoice! This murder is ignominious because this man has tried to open your eyes. Giordano Bruno has revealed to us all the reality and beauty of the world."

As the smoke begins to fill the area near the stake, his mouth dries and he starts to wheeze.

Yet, he continues, "Listen to Giordano Bruno when he says: *For the heaven is declared to be a single general space, embracing the infinity of worlds, though we do not deny that there are other infinite 'heavens' using that word in another sense. For just as this earth hath her own heaven (which is her own region), through which she moveth and hath her course, so the same may be said of each of the innumerable other worlds.*[31] Out of breath, he stops again. Then he concludes, pounded by insults and gibes, "hat is reality. There is an infinity of worlds, stars and lands, like ours. Today, the Inquisition is killing this man because he is right too soon. But he is right! And you who rejoice in his death today... you will all burn in your turn in Hell!"

Just as Phil Caldwell utters this last sentence, the fire completely consumes the pyre and the unfortunate philosopher is writhing with pain in the flames.

Phil Caldwell feels nauseous. He leaps from the wagon and runs at full speed. The moment is well chosen because the spectators' eyes are focused on the spectacle of the day: the horrible death of a man...

Two guards try to catch up with him, but the desire to save the condemned man's life gives wings to the astrophysicist who can smell human flesh burning in the smoke billowing from the flames. He vomits as he runs, soiling himself. But he does not care. He wants to run. Run. Run until his heart bursts in his chest. Until the taste of blood that now fills his mouth becomes his only horizon. His only color. The emblem of his life. And of his death.

Four minutes later he finally arrives at one end of the square. He runs towards a large building with beautiful saffron walls. He rushes into a small dark courtyard.

A lake of mercury takes shape in the center. Without thinking, he plunges into it.

And drowns.

"We almost waited!" says the anomalocaris, laughing, in its inimitable falsetto voice.

"My friends. My friends..."

"Your vocabulary is getting richer from day to day," adds the tiger in a slightly sarcastic tone.

"What happened?" asks Phil Caldwell 3 with her soft voice that is heard so rarely because of the silence that envelopes her, except during a new encounter or after immersion in the mercury worlds.

"At last I am a man. And..."

"And?" asks the white feline.

"And I am proud to be one."

---

[31] First Sentences of the Third Dialogue of *On the Infinite, Universe and Worlds* published in 1584.

CHAPTER 432

For several months, the cyclicality of days and nights has dilated considerably.

In a universe where everything is white, luminous and often aseptic, it is difficult to glimpse aby real flow of relative time which, obviously, is very different here from the time that Phil Caldwell experienced when he was a brilliant astrophysicist at Stanford University. But the foursome is unanimous: the days are growing longer and longer while the nights are similar to what they were from the first night which took him near Magellan the day of his death.

Of course, some of Phil Caldwell's escapades in the mercury worlds feel as if they drag on for several months. Others last only a few minutes. But, for his friends who remain near the wall, the periods of time are equal.

Nevertheless, the days drag on to the detriment of the nights.

It is, however, the only distinctive difference, as the diameter of the central chasm gradually expands. The *outre-blanc* is still as bright. Transparent spheres continue to jostle in the sky. And the giant DNA strands, through which all the representatives of humanity from the earliest prehistory rise, shine, vibrate and seem to bend with pleasure. But the faces that parade here are rarely carved in pleasure, voluptuousness or tranquility. Most are sad, distressed or terrified. Since the execution of Giordano Bruno, a few years earlier, the astrophysicist knows what these convulsed faces mean by pain, agony or torture.

There are too many. Too many!

Phil Caldwell 1 still thinks of Vanessa and Cymbelline. His heart is heavy. He sighs often when he observes this senseless crowd of faces that parade vertically towards the sky because those of his wife and daughter end up occupying the entire abyss. In these cases, he holds his head in his hands bristling with filaments and stays like that. Seated.

His three companions respect these moments of despair which paralyze him because they knew his pain perfectly. His shame too, for the scientist still does not understand why he let them go that way.

Without doing anything at all to hold them back. Without running behind them to hug them.

"I'm a coward!" he thinks. "An idiot and a coward!"

But there is perhaps a very profound reason for this incomprehensible inertia. A reason so structural, so important, that it prevails over all other considerations. Including those of the heart.

Today, they are all climbing happily. Of course, simply raising your head in order to see the extent of the distance that remains to be covered can be discouraging. Despite years of effort, the top of this gigantic cliff still seems so far away. It is even worse when looking at the other side of the abyss. Remoteness certainly diminishes the relative height of this chasm which looks like a volcanic chimney, but it also makes it possible to ascertain the hallucinating number of terraces that still have to be climbed. One by one!

After being made for a long time in the middle of a compact crowd of Phil Caldwells stumbling in all directions and climbing with suicidal haste, the inverted truncated cone is now a great *outre-blanc* desert.

For now, they do not see any living being.

"Where have they all gone?" the tiger asked a few weeks earlier.

But no one was able to answer.

Since some of the paths connecting the terraces are particularly steep along on this part of the cliff, the young woman and the astrophysicist begin to sweat a little. They stop to wipe their foreheads with their filaments.

The fact of having no material need to satisfy has not surprised them for years. But sometimes they still wonder about this oddity, comfortable and destabilizing at the same time. They sweat regularly... without the need to re-hydrate!

The anomalocaris takes advantage of this rest stop to fly gently over the abyss as it does at least once a day.

"So?" asks the tiger, yawning.

"It's deep."

"I am very fond of your ability for brevity," says the great while feeling in a gently mocking ton. The tiger could no longer do without its companion, with its two, large stalk-like eyes, its head with two giant shrimp tails for horns and whips that scour the air as if it wants to punish rebel prisoners.

Phil Caldwell 3 approaches the astrophysicist and writes simply on her arm: "Will we ever get to the top?"

"In a few centuries!" he replies, not knowing whether he is joking or really believes what he writes.

The young woman stands before him. Phil Caldwell cannot help looking at her pubis, then her heavy but beautiful breasts. He swallows, modestly turns his gaze away and scribbles on his arm:

"We can get back to climbing."

The tiger sets out again with the creature from the Cambrian era twirling just above it. The astrophysicist follows and Phil Caldwell 3 brings up the rear. Since all four of them are completely isolated within a luminous abyss of strictly sidereal dimensions, the risk of attack is nil. They climb quietly with only one objective in mind: to reach the peak, brush up against the translucent spheres that hide the sky and finally discover the end of this initiatory climb with the perfectly incomprehensible symbolic value. But the road is still long. Immense.

After a long time that it is difficult to measure because, apart from the alternation of nights and days, every journey within this dense version of Dante's Inferno takes place with a total immutability of the ether, they stop for a moment. The sky is immaculate. The transparent bubbles that mirror ghostly universes continue to jostle in billions at the top of this unprecedented abyss. The four Phil Caldwells who are making the climb are completely incapable of saying whether a luminous period, which can be improperly called a day in the absence of another more appropriate term, lasts twenty hours, fifty hours or a thousand.

But the days are very long.

And, just as the astrophysicist once again makes this bitter observation, night floods the chasm.

Phil Caldwell is very close to the wall. The arthropod from the Cambrian period is almost at his feet. As always, it chirps in its nasal voice that seems to be the result of inhaling too much helium.

"Hey," it begins.

But it does not have time to continue because the eruciform structure extending from a sphere of liquid mercury approaches them both at high speed. The caterpillar of light soon brushes against the wall.

It explodes immediately, engulfing them in a vortex of mother-of-pearl and silver.

A transparent, flexible hose directs them towards a constantly moving landscape where ice and fire unite in a strange orgasm. Icebergs with glowing lights float softly over an ocean of molten lava. But they do not melt. They drift, swirl and break apart.

Then they regroup again, building shimmering cathedrals with extravagant forms that attract the eye and crush the imagination.

Glass peaks, lances and javelins suddenly appear along the ridges of these ice monsters, which are as high as a hundred-story building. Finely honed, these weapons tear the skin of the scientist and the scales of the anomalocaris. The fire creeps into their entrails exposed by their monstrous wounds. Their organs burn and their substance flows towards the magma of this infernal ocean whose glowing and igneous depths are adorned with citrus reflections.

Phil Caldwell 1 opens his mouth to scream. But only a geyser of lava pours out his pain. He looks once more at his talkative friend.

Then they burn up. Slowly. So very slowly.

The room is quite elongated and very decorated. The dominant colors are gold, carmine and very hot browns.

Awakening from a long coma, Phil Caldwell immediately notices that a large scale stands in the center of space. A hard, scaly fin lies on his right thigh and he notices that the anomalocaris is sprawled on him.

He shakes it a little.

"Where are we?" cries the archaic creature.

The astrophysicist motions him to be silent.

"Look and shut up!"

As they are located at the back of the room, they can quietly observe the row of strange characters who are in the center of this place that resembles an antechamber. Or a court.

The large wall on the left is covered with dark hieroglyphics on a gold background. Overhead, forming a frieze, they see the silhouettes of twelve divinities. Although he has never studied Egyptology, Vanessa Caldwell's husband can immediately name them without really knowing why he holds this knowledge. He describes them in detail for his friend who has cautiously gathered the two whips that extend from his tail under his shell.

"Look. From where we are and going towards the back of this room, which we call the room of the two Maats[32]..."

"The two..."

"It is in fact the court of Osiris during the weighing of the body of a deceased person. Harmakhis, Atoum, Shou, Tefnout, Geb, Nout, Isis, Nephtys, Horus, Hathor, Hou and Sia."

"And on the other wall?"

"We find the effigies of the 42 assessors of Osiris who actually represent the 42 provinces of Pharaonic Egypt."

The anomalocaris remains silent for a moment, which is a real feat for it.

"Who is that in front of us?"

The astrophysicist does not have time to answer because the part of the ceremony that involves the *weighing of the heart* of the deceased person begins.

The jackal-headed god Anubis asks the man in front of him a first question: "Do you know the name of this gate Osiris Ouserkaf?"

"Ouserkaf is the name of the dead man being judged?" murmurs the arthropod with the stalk-like eyes.

"Yes."

Dressed in fine white clothes that fall to his feet, the deceased man calmly answers Anubis, "To spread Chou is the name of this door."

"Do you know the name of the threshold?"

"Master of straightness that is on both legs is the name of this threshold."

"Do you know the name of the lintel?"

"Master of force who introduces the cattle is the name of this lintel."

Anubis, god of death and patron of embalmers, seems satisfied with the answers given by Ouserkaf. He concludes this first phase of the ritual with these

---

[32] In the religion of ancient Egypt, Maat embodies the notions of order, solidarity, world balance, equity, peace, truth and justice. On the cosmic level, it is light. In the human world, it symbolizes the cement of the human community whose keystone is Pharaoh. During the weighing of the soul before Osiris (or psychostasis), Maat is as light as a feather. It is therefore the counterweight to the heart of the deceased, which must be as light as it is for the Kâ – the soul of the deceased – to reach the world of the blessed.

few perfectly codified words: "Pass, since you have given the three answers Osiris Ouserkaf!"

The astrophysicist takes the opportunity to observe the other individuals in the room, standing on either side of the giant scale that will be used to weigh the heart. The feather symbolizing Maat has already been placed in one of the trays.

Apart from Ouserkaf and Anubis, the god with the head of a jackal, who has just let the deceased man pass on to the crucial moment of the weighing of his heart, we also see Thot, the god with head of an Ibis, whose knowledge is unlimited. At the back, seated on a massive and highly decorated throne, sits Osiris who is accompanied by his two sisters, Isis and Nephtys. They stand behind him, their hands resting on his shoulders.

Under the giant scale, a strange hybrid creature with the body of a hippopotamus, the head of a crocodile head and the forelegs of a lion opens its maw, armed with countless teeth.

"That's Ammut," Phil Caldwell confirms. "She is also called the great devourer."

"Charming," says the anomalocaris, sighing and tidying up its tail better. "What is her role?"

"She devours the hearts of those who fail during psychostasis. If their heart is too heavy compared to the weight of the feather of Maat, Ammut shreds it. It is for this reason that she is also called the Eater of Hearts!"

"Brrr..."

Just then, the floor and the ceiling are transformed. The gold-covered surfaces disappear. The vision is maddening. The ceiling is nothing more than an immense plate of glass, revealing millions of stars in a serene sky dotted with sparkling carbuncles. Conversely, the floor is replaced by another glass plate. But this one does not draw people's gaze in the direction of an edenic sky. The abyss is but an abundance of hells that intertwine and copulate unceasingly. Magma, lava and flames as high as mountains lick this translucent surface which seems to swallow up the women and men who are led there in procession.

Phil Caldwell tries, absurdly, it is true, not to put his feet back on this ground that both attracts and terrifies him. As he does not succeed, he focuses his mind on the unfortunate Ouserkaf who is positioned right in front of the scales, Thot and the formidable Ammut.

Ouserkaf then speaks, respecting an unchanging ritual and addressing Osiris directly, "Greetings to you, Great God, Master of both Maat! I have come to You, O my Master, to see your perfection. I know you, and I know the name of the two Maats who are near you. Behold, I have come to thee and brought thee what is fair. I have cast out iniquity for you."

He pauses for a moment and then begins the litany of what is called the negative confession which consists in exhaustively listing all the criticized or abject actions that have been carefully avoided during his life on Earth.

In this way, he does not highlight what was done well, but what was not done wrong!

Ouserkaf, without apparently tiring, continues his interminable demonstration of honesty and universal goodwill by specifying, "I am pure, I am pure, I am pure! My purity is the purity of this great Phoenix who is in Heliopolis, for I am really the nose of the Master of breath that makes all men live on this day of filling the eye of Heliopolis..."

After having providing a second negative confession, detailing it divinity by divinity this time, the deceased man finally finishes his long speech with these epic and grandiloquent explanations:

"Hail to you, gods who are in this hall of the two Maats! I know your names. You will say to the Master of the Universe the equitable things that come to me, for I have practiced equity in Egypt: I have not blasphemed Amon-Re. Greetings to all of you who are in this room of the two Maats, you who are free from lies by essence, who live from what is fair before Horus... Here I come to you without sins, without villainy, without accuser. I live on what is fair. I have done what men speak, which the gods rejoice. I have satisfied Amon-Re by what he loves. I gave bread to the hungry, water to the thirsty, clothes to the naked, a boat to the one who had none, and I served the divine offerings for the gods and funeral offerings for the blessed. I am someone whose mouth and hands are pure, someone to whom those who see him say come in peace... I have come here to testify the truth, to put the scale in its exact position within the kingdom of the dead!"

Once the ritual is completed, the weighing of the heart begins under Anubis' guidance. Thot holds a calamus to record the result on a papyrus.

Placed in a canopic vase, Ouserkaf's heart begins gently swinging the tray. Then the it freezes, demonstrating that the feather of Maat and the heart of this pure man weigh exactly the same.

Encouraged by a gesture from Anubis and Osiris, Ouserkaf moves towards the back of the room under the tormented and disappointed gaze of Ammut who has not obtained her pittance and will have to await the negative judgment of another deceased person.

Just then, the god with the head of the jackal sees the astrophysicist and the strange creature born more than half a billion years ago.

Anubis seems surprised. Despite the fact that Phil Caldwell is also dressed in the long white ceremonial cloak that brushes against his feet, it is obvious that he is very different from the Egyptian dead who regularly enter the hall of the two Maats. His complexion is very pale, his curly, red hair and his green eyes are significantly different from the physical features that prevail here. Besides, the extravagant creature who is flying near his shoulder is unlike anything known at the beginning of the New Kingdom and under the glorious reign of Thutmose I.

He turns to Osiris.

With a hieratic attitude and an imperious gaze that seems to turn anyone who dares to look him without blinking to stone, the brother of Isis and Nephtys simply says, "Who are you strangers?"

Even before the astrophysicist manages to discipline the nervous tremors that agitate his arms and legs, the god who judges the souls of the deceased completes his question, "What is this strange creature?"

Phil Caldwell bows respectfully to Anubis, Thoth, Osiris and his two sisters. He does not know how to express himself before these five deities of the Egyptian pantheon.

To use the pompous phraseology of Ouserkaf would doubtless be blasphemous because he is not dead and finds himself, by a capricious whim of fate, in an ancient funeral ceremony that surpasses his understanding.

He decides to be himself. Quite simply.

"I'm Phil Caldwell and I watching the stars."

Unlike Ammut, who starts to open her hungry crocodile mouth, allowing the gold in the room to add a few extra flashes to her sharp teeth, the Stanford scientist continues: "The creature that accompanies me lived on Earth a long time ago. I do not know why I'm here. Because I am not dead..."

Just as he utters those last words, his eyes roll up. He wobbles and seems about to fall. The anomalocaris flies beside him. But it does not really manage to hold him back. Instead, the jackal-headed god steps around the giant scale and helps Phil Caldwell, preventing him from collapsing to the ground.

The glass plate that replaced the floor now serves as a jewel case for the flames of a star at the point of exploding. Flames lick the surface and pieces of molten magma stick to the transparent surface for a moment, before falling back into the fire that grows ceaselessly.

"I'm not dead," the haggard astrophysicist repeats.

Osiris exchanges a few words with his two sisters.

Imperturbable, Thot continues to describe everything he observes. His calamus[33] runs over the parchment which he holds high in front of him.

Anubis takes the anomalocaris' companion by the shoulders and asks him, in a deep voice flirting with the infrasounds, "Who are you really Phil Caldwell?"

"I am, I am..."

His eyes bulge. His forehead is moist with sweat and a little drool begins to flow at the edge of his lips, which are frozen by fear. He trembles as if he were standing on the brink of an immense abyss into which a violent wind could push him.

All the gods look at him.

He finally says, "I am dead and alive!"

---

[33] The calamus is a pointed reed that is used for writing, either dry on clay tablets, or soaked in ink in order to write on a papyrus or a parchment.

He is still agitated. His head nods irrepressibly, blurring as if he has suddenly gone mad.

"I see... death! I see... I see... my death! My death!"

He now howls, which greatly annoys the hybrid creature responsible for devouring the hearts of the unclean.

"Speak!" orders Osiris, eyes flaming like black suns.

"Speak softly," invites Anubis, letting his hands rest on the shoulders of the unfortunate man, who suddenly sees entire sections of the thick wall that has hemmed in his memory for so long start to collapse.

The dark, pointed muzzle of the jackal-headed god is less than twenty centimeters from Phil Caldwell's face. The ears of Anubis, fine, dark and pointed, are attentive and standing upright.

"I'm listening to you. We hear you."

"The veil is tearing. Finally!"

"Yes?"

"I see a forest with gigantic trees. It's hot. I'm in pain."

He stops again.

The anomalocaris in turn approaches very close to the man's head. The face of the astrophysicist, the tapered muzzle of Anubis and the giant shrimp tails that extend from the head of the arthropod from the Cambrian era are now circumscribed within a very small sphere.

Their breaths mingle.

"Continue," says the disheveled creature, gently, without managing to completely reign in its crisp falsetto voice.

"My friends are suffering. A lot of blood has already been spilled. A monstrous man yells incessantly in front of the cold eye of a camera. He insults a red-haired woman. He insults me too."

He pauses for a brief moment and resumes his mad soliloquy under the Osiris' interrogative and angry look.

"He insults me. He insults me!"

"You've already said that. Continue..." says Anubis who seems to have fleetingly taken under his protection this strange man who does not resemble an Egyptian from the time of Thutmosis I and who, above all, should not in any case find himself here in the room of the two Maats.

"He insults me. Hits me. I'm on my knees. He's still screaming!"

Terrified by his own visions that brutally exhort the most dramatic sequence of his life, Phil Caldwell stops again. He looks at the hieroglyphs that cover the left wall, enhanced by the gold lining the wall. All these signs seem to peel off the vertical surface. They rush at him! The astrophysicist moves about disjointedly, trying to dissipate those dark and grimacing hordes that want to insinuate themselves into his eyes, his nose, his mouth and his ears.

"Calm down," says the anomalocaris. "Everything is fine."

"Continue," adds Anubis, pressing more firmly on the shoulders of the unfortunate man, who is dreadfully frightened.

The scientist breathes deeply. He swallows and finally grows calm.

"The cries are so violent! My mind is troubled and foggy. A gray veil and blood obstructs my eyes. I rise a little. That's when I see the saber..."

"The sword!" say Anubis and the arthropod from the days of the Cambrian era.

Phil Caldwell falls to his knees.

Impassive, Thot notes all the details of this strange narrative while the other four deities remain silent. Frozen.

Clearly, they are waiting for a revelation. A sign. An epiphany. Or a second death!

"The light! The man raises the saber. No-o-o-o-o!"

Phil Caldwell falls back. Isis steps from behind the throne where her brother sits to join Anubis. By combining their efforts, the two funerary divinities manage to restore the man. He is pale and drool floods from his mouth.

Rolled back at first, his eyes resume their normal appearance.

"Take the time you need," says Nephtys' sister, in her soft, caressing, almost disembodied voice.

Phil Caldwell revives a little and looks carefully at Isis. The face of the young deity is gentle, full of almost surreal goodness. He realizes at this moment that he is talking with Anubis and the sister of Osiris, Seth and Nephthys.

He shudders and continues his painful recollection of an atrocious moment.

"After the pain: fear! I'm lying on the ground and I look at my body which is bathed in blood. About ten meters away from me!"

"A dozen meters?" whispers the anomalocaris, which just then exceeds all the high-pitched sounds audible by all the beings who have lived on Earth for 3.5 billion years.

"Decapitated?" asks Anubis, whose long eyelashes highlight eyes that glance towards those the unfortunate man who finally discovers how he died.

"Yes. My headless body lies far away and sends me this atrocious yet wonderful message: you are only a head. A brain! And yet... you live!"

"For the time being," Isis comments, widening her lapis lazuli eyes, which shape a miniature universe of unequaled power.

"But... But... I've already seen the sun die!"

Silence falls over the room of the two Maats. This astonishing, mad and totally iconoclastic remark manages to surprise the five divinities of the Egyptian pantheon which officiates in this place for the weighing of the hearts.

How can a man have had his head cut off and yet witness the death of the sun that will take place seven to eight billion years later? That's insane!

It's impossible! It's unlikely.

It is quite possible, in fact, if time does not flow at all at the same rhythm inside and outside this orphaned head of a body which must therefore become... its own universe!

This is what the five Egyptian deities have just brutally realized. This mad, crazy observation sublimates their role in terrestrial life and its slow metamorphosis within a standardized and ritualized beyond in a universe whose limits are known and defined.

But, by the infinite exuberance of the Multiverse, Phil Caldwell gradually becomes his own pantheon.

Osiris understands this at once.

It is he who addresses the man who has just realized this simple, frightening thing: he lives solely within himself and must assume the ritual of a crazy initiation of which he is both the master and the object, the vector and the finality.

"Phil Caldwell! Your destiny is unique in the history of men. By freezing time, your brain becomes both the soil and the finality of your own existence. You will have to investigate all the facets of your intimate being which has become as complex as all humanity since its creation. A mirror of yourself, you concentrate both your hell and your heaven. Your damnation and your sublimity! You have a lot of luck. But you will need a lot of courage too!"

The brother of Isis and Nephthys stops for a moment. He uncrosses his arms, one holding a scepter and the other a ritual fly-swatter.

Then he slowly raises his scepter in a sign similar to a blessing.

"Go in peace!"

Anubis and Isis look at him. Nephtys' sister smiles.

"Thank you..." Phil Caldwell stammers. "Your encouragement gives me unheard-of strength. I will now try to be my own epiphany!"

He smiles in turn and turns on his heels to walk into the lake of mercury that has just appeared at the end of the room he had entered with the anomalocaris.

Ammut tries to grab a leg. But the dry clapping of the teeth of the devourer of hearts demonstrates the futility of this ultimate attempt.

The astrophysicist and the disheveled creature head towards the lake. They immerse themselves immediately.

And they drown.

CHAPTER 433

Ejected on the white terrace like the viscera of fish vomited up by a great shark, Phil Caldwell 1 and the anomalocaris find themselves huddled on the warm, soft soil.

The man is hairy and the arthropod moans as if it has just fallen from the top of a giant waterfall. His faceted eyes greedily capture all the gradations of white and scattered highlights that the *outre-blanc* sublimates so abundantly.

"Are you all right?" asks the young woman, leaning over the still inert bodies of the astrophysicist and the great predator from the Cambrian era.

"They look a little drab," the tiger remarks, with a hint of treachery in its voice.

The two Phil Caldwells who found themselves facing the deities of the Egyptian pantheon alone do not react.

Phil Caldwell 3 shakes her friend while the tall beast licks the lustrous carapace of the insatiable gossip a few times with its rough tongue.

"Where... Where are we?" asks the anomalocaris in a voice even higher than usual.

"With us!" replies the young woman as if this answer were self-evident.

The astrophysicist awakens in turn.

His glazed eyes and his mouth moistened with foam prove that being found on a white terrace at the foot of a cliff higher than the Everest is not necessarily an obvious outcome. Especially when one has just spent quite a long time in the hall of the two Maats, whose gilded and crystal walls house Anubis, Thoth, Osiris and his two sisters in a single place.

"I know... I know..." the scientist stammers.

"You know what?" insists the tiger, opening its mouth to reveal some hyper sharp teeth shining like a thousand embedded crystals.

"At last I know why I am both dead and alive."

"Dead and alive!" splutters Phil Caldwell 3. "That's impossible! Only Schrödinger's cat can be both dead and alive. And still, that's a simple parable to provide a better understanding of the quirks of quantum physics!"

"I repeat: I am alive and dead at the same time. And, above all, I know how I died."

"But..." replies the young woman before falling silent.

"Our stay in the room of the two Maats and our insane meeting with Anubis, Osiris and Isis brutally awakened me. It's totally crazy but... I see my death perfectly! I see and, above all, feel this unbearable sensation, able to observe both my headless, bloody body lying more than ten meters from me," he says.

"But how is this possible?" wonders Phil Caldwell 3.

Suddenly, the young woman hastily pats her limbs, her head, her neck.

"But... But... But..." she begins to bleat without being able to go further.

"Are you rehearsing for a comedy routine?" asks the anomalocaris, awakened by the strokes of the tiger's tongue.

"But, but..."

"We understand!" says the tiger, growing impatient. "Can you go beyond but?"

"We can talk!" exults the young woman. "We can continue talking without needing to write on our skin!"

"I know why," replies the astrophysicist, in a tone that conceals his joy.

"In that case," says the big white cat by sitting on its tail, "You will make us happy. You will make us very happy."

"Yes?"

"You're going to tell us everything in detail and without making us wait any longer!" it roars.

Surprised, the anomalocaris finds itself glued to the pearly wall rippling with light without knowing how it ended up like that.

"I owe you a few explanations."

"One is fine," says the tiger, staring at the astrophysicist.

"At first, we witnessed the weighing of the heart of a man who lived during the time of Pharaoh Thutmose I. This pure-hearted Egyptian was named Ouserkaf. Then we found ourselves..."

"Thutmose I?" interrupts Phil Caldwell 3. "That was about what time?"

"He was the third Pharaoh of the eighteenth dynasty, that is to say, at the beginning of the New Kingdom. He lived in 1500 BCE. So, we found ourselves standing before Anubis in a vast hall with walls that were covered with gold and hieroglyphics."

"The floor and the ceiling!" interrupts the giant arthropod spinning like a top.

Then, staring at the Stanford scientist with its large, faceted, stalk-like eyes, it insists, "Speak of the floor and the ceiling too!"

"You're right! The floor and the ceiling of this space, where a large scale stands and where a hybrid monster with a crocodile's mouth constantly tries to snatch us, are made up of an immense transparent plate. Overhead, a crazy sky such as I have never seen since working as an astrophysicist. Below,.. it's the Apocalypse! Rivers of lava, geysers of magma. Mountains of glittering ashes feeding a monstrous blaze whose flames lick the feet of those who come there to be judged."

"Oups..." comments Phil Caldwell 3, positioning the filaments of her right hand in front of her mouth.

"This environment is actually very surprising. But it is at the precise moment when the deity with the head of Jackal..."

"Anubis!" interrupts the anomalocaris who wants everything to be clear and in the right place. "This god with a jackal's head is called Anubis!"

"Thank you," grumbles Phil Caldwell 1. "So, it was when Anubis asked me, 'Who are you really Phil Caldwell?' a dark veil was torn in my head. First of all, then with much more accuracy right after. I recalled my decapitation and the reasons, some of them in any case, for which we are all here."

He stops just a second, catching his breath, then continues, "This also explains why we are all called Phil Caldwell."

"We are in a hurry to hear you," says the tiger who stares at his friend as wanting to flow into him and wander at will in the confused labyrinth of his neurons and synapses.

The astrophysicist then describes his execution. Strangely enough, the memories linked to the beginning of the Orpheus expedition, to their capture by the mercenaries of the *Blue Macaw*, and their trying conditions of captivity, remain rather vague. Very blurry even. Short sequences arise suddenly. But the linking the episodes is difficult. Certain gaps make the process of unifying memories perilous, if not impossible.

Conversely, the moment of his execution is now very clear.

He recalls word for word the last conversation he had with Felipe Maldorano:

"Turn around!"

"Pity! I have a little girl. You can't!"

"Too late!"

And the blade of the saber fell on his neck...

The most accurate of memories, the most atrocious also, comes just after that. He still feels the very strong pressure of the blood in his temples, increased by the spinning of his head on itself.

Above all, he discovers his own terror with astonishment when he realizes that his inert body is lying very far from him. From his brain. From his thought. From his ability to be intelligent again.

Yet he is there. He sees everything. He hears everything. He understands everything.

Until the magical, hallucinating moment of the *outre-blanc*!

After describing his death to his friends, a long silence falls. Even the hypnotic, repetitive music of the spheres, which seems to be woven into the heart of the terraces, unceasingly emerging from the abyss, fades away. His very texture plots are petrified, giving reason to Schopenhauer, who claimed that architecture was frozen music.

But here the architecture is insane, titanic and quick to satisfy Dante Alighieri or staggering painters like Bosch or Monsu Desiderio.

The tiger is the first to react:

"But then... If you are Phil Caldwell who was beheaded by the leader of the *Blue Macaw*, you should only be a head deprived of its body?"

He pauses for a moment, frowns and continues, "And who are we? Why are we all called Phil Caldwell?"

Phil Caldwell swallows. Then he takes a deep breath to try to describe the unimaginable.

He turns his head a little from left to right. His friends find that he is still pale, that his hair has been replaced by fine tentacles and a myriad of filaments. Similarly, his fingers are merely gigantic brushes ending with filaments dedicated to specific tasks. He does not really resemble the green-eyed, red-haired Phil Caldwell, who immerses himself in the *mercury worlds* every night.

So?

"My friends, your many questions are understandable. I do not have all the elements I need to answer them. I can just draw some assumptions that will be confirmed, or not, when we get to the top of this gigantic cliff. In a few centuries probably!"

"We hear you!" rumbles the beast, stretching itself out to its full length on its belly, its front legs pointing at its friend and its tail beating nervously at the edge of the abyss situated just below.

"It seems to me that everything here is a question of brain and relativistic gravity."

"As for the brain, we agree," the young woman with the full breasts immediately interrupts. "But what does Einstein have to do in this place where colors, life and time no longer have any resemblance to the world that Phil Caldwell knew on Earth?"

"We are no longer on Earth."

"That, we understood!" says the anomalocaris whose two tail whips are now stuck under the claws of the feline's forelegs.

"When I say that we are no longer on Earth," says the astrophysicist, in a learned and professorial tone, "That must be understood in its most congruent sense."

"Con... gru?" asks Phil Caldwell 3.

"What adapts ideally to what you want to express."

"Thank you."

"In this truncated cone shaped like a giant volcanic chimney, we are neither on Earth, nor in our solar system, nor in any galaxy. In fact, we are no longer within the known universe. We are..."

"Yes?" asks the tiger, irritated, opening its mouth so that everyone can appreciate the impressive size of its canines.

"We are in a universe in the making which has been heavily compressed and which, probably when we have completed this initiatory journey, will finally unfold majestically."

"A new universe!" exclaims the young woman, clasping her hands together as if wanting to celebrate this event. "But how is this possible? What is the role of Phil Caldwell in this genesis of an unprecedented world? And us? Our role?"

"Let us take things in order," suggests the astrophysicist, calmly. "Are you familiar with black hole singularities?"

"Hmmm..." grumbles the creature from the Cambrian period which feels a bit overwhelmed by these elements which are certainly very familiar to its friend, but it does not master.

It releases his caudal whips whose ends were still stuck under the legs of the great white tiger. Then it rises gently and positions the two shrimp-like outgrowths in front of the eyes of the unfortunate man who was decapitated by a psychopath.

It then states, "I don't know anything about it. So be clear, simple and precise. Thank you!"

Phil Caldwell 1 smiles. Definitely, this preposterous little is growing on him. And, since they are going to have to climb this cliff together again for several centuries, that is rather a good thing.

"Okay. A stellar black hole is actually the remnants of a very massive star that exploded during a supernova and whose remaining mass is at least equal to three solar masses."

"That's clear," says the young lady, encouraging him with amused expression.

The tiger remains dubious and crosses its legs. Its eyes sparkle. It is easy to see that it will roar again if his friend's explanations get too bogged down in details.

"This matter becomes very dense because of the four great universal forces that govern the universe,[34] of which only gravitation now prevails."

"So?" inquires Phil Caldwell 3.

"The mass of this dead star becomes so significant that its gravitational power manages to capture light. But one of the peculiarities that interests us the most here is that this enormous gravity slows time. And it slowed time down so much that it finally stopped."

"How can time be stopped?" asks the young woman, choking and widening her diamond eyes.

"Everything is relative. Inside a black hole, time flows quite normally. Like here. But when compared to the usual rhythm of time for observers located at the edge of the black hole it gives the impression of slowing down monstrously. Then freezing."

"Is the reverse possible?" asks the tiger, enthusiastically, unsheathing its claws in pleasure.

---

[34] The four elementary and fundamental interactions that govern all the physical phenomena observed in the universe are: strong nuclear interaction, electromagnetic interaction, weak nuclear interaction and gravity. The domain of quantum gravity covers theories that try to reconcile the first three with gravity.

"Exactly! For people inside the black hole, everything that happens outside seems to take place in an accelerated state. One precision is necessary: in a true black hole, it is more prudent to imagine immaterial creatures without substance because a physical body, as solid as it is, would be crushed immediately. Shredded. Pulverized!"

"I understand!" says the anomalocaris, surprising itself.

The archaic arthropod undertakes a formidable series of gyrations around an invisible axis in order to mark its mental feat.

"So?" asks the tiger in a sarcastic tone.

"It is for this reason that we witnessed the explosion of the sun, when it actually died eight billion years later in the normal world," summarizes the eternally chattering creature. "Within this giant funnel, time flows infinitely more slowly than in the normal universe where we lived before you were decapitated."

"Exactly! Congratulations..." says the astrophysicist in an admiring tone.

"All this is perfect," adds the young woman, massaging her forearms as if her skin had suddenly frozen. But what does this have to do with the decapitation of Phil Caldwell? And I repeat my question: what are we doing here? Why are we living in this budding world?"

"These points are more delicate and, considering the present state of things, much more speculative. I have to admit that."

"Speak without fear," says the tiger who would love to know a little more now that his curiosity has been awakened.

The astrophysicist makes a bizarre grimace. He walks over to the chasm, looks at the abyss. The two giant DNA strands where the silhouettes and faces of the billions of men and women who lived on our planet before Phil Caldwell, Karin Stockhausen or the abject Felipe Maldorano continue to rise.

He remains there for a long time, his hands resting on his hips, as if this somewhat theatrical posture could invigorate his mind and his ability to discern.

He turns around, sits down in front of his friends and gives them a reassuring smile.

"The decapitation of Phil Caldwell, or rather, my decapitation..."

The Stanford astrophysicist stops suddenly. He looks desolate and mechanically raises the filaments of his left hand in front of his mouth.

He continues almost immediately, saying "Sorry. I meant our decapitation. In reality, this barbaric act seems to have led – for reasons unbeknownst to me – to an atomic and gravitational concentration of the same order as that which vibrates, snorts and rumbles within the black holes. Don't ask me why. I repeat, I don't know. But, in the present state of our knowledge, this is the only possible hypothesis. I say possible, not plausible. That would be going overboard."

"Good. So what?" insists the feline.

"This would explain why this titanic, monochromatic world is so different from ours and why our relative time has nothing to do with universal time."

"Perfect!" states the young woman, moving very close to the astrophysicist who, by reflex, once again looks down at her pearly nipples. And us? What are we doing here?"

The question returns in a loop: why are there several Phil Caldwells here at a time when the original on Earth at least is now lying with his head very far from his body...

"We are perhaps all the tiny pieces of a gigantic universe in the making that have draped itself behind the name we all know: Phil Caldwell!" says the tiger, rising suddenly on its powerful legs.

"It is possible," interrupts the anomalocaris whose hyper-sharp falsetto voice has not really settled since its forced cohabitation with five divinities of the Egyptian pantheon and a devourer of hungry hearts. "But our astrophysicist friend still has a different role to play than we do because when he is immersed in the mercury worlds, he looks like the real Phil Caldwell who was decapitated in the Amazon jungle. And we don't!"

"But then... the young woman starts to say, "Why are we so different if we actually symbolize a part of the spirit of this man who was unjustly killed by a monster?"

Phil Caldwell 1 turns to his trio of unwavering friends and looking in turn at Phil Caldwell 3, then the feline and finally the exuberant arthropod, says, "Perhaps you represent the part of femininity lurking in every man. You symbolize strength and raw energy. As for you... perhaps you represent the most archaic part of the human being. His brain reptilian."

"A big thank you for the reptilian brain!" says the anomalocaris, choking and waving the two shrimp tails posed on the front of his head like a bullfighter's banderillas. "But, as I am in a good mood after meeting Anubis, I will take this foul remark for a compliment."

"Bravo!" says the tiger, laughing.

"In fact," continues the creature from the Cambrian period, "Every being needs to be re-energized sometimes, thinking of its roots. If I symbolize the origin of Phil Caldwell and the slow evolution that allowed him to be what he was before his death, I'm proud!"

"And you're right," the astrophysicist concludes, hugging his old friend.

The arthropod struggles a bit at first because the scientist chokes it. Then he calms down and nestles for a moment against the pale chest of this man who has become, without knowing it of course, the seed of a new universe. A universe far from everything. Different from everything. But a universe whose fundamental laws will probably be the opposite of a world that has failed. Who betrayed.

And has been irretrievably lost.

"This status suits me well," admits the young woman, unconsciously straightening her chest so that her female attributes are clearly visible.

Apparently, the desired effect is achieved because Phil Caldwell 1 immediately focuses his gaze on his friend's breasts. At the same time, he understands why she had refused to give in during their first fall into a mercury world. She had mentioned the risk of incest.

If they are all fragments of a multiple and complex personality, but nevertheless one in its essence, this notion of incest assumes its full value. To love oneself is common among human beings. It is even an almost absolute standard and one of the driving forces in a world with a thirst for power and a fear of dying. But to reproduce with oneself inextricably combines onanism and hermaphroditism. Phil Caldwell 1 realizes at this moment that he does not want to engage in this dangerous and sterile undertaking.

He looks at the young woman and walks over to her. Then he kisses her on the forehead.

In a universe where the gentle tyranny of the *outre-blanc* is total, they cannot blush. Not even turn pink. But their emotions are intense. They are reflected in their eyes which, as the poets often claim, remain the most reliable mirrors of the soul.

Considering no doubt that the time for hugs has passed, the tiger intervenes, making sure to use a serious, intense voice.

"Now that you can speak without having to doodle on your arms, we will have the opportunity to discuss all this..."

"For several centuries yet!" interrupt Phil Caldwell 1, moving away from his female girlfriend.

"That's it. For several centuries! So, as I said, we can no doubt return to climbing up these millions of terraces?"

"Okay," says the astrophysicist. "We will have plenty of time to examine our situation and what awaits us, I hope in any case, at the top of the cliff."

"This story about a brain that turns into a black hole both fascinates me and bothers me," says the young woman.

"Later, I will discuss with you some of the specifics of the Multiverse like the inflatable, the scalar fields, the Hawking-Turok instanton or eternal inflation, which will no doubt give you some insights into what is happening, since they all lie at the heart of this titanic, *outre-blanc* Dante's Hell, XXL version."

"As you so elegantly pointed out," intervenes the anomalocaris, "I am an archaic creature whose only existence here reinforces your notion of the reptilian brain..."

"My remark annoyed you."

"Not at all! But remember that I have far fewer neurons than you. So, I would like you to share this information in small doses so that I can revel in it without overheating my reptilian brain."

"That's what I said just now. My remark vexed you!"

"Not at all..."

CHAPTER 814

Without it really being possible to know why, new Phil Caldwells continue to appear along the sides of the cliff. Some even extricate themselves from the material almost in front of the quartet of climbers who have spent decades repeating the senseless and vain action of Sisyphus, condemned to an eternal punishment for having dared to challenge the gods. The only difference, although a large one, is that they are not obliged to push an enormous rock which, when they reach the peak of a hill, systematically rolls back into the pestilential waters of Tartarus according to the legend quoted by Homer.

But their climb is infinitely longer. The white cliff is immeasurably higher than the hill overlooked by Tartarus.

"The faces are changing," remarks Phil Caldwell, 3 stopping abruptly in the middle of the narrow terrace overlooking the abyss.

Distracted, the anomalocaris falls onto its back and the outgrowths located under its stalk-like eyes bend under the shock.

It falls to the ground balancing itself with the help of the thin swimming lobes which run along its flanks.

"Hey!"

"Sorry..." apologizes the young woman.

"It's not serious. But warn people when you stop!"

"You were saying?" asks the astrophysicist, taking advantage of this short pause to wipe his forehead.

Phil Caldwell 3 quietly lays her left hand on the back of the tiger and points the filaments of her right hand in the direction of the two colossal strands of DNA. They continue to move in a slow swinging movement starting from the abyss while respecting the helical form that sets them apart.

As the abyss has grown considerably over the last thirty years, the diameter of each of these supple, firm structures has become monstrous.

As it is still easy to distinguish the silhouettes that slip inside while making a climb that is highly symbolic, it is possible to note that each face is several hundred kilometers tall. Since the circumference of the bottomless well exceeds the size of a normal telluric planet, the dimensions are both grandiose and maddening.

But large scale perspectives and ratios are respected, which does not hamper observation. On the other hand, it is impossible to see the other side, which is no more than a fine strip at the edge of a crazy horizon that is constantly permeated by thousands of shades of white that unite this monochromatic symphony that would amaze a painter who has dedicated his life and his art to color.

Luckily, there are no painters among the millions of Phil Caldwells who have passed by here and have stayed here. As is the case for the anomalocaris and its three friends.

So, they all look in the direction of the closest DNA strand.

The observation is obvious, the silhouettes have grown a little longer, the features have become more refined. Imperceptibly, we are approaching the aesthetic criteria that were in force and prevailed at the time of the execution of the red-haired astrophysicist who had left for Mount Roraima in order to discover strange molecules likely to be compatible with extraterrestrial life.

"These humans are very close to us," says Phil Caldwell 1, gently nodding his head.

"So much the better," said the tiger.

"Why?" asks its companion, waving its stalk-like eyes in circles.

"That means we are approaching the top."

"You think so?" says the young woman, looking in surprise at the top of the cliff, which is still lost in the sky filled with billions of transparent spheres.

"We are actually approaching the peak because we have been climbing constantly for many years," confirms the scientist in a tired tone. "A hundred if my estimates are right. But we still have a long way to go because the vast majority of the entire human population was concentrated in the last two or three millennia."

"So?" asks the white feline, a little annoyed.

"This is all heading in the right direction. But the fact that the women and men who float through these tubes propelling them to the sky resemble us more and more does not mean that our vertical odyssey will end soon."

"We suspected that a little!" squeaks the anomalocaris, taking advantage of the opportunity to free itself from the floor of the terrace and rise to the eyelevel of Phil Caldwell 3 and the scientist.

All four of them remain on the edge of the abyss.

This ritual occurs frequently. For, it must be admitted, except for going up thousands of paths that lead to thousands of terraces and looking inside the well or up at the sky, there is nothing else to do within this constantly expanding volcanic chimney whose dimensions are in keeping with those of a giant gaseous planet. But they are not in the heart of Jupiter.

Nor are they in the center of Saturn.

They are... elsewhere!

Satisfied with whiteness, sparkling mother-of-pearl and vertiginous spikes, they set off again, not without realizing, once more, that 90% of the human faces that slide along the two closely intertwined strands are tense with hatred, congested by enjoyment or terrified by fear. A kaleidoscope of emotions, love and horrors. With an absolute preponderance for hidden or cruelly unveiled horrors.

A few hours later, they stop for a while and settle under one of the arches that draw patterns and half ellipses on this white, warm and vibrant wall.

As is usually the case now, the arthropod settles between the tiger's front legs and the two humans lean against the almost infinite vertical wall of the cliff sculpted by titans. Or demented demi-gods.

Just then, the radiant night spreads its veil of darkness over the abyss, the layered terraces and the sky.

The astrophysicist turns around.

The mercury sphere with its extensions that make it look like a giant worm or hysterical caterpillar rushes towards him. Towards them rather, as the young woman is sitting right next to the man who was beheaded by Felipe Maldorano on the border between Brazil and Venezuela.

The bubble, with its amazing mercurial reflections, brushes against the surface, expands and grows more refined. Then it explodes, engulfing the two Phil Caldwells.

Cold. Always.

Phil Caldwell 1 and his three companions have become accustomed to these transitional spaces which constitute a corridor for the strange, the baroque. Or the monstrous.

They know that their bodies will freeze. Turn to stone. Then, a greedy ogre or a diabolical machine will tear their skin, shatter their bones or stab them with a few thousand carefully tapered ice daggers.

They experience the worst of nightmares. They both slide along a continuously narrowing tube. They finally find themselves trapped in a rolling mill, one that grinds each of their cells. Their bones crack like crystal stems under the hammer of a mad blacksmith.

Their eyes finally explode under the pressure. The vitreous humor then flows into their mouths, distorted by pain and the effects of rolling that reduce the thickness of their body to that of a phosphorus atom.

A mound. Or the top of a hill. In the distance, the sea.

In front, a man sitting on a bench. He is up on himself and holds a sheet of paper in his hand.

Contrary to the image transmitted by history books and those dedicated to French literature, which almost always represent the poet with a carefully trimmed, thick white beard, Victor Hugo is beardless at this moment.

It is in 1854, near Jersey. Hugo is 52 years old.

With dark hair, a high forehead, chiseled features and a thick nose, the illustrious novelist, dramatist, draftsman, pamphleteer and poet, is looking at the dark gray waves over which a tormented sky casts a pall. In the distance, a curtain of rain falls and it will soon swallow up the coast of the island of Jersey,[35]

---

[35] Victor Hugo left the island of Jersey in 1855 and settled for 15 years on the island of Guernsey where he wrote some of his masterpieces: *The Legend of the*

where Hugo has taken refuge since 1852, a few months after the coup d'état of December 2, 1851, which led, following six decrees enacted by Louis-Napoleon Bonaparte, to the birth of the Second Empire.

The poet is looking at the sea.

He turns about suddenly as Phil Caldwell and the young woman appear in the middle of a small grove of puny shrubs swept by the wind.

"Who is that?" asks Phil Caldwell 3, wide-eyed.

"One of the greatest writers of all time: Victor Hugo."

As he speaks, the red-haired man does not understand why he knows that they are both on the largest of the Channel Islands, that it is the middle of the nineteenth century and that this man with the massive stature and sad, sullen face is Victor Hugo.

But he does know it. And he knows why the novelist is sad.

He also knows why they're both here. Facing him. In a gloomy atmosphere where the drizzle veils the landscape and coats the skin with water droplets. Such knowledge now seems to be anchored in him every time he is immersed in the *mercury worlds*. And this has been so ever since he found himself face to face with Osiris and Anubis. A moment that he is not about to forget because he finally revealed himself to himself through his own death.

The astrophysicist observes Victor Hugo, who is in the prime of his life. But the master is downcast. And has been for a long time.

Since September 4, 1843, to be precise. The day when his beloved daughter, Léopoldine, drowned in the Seine along with her husband, Charles Vacquerie. Four people were on board the boat that sank after capsizing following an unexpected whirlwind. In addition to Léopoldine Hugo, who was only 19 years old, the boat also held her husband, Charles Vacquerie's uncle Pierre Vacquerie and young Arthur Vacquerie who had just celebrated his 12th birthday.

Since learning about that tragedy only four days later – and through the press – the poet has languished. His drawn features and his almost crazed look show that the wound is still open today.

The author of *Hernani* examines the two newcomers whom he does not know. But the red-haired man and young woman do not appear threatening. They are dressed very simply and look like all the people of Jersey who live mainly from agriculture or trading.

Victor Hugo does not move. The sheet of paper he holds in his left hand droops gently. As the wind rises, it jerks, giving the absurd sensation it lives, sighs and suffers.

Ages, Les Misérables, The Toilers of the Sea, or *The Man who Laughs* for example. In 1870, at the fall of the Second Empire and the advent of the Third Republic, Victor Hugo returned to Paris, where he was received triumphantly.

Mistake! The one who lives, sighs and suffers here is Victor Marie Hugo, son of Joseph Léopold Sigisbert Hugo and Sophie Trébuchet.

The scientist decides to walk over to the stone bank that looks down on the shore from a steep cliff about ten meters high. Phil Caldwell 3 follows him, somewhat intimidated by this man whose works are known to all.

The astrophysicist is now less than three meters from the poet. He stops and waits. His mouth is half open, his lips tremble a little. But no sound comes from his throat. Clearly, he does not know what to say by way of introduction. The young woman pushes him a little bit, patting his shoulders, as if this simple gesture could release his inhibitions.

He breathes deeply, taking advantage of the revitalizing effects of the salty, sea air.

Then he says, "Good morning, Mr. Hugo."

Then red-haired man curses himself internally.

"There was no point standing there for a good minute only to come up with such a banality," he muses, as he digs his fingernails into the palms of his clenched hands.

The inconsolable father watches them for a long time. Then, in a grave and warm voice, he simply says, "Come to sit beside me."

The two Phil Caldwells are eager to obey.

The exiled novelist remains silent. Then he looks at the man and the woman he has just invited to sit next to him.

"The gloomy intimacy of evil and abyss defeats me," he says.

The astrophysicist hesitates a moment. Then he says, "We have both lost a daughter."

"Your child drowned?"

"My case is the opposite of yours, actually."

"Meaning?" Hugo asks, frowning.

"Léopoldine was swept away by the river and you are have to face the horrible challenge of surviving her. I let my daughter go twice. First, by dying prematurely. Then, by finding her in a place outside our world and without trying to hold her back..."

Hugo then turns the hand holding the sheet of paper and shows Phil Caldwell the only line he has written there:

"Man, thinking, descends into the universal abyss.

Phil Caldwell asks, "What do you mean by the universal abyss?"

"You! Me! Every man is his own abyss..."

This remark suddenly blazes in the mind of the Stanford scientist. Like a geyser of light, this simple, eight-word sentence finally opens his eyes. Without realizing the incongruity of his gesture, he grasps the writer's hands and takes them in his own. He drowns his gaze in that of one of the greatest literary geniuses in the world. But at this moment he does not see the author of *Les*

Misérables. He immerses himself in the gaze of the one who has just clarified a part of his personal darkness.

"You're right!" he exults. "You are a thousand times right. In one of your poems, you perfectly define the bronze walls in which we delight, for we are at once the jail, the prisoner, and the guard who shuts away our hopes."

Caught in the grip of an exultation that borders on hysteria, he moves even closer to Hugo, who is perhaps beginning to wonder whether he was right to invite two strangers to sit down near him.

But Cymbelline's father continues his speech, his tribute.

"I remember. I remember…"

"We understand," says the young woman, fearing that the poet will go away, realizing that the red-haired man with the bulging eyes has lost his mind.

"I recall this extract from the poem of which you have just shown us the first verse, word for word. Wait! Here. That's it! You wrote: *in this abyss where the abyss in the abyss melts, the wretched deeds are transformed into tortures, fear, mourning, evil, complicit shadows, tears under the fleece, the expired sigh in the flower, and the cry in walled stone!*[36]"

The astrophysicist stops for a moment to calm the chaotic pounding of his heart.

He then concludes:

"*The cry in walled stone*! That's exactly what we've endured! In the light of the senseless experience that we've been experiencing in a well of light without beginning or end, the premonitory and almost prophetic character of your poems is striking. Striking and wonderful too!"

Hugo then opens his mouth to answer. But the feverish scientist, who has been decapitated yet is still alive, continues in a jubilant tone, "Man is the only point of creation in which, in order to remain free by becoming better, the soul must forget its inner life! You wrote this in the last poem of *Les Contemplations*. It's crazy! Our situation is exactly the same! All of Phil Caldwell's components must forget their past lives in order to be free and become better. That's fantastic!"

Totally losing his sense of reality, he kisses Victor Hugo on the cheeks.

Disturbed by the excess of his own behavior, the red-haired man immediately moves at least twenty centimeters back.

Then he says, "I'm confused. Confused… You must think I'm mad."

"Not at all," the writer says, in a reassuring tone, nodding his head gently. "You are simply a man who is suffering. Like me."

---

[36] "Dans ce gouffre où l'abîme en abîme se fond, se tordent les forfaits, transformés en supplices, l'effroi, le deuil, le mal, les ténèbres complices, les pleurs sous la toison, le soupir expiré dans la fleur, et le cri dans la pierre muré."

"We're sorry," says Phil Caldwell, 3 avoiding sticking her full bosom too ostensibly under the playwright's eyes. "Losing a child so young and so tragically is a terrible trial. I would like to be able to find some words of comfort. But I cannot."

Hugo then notices that the young woman's eyes are misting and that several tears are starting to trickle down her cheeks. The poet approaches and, with a delicate gesture, he wipes away the profuse, warm pearls of light.

"Thanks..." she says, sniffling.

"No, I thank you. Your presence brings me a little comfort during this formidable trial, the outlines of which I understand crudely, but whose end I never discern."

"Mourning is like climbing a mountain without being able to see the peak. Your heart pounds, emotions overwhelm us and we remain there. On our knees. Begging for an impossible redemption for the faults we have committed and for those we will commit. The climb then becomes trial. And the trial becomes a calvary."

"Climbing is immolation!" replies Hugo, passionately.

"In our case, climbing is probably also burning in order to be reborn," replies the young woman whose tears have dried.

"Such a phoenix!" concludes the poet, rising suddenly.

While remaining between the two Phil Caldwells, he looks again at the sea and its dark waters where slate competes with mud.

Hugo sits down. He looks again at his two strange companions and asks them, "Who are you really?"

The astrophysicist then describes in great detail what happened to him in the Amazon jungle.

When Victor Hugo discovers that the brain of a man whose head has been cut off can survive well beyond a few seconds, as confirmed by observations made during executions, he pales. Then his eyes light up. It is immediately obvious that his fascinating poetic and epic imagination already overlapping with golden ringlets encrusted with diamonds in order to describe the unspeakable.

That is the most dazzling and magical quality of poets. They are sometimes able to put into words what reason rejects out of fear. But the poet is not afraid. He can shamelessly investigate the ignored areas of the human soul and pick up here and there the drops of an emotional and psychic nectar that surpasses our ambitions. Our dreams. Yet, this work is hard, difficult, grinding. Generally frustrating. But when the veil tears, a jewel can be born. A few words suffice to create the purest emotion. One that makes us proud to be a human being. A rare ecstasy...

Satisfied with the oddity, the author of *Les Misérables* then demands a meticulous and almost exhaustive description of this unique place of cosmic dimensions in which all the components of a human soul gradually rise towards a still-distant heaven.

The novelist also asks questions about the mercury worlds that pop up every night, snatching the astrophysicist in their nets. The expedition to accompany the King of Uruk in his quest for immortality and the dreamlike passage in the hall of the two Maats attract his attention in particular.

Suddenly, he warns Phil Caldwell and his friend, saying, "We must never forget this, for this observation singles out our existence: the universe has only me in its gloomy depth. On this side, it's night. Beyond that, it's dream.[37] Do not forget it. We are prisoners of the present and of ourselves. The opportunity offered to you is a great one because you can transform the usual laws of the universe and become your own horizon. The Alpha and Omega of your sensitivity. The Orpheus of your emotions. But..."

"But what?" asks Phil Caldwell 3, observing that Victor Hugo's expressive face has suddenly shrunk.

"Without reflection, without humility, without courage, this step can lead to the worst extremes. Do not take yourself for an omniscient deity. You are a man. Be one to the end! Majestically. But keep the values and everything that made the man that your wife and your daughter have been mourning for since your decapitation. If you fail to do so, you will be damned. For all eternity!"

Coming from the mouth of a genius and inspired poet who wrote *La fin de Satan*[38], this recommendation is priceless.

After making this last observation in the form of a purely Hugolian apophthegm, the poet turns to the red-haired man.

"You are a specialist in the universe and stars?"

"Yes."

"Could you then explain to me how the brain of a decapitated man could become a universe in itself? A monochromatic world totally different from the one our astronomers have described for us?"

"It is difficult to explain. To be quite frank, I don't know or, more exactly, I'm not sure of anything."

"Your frankness is honorable. Still, do you have any ideas?"

"At the beginning of the twentieth century, we discovered the principal mysteries of the infinitely great and the infinitely small. These are the theories of relativity and those of quantum physics."

"I'd like to live again at the beginning of the 20th century..."

"Alas, this century was atrocious, filled with countless wars, hideous ideologies and daily barbarities. And the 21st century will be even worse!"

"Let us therefore set aside regrets. Tell me about these cosmological marvels!"

---

[37] Extract from *Au bord de l'infini* – Les Contemplations.
[38] Long epic poem (5,700 verses) written between 1854 and 1862, *La fin de Satan* would be published posthumously in 1886.

Phil Caldwell spent a few minutes evoking the discoveries of Einstein, the great physicists who laid the foundations of quantum physics, the discovery of the universe with its hundreds of billions of galaxies and space exploration.

Then, comes the inevitable question, "Are there other universes beyond ours?" Hugo asks with a bit of malice in his eyes because he finds this concept, both iconoclastic and destabilizing, highly seductive.

It fills him with enthusiasm.

"Yes. Our universe is only a fragment of a larger, infinite and perpetually expanding whole, known as the Multiverse. Now, some of these universes can be quite similar to ours. But others, baroque, lush and crazy, can be born under such strange conditions that physical laws differ totally from those prevailing here. Better still, some universes may be colossally larger than ours, while others may be infinitely smaller than an atom."

"Amazing!" says Hugo who, at this moment in any case, seems to have completely forgotten his sentence following the death of Léopoldine.

"These ever-fluctuating universes form a majestic and crazy tree that is the fruit of a fascinating phenomenon known as eternal inflation," sums up the young blonde woman whose opulent chest overflows from a blouse that is very cautious in both its cut and its texture.

Victor Hugo cannot be insensitive to this. Indeed, all France knows that he loves feminine curves and about his passion for one of his mistresses, Juliette Drouet, with whom he has been in a relationship with since 1833 that would remain intact for nearly 50 years. As for the author's official wife, Adèle Foucher, she eventually expelled him from the marriage bed after the birth of their fifth child for the benefit of another writer, Charles-Augustin Sainte-Beuve. Driven by an extraordinary sexual appetite, Hugo made one conquest after another in all circles: ladies from the best society, courtesans or simple maids. And all this, despite the efforts of Juliette Drouet who tried, without success, to fight back against the mistresses of the great man.

But today, at least, Hugo concentrates on the extraordinary revelations that this green-eyed, red-haired man distills and not on the graceful curves of the young woman who, if he understands correctly, symbolizes the female part of one and the same person: Phil Caldwell.

"*Eternal... inflation...?*" says the poet, choking, widening his eyes and sweeping away the locks of hair blown over his forehead by a growing wind.

"The scientists of our time, excuse me... from the time when I lived before being killed, now trace the genesis of our universe by relativizing it," the astrophysicist adds.

"Meaning?"

"The birth of our universe, which is defined with a barbaric expression: big bang, would in fact be nothing but a spasm of emptiness. More precisely, the work of the best specialists has revealed the existence of a scalar field that would be the source of an inflation phase of our universe bubble and the origin of other bubbles of universes with different properties."

"*A scalar field?*"

"A scalar field is a place of space where a force is not directed, unlike vector fields. Scalar fields play a very important role in cosmology. These fields, in fact, are at the origin of the expansion of the universe and the phenomenon of inflation. Indeed, a scalar field is uniform throughout space. Its temporal behavior is analogous to that of a ball rolling along a slope. This movement corresponds to its potential energy. But it is subjected to a force of friction due to the expansion of the universe. When the slope is sufficiently gentle, this scalar field so peculiar to inflation – and called *inflation* for that reason – is practically immobile. Its potential energy is almost constant. This has the effect of generating an exponential growth in the size of the universe that is much faster than light. The observable, gigantic universe, which seems infinite to us, would in reality be only the result of the extraordinary inflationary expansion of a very small part of the universe before the onset of inflation."

"My head is going to explode," says Hugo.

The playwright places his hands on his neck in order to help relax him a little.

Then he continues with an obvious touch of masochism, "But what about you then? If I have understood your previous explanations, you are no longer part of this universe and you find yourself, with this charming girl, in a world that is not governed by you, but is orchestrated around you?"

"Perhaps. We will probably know when we reach the peak of this gigantic white cliff. What is certain is that current research in cosmology does not prohibit the creation of a universe in a place as absurd as the brain of a man who has just been decapitated."

He stops for a moment so that this last sentence takes on its full scope. Then he continues, "Afterwards, the laws of time and matter can be totally jostled, manipulated and rearranged in an incredible way. We have already witnessed the death the sun and its ultimate twilight."

"Imagine watching the death of the sun!"

The poet's gaze strays far beyond the sky. He imagines extravagant landscapes, rubicund lights that form haloes around and encapsulate stars bent on eternal wandering. He sees orbs of black lights that twist, weave and bruise giant planets.

He blinks again and contemplates the majestic poisonous beauty of monstrous rings. Cosmic chimeras assail him, crush his heart and cause his eyes to glaze. Without really realizing it, he is bringing forth the sequel of the poem, of which he has written only one verse so far: *Ce que dit la bouche d'ombre*. He also feels entire passages of his future poem, the most epic and somber of all, *La fin de Satan*, weaving within his mind.

Hugo looks at the two young people. He takes their hands in his and clasps them tightly. Phil Caldwell 3 jumps and grimaces a little. But she says nothing.

The fertile and inspired novelist waits, probably filling himself with the warmth of their skins. He scans the sky where heavy black clouds gradually obscure the moist, cool atmosphere of Jersey.

Then he whispers simply, "L'homme est brumeux, le monde est noir, le ciel est sombre, les formes de la nuit vont et viennent dans l'ombre; et nous, pâles, nous contemplons[39]."

He stops and finally concludes, "But you, my friends, live in a world amazed by an immaculate whiteness and you are not content to contemplate. You climb up a titanic mountain that would have dazzled Dante Alighieri as he began to write *The Divine Comedy*. You may live beyond eternity! I envy you..."

The young woman embraces the poet. The astrophysicist does the same. Then they both move gently towards the grove where they first appeared an hour earlier.

They walk around it and find themselves in front of a mercury pool whose silvery reflections capture the last rays of light from the stormy sky. They walk into it.

And they drown.

---

[39] *Au bord de l'infini* : poème XIV – Les Contemplations. Translation : Man is foggy, the world is black, the sky is dark, the forms of night come and go in the shade; and we, pale beings, we contemplate.

CHAPTER 997

The sharp cry of the anomalocaris immediately captures the attention of its three companions who have been walking for a long time along a particularly narrow terrace. The arthropod is agitated, pointing at in a very precise direction at the one of the strata located just above them.

The tiger and the two humans come to a stop. Their bulging eyes reveal their terrified surprise. Coming from the abyss, an immense quetzalcoatlus[40] the color of the night has just taken possession of one of the Phil Caldwells marching ahead of them. Because of his corpulence, it is possible to imagine that it was Phil Caldwell 8 whom they had already found, and lost, twice.

The spectacle is horrible. The feeling of impotence that prevails at this moment constricts their throats and crushes their chest. Trapped in the beak of the giant pterosaur, the man struggles. But he cannot prevail against an animal whose wingspan is equal to that of a fighter plane. In addition, this titan of the airs has long, slender and clawed legs capable of shredding anyone who tries to resist it.

The man, although very muscular, struggles and strikes with his arms, but the quetzalcoatlus does not care. It begins long spirals over the bottomless pit, remaining closer to the edge than the two giant DNA strands that continue to rise with the vast caravan of all the human beings who lived before Phil Caldwell and his contemporaries.

Suddenly, the predator releases the man who screams as he falls into the abyss.

Phil Caldwell 3 closes her eyes. The astrophysicist covers his ears with his filaments to block the cries of the damned man who falls back to Hell.

The odd events had begun a few weeks earlier. But no one could imagine that the situation would become so dramatic after climbing for more than two centuries.

The tiger was the first to notice that one of the Phil Caldwells near them, an elderly woman who was climbing at her own pace, had suddenly disappeared. Without noise or light. The fragile silhouette was there. In front of them. Then it vanished like a bubble of soap bursting in front of amused children.

Then a second. A third.

---

[40] Quetzalcoatlus northropi is one of the two biggest flying animals of all time. The other is the Hatzegopteryx which also had a wingspan of between 12 and 14 meters. These giant pterosaurs lived during the Upper Cretaceous, that is in 95 and 65 million years.

These discrete disappearances naturally fueled a long discussion among the four comrades.

They thought that this process of elimination was natural and part of one of the phases of initiation involved in their almost infinite climb towards a peak that would normally be the source of all truths. Of all revelations. Of all hopes, even if one were to rely on the remarks made by Osiris and, much later, by Victor Hugo, still under pall of the tragic disappearance of Léopoldine.

But now the situation is very different. It has even become very serious.

It is no longer bits of the custodial Phil Caldwell tutelary that fade without leaving traces. It is a satanic, aggressive creature who takes his tithe, selecting Phil Caldwells, apparently at random, and dropping them into the well which is now twice the width of Mars.

There has been a brutal shift from mysterious evaporation to organized massacre.

"A programmed mass extinction..." the astrophysicist immediately thinks, while making sure that his thoughts do not transform into words so as to avoid frightening his three faithful companions further.

The scientist does not really have time to let his mind wander because the huge pterosaur is already attacking a second victim. Skilled, despite the amazing size of its membranous wings inlaid with black on a slate-gray background, the monster from the incredible depths of the volcanic chimney sows panic among the few Phil Caldwells who climb above the stunned quartet. With a violent blow of wing it unbalances another man who tilts back. As the long membranous veils of the monster are equipped with embryos of extended legs, as well as long sharp claws, the effect of the blow is multiplied.

The prey is destabilized with each attack.

The quetzalcoatlus makes a complete circle around an invisible axis vertical to the abyss. Then it opens his mouth wide. It is more than two meters wide. The pterosaur then takes picks up the body of the unfortunate man he has already caused to fall.

In turn the white man tries to struggle. It must be admitted that hands that end in thousands of filaments and very fine tentacles are less effective than fists in such a case. But what could human fists do against the power of an archaic animal as large as a bus, with a beak the size of a bear?

The man's fate is sealed.

The trapped Phil Caldwell prisoner twists impotently. He tries to hang on when the animal dives. But his strength quickly fades and the taut muscles of his arms fail at the worst moment, just as the giant from the abyss flies over the maddening vertical wall that plunges several billion kilometers down.

Two about-turns later, a new victim falls in turn into the abyss located in the center of this volcanic chimney that defies the most complex stellar systems and the most arrogant Uranian deities.

The arms of the Phil Caldwell falling into the abyss, continue to stir in the void for a few moments. He screams in terror and his screams bounce from one wall to the other, echoing over and over.

Then he is no more than a white spot in a deep white thebaid that engulfs him forever.

At the same time, the gentle, ethereal, seraphic music which has been weaving its mesmerizing, hypnotic webs for two centuries weaves is brutally covered by a telluric tinkling. Giant metal sheets seem to collide, rocks crumble and burst. Demons scream like a thousand werewolves backed by their peers into an isolated canyon, knowing that they will be slaughtered in a few moments.

A dull and terrifying roar completes this funereal symphony where sinister terror weaves its way between each of us. Between each vibration.

Observers have the unbearable impression that it is the whole lower part of the abyss that is roiling, about to expel the dregs of the world into an ultimate vomiting of sound.

"Let's go!" yells the terrified anomalocaris.

"But where?" asks the astrophysicist, panicking as he realizes there is nowhere to hide.

The quartet is still far enough from the summit. Their immediate horizon is the simple accumulation of a hallucinating stratification of terraces connected by gently sloping paths.

On one side: the cliff, smooth, rigid, tepid and soft. But without a cave, or labyrinth in which to hide. This Dantesque wall opens only at night when the *mercury worlds* brush against its surface. On the other side: the void where the colossal bird drags its prey.

"We cannot escape anywhere!" scolds the tiger, revealing its powerful canines.

But, once again, what can sharp canines do against a Titan armed with long claws, whose power is equal to that of ten elephants?

"Things are getting really complicated!" says the young woman indicating a point that is rapidly growing behind the two strands of crystallized DNA of light in which thousands of dead people continue to flow.

"My God! cries the exoplanet specialist, without really knowing who is addressing this useless supplication.

"A second monster," says the large white cat.

A second quetzalcoatlus emerges from the abyss.

"But how many of them are there?" beseeches the anomalocaris its voice rising so high it is almost beyond hearing.

"I don't know," admits Phil Caldwell 1, shaking his head desperately. But if there are more and more of them, our quest will soon come to an end."

"How can we resist them? Where can we hide?" asks Phil Caldwell 3 who snuggles up against the astrophysicist for warmth.

She is quickly disappointed because her friend is frozen. From inside out. His skin, already pale in the normal state, is now almost cyanotic. The Stanford scientist has the excruciating, confusing feeling that all his blood has gathered in his heart, fleeing there from the rest of his body.

The tiger looks everywhere. It measures the distance separating them from the lower terrace.

But it quickly realizes that a leap of this type would be impossible for both the human Phil Caldwells. Moreover, the two giant pterosaurs seem ready to attack anywhere. They can cross 30 terraces in a matter of seconds and with a single stroke of their wings.

"We'll have to fight!" howls the tiger, communicating its energy and taste for predation.

It receives a very modest success because the only answer comes from the pale astrophysicist.

"And die..."

The beast remains motionless. It scans the two-winged monsters that swirl about as they identify their next prey.

They find one very quickly in the midst of the crowd of Phil Caldwells scattered along this part of the wall of the cliff.

After long moments of petrified fear in which the palms and filaments of their hands grow moist with cold sweat and the hair on the tiger's back bristles, the beings from the abyss head straight for the cliff. Using their a formidable ability to move about and highly develop vision, they seize a woman and a man. They are unstoppable. And the result is always the same. The unfortunate victims twist about in all directions trying to extricate themselves from the gigantic beaks that serve as yokes or, more exactly, the powerful jaws of bear traps.

The snap of the beak is almost similar. And the victim howls in despair and fear. But terror is not enough to free oneself from such an atrocious trap. With a few well controlled movements, the two quetzalcoatlus totally disorient their prey who no longer know where up and down are.

With broken ribs and unable to breathe, the captives are already in a very bad state when the two infernal creatures finally open their beaks wide and let them fall.

Some wild contortions. Panic dominates everything. Then the fall. Bottomless. And endless.

The screams of the damned recall the worst pages of human history when women and men, for often futile or perfectly unjust reasons, were burned alive, cut up, eviscerated, quartered or immersed in baths of boiling oil.

"We cannot get there," says the arthropod. "They will exterminate us!"

"The end of this insane initiation is, perhaps, a fall into the abyss," says the young woman, who seems a little calmer.

Her lucidity scares her companions. But they are by no means able to demonstrate to her that she is wrong. This impotence terrifies them as much as the spectacle of desolation that spreads before them.

After a moment of heavy silence, the astrophysicist replies while making a horrible grimace that belies his query, "In this case, we must prepare ourselves psychologically for this last leap."

"That's ridiculous!" says the tiger, losing patience. "Why have we climbed thousands and thousands of terraces if, after all these efforts, the ultimate goal is to crash and shatter a billion kilometers below? That does not make any sense!"

"I must admit that I agree with him," adds the anomalocaris who spends his time looking towards the abyss and then towards the two powerful winged monsters that constantly fly between the wall and the two helical DNA structures. "We have not made all these efforts for nothing! What was the purpose of all these immersions in the mercury worlds if, in the end, we are to fall like stones into a bottomless pit?"

"Is this not the goal of every being?" the young woman asks, raising her eyebrows.

This tense remark temporarily puts an end to the discussion. Above them the carnage continues with the implacability of a metronome gathering seconds of death. Seconds of fright.

The Phil Caldwells run in all directions. Their desperate flight scatters them like ants in the middle of their anthill disturbed by a wild animal. But here they do not scatter to preserve the queen's eggs. They are quite simply trying to save their lives. Some do. Others do not. They find themselves trapped in the monstrous beak of a monstrous bird that pursues a monstrous goal: to kill the maximum number of Phil Caldwells! Why?

The absence of a logical answer, or of any answer, drives the astrophysicist mad with rage.

"Fine!" he says as he approaches the edge of the abyss so that one of the pterosaurs can see him at last and heads straight for him.

"You're crazy!" roars the tiger as he stands before the astrophysicist. "We haven't done all this for nothing. We're going to fight! We're going to get away! There is a solution! But we are not going to die!"

The beast's three companions are dumbfounded. They suddenly realize why one of the facets of the personality of the unfortunate scientist who was decapitated by Felipe Maldorano has been reincarnated here as a tiger.

"Let's look for an exit near the wall," recommends Phil Caldwell 3, beginning to slide the filaments of her hands along the wall just behind them.

As is the case of the millions of absurdly stacked floors, it is topped by an elliptical arc which is slightly flattened in the center.

They wait for her to complete her investigation. Two minutes later she turns around. Her expression is grave. Sad. Her eyes shine and two tears start to flow down her cheeks.

"Nothing. I've found nothing."

"No way to escape, then?" asks the anomalocaris of a voice, for once, almost gentle.

"No."

Grimly, they huddle along the cliff, hoping that the monsters with the immense beaks will not see them. Or that they prefer other prey.

The spectacle that unfolds before them is appalling because the quetzalcoatlus conscientiously collect all the Phil Caldwells that they locate throughout the terraces lie in layers around the abyss. Most continue to run, which immediately attracts the attention of the large winged predators. But even those who, like the members of the quartet, freeze in order to remain hidden as long as possible, end up being spotted. In this case, the sentence is always the same. Capture. Then the fall.

The sonic cataclysm that has invaded the volcanic chimney of cosmic dimensions naturally attenuates the horror of the screams of the unfortunate victims who are thrown into the abyss. But this superimposition of a demonic noise and unspeakable suffering is maddening.

The young woman with the full bosom is now ground against the torso of Phil Caldwell 1 while the arthropod with the falsetto voice has slipped between the tiger's front legs. They all wait for a very unlikely calm, frozen in silence and fear.

Suddenly, the anomalocaris tries to scream but his shrill voice is lost in the hubbub, "Attention, they..."

His friends immediately understand what is going on. One of the two pterosaurs has already flown around them near the terrace where they are hiding.

It gains a little altitude and approaches one of the giant DNA strands where thousands of faces filled with anger, fright or pleasure constantly parade. Then, suddenly, it turns 180° and heads straight for the quartet huddling against the cliff wall. White against an *outre-blanc* background, they are not easy to see. But the flying monster has excellent vision. Vision that allows it to grasp his prey while gauging their weight.

This point is important because the tiger's companions have noticed that the quetzalcoatlus has carefully avoided attacking the stegosaur, despite flying over it three times.

"Weight is their only enemy," the astrophysicist says, pointing out the only weakness of these winged creatures.

Indeed, the diabolic creatures cannot carry prey that is too heavy over the abyss or they will run the risk of falling along with their unfortunate victims. The stegosaurus, which they encountered many years ago and which they still see regularly, has been saved by its size and the power of the bony darts that adorn its tail.

This gives the big white cat a small chance, but none at all for his three friends.

The giant creature rushes towards the quartet cornered against an immense wall along a narrow terrace that looks more like a cornice than a shelf. The animal dives at them. Its coal-gray silhouette grows gigantic. Little by little it obscures the sky and the abyss.

"It is the end!" screams Phil Caldwell 1, squeezing the shoulders and torso of the young woman to whom he is so close and so distant at the same time as hard as possible.

"Not necessarily!" whispers the anomalocaris, darting its stalk-like eyes towards the wall wedged beneath the elongated arc.

Although night has not fallen and the *outre-blanc* is radiant, an enormous mercury sphere moves horizontally towards them. When the quetzalcoatlus is fewer than ten meters from the quartet, the bubble with its mercury streaks breaks through the surface of the wall. Without stopping to think, they all dive into this life-saving, icy sphere.

Followed by the dry snap of the beak of the angry monster as it turns away from edge at the last moment.

CHAPTER 998

The interior of the perfect sphere is almost translucent.

The four silhouettes inside are positioned perpendicularly to this soft surface which constantly grows more iridescent. Unlike all other the other times the Phil Caldwells have been immersed in the mercury worlds, there is no feeling of cold or pain here. The feeling that prevails is an almost absolute tranquility, close to ataraxia[41].

It is impossible to say whether this modification is related to the fact that the foursome was swallowed up by the silvery worm extending from the sphere of liquid mercury occurred in broad daylight and not at night. This emergence of the sphere in the very heart of the cliff allowed the four unfortunate Phil Caldwells to escape from the claws and beak of the winged monster that was about to massacre them.

They awaken gradually. Their surprise is total.

In this space connecting two worlds, which is usually filled with suffering, the explosion of the viscera and the pounding of bodies, they find themselves instead in a sphere that sails gently on a stream of calm, clear water. Around them, clear silhouettes. Men and women. Naked. Like them.

Animals too. Exuberant flowers and a tender green meadow. Some comical objects: a giant mollusk, men upside down in a squash as large as a small house or a small mouse in a transparent tube near a human face that scrutinizes it, looking for infinity in the hairs of its mustaches finally reveal the truth to them.

They are in the central panel of the triptych by Hieronymus Bosch entitled *"The Garden of Earthly Delights"*.

Colorful birds observe them and dozens of humans prance on titmice and finches the size of a donkey or a horse.

"The... Garden of Earthly... The Garden of Earthly Delights," mumbles the astrophysicist who immediately recognizes the dominant colors: light green, pale blue and pink.

"But what?" asks the young woman, without knowing whether the rest of her sentence makes sense or not.

As a result, she falls silent, filling her eyes, her mind and her heart with the rustic, burlesque and baroque images.

Worrisome as well, as Phil Caldwell 1 immediately points out:

"We are in the central panel of the triptych. But the one on the right focusses on Hell!"

---

[41] Notion already defined by Democritus, and later Epicurus, the ataraxia symbolizes total tranquility linked to the absence of troubles, sorrows or pain.

The serene enjoyment gently transforms into fear. Then the fear changes into terror.

This development is justified, moreover, because the sphere that serves as a crystalline ship begins to move gently downstream in this small brook that is growing incessantly. It accelerates.

There are still many humans, eccentric plants and comical animals in the surrounding landscape. But their features harden and their shapes lose their natural grace. The colors bleed and the light flickers. Like a phantom vessel in a monstrous storm, the bubble in which the astrophysicist and his companions are still held in a hieratic and stilted posture twirls on itself.

The wind roars and a terrifying noise grows louder and louder ahead of them.

The humans try to determine the source of this appalling roar while the anomalocaris feverishly focuses its faceted eyes on an invisible spot.

Not a spot... A line! A line that runs along the horizon, separating, as with a scalpel, the world of water from that of air.

"We're going to fall!" yells the young woman, clenching her fists as if this innocuous gesture could slow them.

But, trapped in the crystal sphere, they can do nothing. The tiger roars and the translucent ship shakes. Five seconds later, they all pour into the abyss, following millions of tons of water from a waterfall that would make Victoria Falls look ridiculously small if they were located on Earth.

And they drown.

The sky is deep blue. The burning sun of the Mycenae quickly warms the bodies still languishing on the ground.

In the distance, cyclopean ramparts protect the city of Argos. In front of that, there is a carefully maintained park with manicured lawns. Many Mediterranean trees are stand there with the elegance and majesty of the plants that defy time. The branches of the thousand-year-old olive trees bend under the countless fruits waiting for a gust of wind to be harvested.

A pond with large white birds is located just in front of the palace.

Several figures dressed in white walk quietly under the blazing Greek sun of the second millennium BC.

The tiger wakes first.

It growls a little, rousing the young blonde woman who is now wearing a linen peplos, the earthy color of sienna. Essentially a rectangular piece of wool or linen with large folds, the peplos is a practical, ample and light garment. The top of the garment forms a flap over the chest and the two halves of the fabric are attached by a large clip on each shoulder. It is cinched at the waist by a narrow belt which, in the case of Phil Caldwell 3, is of a beautiful indigo shade that contrasts pleasantly with the deep red of the peplos.

Dressed in the traditional chiton, the astrophysicist wakes in turn, roused by licks of the tiger. The arthropod continues to snore as if the drop in the waterfall had not really affected it and the redhead begins to shake it firmly like a toy whose batteries have died.

Finally, it wakes up and utters a shrill cry that could no doubt be heard all the way to Crete.

"Where are we?" it asks, after its previous cries have been carried off by the light wind that comes from the sea.

"In Greece," replies the astrophysicist.

"But during which period?" asks the tiger, worried.

"We are in Mycenae. But I don't know exactly when."

Silence falls.

The young woman carefully observes the landscape from the hill in the northeast part of the plain of Argos where they have just awakened. On this hill, and behind the tall trees, stands a sumptuous, white marble palace. From here, it is easy to see Argolis and the Saronic Gulf, where the Mediterranean nestles, creeps and cajoles, dazzling the horizon with its sapphire waters.

Encircled by high walls made up of enormous blocks of stone, the site is closed by the Lion Gate. In front of this impressive opening, it is easy to see a vast circular space littered with the tombs of the ancient kings of Mycenae. From the Lion Gate, terraced staircases run down to a small harbor. Several boats, whose sails have been cautiously lowered, lie motionless in the harbor nestled at the edge of the Saronic Gulf. Their slender silhouettes dot the azure see, reflected in the waves.

The red-haired scientist seems in a hurry to head for the palace that overlooks the city and the surrounding wall while his three companions hesitate.

"Are you coming?"

No answer.

"Fine. I'm going. Join me when you finally manage to peel your feet, scales and legs from the grass."

He smiles slyly, giving him a particularly playful look.

Suddenly, a procession appears at the bottom of the steps nearest to the wharf where the ships dock. It is composed of about thirty men. Some women follow, all dressed in white or ocher.

The majestic, stiff character of the procession immediately confers on it an official character, much like a reception with great pomp in the royal palace of Argos.

"An embassy, no doubt," thinks Phil Caldwell 1.

In the middle of the hubbub, two names are repeated cyclically. The names of two kings. The names of two brothers united by the same story. By the same hatred: Atreus and Thyestes!

The scientist turns pale. The young woman, the giant feline and the anomalocaris flee immediately!

286

Ten seconds later, the astrophysicist can no longer see them. Obviously, they are hiding behind a group of trees with gnarled trunks that stand along the edges of the royal park standing over the palace and the city. What can terrify a tiger?

The Stanford exoplanet specialist has an idea. He too would like to run away, for the mythological legend related to the fatal destiny of the Atrides family is atrocious. It is even said that the crime which took place here in Atreus' Mycenaean palace was so terrible that it made the sun move backward!

What unspeakable terror, what monstrous crime can make a tiger flee and cause the sun to move backward?

Turning back to the palace and the sea, Phil Caldwell 1 realizes that the procession has almost completed the long ascent of the path that winds through stairs to the entrance of the palace. The procession is about to enter state rooms of the palace through a vast terrace with a majestic portico with columns.

The palms of his hands are moist. Icy. He knows this detestable sensation well. Fear. Despite the terror that crushes his heart, he forces himself to look.

Once the last person has finally entered the palace, followed by two watchful guards, wearing armor and armed with long spears, the astrophysicist finally decides to approach. He does not know why he is driven by this irresistible desire to know what he already feels. Perhaps, simply because the sudden appearance of this mercury world in broad daylight saved his life, as well as those of his three companions, from the claws and beak of the monstrous quetzalcoatlus that wanted to pitch them into the abyss. He tells himself that this is reason enough to justify having to face this absolute horror.

"An additional element of a redemptive initiation?" he wonders, knowing that the one or ones who could respond to his request had remained desperately mute for more than two centuries.

Absolute horror? The use of words is sometimes outrageous when humans express themselves and converse. But the legend of Atreus and Thyestes surpasses the worst stories. It is so terrifying that it only inspired three dramatic authors in two millennia[42].

The others have fled. Or, have cautiously avoided staging an abomination likely to make the sun moved backward...

The legend starts simply in a manner quite common in Greek mythology. Atreus and his twin brother Thyestes occupied the throne of Mycenae in the absence of King Eurystheus. Then, the two scoundrels murdered their half-brother Chrysippus. All this is distressingly banal, as is the fact that Thyestes became the lover of Aerope, Atreus' wife. Similarly, Atreus learned that his brother had an adulterous relationship with his wife and decided to take revenge.

---

[42] Seneca, in the first century AD, De Monleon in the seventeenth century (1638) and Prosper Jolyot de Crebillon in the eighteenth century (1707).

All the above is so commonplace, so common in mythology as in the usual life of men, that it could very well have constituted only a few lines in a very long chronicle dedicated to the vicissitudes of a humanity torn by its desires and appetites for power. But what will happen in a few minutes, and under the eyes of the astrophysicist, terrified and horrified all the commentators who took the trouble to relate this monstrosity.

Well-versed in mythology, the red-haired man knows perfectly what is about to happen. His father, William Caldwell, was passionate about Elizabethan theater and French classical theater. When he was twenty years old, the future Stanford astrophysicist had the opportunity to read one of the two best tragedies written by Prosper Jolyot de Crebillon: *Atrée et Thyeste*.

In particular, he recalls the last three scenes...

And the idea of being here at this moment is freezing his blood.

But he walks ahead anyway. Cautiously.

Some Mycenaean soldiers walk along the ramparts. But they are mostly looking towards the plain below and the harbor where the boats that ply a fruitful trade with Crete and some towns of the Peloponnese sleep peacefully. The path is clear. The sound of voices quickly make it obvious that Thyestes and his companions have already entered the Atreus' palace.

For it is indeed at the heart of his palace that the King of Argos is planning to organize a great feast to symbolize the peace found by the two enemy brothers.

Moving slowly under the implacable Mycenaean sun, Phil Caldwell finally reaches the entrance to the palatial residence. He straightens his chest and passes quietly by two helmeted and armed guards who barely glance at him.

The first room, a vast vestibule, is cool despite the ambient heat. The walls are covered with frescoes inspired directly by the Minoan art for which Crete was renowned a few centuries earlier, during the time of Knossos.

Since the noise of conversations is growing, Phil Caldwell 1 decides to mingle with the crowd of the two kings' servants. He walks into a second room, also decorated with paintings and frescoes representing scenes from everyday life, in a colorful mixture of green, purple and saffron. Unlike most of the civilizations of the time that favored pomp and feats of arms, the art of the Minoan and Mycenaean civilizations were inspired by life. The movements were fluid and supple. Often voluptuous.

But the astrophysicist knows perfectly well that he is not here to study Mycenaean art, or to feast his eyes on comical or libertine images.

He must focus on the very essence of what the human mind can conceive when the roots of evil plunge so deeply into us that they reach and go beyond hell!

He is still walking towards the place where the banquet will take place, while exchanging some banalities in a language he did not know five minutes earlier when he arrived here with a blonde young woman, a fearful tiger and an extravagant creature which speaks in a falsetto voice. The men and women he meets are all wearing peplos or chitons. They seem calm. It is easy to imagine that the reconciliation between Atreus and Thyestes symbolizes a new era for the people of Mycenae.

An 18th-century poet, painter and engraver of the eighteenth century stated: *exuberance is beauty*[43]. At this moment, Phil Caldwell must admit that here, exuberance really is the reflection of beauty. But a fleeting one. It always withers. And today, this radiant beauty in which innocence still permeates will wilt at an almost unthinkable speed.

After a few moments of discussion with a man with impressive muscles and am elegant, young woman, he finally reaches the entrance to the megaron, the great throne room where Atreus receives his people, his advisers and the various ambassadors that come to Mycenae to sign treaties or endorse trade.

A gigantic, sumptuous banquet table has been set up to welcome his brother. The King of Argos has ensured that the presentation and nobility of the dishes symbolize his willingness to reconcile with Thyestes.

The astrophysicist rapidly notes the details of this vast room which is more than ten meters long and built as a perfect square. Fruits are displayed everywhere, giving a sensation of abundance which the large, horn-shaped cup amplifies much better than a long speech.

The king's munificence is unparalleled. Drinks flow and the ruby color of the wine promises brilliant drunkenness.

"Dionysus seems to be in attendance..." murmurs Phil Caldwell 1, without anybody being able to hear him.

Indeed, a troupe of musicians orchestrates a racket that is somewhat dissonant for the ears of a 21st-century man. Percussion instruments pound and thunder after each speech by the monarch or his brother. The guests eat either sitting or standing and the ambient mess is a bit the norm here.

Phil Caldwell then said to himself that the ceremonial, solemn, stilted and sometimes even austere character sometimes associated with this pre-Homeric period hardly corresponds to the atmosphere that prevails here.

Apparently, the Minoan and Mycenaean civilizations were festive, cheerful, and lustful and very far from a warlike or theocratic structure that promoted the worship of weapons or that of demanding and distant gods. Here Dionysus reigns supreme and wine flows without stop.

The astrophysicist leans against one of the forty columns supporting the ceiling of this vast megaron reserved for royal receptions, banquets and rituals aimed at attracting the favors of a propitiatory divinity that would be capable of protecting the ancestors of Atreus and Thyestes and their descendants.

The mythological legend proved, alas, that this hope was in vain. But, at this moment, none of the guests knows that yet. Thyeste less than anyone else.

---

[43] William Blake in *The Marriage of Heaven and Hell* (1793).

The scientist takes advantage of this moment of effervescence, allowing himself to be lulled by the euphoria affecting all the guests present. A servant brings him a cup filled with an amber liquid whose surface vibrates and reflects. He raises it to his lips and chokes at once.

"That's strong!" he says, wiping his mouth with the back of his hand.

But, determined not to remain a failure, he makes a second attempt. The green-eyed, red-haired man seems to take a liking to this rather alcoholic beverage, which is fruity, yet harsh on his throat.

He then turns to look at one end of the table. Atreus is clearly visible, with a fairly corpulent stature, black hair, bushy eyebrows, and chiseled features, demonstrating a shady character, quick to anger. Or revenge...

Sitting next to him, Thyeste is thinner. But he shares the same physical family features, indicating a difficult temperament. His fleshy, greedy lips also confirm his appetite for sex and Aerope would certainly not claim otherwise. But the connection between Thyeste and his brother's wife seems to be forgotten today.

Joy reigns and sentimental torments seem to have no place in their present concerns. A young man sits to them. He is Pleisthenes, the fruit of the illegitimate relationship between Thyestes and Aerope.

The reunion is moving. With forgiveness becoming the norm in Mycenae, everyone can rejoice in this reconciliation, which will probably prevent innocent victims from paying a heavy price for the hatred that can sometimes overwhelm the two brothers.

The three men have been talking for a while.

Suddenly, Atreus makes a sign to the captain of his guard: Alcimedon. He whispers a few words in his ear. Then the captain of the guards does the same with Pleisthenes. The two men walk away.

It is at this moment that a beautiful brown girl, settles down next to Thyestes. Theodamia is one of Thyestes' daughters. She is accompanying him on this long journey of reconciliation which is supposed to calm family quarrels that have lasted for far too long.

The banquet continues and the master of ceremony announces that the large cup will soon appear and be placed in the center of the table.

Phil Caldwell approaches an elderly woman who eats greedily as if she had been hungry for six months crossing a hostile desert.

"What is this great cup?"

"The cup of reconciliation, of course!" replies the old woman, as if this question were absurd. "It is the cup that symbolizes the peace between the two brothers who have reigned, reign and will reign for a long time still over Mycenae!"

The astrophysicist thanks her. Then he moves away from the old woman and a little closer to the table. He must force his way through since the women and men who are part of the delegation accompanying Thyestes are elbowing one another in order to obtain the best pieces of meat or poultry. He smiles inwardly, thinking that this kind of behavior has not really changed over 3,300 years!

The drums pound and all eyes turn in the direction where this famous cup will appear carried by the cook who has prepared an exquisite meal exclusively for the two brothers. From where he is standing now, the astrophysicist can finally hear and see well despite the music that hurts his ears a little, the noisy discussions and the chewing and repeated clashes of cups and dishes that regularly fall from the hands of guests already a little tipsy.

Atreus is talking to his brother, who has been scowling since the Pleisthenes' unexpected departure. He looks for his son. But he does not see him.

Atreus stares at his brother and says[44]:

Dear Thyestes, come near: where does this fright come from?
What displeasure so quickly disturbs your heart?
You seem to be in the grip of a secret sorrow,
And no longer show me that satisfied soul
Who seemed to breathe the sweetness of peace:
Is it no longer your most tender wish?
What! What suspicions does your soul harbor?
This day, is this happy day made for fear?
My brother, you must banish fear from now on;
The cup will soon unite us forever.
Do you taste the sweetness of such a perfect peace?
And do you want it as I want it?
Are you not aware of this rare happiness?
Thyeste replies:
Who? I suspect you, or hate you, Lord?
The gods stand as witnesses for me, these gods I vouch for here,
Who read Thyestes' soul better than you do.
Do not be offended by a vain terror
Which seems, despite myself, to seize my heart:
I feel it troubled with mortal pain;
My constancy succumbs; in vain I call it back;
And, for a moment, my downcast spirit
Allows a shameful weight to overwhelm its virtue.
However, near you, an indescribable charm

---

[44] From this moment on, the dialogues that follow in italics are a translation of verses 1408 to 1525 (scenes 6, 7 and 8 of Act V) of the tragedy written by Prosper Jolyot de Crébillon: Atrée and Thyeste. This play was presented for the first time on March 17, 1707 at the Comédie Française. The French text is provided in an appendix at the end of the novel.

Suspends for now the turmoil that alarms me.
To reassure my timid mind again,
Give me back my children, bring my son to me;
That he may witness a union so dear,
And share, my Lord, the kindness of my brother.
Atreus looks at Thyestes for a moment before replying:
You will be satisfied, Thyestes; and your son
Forever in these places will be given back to you.
Yes, my brother, it is no more than the inhuman Fate
That can separate Thyestes from Pleisthenes.
You will see him soon; my order
Hastens your departure from this palace.
To provide the most certain proof of my good faith,
I want to send you back this day to Mycenae.
Despite what I do, unsure of this faith,
I see that your heart is alarmed by me.
However, I believed that full insurance
Should follow...
His brother interrupts him then:
Ah! Lord, this reproach offends me.
Atreus then addresses one of the guards located nearby:
Let someone go look for the princess; go, and in these places
Have Pleisthenes appear before my eyes without delay.
It must be so...
At this moment, Eurysthenes, the master of ceremony, brings in the great
cup holding a stew that looks succulent.

A few pieces of meat spring up from the surface, forming small mounds.

Atreus is delighted. He claps his hands and says:
But I see the cup of our fathers:
Here is the sacred knot of the peace binding two brothers;
It comes at the right time to reassure on e's heart
Alarmed just now by an unworthy terror.
One that could still challenge Atreus
May perhaps believe better in the sacred cup.
Does Thyestes want it to succeed this day
In uniting two hearts torn asunder by love?
To inspire a brother to greater trust,
To convince him finally, that I begin.
At this moment, Atreus grasps the cup which Eurysthenes had so carefully
held in his hands. He conspicuously shows it to his brother and the other guests,
raising his arms slightly.

Thyestes observes what his brother does and immediately says:
I have already told you, you are insulting me, my Lord,

If you take offense over a vain fear.
What would henceforth your hatred wish to steal from me,
After having restored my estates and Pleisthenes to me?
From the most frightful wrath, whatever the project was,
Are my unfortunate days worth this blessing?
Eurysthenes, give it to me; give me the advantage
Of swearing this precious pledge first.
My heart has apparently recovered from its distress;
Give it to me. But I do not see my son.

While talking, Thyestes takes the cup from Atreus.

Atreus first addresses his guards when he speaks of Pleisthenes:

Has he not returned?

Then he turns to Thyestes:

Rest assured, my brother;
You will soon see a head so dear:
It is the most sacred knot of our union;
Fear less than ever of being separated from it.

On hearing this phrase, Phil Caldwell starts to shudder uncontrollably. His hands are icy. And sweaty.

However, he is to observe this scene, of which he knew, alas, all the details.

Thyestes immediately replies to his brother:

Vouch for the safety of Thyestes,
Cup of our ancestors, and you, gods whom vouch for.
May your wrath now strike
The first of us who breaks the peace!
And you, brother as dear as my daughter and Pleisthenes,
Receive such proof of my good faith.

Suddenly, Thyeste looks into the cup. He immediately sees human remains floating in this abject stew. A few seconds later, he sees his son's head, two hands fingers partially cut off. A piece of a foot.

His eyes bulge. He turns pale.

Thyestes is terrified and, at the same time, he has just come to understand the real frightful vengeance his brother has exacted for his adulterous relationship with Aerope.

He screams:

But what do I see, traitor? Ah! Great gods! How horrible!
It's blood! All mine blood is freezing in my heart.
The sun is growing dark; and the bloody cup
Seems to flee on its own from this trembling hand.
I'm dying. Ah! My son, what has become of you?

He continues to shriek and tear his hair in fright and rage.

Theodamas, his daughter, then intervenes, discovering the absolute horror of an act combining vengeance, murder and cannibalism.

Did you suffer, cruel gods? What have I seen?
Ah, Lord! Your son, my deplorable brother,
Has just been deprived of light forever.

Thyestes is overwhelmed by pain. He wants to vomit and curses his brother who just committed the worst outrage imaginable: having his brother's child murdered and inviting him to feed on his corpse!

He curses his brother who smiles diabolically:

My son is dead, cruelly, in this very palace,
And at the very moment when they offer me peace!
And, horror of horrors,
Barbarian, you offer me blood with your hand!
O earth, at this moment, can you bear us?
O my dreadful dream, sad memory?
My son, was this your blood offered to your father?

Drunk with pleasure, Atreus then asks:

Did you not recognize this blood?

Thyestes responds in tears:

"I recognize my brother.

Atreus grows impatient. He roars and spits as he speaks:

You must have acknowledged him and no longer offended him;
Wretch, do not force this brother to avenge himself.

A short silence fills the room.

All the guests of the king of Mycenae are petrified. They do not fully understand what has just happened. But they know one thing: the universe and the gods will never forget that terrible crime which made the sun move back!

The unhappy Thyestes continues:

Great gods, for what crimes do you release the thunder?
Monster, which the hells have vomited up on earth,
Quench the fury with which has washed over your heart;
Join an unfortunate father his unfortunate son;
Give this victim his bloody manna,
And do not stop in the middle of your crime.
Barbarian, can you spare me in places
From which you have just chased away the day and the gods?

Atreus replies dryly:

"No, to see the misfortunes in which I have plunged your life,
I would repent pf taking it from you.
By your groans I know your pain:
I so wanted you to feel your misfortune;
And my heart, losing the hope of its vengeance,
Find its only hope in your tears.

You wish for death, you beseech it; and me,
I give you the day to take you vengeance on me.

Thyestes watches his brother. He slips the worst poison he can conceive of in this moment of pure terror into his gaze, already turned towards the afterlife.

Then he simply says:
You flatter yourself in vain, and the hand of Thyestes
Will be able to deprive you of such a disastrous pleasure.

He takes his short sword and stabs himself through the heart.

His body wobbles. Then he falls back with a great crash.

His eyes remain wide open until the moment when Atropos[45] definitely cuts the thread of his destiny.

Theodamas rushes to her dying father.

She tries to take him in her arms. But his blood already covers his tunic and the ground.

She does not know how to express her pain and distress and simply says:
Heaven!

Hiccupping and spitting blood, Thyestes finds the strength to utter these words to her before he dies:
Console yourself, my daughter; and from these places
Flee, and turn your vengeance back to the gods.
Content, by your tears, to implore their justice,
Get away from this traitor to wait for his torment.
The gods, whom this breach of oath as caused to grow pale with fright,
Will make him some day more unfortunate than I am;
Heaven promises me this, the cup is pledges this;
And I die.

With a ruby face and eyes sparkling with unhealthy joy, Atreus concludes:
At this price, I accept the omen:
Your hand, by immolating yourself, has fulfilled my wishes,
And I at last enjoy the fruits of my crimes!

Phil Caldwell has the horrible feeling that his heart has just stopped beating. He tries to swallow. But he cannot. One part of his body no longer responds: his eyes. They stubbornly stare at the large cup that Atreus has placed on the large table. From where he stands, he easily sees Pleisthenes' skull and one of his hands.

The astrophysicist wants to look away from the symbol of the absolute horror committed by the King of Mycenae. He wants to run away and vomit. Or vomit and run. But his eyes refuse to obey. He curses himself to restore strength and vigor to the muscles of his legs, which are also frozen by fear.

---

[45] In Greek mythology, the three Moirai are the goddesses of fate and destiny. Clotho spines the thread of life, Lachesis measures the length of it and Atropos cuts its.

After several ineffective attempts, the astrophysicist finally manages to control his distress, his emotions and mind tyrannizing his body.

"To run away. Run away... Right now!" he says, without worrying about the other guests.

It is true that the women and men who rejoiced, drank, stuffed themselves and sometimes embraced behind some of the forty columns are now also completely overwhelmed.

The agitated behavior of Phil Caldwell 1 has no chance of grabbing the attention of human beings who gradually feel the abysses of hell open under their feet.

The other guests share the astrophysicist's gut reaction: to flee from this accursed place. Most of Thyestes' companions set off down to return to their boats. The astrophysicist heads in the opposite direction.

He runs to the curtain of thousand-year-old trees that cover the top of the hill above the royal palace, with its impressive wall of stones carved by titans.

He runs. A taste of blood fills his mouth. But he persists.

A few minutes later, he finally reaches the majestic trunks whose thick bark protects them from the monstrosities of the world.

"The trees are very lucky," whispers Phil Caldwell 1, slowing a little.

In front of him a pond of mercury awaits him. His three friends are there.

"So?" asks the anomalocaris in a voice even higher than usual.

While diving with them into the mass of liquid mercury in which they will drown, yet again, he merely finds the strength to say, "I'm my worst nightmare!"

CHAPTER 999

Finally, free of the two quetzalcoatluses that had pitched the Phil Caldwell into the abyss before their trying passage in the mercury world reserved for the revenge of Atreus, the gigantic white volcanic chimney is almost an Eden.

Spit out by the mercury sphere that extracts all the aspects of a personality as complex as the 10^{80} nucleons that make up our visible universe from the mind of the decapitated scientist, those who explore the abysses of the soul are in poor condition. Phil Caldwell 1 is sprawled on his stomach. The tiger is curled up in a ball. The young woman is on her knees and the anomalocaris is lying on its back like a tortoise swept over by the wind.

Amazed, they take time to recover following their frightful stroll in the Mycenaean era. With a slowness dictated by the pleasure of finally finding themselves in a place where no one boils the body of his brother's son after having first dismembered it, the quartet stirs a little.

The humans are massaging some still sore muscles as the arthropod from the Cambrian era settles back in its favorite place, between the legs of the big white cat!

"Happy to be back here!" says Phil Caldwell 3, rubbing her hands in satisfaction.

"What could I possibly say after the ordeal I have endured?" adds the astrophysicist whose face still bears the stigmata of the horror which he witnessed an impotent bystander.

"Can you explain your last sentence?" asks the tiger, frowning.

"Uh..."

"Before diving into the pool that allowed us to leave Mycenae, you clearly said: I'm my worst nightmare! Can you clarify?"

"That is really what I have believed since I witnessed Atreus' horrible vengeance on his brother."

"So?"

In fact, the mythological tale of the frightful destiny of the Atrides is well known and is similar, in terms of horror in any case, with tragedies like that of Oedipus or Medea, the child-murdering mother.

"I did not quite understand this story of brothers who hate one another and then reconcile. And then they end up killing each other?" insists the anomalocaris whose prominent eyes are moving about in all directions, making their 16,000 facets shine.

"It's simple," interrupts the young woman, still arrogantly thrusting her bosom forward. "To take revenge on his brother, who seduced his wife, Atreus, feigned reconciliation, invited Thyestes to his palace and gave him his children, whom he had just killed to eat."

"But... but..." stammers the anomalocaris.

"I know," she says, sighing. "Human beings are often much worse than the bloodiest of animals. Compared to some men, hyenas are gentle, candid and affectionate as newborn lambs."

"The history of humanity is filled with men like Atreus," adds the astrophysicist. "After tragedies, mass executions and holocausts, people always utter this meaningless sentence: never again! We weep. We lament. Our voices quaver. We hug one another for reassurance and to affirm that we all finally understand. That the world will be less ugly. That the ferocity inherent in the human heart will fade somewhat. But barbarism always creeps back. Often the very next day. Imposing its law. Again, and again!"

A heavy silence falls at this moment, betrayed only by the music of the spheres that resumed its rights following the disappearance of the two giant pterosaurs.

"This myth was taken up by Seneca in one of his tragedies," says Phil Caldwell 1, whose face gradually relaxes. "The guiding thread that shaped this dreadful re-enactment which I forced myself to watch was inspired by Crebillon's play, which my father made me read when I was a teenager. I delightedly discovered the workings of the human soul by reading Shakespeare, Racine, Rotrou or Corneille."

"But Crebillon is less known," observes the young woman. "He is particularly well-known for his libertine novels. I remember reading *Le Sopha* and *Les égarements du cœur et de l'espri...*"

"You're mixing things up."

"How?"

"The libertine tales and stories were written by Crebillon's son. The father was an academician and wrote mainly tragedies, of which the two most known are *Rhadamiste et Zénobie* and *Atrée et Thyeste*. But the singularity of this play, and of its principal character, have made me suddenly understand that I carry such monstrosities within myself. It is for this reason that I say, and I now confirm, that I am my worst nightmare! Hell lies within in us. Even when we try to convince ourselves otherwise."

He remains silent for a moment and then continues, "That's what worries me. If this climb has an obvious initiatory and symbolic character, why then select this monstrous character, Atreus, who is not content with being the author and director of his own vengeance but who is also an actor and spectator of the violence he caused to his own brother? It is his enjoyment as a criminal discovering his victim's terror that terrifies me when I think of the abyss of ignominies and sorrows that I carry in me."

"Perhaps it is the fact of having been executed in such a barbaric manner that exhumes in you these recurring dreads, and gives substance to similar monsters. To the worst ferocity. To the worst crimes!" concludes the tiger.

"Probably," agrees the Stanford scientist. "But these hideous horrors have probably existed in me for a long time. Such a very long time."

"Finally forcing them to emerge from the depths in which they have hidden themselves may perhaps have a therapeutic function as well," says the obstinate young woman who knows that she is totally and unfailingly linked to the fate and psychic survival of the astrophysicist.

"A kind of catharsis?"

"Without a doubt."

"I don't understand anything!" says the anomalocaris, waving the two shrimp tails that adorn its head. "But I do know one thing. Now that we are rid of the two winged dragons, let's continue our climb! And reach the summit at last!"

"You are right, old eccentric chatterbox!" says Phil Caldwell 1, sighing. "There are still many terraces above us to climb."

Before returning to the climb that will take them to the peak, in a few more decades, the astrophysicist examines their environment that is once again peaceful after the disappearance of the two winged monsters.

The gulf has widened further. But it is so vast now that it is quite difficult to measure how much it has grown. It is no longer possible to see the other side where the horizon blends into the thousand shades of *outre-blanc* that are constantly being refined in this Dantesque universe. The layers above them are still clearly visible. But the slope of the cliff has diminished slightly, probably about 70 degrees from this point on. The top is still lost in an immaculate whiteness like a mirage in a desert of salt.

Overhead, the billions of translucent spheres pursue an unfathomable ballet. They slip, jostle, move this way and that. Sometimes, they collide, without causing any explosion or particular noise.

Everything is silk, powder and beauty here.

The sky boasts sparks and gleams that seem to draw the eye and invite the viewer to take part in a sensual and mystical experience.

"A crystal world where the mind is ready to immerse itself in a fascinating and burgeoning fractal geometry..." says the scientist in a low voice.

Automatically, he raises his hands to his neck.

Since he passed through the hall of the two Maats and following his discussions with Anubis and Osiris, he knows how he died. He is obsessed with the image of a head rolling before stopping a distance from his body. It both obsesses and delights him. The paradox may seem absurd, even unhealthy. But knowing that his mind continues to fantasize, to function intelligently, and to travel through a universe of which he now appears to be the Alpha and the Omega, brings him more enjoyment than fear.

But sometimes he automatically makes sure that his head is still attached to his neck, even though his hair has been replaced by a multitude of extremely white, fine tentacles and filaments.

After checking once again that his body is not headless, he carefully observes two giant DNA strands. They continue to grow in unison with the central crater that dominates the abyss. The human silhouettes and faces that continue their crazy ascent to the empyrean are probably thousands of kilometers high since they can still be seen easily from the terrace where he stands with his trio of friends.

This vibrant, vertical dance continues to terrify him. The faces and silhouettes are much more contemporary now.

"The sixteenth or seventeenth century, maybe..." he whispers, observing the hairstyles that can provide useful information in this regard.

Women and men change. But the emotions that sum up the most important moments of their respective lives are always the same. Cries and howls of agony take precedence. Countenances that are cheerful or frozen in ecstasy are too rare. Fear dominates. Sometimes terror. Hate, too. A desire twists many faces.

Suddenly, Atreus' abject mask, his face disfigured by the sadistic joy that fills him when Thyeste discovers that he has almost eaten his own son appears at the head of the carousel of those parading in the abyss.

Phil Caldwell 1 reels backwards, falls back and strikes the shell of the anomalocaris. He stands up. Stammers some apologies.

Then, eyes wild and skin dripping with sweat, he says, "I see him everywhere!"

"Who?" asks the tiger.

"Atreus! Everywhere I look, I see his hideous face just as his abominable vengeance finally comes about. I still hear his frenzied roar of pleasure when his brother made the macabre discovery, seeing the scattered limbs and head of his son in the great ceremonial cup. I am obsessed with this image of absolute hatred and ultimate vengeance. It takes precedence over all others."

The astrophysicist leans forward a little. He takes his head in his hands and says, "Atreus will drive me completely crazy!"

The girl walks over to him. She tries to comfort him. But Vanessa's husband remains tense, his eyes bulging. His jaws clenched to the point of breaking. Phil Caldwell 1 hiccups at time s. His muscles are frozen, making his body stiff and he seems about to break, like a fragile glass statue placed on an unstable piece of furniture.

He sits on the white, warm and pearly surface of the terrace.

His companions wait a few minutes so that he can grow calm before resuming the climb. While watching him, they also observe this hallucinating parade of all the human beings who lived on Earth before a humble astrophysicist from Stanford University was decapitated by a kidnapper overwhelmed with his fake power. Each face, petrified in an ultimate emotion, slips into these two transparent, titanic tubes that halo skin and eyes with a light that scatters into billions of sparks.

The spectacle is esthetic, majestic and impressive. But it is especially tragic because joy is tiny and pain immense.

"That's better..." says Phil Caldwell 1, sniffling.

He stands up painfully, leaning on tiger's back.

"Please forgive me for those moments of weakness. But some visions obsess me so much that I cannot get rid of them. Worse still, the scene in the megaron of the Mycenae palace frightens me even more than the first time, in the room of the two Maats, my frightened eyes contemplated my headless body lying nearly ten meters away from my head! I mean..."

"We forgive you all the more easily since we fled like cowards while you had the courage to witness this horrible scene of vengeance that horrified the gods and the sun. You wouldn't really be a man if your mind was not affected by such a horror," replies the tiger in its grave voice.

"That's true," admits the scientist.

Then he turns back to the thousands of faces that rise towards the sky, as if a giant hand were pulling them upwards. He watches them for a few seconds and concludes, "At the same time, I wonder if being defined as a human being something I really I aspire to. Humanity is filled with people like Atreus! I do not want to be like them. To be more precise, I no longer want to be like them!"

The young woman with the long, *outre-blanc* tentacles and filaments walks over to the astrophysicist. She sits down facing him and, once again, the tips of her nipples graze Phil Caldwell's chest.

Their breaths mingle and the scientist wonders just then if this beautiful, curvaceous, young woman is really a part of himself. The answer, it seems, is yes! This observation distresses him.

Phil Caldwell 3 looks into astrophysicist's eyes.

Then she softly says, "In one of his tales, Austrian poet Hugo von Hofmannsthal spoke in a very premonitory manner about the situation in which we find ourselves. He said: *The landscapes of the soul are more wonderful than the landscapes of the starry sky. Not only are their Milky Ways thousands of stars, but their shadowy abysses, their obscurities, are a life multiplied by a thousand, a life whose tangled web has dimmed the light, which profusion has been stifled. And these gulfs which life itself swallows up, can for a moment illuminate them, deliver them, make Milky Ways*[46]. So, I think that all these horrors which sully

---

[46] Translation of an extract from: L'entretien sur des poèmes (1903). Complete extract: *Les paysages de l'âme sont plus merveilleux que les paysages du ciel étoilé. Non seulement leurs Voies Lactées sont des milliers d'étoiles, mais leurs gouffres d'ombre, leurs obscurités sont une vie multipliée par mille, une vie dont la cohue a terni la lumière, que la profusion a étouffée. Et ces gouffres dans les-*

mankind and continue to blind us, will gradually disappear as we climb up. These shadows, symbolized by the Hecatonchire, the giant pterosaurs, the grimacing faces that rise from the abyss and some of the horrors you have encountered within the mercury worlds, will illuminate and generate, one day or another, the Milky Way and new galaxies."

She stops for a second and then continues, "We must always listen to poets..."

"You're probably right. But, there are no galaxies here."

"Perhaps, the translucent spheres that stand in line with this volcanic chimney of colossal dimensions serve as galaxies?" interrupts the anomalocaris, which has been strangely silent for some minutes.

"You know what galaxies are?" asks the tiger, astonished.

"Drat!"

Phil Caldwell 1 suddenly realizes that his friends are still with him. That they support him. Encourage him. He has no right to disappoint them and give in to the unhealthy flow of anxieties and dysphoria.

He decides to react.

"You're totally right. Let is leave Atreus, his imitators and his followers behind us. Let's keep climbing. I have no idea what we will discover once we have climbed up the last terraces and finally approach the summit of this titanic cliff. But we must complete our quest. Whatever it costs us!"

The emphatic and martial character of the last two sentences does not leave his companions indifferent. The young woman takes him in her arms while the big white feline caresses his legs grunting with pleasure

Finally, the anomalocaris settles squarely on his head and completes the confusion of his tentacles and filaments by adding a strange convoluted helmet with two weird horns in front and two long whips behind.

The humor of the situation does not escape him.

He sums up his satisfaction in two words, "Let's go!"

Immediately, the small group returns to their endless climb, which had been interrupted by the attack of the quetzalcoatlus, then their immersion in the Mycenae palace a few decades before the capture of Troy[47] described by Homer in the *Iliad*.

A few months later, a two-fold observation is necessary.

Although the cyclicality of the radiant day and night is respected, when compared to previous years, the mercury worlds no longer touch the white walls. When the relative darkness spreads its silk veil over the abyss, the quartet settles

---

quels la vie s'engloutit elle-même, un instant peut les illuminer, les délivrer, en faire des Voies Lactées.

[47] Indeed, Agamemnon and Menelaus are the sons of Atreus and Aerope.

quietly along the pearly surfaces that still stream with a light scarcely thwarted by the furtive darkness.

They do not sleep, of course, because all their vital mandatory functions: feeding, sleeping, eliminating waste or drinking, are useless and unnecessary here. Only fatigue still prevails when climbing is too rough and the ability to perspire when effort is violent.

Another characteristic preserved and directly correlated with emotions remained intact: the ability to cry.

But it must be admitted that the four Phil Caldwells who are climbing together, while so disparate in their physical appearances and so united in their desire to finally know what is controlling their lives at the top of the cliff, have no reason to cry.

The human faces that are flying upwards are of course always clenched, distraught or torn by contradictory or obscene emotions, but it is the only realization of a reality that they are now perfectly familiar with: each man is his own hell and his own paradise. Apart from this overwhelming observation, their wandering towards the summit is unhindered.

A second point now attracts their attention.

While they were almost alone on the road after the frightful Mycenaean interlude, the paths that connect the terraces are once again populated with Phil Caldwells. As all the members of the quartet had been swallowed by the mercury world, they could not know if the pterosaurs had decimated all the other Phil Caldwells present at that time.

It is therefore impossible to know whether all those seen now, mostly on the upper layers, survived the attack of the winged monsters or whether they have recently been born from the very wall of the cliff.

A symbolic and comforting wall, a magical material whose immaculate whiteness is at the same time the matrix of all the facets of the personality of a decapitated astrophysicist named Phil Caldwell and materialization of the long vertical initiatory journey to be undertaken.

Another element, however, attracts their attention: the vast majority of the white silhouettes that are cut out on the wall and along the terraces are not human.

"This is an astonishing bestiary!" confirms Phil Caldwell 3 as she watches mammals, giant frogs, stinking birds and stocky reptiles walking slowly near her.

"Why so many animals and so few people?" asks the astrophysicist, knowing that the answer lies within him and that there is little chance that a tiger and a creature from a period a billion years earlier can give him an answer.

Yet this is what is happening.

The anomalocaris rises a little above the smooth and warm terrace. It looks Phil Caldwell 1 straight in the eye and simply says:

"You are gradually becoming your own Noah's Ark!"

CHAPTER 2000

Almost a century later, they finally arrive near the summit. Very close…

"I never thought we would finally reach the summit!" marveled the young woman, men tally counting the last terraces to climb.

There are only five left.

The tiger stops for a moment. He looks attentively around him.

The astrophysicist does the same and, comically, their heads oscillate in the same direction each time. It is as if the two Phil Caldwells were synchronized to an ancient rhythm, preeminent to any other. But this is probably merely by chance. They share a common curiosity that is manifested in the same way.

On the terraces above and below, there are no longer any silhouettes.

"Are we alone?" asks the worried arthropod from the Cambrian period, waving the two shrimp-like tails that serve as appendages in all directions.

"Apparently," replied the astrophysicist, who has been growing more and more silent while approaching the goal they have shared for more than three centuries.

The sensation is strange. For several nights, the last Phil Caldwell animals to be seen have disappeared. They have not fallen into the abyss. They were not attacked by any demonic creature. They are simply not there..

These discrete disappearances always occur during the long periods of bright, diaphanous nights that characterize this Dante-like inferno devoted to the *outre-blanc* and to the exuberant gloss of a world that is constantly growing. A vertical universe that vibrates, streams with light. An extravagant world from which flows a haunting symphony created by seraphs, who have been long-time followers of Bach or Mozart.

Now there only four adventurers left to cross these last terraces connected by gently sloping paths. The paths are structured in a zigzag pattern and increasingly symbolize the staircases built in the time of Gilgamesh and the other rulers of Sumer or Akkad.

"The day has finally arrived," says the astrophysicist, voice breaking with obvious emotion.

"Let us make the most of this moment!" says the anomalocaris, giggling and whirling around an imaginary axis as if a pack of ants or fleas were attacking its lustrous shell.

"Above all, let hurry!" concludes the wild beast who is really in a hurry to know what they are going to discover at the top of this gigantic cliff.

Phil Caldwell 3 then walks over to the astrophysicist. She takes his hands in hers and looks at him intently. Her diamond-like eyes shine like carbuncles plunged in ass' milk and frosted by the intense cold of interstellar space.

Thirty centimeters separates them. Then twenty. Then ten.

With a quick gesture, she kisses him on the forehead. Then the young woman disentangles herself and says, "Excellent idea. Do you want to race?"

"There's no point," replies the arthropod with its stalk-like eyes. "I will always be a little ahead of you."

Naturally, the strange creature's capacities for levitation and flight give it an undeniable advantage which makes any race pointless.

"Let's walk at a good pace. That will be fine," concludes Phil Caldwell 1, with a broad, genuine smile.

After their immersion in Atreus' Mycenaean palace, it had taken the astrophysicist a long time before he finally reappropriated the real meaning of the word smile. But the stigma of the horror he had been forced to witness had gradually faded. Even though he still knows that this ultimate monstrosity is still anchored in him and will never leave him.

Nevertheless, he often told himself: there are also jewels in the heart of man...

The question is, and remains: how to bring to light this wonderful part of humankind without also exhuming mud, shame and ferocity?

The answer perhaps lies a few terraces above them.

Five. Exactly.

Before leaving for this last, challenging climb, the quartet continues to watch the vertical parade of billions of human beings born before the atrocious death of Phil Caldwell in the Amazon jungle and in the far north of Brazil.

The faces are totally modern now. However, their expressions still alternate between pleasure, suffering and hatred. An implacable triumvirate that has ruled mankind for seven million years. But, in this world where the *outre-blanc* reigns, the problems inherent in the community of men are probably obsolete.

The ghosts, imbued with a light which comes simultaneously from themselves and from this translucent sheath in which they circulate from bottom to top, continue to be lost in a sky titillated by the ends of the two giant DNA strands.

The astrophysicist stands there a few seconds.

His eyes follow the movement with a rhythm similar to the spectacle of two tennis players hitting a ball back and forth with the regularity of a metronome. The only difference is that these volleys do not take place in the horizontal world, but vertically, first climbing towards the sky the plunging into the abyss.

Apparently, he has been looking for familiar faces for several weeks.

The tiger had asked him about that a short while earlier, "Are you looking for someone?"

"My wife and my daughter," the astrophysicist replied, as he licked his lips to moisten them.

After a very short silence he had added, "As we finally approach our goal, I tell myself that the humans who pass before our eyes are my contemporaries. I would love to see Vanessa and Cymbelline again even if I can't hold them in my arms."

As he spoke those last words, his eyes filled with tears.

After so long, he still does not understand why he had done nothing to hold them back when he had seen them after sharing the astounding epic of Gilgamesh for a few days.

Absurdly and pointlessly, this attitude of renunciation continues to crucifies his conscience. He sometimes curses himself. When he does so, his three friends must deploy treasures of ingenuity in order to appease his pain and the anger he often turns against himself.

Today he is once again scrutinizing these two incredibly luminous, twisted elevators that carry 200 billion human beings up towards a translucent white sky where billions of transparent spheres continually twist and writhe.

A sphere for every human? he wondered sometimes. Of course, his friends cannot provide even an embryonic response. But that will change soon. In a few hours, perhaps? Once this monstrous cliff has finally been defeated.

However, is it meaningful to talk of defeating a cliff? Phil Caldwell 1 has no idea.

So, they set off.

Three more terraces. Two.

Just then, the situation becomes more complicated.

"The muscles of my thighs are knotted," says the young woman, surprised, as she tries to massage her legs to make them supple again.

"Me..." the anomalocaris starts to say, collapsing at the astrophysicist's feet.

The latter immediately asks, "Yes?"

"A giant is pressing on my back, head and tail. I cannot move."

It panics. Its faceted eyes turn in all directions and it ends up yelling in its inimitable falsetto voice.

"Help me!"

Phil Caldwell 1 takes it in his arms.

"I'm stuck too," says the tiger.

"A muscle problem?" inquires the young woman, struggling with her rebellious legs.

"My legs! I have the impression that they are sinking into shifting sands. The slightest movement requires considerable energy."

"Same for me!" admits Phil Caldwell 1, fighting against a detestable sucking phenomenon while protecting the anomalocaris which he holds tightly against his chest, pushing its shrimp tail appendages into his nose and mouth.

"Why are we having so much difficulty moving forward?" roars the tiger who is really annoyed by the fact that their journey is growing arduous just as climb the last two terraces.

"An ultimate test before our deliverance, perhaps?" suggests the young woman, grimacing more and more.

"This test is really stupid!" says the scientist, losing his temper. "To cross millions of terraces just to find oneself having to wade through a marsh with cramped muscles is moronic!"

This anger seems to be liberating since his constraints fade a little.

But just a little. But this demonstrates that the material difficulties endured today are the result of a psychic agitation affecting the first Phil Caldwell. The very one that has been embodied for three centuries in these four courageous and pugnacious individuals climbing up the volcanic chimney with its truly cosmic dimensions.

"Let us take advantage of this moment of calm to reach the summit!" says the astrophysicist starting to walk again.

He still holds the trembling anomalocaris in his arms because it has expressed the wish to remain nestled there.

Their progress is much slower than before. But, taking care to focus on each step and making their steps as regular as possible, they do move ahead.

Taking a small, narrow path, they finally arrive at the top of the next-to-last terrace just under the last. Its height is insignificant when compared to the distance traveled: less than fifty meters high.

"One last effort!" says the tiger, encouraging them.

But, just then, one last night falls over the abyss and its millions of layers stacked to infinity.

"Do we go on?" asks Phil Caldwell 3.

"We go on!" answers the astrophysicist, slapping his fist against the palm of his left hand, filaments shuddering with pleasure at this idea.

Putting word into action, he takes the lead with the archaic arthropod because the path is so narrow it is dangerous. To fall down so close to the goal would be much more than a tragedy. It would be a failure. The young woman follows with the tiger on her heels.

They climb for a few minutes as they continue to experience the effects of a colossal pressure on their shoulders, even though the sensation of wading in a murky cesspool has disappeared.

Hypnotic and throbbing, the seraphic music continues to weave its sound-tracks when suddenly... everything stops!

"What is going on?" demands the anomalocaris whose shrill voice takes on even greater magnitude in the face of a total and unprecedented silence.

"I don't," acknowledges Phil Caldwell 1, nervously biting his lower lip.

"I don't like this!" adds the tiger in a rumbling voice.

They remain there, listening to the silence.

Moved by a presentiment, the astrophysicist looks once more at the abyss. And more particularly in the direction of the two giant helical structures.

"But... but..." he whispers, unable to say anything else.

The two titanic luminous elevators have just interrupted the immeasurable procession of lives.

Phil Caldwell 1 immediately recognizes the dozens of human beings who are located at the upper ends of the two giant DNA strands. A young red-haired woman, another blonde, two men with shaved heads and the eyes of fighters. Some have darker complexions than others.

He immediately recognizes his friends from the Orpheus expedition.

They all look at him, their eyes bulging in unspeakable terror.

They all seem to implore a merciless deity who brutally raises a sword of fire over their heads.

A long, still, petrified silence.

Then everything explodes!

The ghosts, iridescent with light, suddenly break up in the midst of a gigantic explosion that completely destroys the two structures rising from the abyss to the sky.

Two hundred billion silhouettes shatter, scatter and fall. Two hundred billion bells ring at the same time. The sound is crystalline. Light. Almost a breath... But, multiplied by 200 billion, it becomes a din, roaring like a tornado.

Followed by a sound tsunami. A colossal tidal wave that defeats courage, snapping all hopes.

Silence returns.

"Why? Why?" repeats the astrophysicist, holding his head in his hands.

Thin white filaments adorn his face with a beard, which he never wore. The young woman sits down beside him and caresses his shoulders. Worried, the anomalocaris lowers itself onto the man's thighs like an animal looking for a hug.

Only the tiger remains frozen, looking at this gaping hole, now freed from its luminous garlands of human heads that once rose to the sky.

It stays that way for a long time. Then it stands before the astrophysicist and simply says, "Now we are alone!"

It lets the obsessive silence that has reigned here for a few moments flow gently in.

The large white feline then adds, "Only for the last test."

Phil Caldwell sighs violently. And this sigh is pain. He looks at his three companions who have been with him for so long. He opens his mouth. Thinks a little. Is silent.

Then he finally states, "I'm ready for this last event."

"We are too!" they answer together.

The astrophysicist once again places the disheveled creature against his chest. He passes his right hand under its armored tail, making sure not to pinch the two whips that extend from it. And they set off.

The slope is gentle, forming an angle of five or six degrees, but the abnormal pressure at the top transform the end of their climb into Calvary.

"A hundred yards more!" says Phil Caldwell 1 to en courage them, turning quickly to the young woman and the tiger.

He pants, coughs and moans because the effort is immense. He sags. He struggles. He wavers.

Then he falls to his knees. Phil Caldwell 3 does the same and the white tiger is flattened against the ground and must now crawl. How humiliating for a tiger!

"Hang on to my back!" the astrophysicist orders the arthropod, which immediately grasps its friend's shoulders.

The two human Phil Caldwells are now crawling on their knees.

"No more than ten yards!"

The pressure is increasing. They are all now crawling. Fortunately, the surface is still smooth.

"We're getting there..." says the astrophysicist, whose throat is so tight that he can no longer speak. He is held in a vise and has the horrible feeling that his nerves are about to be shredded and his eyes will be expelled from their sockets.

The last two meters take a long time. A few minutes maybe. Or a few centuries.

They have no idea.

In a last, almost desperate effort, Phil Caldwell 1 finally manages to reach the top, using his filaments like the scansors and setae[48] of geckos that those creatures to adhere to any surface, under any conditions.

He raises his head and says in a completely broken voice, "The top. We've reached the top!"

Then he collapses to the ground.

---

[48] Geckos' legs comprise a series of lamellae, called scansors, which are covered with supple fibers, setae. A gecko has about 6 million setae. Adhesion is maximal when the gecko's foot rises, rests and retracts.

CHAPTER 2001

His surprise is immense.

First, the sky. The spheres seem much closer than when they were in the abyss.

The cosmic acceleration that has affected this virginal world since he first awoke continues because, above the astrophysicist, space is constantly swelling. He sees thousands of creatures, all white and diaphanous, encrusted within these spheres that jostle and collide. Some look like him. Just a little. But he also sees women, animals, shrubs and flowers enclosed in these magical and yet indecent transparent bubbles .

They are all perfectly white. Without any consistency.

"Ghosts... Or holograms!" the scientist whispers before looking at what was really right at the top of this colossal cliff.

His amazement is in keeping with his hopes. At the top of this structure with its infinite layers there is nothing! Well, almost nothing.

He hears his friends who, finding recovery difficult, also reach this immense *outre-blanc* plateau. Their first observation confirms that of the astrophysicist: the top of this vertiginous cliff is dreary, banal. Almost innocuous.

"That's it?" roars the tiger.

"Let us beware of appearances," says the young woman with the full bosom, the skin of her arms vibrating with pleasure.

"Meaning?" asks the beast.

In Phil Caldwell's old life, everything was just appearance. This place, while apparently monotonous, probably holds some surprises.

"What I would like above all," says the scientist, "Is explanations. But I cannot find any here!"

"Patience..." whispers the anomalocaris, once again rising into the sky without difficulty.

Indeed, the hated constraints imposed by an unbearable pressure, or very serious gravity, have totally disappeared. This, at least is positive...

Standing in a circle, the four friends observe their new environment.

Behind them: the abyss, which is now completely empty because the two giant helical structures have collapsed into the bottomless pit. In front: some softly rolling hills and myriads of spheres. Half-spheres to be more precise. Arranged without any apparent order, these immaculate shells are most often directly placed on the ground. In this case, their generous convexity makes them look like melons half sunk in the ground and covered with a few thorns or small pipes with obscure ends. Sometimes they too are embedded in the same pearly white material that makes up the cliff and all the Phil Caldwells wandering in this eternally expanding world. In this case, their welcoming concavity gives them the appearance of the peel of a half-orange carefully peeled and pierced with small openings equipped with translucent cylinders.

But, unlike a melon or an orange peel, these hemispherical structures are desperately white and their surfaces are polished. Shimmering. Streaming with light!

"What is that?" asks the tiger, tilting its head in the direction of one of the hollow hemispheres.

"The bubble that has been cut in two or the small translucent pipes that decorate it?" asks the young woman while walking over to the incongruous object.

"Both!" replies the beast, grunting.

"Be careful!" whistles the anomalocaris. "It may be dangerous."

Without paying attention to the remark made by the disheveled creature, the astrophysicist walks over to the white bubble that has been cut in two and brushes it with the filaments of his right hand.

"It's not safe!" insists the big white cat.

"I've already been decapitated," replies the scientist with a smirk. "So, I'm not risking much now..."

In fact, nothing happens. Apparently anyway.

But, a few seconds later, the empty hemisphere begins to vibrate. To shudder. Immediately, the four courageous explorers of this vertical and infinite universe also begin to tremble.

"Look!" yells the young woman, pointing at the sky.

"You've done something stupid..." the arthropod insists, nesting once again against his friend's chest.

He remains silent for a moment, then adds, "Something immensely stupid."

Reality seems to corroborate the worries of the little, cowardly predator. The sky, which until now has been calm, is filled with disorderly movement. Disturbing.

The translucent bubbles, some of which still bear the watermark of the countless Phil Caldwells who emerged in this universe and hallucinating landscapes from abyss, begin to jostle. Growing oval before returning, for a fleeting moment, to reassuring roundness.

Such clashes and gyrations are not new as the four explorers in the stratified volcanic chimney with its millions of terraces had already noticed similar movements. But now the phenomenon is widespread. Moreover, and this is very surprising in an environment governed, until now, by a celestial, comical and debonair disorder, a certain hierarchy appears.

Some spheres shrink and are ejected upwards. Then they disappear. Without exploding. Noiseless. Without flashes of light. Nothing. They simply disappear.

"But... I didn't do anything!" says Phil Caldwell 1, defending himself against the somewhat angry looks of his three friends.

"You touched one of the hemispheres wrapped in transparent pipes!" says the tiger in a voice halfway between a hoarse rumble and a roar of anger.

"I know. But..."

"That simple gesture seems to have heavy consequences," says the young woman, walking over to the astrophysicist.

She looks at the sky again and realizes that the billions of spheres are still reorganizing into two categories. There are spheres that gently vanish in the *outre-blanc* and those that remain. The latter grow. Grow! Not knowing how to interpret this strange ballet, she now stands in front of Phil Caldwell 1 She holds out her arms in his direction and embraces him. Their bodies meet. Always warm and welcoming, the young woman's breast, nipples now hard, deliberately rest against the scientist's chest.

Then their pelvises brush.

The astrophysicist immediately senses that penis has grown hard. For the first time in several years. He swallows, passes his tongue over his lips and pushes his friend gently away.

"She's much more than my sister," he muses, his eyes fluttering slightly.

The astrophysicist knows perfectly well that any intimate relationship with this charming, sensuous young woman is totally impossible. It surpasses incest, because Phil Caldwell 3 is not his sister. She is an important part of himself or, more exactly, of that almost infinite mosaic of behaviors, desires and emotions that one day on Earth was called Phil Caldwell.

The young woman understands this perfectly. She is not at all offended by this reticence which guarantees an indispensable psychic stability under such circumstances.

"What are we going to do?" yelps the anomalocaris whose falsetto voice has not really improved since they have reached the top of the giant funnel.

"We go ahead a bit?" suggests the tiger who dreads inaction and who is still watching the strange rearrangement of the translucent bubbles teeming with a ghostly life, the expression on his face tormented.

A ghostly realm? Or perhaps somewhere located in a dimension adjacent to ours?

The astrophysicist is looking at the sky almost frantically. Every thirty seconds. This agitation quickly causes pain in his neck. But, since these upheavals at the peak of their new world are evolving at a rate that seems hardly correlated with that of the Phil Caldwells present on this desert plateau only occupied by empty half-hulls, reason prevails.

"Let us walk towards those gentle hills that lie along the horizon," states the astrophysicist.

They begin to move towards the very gentle slopes that seem reminiscent of the bucolic, agricultural landscapes that can be found in many parts of a planet Earth that was burnt to a crisp by the death of its sun. Probably several thousand million centuries ago.

They seem to progress easily. But the half-spheres quickly temper their optimism. As they generally measure five to ten meters in diameter, it is more prudent to walk around them. But, there are so many of them. So many! As a result, the only possible path is particularly convoluted. It winds incessantly, quickly transforming into a labyrinth designed for lost Titans fleeing the wrath of their gods.

First, the astrophysicist took the lead. But after a while, he must admit that they are not advancing. As a result of the narrowness of potentially accessible passages between the concave or convex half-spheres, they have to deviate from their primary objective, which is to reach one of the hills.

Worse still, the more they walk, the closer they are to their starting point.

The great tiger then takes charge of operations. He calls the talkative arthropod, asking it to fly over the area to identify the paths that head in the right direction.

This process fails at first because the anomalocaris makes pointless comments and digressions. As a result of its constant chatter, its first indications are of little use. The tiger grows angry, roars loudly, and tells the archaic predator, "Concentrate! Give us clear indications: front, left, right! No more idle chatter!"

The creature then pivots its stalk-like eyes in all directions, an evident sign of its discontent. But it obeys and its incessant babble finally stops.

Providing some accurate information this time, the anomalocaris leads the trio in the right direction, although the road remains winding, long and complicated.

After a time that it is difficult to measure in earthly terms in a very bright, monochromatic, universe, the four Phil Caldwells finally arrive at the foot of the first hill. They walk up the slope, which is almost totally barren of the hemispheres that cover the lower part of this slightly mountainous landscape.

With its old friend flying overhead, the tiger arrives first. The two humans arrive a few seconds later. They are vexed.

"Hills! More hills!" says the astrophysicist. "We have not traveled up these millions of levels for centuries just to find ourselves facing an infinity of white hills that stretch to the horizon!"

His comment is bitter. The hills are all very similar. All white. All banal and without much interest.

"I don't understand..." admits the young woman, sitting on the warm, glazed floor.

"Oh! Oh! Oh!" shouts the anomalocaris, darting its faceted eyes upwards.

During their long stroll through the labyrinth of paths, striving to avoid obstacles and finally reach the hill, they had stopped looking at the sky. That was a mistake. The spectacle is now... dantesque!

Colossal, monstrous even in its exceptional dimensions, a single transparent sphere now hides the zenith. Many other translucent bubbles are also clearly visible, stretching behind it to infinity. But the one that fills the sky above the dreary expanse of white hills surpasses them by far.

Similar to the view seen from a satellite orbiting very close to a giant planet, the vision is maddening. The astrophysicist and his friends have the crazy feeling that they are literally falling on this twisted ball of lights on which whole worlds are stacked. Swirling galaxies. Chaotic, erratic, tortured worlds. Giant caves where whales fly in squadrons. Volcanoes which open in two and allow tsunamis of sparkling gems to flow from their flanks, moistened with foam.

"I'm scared!" yelled the young woman, putting her hands over her eyes.

The other three Phil Caldwells stand there. Petrified.

Now larger than a giant planet, the sphere overhead continues to grow. It moves closer. And closer.

The Stanford scientist and his friends have the sensation that they could almost touch its shiny surface which seems extremely fine. The quartet sees themselves mirrored on its surface, which further increases the feeling of strangeness. The landscapes that jostle and fluctuate incessantly within this world, whose interior seems a thousand times greater than its colossal external film, are dizzying. Watching them, even for a fleeting moment, is hypnotizing.

The sphere continues to move closer. This crazy world is going to the top of the hill where the four Phil Caldwells stand. Dumbfounded. Paralyzed.

"It's going to..." says the tiger.

But its rumblings stop in his throat squeezed tight the anguish of a wild, dream-like moment of panic.

"Yes!" the astrophysicist says simply, closing his eyes in which all the diamonds of the universe shine.

The thin film now brushes against them. It rustles a little and delicately, almost voluptuously, envelopes the disparate forms of the four members of this expedition within the confines of the mind of one man. Or of all! They do not know.

The translucent wall sticks to their skins, hair, scales. To their filaments.

And the giant translucent sphere engulfs them...

CHAPTER 2002

"Why?" moans Phil Caldwell 1 who has fallen to his knees.

"What happened?" asks the tiger, sprawled on its back after the mind-boggling immersion.

"Everything has changed..." murmurs the young woman.

That's an understatement!

The *outre-blanc* is nothing but a vague memory. Here, extravagant colors reign. Billions and billions of colors dance before their eyes, undulate on their skin and quintessential, exuberant and crazy atmosphere

The astrophysicist stands up and discovers three things. First, they are all in a grassy valley crumbling under foliage, bouquets of flowers, and lush vegetation. Second, the young woman and he now have hair, fingers, and no filaments. Moreover, they are soberly dressed in rather short, cobalt blue tunics made of a supple, sensual fabric.

Third, the anomalocaris is silent for once, stuck head down, in a thick, almost spongy soil. Its tail flicks in all directions, a sign of its distress.

Phil Caldwell 1 rushes and finally pulls it out of the dense grass in which it had plunged.

"Thank you!" it whispers in its his exasperating falsetto voice.

"At least... that hasn't changed!" says Phil Caldwell 3 laughing, delighted to be wearing clothes in a world where color prevails.

After enjoying a few moments of pure joy, they all look carefully at their new surroundings.

Their surprise is total. For while they are clearly in a sphere of cyclopean, even cosmic, dimensions- the atmosphere and the sky are absurd.

Such a gigantic bubble, regardless of whether it is artificial or natural, should logic ally have either a source of light, a small star for example, or a clear sky with true depths. An infinity in miniature somehow!

That is not the case. Instead of a sun or clouds, they see a real hodgepodge of unconnected landscapes. A piece of mountain fringed with soot runs through a large waterfall spewing crimson water that looks very much like fresh blood. Enormous toothed wheels grind ice masses that appear more reflective of fractal geometry than the frigid elegance of the boreal zones. Between these horizons, shattered by the ax by a demented deity, they can see lakes with milky green water, colossal pyramids split in two from which chatty, multicolored birds escape. Dark monoliths stacked vertically in a forest that swells and stirs like a dinosaur of greenery...

The scene is cluttered. Extravagant. Filled with a warm chaos, both colorful and maddening because the dimensions of space seem to take some liberties with logic. Vertical lines curve, twist and sometimes end in a Moebius strip or in a Bernoulli leminscate curve designing infinity.

Unsettling for the mind and tiring for the eye, this confusion of shapes, structures, landscapes and colors, makes them feel as if they have in the cave of Ali-Baba, redesigned by a mad painter .

"Overabundance of spaces. Overabundance of spatial dimensions. Overabundance of worlds..." murmurs the astrophysicist, letting his lower lip hang in a grotesque manner.

Phil Caldwell 1 is familiar with certain singularities and incongruities of our universe. But here, this almost hysterical abundance amazes and terrifies him at the same time.

"Where will we go?" asks the tiger with its usual pragmatism.

"Uh..."

What else is there to say in such a place?

The Stanford University scientist is thinking of Giordano Bruno and his impressive foreknowledge of the multiplicity of worlds which, alas, turned out to be fatal for him.

For a moment, he observes for a moment the young woman in her cobalt blue tunic which perfectly highlights the shapeliness of her legs, her beautiful face and her blonde hair that is no longer overgrown with tentacles. The astrophysicist walks over to her. He takes her hands in his and nods in the direction of a small building located a hundred meters below.

"We'll go there!" he says, pointing at the gazebo.

Inspired by ancient Greek or Roman art, these small circular temples were very much in fashion starting in the Renaissance. Consisting of a dome surmounting several columns, either smooth or fluted, these buildings adorned the parks of great estates, manors and castles.

The presence of such a building here is a complete surprise since such antique gazebos were often places of relaxation for lovers in search of privacy or for aristocrats wishing to take tea while protecting themselves from the harmful effects of the summer sun.

But here? Far from our universe, far from any landmark and under the threat of fabulous landscapes embedded in the sky or compacted at the zenith of a wild, unfettered imaginary place, the presence of this ten-meter-tall glory is totally unexpected.

What is even more amazing is that this gazebo is already occupied by four characters. Three men and a woman sit on the circular bench running inside the stone circle where the bases of eight elegant and finely decorated columns are anchored.

The whole look is very esthetic, almost bucolic and rewarding. But the four Phil Caldwells are wondering what they're doing here. And who are the four humans quietly talking without paying any attention to the newcomers, or the clouds of baroque and tortured worlds that clutter the sky like thousands of chandeliers hanging from a ceiling of titanic dimensions.

"Let's go?" says the anomalocaris growing impatient and by convulsively waving its two outgrowths.

The tiger has recovered its beautiful orange and black colors and the scales, back and tail of the archaic arthropod cast metallic reflections. Only its two caudal whips remain dark charcoal in color.

The disheveled creature does not wait for the answer from its friends. It begins to gently flutter in the direction of this round structure topped by an elegant dome made of very light stone.

Less than a minute later, they arrive near the gazebo.

Just above them, the zenith is filled by two almost similar mountains, nervously separated by a powerful waterfall from which streams of emerald and indigo water pour. Phil Caldwell 1 and the tiger immediately recall the Twin Mountains they crossed with Gilgamesh such a long time ago.

The astrophysicist stopped for a moment and immediately recalled the phrase of Martin Heidegger, who had impressed him when he was younger and completing his studies: *it is there only where there is the peril of terror, there is the beatitude of astonishment, that lively rapture which is the breath of the art of philosophizing*. Looking at this disturbing sky filled with Baroque worlds, then at this serene structure, in which four elderly individuals, who seem to be imbued with real wisdom, are talking with one another, he says that he is probably at the perfect conjunction between *the peril of terror and the beatitude of astonishment*.

Which would win?

"Can you tell us where we are?" he asks the woman and the three men who are still sitting on the circular stone bench that forms the base of the gazebo.

A long silence.

Then, one of the men with very white hair stands and says to him, "Come and sit with us!"

This invitation is accompanied by a broad, friendly gesture.

Phil Caldwell 1 and the young woman walk over and settle between the columns. The anomalocaris also rushes in and settles between the unknown woman and the astrophysicist. Since the tiger is too large to fit into the space allowed for each individual, it settles outdoors and is content to put its big round, furry head on the vacant bench.

"Thank you. But who are you?" the Stanford scientist asks again, since his first question has not yet been answered.

"Our names are of little importance because our presence here is fleeting and symbolic. But, to simplify, know that we are respectively called..."

While speaking, the man who, a few seconds would identify himself as Master Eckhart, began a circular gesture pointing first at the elderly woman, whose beautiful face radiates a singular kindness.

"This is Hadewijch of Antwerp, next is Proclus, and finally that is John Scot Erigena. As for me, my name is Eckhart von Hochheim, but I am often called Master Eckhart[49]."

"That's... That's..." stammers Phil Caldwell 1.

"Do not look for your words. Let them come quietly when astonishment has been replaced by reason. We are here to help you become your own. Or, more exactly, to become the Alpha and Omega of your own universe."

"I don't understand."

"Neither do I!" laments the arthropod whose beautiful colors are moist with light, looking more and more like the bark of some prune tree or, in its astonishing chromatic diversity, that of the rainbow eucalyptus.

"That's the problem when you have a reptilian brain..." says the tiger treacherously, barely opening its powerful jaw.

"Shut up, both of you." Says Phil Caldwell 3, glaring at them.

The two companions look at one another for a moment like boxers just before a fight, then they look at the angry young woman whose cheeks immediately turn red.

The anomalocaris then turns away with an expression of disdain that is particularly comical when one has a mouth shaped like a pineapple slice.

After a very short silence, Mr. Eckhart continues, "One of the great thinkers of the twentieth century, Jakob von Uexküll I believe, specified that every organism is a melody that sings itself. The time has come for you to sing yourself."

"That idea is enticing," admits the astrophysicist. "But, my friends and I would like to know where we are. And why?"

Proclus speaks then. Unlike Master Eckhart, who wears a long gray beard and whose clear green eyes are in perfect harmony with the luxuriant vegetation surrounding the gazebo, the Greek philosopher has long, very brown hair, and expression is indicating of a skittish temperament.

"You are the four ultimate facets of Phil Caldwell who perished under the hand of a barbarian armed with a Japanese sword. But millions were present throughout this vertical odyssey, this initiatory climb to the center of your inner being nestled in the core of a brain now deprived of its body. The time has come for you to make the big leap. Both allegorical and fictitious, this place is only the antechamber for your dive into a new universe whose contours are still un-

---

[49] Proclus (or Proclos) was a philosopher of the Neoplatonic school of Athens. He lived from 412 to 485. John Scot Erigena was an Irish philosopher and theologian. He lived from 800 to 876. Hadewijch of Antwerp was a Flemish mystic and poetess. She lived from 1210 to 1260. Master Eckhart was a German mystic, theologian and philosopher. He lived from 1260 to 1328. All of them were part, in different ways, in the Neoplatonic logic initiated by Ammonios Saccas and Plotinus in the third century.

known to you. This unprecedented universe, unlike any other in the heart of the Multiverse, is..."

"You!" exclaims Hadewijch of Antwerp rising with some difficulty.

Despite her fifty years of age, the poet seems unusually old. Her almost white hair leaves no doubt in this respect. But her eyes, a superb lavender blue, still sparkle with mischievousness, revealing a spiritual agility never denied.

"But... But..." the astrophysicist stammers, who has broad experience with the singularities of the Multiverse. "How could I become a universe all by myself? That's impossible! It is the work of God, if He exists! But not the work of a man. Even though he is now reduced to just his brain..."

"It costs us a lot to acknowledge it here," says John Scotus Erigenius, staring at Phil Caldwell 1 with his black eyes, "But the creative principle of the Multiverse and of all the universes that are constantly born in infinite arrays of it, is a simple scalar field!"

"That's less exciting and less glorious," remarks the great beast, in a rather strident tone.

"Even less so, for an archaic creature with a reptilian brain..."

"And a falsetto voice caused by inhaling too much helium!" interrupts the young woman in order to prevent the tiger from getting involved.

"That's it! Laugh... Fine," continues the anomalocaris. "So, I ask my silly question: can anyone finally tell me what a *scalar field* is?"

The astrophysicist hastens to respond in order to justify his specialization in the study of the universe and, in particular, of exoplanets.

"A field is called scalar when it concerns a physical quantity described only by its value. It is different from a vector field, which refers to a physical quantity described not only by its value, but also by a direction and a sense enabling it to be represented by a vector."

"For example?" asks the arthropod, wriggling on the stone bench as if it being attacked by a pack of scorpions.

"For example, scalar fields are used in meteorology to describe the pressure or temperature values over a certain geographical area. People use the expressions temperature field and pressure fields. So, a weather map with atmospheric temperatures or pressures is a scalar field. A weather map indicating the strength and direction of the winds is a vector field."

"Thank you!" barks the anomalocaris. "I understand! All you have to do is explain using clear words and speaking slowly."

Unfortunately, they are not totally out of the words since the astrophysicist immediately continue s speaking, while beginning to understand the totally crazy notion that Proclus and Hadewijch of Antwerp have clarified in a few remarks.

"In the theory of inflation, which has now been validated by the entire scientific community, the scalar field responsible for the monstrous expansion of our universe in the first billionth of a billionth of a second after the big bang is called the inflaton field[50] ."

"They weren't exactly wildly original," says the young woman, looking disappointed.

"Indeed. Within all the universes of the Multiverse, all it takes is for a part of this inflaton field to acquire a negative pressure to trigger a new inflation and create a new *universe-bubble*."

"What is the effect of negative pressure?" asks Phil Caldwell 3, hanging on a bit in order to follow her friend's reasoning and their hallucinatory cosmological consequences to the end.

"The energy and the negative pressure of a uniform scalar field, such as the field of inflaton, immediately create repulsive gravity."

"So... a colossal new inflation!"

"Exactly! And one that can occur everywhere..."

"You are starting to understand what was set in place right after your execution and, above all, what will open a field of consciousness and totally infinite investigation for you," intervenes John Scotus Erigena.

"The circle of things must shrink and perish so that the circle of nakedness grows and widens in order to encompass the Whole," adds Hadewijch of Antwerp, repeating a phrase from her poem *Mengeldichten*.

"Uh..." says the blonde young woman, realizing that a small explanation of text will no doubt be necessary.

"At the dawn of a new world or, better still, of a new universe, we must first of all divest ourselves. Be annihilated. Disappear to oneself so that, like the phoenix, we can be reborn. Naked. Purified. Relieved of the dross of a mind stuck in the miasma of everyday life," says Hadewijch of Antwerp. "It is at this moment, and at this moment only, that your destiny will be fully awakened. It will even become an epiphany. You will finally be able to serenely understand your new life and plant a universe for which you will be the driving force, the center and the horizon. You will not be God, nor any shoddy deity. You will be you! All thanks to a simple field of inflaton that will dilute space and time into a motionless sphere. An infinitesimal sphere that will grow. Quickly! That will explode! Phil Caldwell will no longer be. A new world will be born. Soon. Very soon!"

---

[50] The inflaton is the energy quantum of this particular scalar field that can generate billions of different universes. The energy density of the inflaton is considerable: nearly 10^{110} times higher than the current density of the universe. At the end of the inflation phase, the pressure of the scalar field, which was negative during the inflation phase, increases to near zero. At that moment, the inflaton field enters a new dynamic phase and it yields its primitive energy to the first elementary particles (quarks and electrons) which are formed, little by little.

Astonished, the astrophysicist, Phil Caldwell 3, the great beast and the talkative anomalocaris freeze on the spot.

They are trying to think. But this effort exceeds their capacities for the moment.

With his eyes still wide open, the astrophysicist simply asks, "But then, this gigantic white cliff and bottomless well was..."

"Quite simply you!" replies Jean Scot Érigène, whose balding skull shines beneath a vermillion light that does not come from a star but from a very high mountain that is bleeding, just above them.

"Your decapitation caused the brutal emergence of the millions of Phil Caldwells that were in you, as they are at the heart of every woman, every man."

"So, we are always both one and millions?" says the surprised blonde young woman whose magnificent aquamarine eyes shine like fires in the darkness.

"Indeed," Proclus adds, "The complexity of the human soul concentrates all the possible and imaginable behaviors into several strata. These same strata that your immersion in the large *outre-blanc* funnel symbolized in the form of millions of terraces."

"Every being conceals his Hell and his Paradise within himself?" asks the tiger, raising its head slightly.

"Hell and Paradise do not exist!" says the old woman, smiling again, her pale eyes sparkling. "Every human being must conjugate all the paradoxes within himself. Certain traits of character, or certain impulses, often appear at the edge of consciousness. They structure our personality and shape our relationships with others. But almost all of these positive potentials and hideous horrors remain buried."

"When they finally rise from the depths..." says the arthropod, feeling enthusiastic that it can finally say something without being rebuked by its friends.

"Man is simultaneously an angel and a demon. Everyone knows that," murmurs the astrophysicist. "But..."

He pauses for a moment.

Phil Caldwell 1 observes the bucolic environment, then the fractal worlds that fill the sky , worried by their profusion. He stands there. Dumbfounded.

Then he looks again at the four philosophers who have been temporarily extracted from the history of a world that is no longer his own. That will never be his again.

That bothers him and astonishes him at the same time. He asks, "What should we do now?"

"Live!" says John Scotus Erigena.

"Create!" says Proclus.

"Exult!" says Master Eckhart.

"Love!" says Hadewijch of Antwerp, last.

Taken aback, the astrophysicist looks at them one by one. Then he opens his mouth to respond to the four orders that sum up his current state of mind so well.

But the words freeze in his throat.

In a fraction of a second, the four characters have vanished, leaving in their respective places only a mist that the wind immediately sweeps away.

CHAPTER 2003

The anomalocaris swings around an invisible axis like a dog running after its tail.

"But where are they? But where are they?" he repeats, waving his faceted eyes in every direction.

The tiger freezes and the young woman locks her emotions up behind a questioning expression.

The astrophysicist tries to recover his spirits. But these few revelations and the brutal disappearance of the four individuals who could, perhaps, guide him through the meanders of his own brain, leave him helpless. At this moment, and without showing any lack of gratitude towards his three faithful companions, Phil Caldwell 1 feels alone.

"What are we going to do?" asks the tiger with its customary pragmatism.

"I don't know."

"How can you not know? You were beheaded. It is you who have been promised this mad destiny that our four visitors have elegantly described. It is you who must build a new world and get rid of its slag, as Hadewijch of Antwerp would say. So, it is you and you alone who can tell us what to do and what is going to happen."

"I don't know... I don't know..." stammers the astrophysicist, whose green eyes seem to gradually grow dull.

He stands there. Motionless. Overwhelmed by the weight of revelations that brutally give him almost divine power.

Power he does not have. Of course.

His friend places her left hand on his right shoulder. She stares at him, seeking to awaken a new light in him. An igneous power that, in a few seconds, will spring from his skin, from his mouth. From his heart.

But silence alone prevails. Above them, rivers of molten lead curl, mingle and convulse near a blue and gray desert landscape where gigantic fairy chimneys oscillate on their bases before collapsing.

The light grows more and more orange, almost saffron.

Blood flows. But where? And for whom?

"Maybe the driving force behind this eternal inflation..."

"The inflaton?" interrupts the anomalocaris which has finally decided to concentrate and has retained the name of this strange scalar field that seems to be at the origin of everything.

"For a creature with a reptilian brain you are doing very well," observes the astrophysicist whose eyes shine once again to the great satisfaction of his three friends. "Indeed, if the inflaton suddenly creates a repulsive gravitation, we will undoubtedly explode..."

The Stanford scientist does not have time to finish his sentence.

The horizon suddenly starts to pitch like a frail skiff lost in the midst of a wild sea, with waves thirty meters high!

In the midst of this tempest which simultaneously upsets the forms, the lights and the colors, the pavilion gradually takes on an oval shape. The columns, which had been elegant and straight until then, become curved, giving the building the incongruous silhouette of a rugby ball held at both ends by a brilliant dome and benches of stone that crack rapidly.

"Let's go before it collapses on us!" roars the tiger.

Its companions hasten to follow the judicious advice of the wild beast, for the cupola shakes. Crumbles. Then finally collapses with a horrible crash.

The great feline leads the way. The two humans follow with difficulty because the quiet grassy valley has now been transformed into steep valleys whose walls are rising more and more vertically, in an absurd geometry that is reminiscent of the walls of the white cliff. The arthropod follows, fluttering.

But gusts of wind gradually distance it from the group.

The astrophysicist tries to call him. In vain.

Just then, the red-haired man realizes that the cat and the young blonde woman are also moving away. She waves her arms and the tiger roars in rage. But these desperate attempts are pointless.

Suddenly, their silhouettes begin to change. They swell, swell, grow enormous and now resemble frightened moon fish. They turn into almost perfect spheres.

The astrophysicist's eyes itch. He then tries to run his fingers over the eyelids. But he, too, becomes expands, swells, and quickly turns into a reddish bubble with green eyes that grimly decorate a hideous surface stretched like a sail ready to tear under the impact of a tumultuous wind.

Phil Caldwell 1 tries one last time to speak.

But it's too late! His lips, eyes and tongue explode.

CHAPTER $10^{100\ 000}$

Darkness.
Darkness again.
No sound. No energy. The void.
Four consciousnesses arise within an absolute that is singularized by absence. Total absence. The absence of everything.
Except four petrified consciences.
Dark, dreary, inert, this thebaid is corseted by the tiny quantum fluctuations of a vacuum that flows from abysses. But these abysses are empty. Them too.
Suddenly... a vibration. Terrifying! A spasm of energy in the hollow of a totally inert scalar field one billionth billionth of a billionth of a second earlier.
The first quantum of energy is sufficient. An inflaton. Only one! Negative pressure of unimaginable force. And the explosion tears the complex mesh of the Multiverse.
The four consciousnesses have been compressed so far in a bubble of energy infinitely smaller than a quark, and they suddenly awaken.
They grow. Grow. Grow. Grow again.
The quark becomes an atom. The atom becomes orange. The orange becomes a planet and the planet becomes a universe. In less than a billionth of a second!
The tearing is painful. Atrocious.
The world swells. Dilates. Multiplies. Diversifies. Enhances all colors that give meaning, nourish life. That jubilate, forming tsunamis of photons scattering in all directions in a universe whose dimensions have just been increased by a coefficient 10^{60} in less than a billionth of a nanosecond!
The storm rumbles, the volcanic outburst is near.
In one, brief and unbreakable moment, the lava seeds the universe in a chthonian orgasm likely to cause mountains to quake, to crack the giant rocky planets and to dismantle the heart of the largest stars.
The tsunami rumbles, splashes, engulfs. And fertilizes.
Life is there, profuse and luminous. The soul of the World is there too.

Four consciousnesses are incarnated. Four consciences awaken.
Four consciences move.
Four silhouettes finally emerge from a very long lethargy which could have lingered for a few centuries. Or a few million years. Nobody really knows. And it does not matter.

The young blonde woman is the first to open her eyes. She's lying on her back. Naked.

Before looking to each side to see if she is alone or not, she watches the sky above her for a long time.

Her amazement is intense because there is really no sky in the earthly or even universal sense of the term.

The atmosphere is tinged with lemon and indigo tones. Instead of satellites, planets and stars, it is filled with strange and particularly complex forms. Shaped like the ribbons used by gymnasts, they mingle, overlap or form Moebius strips. They all start from a height already impressive enough to lose themselves to infinity in a multicolored abundance governed by four ribbons that are wider and much more twisted than the others. In the midst of this skein of strips that shudder as they twist about themselves, vortices of warm, pulsating lights multiply ceaselessly, dancing a strange ballet.

No sun here. No stars either. But darkness is banned from this place, which beyond anything that humans know and have observed with their instruments.

A diffuse light is constantly exuded of these long frames that wind and unfold, structuring the sky and giving it an insane depth.

The young woman turns her head in all directions. But she is located in a slight hollow covered with motley, diversified vegetation with a general structure based on a logic of exacerbated verticality.

Everything is grand here. Everything rises as an offering to the sky.

She tries to talk. Without success, because her mouth and throat are dry. So, she sits up, leaning on one elbow. But the small cavity is too deep. She decides stand up and realizes that this is facilitated by a gravity that is lower than that on Earth or in the *outre-blanc* well of which she recalls each detail, each terrace. Each episode.

Finally standing, the young woman looks about her.

The landscape is almost as strange as the sky, which is still cluttered with ribbons, strings of light and flat, extremely long filaments. She woke in a valley sitting beneath high mountains. But once again, the logic that prevails here defies the laws of earthly gravity. Some parts of these shattered mountains stand in equilibrium above the void and seem to be maintained and held together either by magic or by the astonishing effects of the repulsive gravitation mentioned by the astrophysicist when they talked with the four Neoplatonist philosophers in the gazebo.

Some mountains slope over deep valleys that run in all directions. But these colossal pieces hold on to a point, by a very fine end or... not at all! But they do not fall, demonstrating that the effects of gravity here fluctuate, and are random and contrary to human logic.

In the distance, an immense lake or a sea obscures the horizon. The water shines as if it has been polished by the hand of a giant. It looks as if it is essentially composed of silver and liquid mercury.

This detail immediately reminds the young woman of their many immersions within the white cliff.

"But..." she says to herself, "This water certainly has nothing to do with the mercury worlds which we have known, and which have held so very many surprises for us."

She immediately thinks of her first adventure with the astrophysicist when she saw a couple killed by a crazy warrior who split the chest of one of his victims in two in order to seize the heart of his victim and show it to his companions. She also recalls the frightful vengeance that Atreus had on his brother, Thyestes.

The blonde woman says to herself that this place, with all its cosmic and architectonic oddities, is a far better eden than the Earth of men.

Between the flat surface of the sea and the foothills of the mountains that circle the valley like a giant horseshoe, the young woman discovers several herds of very surprising animals. Some seem to be inspired by the great mammals of the tertiary era. Others, with long, very thin legs, look like the disheveled plants that grow in the most arid deserts.

Near these almost spherical and feathery animals, deer and fawns graze, eating plants of an intense, very astonishing blue. In the distance, massive, comical, gold silhouettes slowly wander with the tranquil serenity of beings who live as long as the atoms that compose them. She finally sees a few humans. Naked, like her. They are beautiful and their skin dazzles with saffron reflections constantly enhanced by the gold of an eternal twilight.

Just then, she finally discovers her three friends.

The tiger wakes slowly. It moves towards the scientist who, a few billion years ago, was called Phil Caldwell. The big cat licks his face.

The astrophysicist finally regains consciousness following the titanic shock resulting from the inflation of this scalar field born from him. And in him. And... for him!

Phil Caldwell rises with an ease that he finds disconcerting after such a long trial. He immediately notices that stars no longer exist in this universe where space is woven into long multi-colored ribbons. He lifts a mass of shaggy vegetation and finally discovers the anomalocaris trapped just below.

The arthropod from the Cambrian period immediately says, "Where are we?"

"With us!" roars the tiger.

The red-haired man and the young, blonde woman move closer. They look at one another. Smiling.

Their eyes fill with tears. They also shine with a light unknown until then: that of the crazy hope of a life finally serene in a welcoming new land with infinite potentialities.

Then they hug each other. In the distance, a fawn calls. The astrophysicist moves off a little.

After observing the women and men with the honey gold skin, who are placidly heading towards them, he takes the hands of the young woman in his. The great beast approaches with the anomalocaris, perched on its back like a mighty conqueror would crown a fierce cavalier. Phil Caldwell looks at them all in turn.

Then he simply says, "Atreus is definitely dead in us! A new world opens up before our eyes, finally free from the horrors we have conquered. Our world!"

Multifaceted, exuberant and generous, this new universe is embedded at the same moment in the infinite puzzle of the Multiverse.

Appendix

French text of Atrée et Thyeste
(scenes 6, 7 and 8 of Act V)

SCÈNE VI.
Atrée, Thyeste, Gardes.

ATRÉE.

Thyeste vient ; feignons ; il semble, à sa tristesse,
Que de son sort affreux quelque soupçon le presse.
   Cher Thyeste, approchez : d'où naît cette frayeur ?
Quel déplaisir si prompt peut troubler votre cour ?
1410   Vous paraissez saisi d'une douleur secrète,
Et ne me montrez plus cette âme satisfaite
Qui semblait respirer la douceur de la paix :
Ne serait-elle plus vos plus tendres souhaits ?
Quoi ! De quelques soupçons votre âme est-elle atteinte ?
1415   Ce jour, cet heureux jour est-il fait pour la crainte ?
Mon frère, vous devez la bannir désormais ;
La coupe va bientôt nous unir pour jamais.
Goûtez-vous la douceur d'une paix si parfaite ?
Et la souhaitez-vous comme je la souhaite ?
1420   N'êtes-vous pas sensible à ce rare bonheur ?

THYESTE.

Qui ? Moi vous soupçonner, ou vous haïr, seigneur ?
Les dieux m'en sont témoins, ces dieux qu'ici j'atteste,
Qui lisent mieux que vous dans l'âme de Thyeste.
Ne vous offensez point d'une vaine terreur
1425   Qui semble, malgré moi, s'emparer de mon cour :
Je le sens agité d'une douleur mortelle ;
Ma constance succombe ; en vain je la rappelle ;
Et, depuis un moment, mon esprit abattu
Laisse d'un poids honteux accabler sa vertu.
1430   Cependant, près de vous, un je ne sais quel charme
Suspend dans ce moment le trouble qui m'alarme.
Pour rassurer encore mes timides esprits,

Rendez-moi mes enfants, faites venir mon fils ;
Qu'il puisse être témoin d'une union si chère,
1435 Et partager, seigneur, les bontés de mon frère.
ATRÉE.
Vous serez satisfait, Thyeste ; et votre fils
Pour jamais en ces lieux va vous être remis.
Oui, mon frère, il n'est plus que la Parque inhumaine
Qui puisse séparer Thyeste de Plisthène.
1440 Vous le verrez bientôt ; un ordre de ma part
Le fait de ce palais hâter votre départ.
Pour donner de ma foi des preuves plus certaines,
Je veux vous renvoyer dès ce jour à Mycènes.
Malgré ce que je fais, peu sûr de cette foi,
1445 Je vois que votre cour s'alarme auprès de moi.
J'avais cru cependant qu'une pleine assurance
Devait suivre...
THYESTE.
Ah ! Seigneur, ce reproche m'offense.
ATRÉE, à un garde.
Qu'on cherche la princesse ; allez, et qu'en ces lieux
Plisthène, sans tarder, se présente à ses yeux.
1450 Il faut...

SCÈNE VII.
Atrée, Thyeste, Eurysthène, Gardes.

Eurysthène apporte la coupe.

ATRÉE.
  Mais j'aperçois la coupe de nos pères :
Voici le nœud sacré de la paix de deux frères ;
Elle vient à propos pour rassurer un cœur
Qu'alarme en ce moment une indigne terreur.
Tel qui pouvait encore se défier d'Atrée
1455 En croira mieux peut-être à la coupe sacrée.
Thyeste veut-il bien qu'elle achève en ce jour
De réunir deux cours désunis par l'amour ?
Pour engager un frère à plus de confiance,
Pour le convaincre enfin, donnez, que je commence.

Il prend la coupe de la main d'Eurysthène.

THYESTE.

1460   Je vous l'ai déjà dit, vous m'outragez, seigneur,
Si vous vous offensez d'une vaine frayeur.
Que voudrait désormais me ravir votre haine,
Après m'avoir rendu mes états et Plisthène ?
Du plus affreux courroux quel que fût le projet,
1465   Mes jours infortunés valent-ils ce bienfait ?
Eurysthène, donnez ; laissez-moi l'avantage
De jurer le premier sur ce précieux gage.
Mon cour, à son aspect, de son trouble est remis ;
Donnez. Mais cependant je ne vois point mon fils.

Il prend la coupe des mains d'Atrée.

ATRÉE.

À ses gardes.
1470   Il n'est point de retour ?
À Thyeste.
         Rassurez-vous, mon frère ;
Vous reverrez bientôt une tête si chère :
C'est de notre union le nœud le plus sacré ;
Craignez moins que jamais d'en être séparé.

THYESTE.

Soyez donc les garants du salut de Thyeste,
1475   Coupe de nos aïeux, et vous, dieux que j'atteste.
Puisse votre courroux foudroyer désormais
Le premier de nous deux qui troublera la paix !
Et vous, frère aussi cher que ma fille et Plisthène,
Recevez de ma foi cette preuve certaine.
1480   Mais que vois-je, perfide? Ah! Grands dieux! Quelle horreur!
C'est du sang ! Tout le mien se glace dans mon cour.
Le soleil s'obscurcit ; et la coupe sanglante
Semble fuir d'elle-même à cette main tremblante.
Je me meurs. Ah ! Mon fils, qu'êtes-vous devenu ?

SCÈNE VIII.
Atrée, Thyeste, Théodamie, Eurysthène, Léonide, Gardes.

THÉODAMIE.

1485   L'avez-vous pu souffrir, dieux cruels ? Qu'ai-je vu ?
Ah, seigneur ! Votre fils, mon déplorable frère,
Vient d'être pour jamais privé de la lumière.

THYESTE.

Mon fils est mort, cruel, dans ce même palais,
Et dans le même instant où l'on m'offre la paix !
1490   Et, pour comble d'horreurs, pour comble d'épouvante,
Barbare, c'est du sang que ta main me présente !
Ô terre, en ce moment, peux-tu nous soutenir ?
Ô de mon songe affreux triste ressouvenir ?
Mon fils, est-ce ton sang qu'on offrait à ton père ?

ATRÉE.

1495   Méconnais-tu ce sang ?

THYESTE.

    Je reconnais mon frère.

ATRÉE.

Il fallait le connaître, et ne point l'outrager ;
Ne point forcer ce frère, ingrat, à se venger.

THYESTE.

Grands dieux, pour quels forfaits lancez-vous le tonnerre ?
Monstre, que les enfers ont vomi sur la terre,
1500   Assouvis la fureur dont ton cœur est épris ;
Joins un malheureux père à son malheureux fils ;
À ses mânes sanglants donne cette victime,
Et ne t'arrête point au milieu de ton crime.
Barbare, peux-tu bien m'épargner en des lieux
1505   Dont tu viens de chasser et le jour et les dieux ?

ATRÉE.

Non, à voir les malheurs où j'ai plongé ta vie,
Je me repentirais de te l'avoir ravie.
Par tes gémissements je connais ta douleur :
Comme je le voulais tu ressens ton malheur ;
1510   Et mon cœur, qui perdait l'espoir de sa vengeance,
Retrouve dans tes pleurs son unique espérance.
Tu souhaites la mort, tu l'implores ; et moi,
Je te laisse le jour pour me venger de toi.

THYESTE.

Tu t'en flattes en vain, et la main de Thyeste
1515   Saura bien te priver d'un plaisir si funeste.

Il se tue.

THÉODAMIE.

Ah ciel !

THYESTE.

Consolez-vous, ma fille ; et de ces lieux

Fuyez, et remettez votre vengeance aux dieux.
Contente, par vos pleurs, d'implorer leur justice,
Allez loin de ce traître attendre son supplice.
1520   Les dieux, que ce parjure a fait pâlir d'effroi,
Le rendront quelque jour plus malheureux que moi ;
Le ciel me le promet, la coupe en est le gage ;
Et je meurs.

ATRÉE.

À ce prix, j'accepte le présage :
Ta main, en t'immolant, a comblé mes souhaits,
1525   Et je jouis enfin du fruit de mes forfaits.

Bibliography
(in French)

Novels:
Cathédrales de brume (2009)
Katharsis (2010)
Tomyris et le labyrinthe de cristal (2013)
Un matin différent (2015)
Zalmoxis (2016)
L'outre-blanc (2016)
La crypte des fantasmes (2017)

Essay:
Les métamorphoses d'Éros (2011)